LAW & DISORDER

BOOK 3 OF THE MASTERS OF MARQUIS SERIES

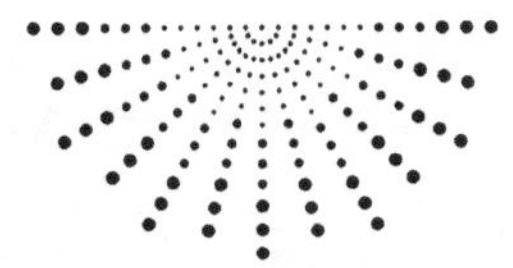

GOLDEN ANGEL

PROLOGUE

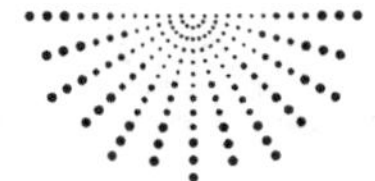

One Month Earlier

Iris

Hello again, consequences of my own actions... how I loathe thee.

Slumped in the chair in front of Master Patrick's desk, arms crossed over her chest, Iris felt as if she was in high school, sitting in the principal's office all over again. She'd spent an awful lot of time there as a teenager, and she didn't like it any better now as an adult. Schoolgirl role play would never be her fantasy for that reason alone.

Although it really wasn't a fair comparison. She had absolutely no attraction to Master Patrick, who was currently standing in as the principal figure, but she absolutely had an unwanted attraction for the man standing next to him. He was scowling as if he was her eleventh-grade history teacher and she'd just thrown a spitball at him. Why she found Master Law so hot when he could be such an uptight prick, she didn't know, but he made her tingle in all the right places, even when he was lecturing her.

And man, did he lecture her a lot.

Which was also her own fault since she'd been volun-told to be a submissive for the Dominance 101 class. It was supposed to remind her of all the things she'd learned in her Subbie 101 class. The upside was she'd met some new friends. The downside was she'd been reminded on a weekly basis just how attracted she was to Master Law, who only noticed her when she was acting up. That seemed to be her lot in life—men who only cared about her behavior when she wasn't behaving.

"Iris, I thought we talked about this." Master Patrick—she made a point of thinking about him with his honorific when she was at Stronghold and not as her big brother's friend Patrick—ran his hand over his bald head, rubbing the back the way he did when he was extra annoyed but trying to be calm. "You cannot interrupt people's scenes, even if you don't like what's going on in them."

"I'm sorry," she muttered. She really was sorry this time. The Dom hadn't deserved the way she'd yelled at him. Humiliation kink was not her thing, but she shouldn't have interrupted the scene. She got it, and she really hated having to have it rubbed in her face that she'd done the wrong thing with the best of intentions.

Again.

She would never like humiliation kink, but next time, she'd remember to look and make sure the submissive really wasn't okay with it before she jumped in. Probably.

"If you were anyone else, we'd be having a discussion about kicking you out right now." Master Patrick's gaze met hers, and Iris sat up straight in her chair. He wouldn't... would he? "The fact is, I have been far too lenient with you because you're Andrew's little sister."

"You aren't going to actually kick me out, are you?" she asked worriedly and saw his gaze soften.

Others might look at the kink club owner and find him intimidating—considering he was well over six feet tall and built like a linebacker, plus the scar that ran down his face thanks to a childhood incident involving his best friend and some swords—but Iris knew he was a teddy bear. It didn't hurt that his submissive, Lexie, had a soft spot for Iris, but Lexie wasn't here right now, and she couldn't help but wonder if that was deliberate.

Behind Patrick's chair, Master Law shifted his stance slightly, but she didn't look at him. If she saw hope on his face, it was going to crush her. Not that Iris wanted to be bad or didn't want to be liked, it was just something that kept happening. And Mr. Burly, Brooding, and Hot really got under her skin.

"I'm not kicking you out," Patrick said, and Iris sagged back down with relief. Patrick raised his eyebrow at her. "But you're running close to your last chance, no matter who your brother is."

Yeah, that was bullshit, and they both knew it. Andrew would throw a fit if she was kicked out and ended up going to some of the other local clubs, where he wouldn't know whether or not she was safe. For that matter, she was pretty sure Lexie would throw a fit.

That he would say it meant he was down to his last nerve with her, and the last thing she wanted to do was cause an issue between her brother and one of his friends. Andrew already thought she was a fuckup of massive proportions, no matter how hard she'd tried to clean up her act, so she didn't need to give him more ammunition.

"Okay, so what now?" she asked, pressing her fingers together nervously in her lap.

Master Patrick leaned forward, holding eye contact with her. His dark face was serious, without a hint of humor or his hidden teddy bear interior. If he wanted to make her nervous, he was doing a good job.

"You're going to spend the next month as a server at Stronghold. For free. You will not be allowed to scene. While you are there, you will spend one hour of every shift watching scenes in the Dungeon and taking notes on what is happening in the scene and how the submissive is reacting. Not how *you* are reacting, how the submissive is." Master Patrick's lip quirked slightly when she made a face, but she didn't protest.

The 'punishment' was more than fair, and it fit the crime, as it was.

If Iris had paid more attention to how the submissive was reacting to the name-calling from her Dom, rather than just hearing the words and seeing tears, she might not have jumped in. Because the submissive had been way more embarrassed by Iris interrupting the scene than she had been by being insulted.

"Yes, Sir," she said, nodding.

"You will not interrupt any more scenes. If you do see a submissive in distress, you will get a Dungeon Monitor. And you will listen to and respect all the dominants in the club." There wasn't any discernible change in Master Patrick's voice or his demeanor, but suddenly he was very much *Master* Patrick, and Iris felt herself sitting up straighter without thinking about it. Some Doms could have that effect.

"Yes, Sir."

"Now get out while I have a discussion with Master Law." Patrick waved his hand at her, the switch flipping back off again as soon as it had flipped on.

"Thank you, Sir." Iris bounced to her feet and booked it to the door before he could change his mind. Unfortunately, she wasn't fast enough to outrun the sound of Master Law's furious exclamation as the door to Patrick's office started to swing shut.

"Are you serious, Patrick? That girl is nothing but trouble."

Iris winced, pressing her lips together against the emotion that suddenly welled in her chest. It wasn't like the first time she'd heard someone say that. It wasn't even the hundredth.

So why did it hurt so much more to hear Master Law say it?

Her mood, which had been a lot lighter after she realized Patrick would not kick her out or go to her brother, plummeted.

Law

Normally, Law would never even think about addressing the owner of an establishment in such a tone, but he was at the end of his rope. Iris Baez was practically the poster child of special treatment at Stronghold. In any other kink club, she would have already been spanked to true regret and turned into a very sorry submissive. One that was intent on behaving.

Everyone was hands-off merely because she was the sister of one of the owner's friends, which grated on his last nerve.

Any other submissive interrupting a public scene would have received a public punishment. Though he supposed Patrick would argue that her punishment would be public, it was lenient. All three of them knew it, and so would everyone else. Granted, Law understood how hard it could be to subvert expectations in the club—hell, he'd started thinking of himself as "Law" rather than Lawrence, thanks to the submissives who had given the nickname and made it stick.

Swiveling around in his chair, Patrick leveled a stern look at Law, who refused to be intimidated, even though Patrick was practically a head taller than him. Law was of perfectly average height, just below six feet, which made him the tallest person in his family, but size wasn't everything. He'd never allowed himself to feel smaller because of someone else's height.

"She's not trouble. She's just constantly *in* trouble because she acts before she thinks."

"That amounts to the same thing." Law felt a muscle in his jaw tick. Iris was the epitome of the phrase 'Ready, fire, aim.' Sure, she might feel bad for going off early afterward, but by then, it was too late. The damage had already been done. From the way things were going at Stronghold, apparently, she would never be held to a standard that required her to learn to think before acting.

Yet again, she was getting off easy.

"She'll learn. But I agree that I'm too soft with her. Most of the Doms that I would normally assign to her are going to be." Patrick leaned back in his chair, elbows resting on the arms, fingers steepled in front of him.

Crap.

Law sensed the danger too late. He'd walked into an ambush. Sighing, he reached up to rub his hand along the scruff on his jaw, knowing it was already too late.

"I think, as someone who is friendly but not friends with Andrew and does not have a personal history with him or Iris, that you will be the perfect person to oversee her." Patrick grinned wide, white teeth flashing in his dark face like a shark's grin. *Chomp, chomp.*

"Why not Julie?" Both he and Julie, who was a Domme, had run the recent class, and he hadn't noticed Julie taking any shit from Iris.

"Because Iris doesn't have any trouble with any of the dominants who don't identify as male. Besides, Julie definitely has a soft spot for Iris, even if she doesn't allow it to show. You, on the other hand, will have no problem spanking her ass if she deserves it." Patrick pointed at him, still grinning, clearly pleased with himself. "That makes you the perfect man for the job."

He opened his mouth.

Closed it.

Patrick was right, although Law hadn't really thought about it before.

Iris behaved for Julie in a way that she hadn't for him. She'd even behaved for Samantha, a switch exploring her Domme side in the class, in a way she hadn't for him.

"You think she has a problem with men, and you want me to figure it out for you?" he stated flatly. It didn't take a genius to read between the lines, especially when Patrick was half spelling it out for him.

"That's part of being a Dom sometimes." Patrick flashed him another grin and turned back toward his desk.

Exasperated, Law moved around to the front of it so he was still facing the other man.

"She's not my submissive."

"Nope, but she's a club submissive, and you're one of my Dungeon Monitors, which means you get the extra duties." Patrick gave him a thumbs up. "By the way, thanks for agreeing to take that on. It's appreciated. And hey, if you can help her find a Dom, you can pass along that responsibility to him instead."

Dammit.

Law didn't have a good argument against that. Helping the club submissives *was* one of the duties he'd agreed to take on. Normally, it was the exact thing he loved to do and gave him some fulfillment and some peace.

Thinking about doing it with Iris did not give him feelings of fulfillment and peace.

Probably because he was attracted to her, and he really didn't want to be. He needed serenity and calm in his life. Not a hot mess who liked to push all his buttons.

CHAPTER ONE

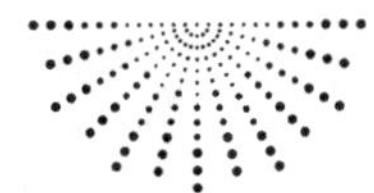

Law

Watching Iris moving across the floor of Stronghold, wearing nothing but a tight miniskirt and electrical tape over her nipples, Law reminded himself—again—she was off-limits. It wasn't that her outfit was particularly risqué, not for Stronghold. The kink club was filled with people wearing regular clothing, fetwear, or nothing at all. Having her abundant curves on display was nothing new and nothing he hadn't seen before.

Yet he had trouble keeping his eyes off her, even though he knew he should. He was supposed to be keeping an eye on her, but not *this* closely.

Sure, she was beautiful, and for some reason, her sassy mouth appealed to him—even though he wanted a well-behaved submissive who did as she was told—but there were so many other reasons he needed to stay hands-off. One of which was standing behind the bar, glaring at him... as usual.

Andrew hadn't been a fan of his since Law had threatened to spank Iris a few days ago if she didn't shape up, right in front of her brother. He was pretty sure what set Andrew off was that Law had meant it.

The brother and sister should not be allowed to work the same shift, but since when did anyone around here listen to his opinion?

"How goes the watch?" A heavy hand clapped the back of his shoulder in greeting, and Connor's deep voice filled with amusement.

Scowling, Law looked up at his giant friend. For someone who stood close to six and a half feet, Connor could be surprisingly stealthy. Then again, Law was distracted.

"You'd think after almost a month, you would be tired of that joke." Law was tired of hearing it, even if Connor wasn't tired of telling it.

The big guy grinned down at him. With his auburn hair and beard and massive stature, he looked like he belonged in Game of Thrones. Throw a few furs on him, give him an axe, and he'd fit right in.

"You're the one who wears all black, takes life way too seriously, and has been celibate for months," Connor replied easily. He smiled widely at the submissive who came up to take his drink order as he sat down at the bar table with Law.

Iris was serving in the Lounge area, which is where Law deliberately had her assigned all the time, rather than letting her serve in the bar. That way, he could keep an eye on her but still relax with his friends.

What he could not do was scene. The one time he'd gone to help with a scene, she'd tossed a drink in a Dom's face. Granted, the Dom in question had said something offensive and had been kicked out of Stronghold for his troubles, but Iris should have told him, her brother, one of the Dungeon Monitors, or *anyone*, but instead, she'd reacted without thinking. As usual.

The only reason he'd only warned her instead of actually spanking her was she had been pretty well behaved for the past few weeks, the Dom really had deserved it, and... her brother had been looming beside him.

Yeah, add him to the softies who were having trouble giving her the discipline she really needed because of the circumstances.

He wasn't afraid of Andrew, but he didn't want to face off with big brother unless the reason truly warranted it, and that particular incident hadn't. Especially since she was so close to finishing out her month.

She really had been good. He'd only had to dole out a few punishments, none of which had been a spanking. She'd hated writing the essay about why, in Stronghold, all Dominants deserved to be spoken to with respect. Overall, though, she'd been a lot less trouble than he'd initially thought she would be. Sometimes, he wondered if he was disappointed because part of him was itching to spank her delectable ass. Just once.

Which was another reason he had only warned her instead of doing it. She tested his control in a way he wasn't proud of.

"Any plans for tonight?" Law asked Connor once the other man had ordered. As usual, Law was drinking iced tea. One of the things he really appreciated about his friends here was they never asked why that was all he drank.

"Not yet," Connor said affably. "I figured I'd sit down and see what I feel like doing."

Connor was a very 'go with the flow' kind of guy. Just thinking about it made Law itch. He hated not having a plan.

"Oh, hey, there's Asad." Connor raised his hand, waving across the room as a dark-haired Dom came into the main room. Considering how tall he was, Connor waving was impossible to miss, even sitting down. Asad saw them and grinned widely, heading toward them.

Law waved too, glancing over at Iris before he focused on greeting Asad. Just to make sure she was staying out of trouble. Not because she happened to be bending over with her cute little ass pointed right at him. That definitely wasn't why.

Iris

"He's staring at your ass," Amy whispered to her.

"He is not." Iris straightened and glanced over her shoulder. Her Watch Dom was saying hello to Master Asad, not looking at her ass.

She looked back at Amy, scowling, and the blonde spread her hands wide.

"He was looking, I swear. He watches you a lot when you don't realize." Amy's smile was mischievous.

If she was someone else, Iris might not have believed her, but Amy was nice, even if most of her friends weren't. Iris tried not to judge Amy by her friends since she was hardly one to talk. Besides, she was pretty sure Amy's niceness was exactly how she'd gotten caught up in that particular group of Stronghold subs—she was too nice to break away from them.

Iris snorted.

"That's because he's sure the second he takes his eye off me, I'll get into trouble." Something flipped in her stomach—she really didn't want to get into trouble.

Every night, at the end of her shift, when she'd done a good job, Master Law told her she'd been a good girl in that gruff way of his. Sure, he'd said it almost suspiciously the first few nights, but now he just said it, and every time it happened, it was the best moment of her day.

There had only been a few days when she'd missed the mark. Though when he'd threatened to spank her for pouring a drink out on Chad's lap, it hadn't been her worst moment.

The worst day had been when she'd mouthed off to her brother—who'd deliberately been a dick—and Master Law just shook his head and looked away. No 'good girl' that day. No praise. No reaction.

Iris was willing to be very, very good if it meant avoiding another day like that.

"You've barely gotten into trouble all month," Amy replied, shaking her head. "By now, he should know he doesn't need to worry about that. The only times you do something are when it's deserved."

Warmth filled Iris' chest, and she smiled. It was nice to have that acknowledged. Why was it so much easier for women to notice her effort and praise her? Master Law was the only one who seemed to notice out of the Doms. Her brother sure as hell didn't. He'd spent his whole life only paying attention to her when she was affecting him, which hadn't changed now that they were adults.

"I'm trying. Only a few more days and I'm free of my Watch Dom." Oddly, she would miss it. She'd been pissed when she'd realized Patrick had assigned Master Law to keep an eye on her, but with every 'good girl' she'd received, she was a lot less mad about it.

What was she going to do when it was gone?

Oh, go cry about it, why don't you?

Yeah, melancholy was not her normal state.

"Who are you hanging out with tonight?" she asked Amy.

"Morgan's coming by soon, and I think Zach might be in later, but I don't know if he'll be available to scene." Though Amy's expression didn't change, there was something in her voice whenever she said Zach's name. She was still wearing another man's ring on her finger, and she was devoted to her fiancé. Iris' understanding was Amy only scened platonically because her fiancé was completely vanilla but knew about her kink and was 'understanding.'

They were also monogamous, so either he was one *really* understanding guy, or he didn't care about Amy. Iris hoped it was the latter because she was pretty sure Zach was in love with Amy, and he was a nice guy. He also had a boyfriend, who didn't mind that Zach and Amy scened together, and Kincaid was definitely completely in love with Zach.

Kink was very complicated sometimes.

"Great, well, I'll be right back with your drink." She gave Amy a smile and straightened. Back to work.

She had a 'good girl' to earn by the end of the night.

Law

Hanging out with Connor and Asad was always interesting. Connor rarely glanced over at the Lounge area, where the submissives were gathered, hoping to be approached by a Master who wanted to scene, and Asad never took his eyes off it. Commitment-phobe was Asad's middle name, but he loved to scene, whereas, so far, Connor had to be pushed into finding a submissive to connect with. The Dom class had been to help him find confidence, but he was still shy, even though the subs loved him.

"Only a few more weeks until Renn Fair. We're still going Opening Day, right?" Asad asked, grinning as Connor groaned.

"I hate Opening Day. It's too hot. Can't we wait a few weeks until the weather cools down?"

"And miss out on the day when the women will be wearing the least amount of clothes? Absolutely not."

"It's not like you can't come here to see half-clothed women," Connor grumped. "You'll even see a lot of the *same* women there." The kink community and the Renn Fair community as a Venn Diagram were basically one big overlap. Add in cosplay and nerds, and the Venn Diagrams turned into a stack of pancakes.

Law's lips twitched. Connor had a point, but he didn't think that would stop them.

They'd met at Renn Fair, and it was tradition to go to Opening Day together.

"Some, but not all." Asad's grin widened. "And some I haven't met might be eager to ride the Persian Excursion."

Connor and Law groaned. Asad had found out that was what the Stronghold subs called him, and he'd embraced the nickname whole-heartedly. Even used it as a pickup line.

"The fact you actually like to be called something that makes you sound like a tourist trap is really telling," Law said, shaking his head, but he couldn't stop smiling.

"It's not a trap, more of a catch and release program. Thank you, love." Asad turned his attention to their server, who blushed bright pink as he took his drink and winked.

"Thank you, Sir… I mean, you're welcome, Sir." She blushed even deeper and practically fled.

Asad tended to have that effect on the submissives.

"Speaking of traps," Asad murmured, his eyes shifting.

Law knew Iris must be coming up behind him. It was about time for the end of her shift.

As if on cue, he could see her friends, Domi, Rae, and Avery, walking into the club with Domi's boyfriend, Mitch. They usually showed up to hang out with Iris on the nights she was working once she was done.

Law turned before she reached him, enjoying the look of surprise on her face as he swiveled around to face her before she'd said his name. It wasn't often he got to throw Iris off balance. Normally, it was the other way around.

"All done?" he asked. She nodded, hands clasped in front of her, shifting back and forth nervously on her toes for a moment. Over the past few weeks, Law had come to realize she wasn't quite as self-assured as she liked to pretend. "Good girl. Go have fun with your friends."

Lighting up, Iris smiled and took off, heading for the little group already sitting at one of the bar tables.

"Man, that girl has got it bad for you," Asad said.

Law jolted in his seat.

"What?" He couldn't have heard that correctly. Turning, he stared at Asad, who was looking back at him with a bit of consternation. Even Connor was staring at Law, not Asad, even though Asad had just said the most ridiculous thing he'd ever heard.

"Iris? The cute little subbie you warned me off three weeks ago?" Asad tipped his head. "Did you not notice how she lit up the moment you called her a good girl? I assumed you warned me off because you want her for yourself, but you really didn't know, did you?"

"There's nothing to know." Law's scattered thoughts came back online, and he shook his head as though he could shake off Asad's words with the motion. "You're reading too much into things."

There was no way Iris liked him like that—she didn't actually *like* him at all. Besides, he was far too old for her, and she was too young and bratty for him. She needed someone younger and happier. Someone who would enjoy bringing her in line and who could put up with her wildness.

Someone who was definitely not him.

CHAPTER TWO

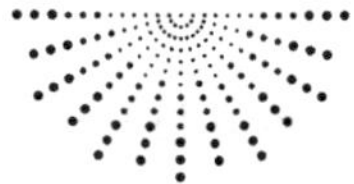

"Hello, hello!" Iris gleefully accepted the hugs from everyone, including Mitch. He might be a bossy Dom and kind of terrifying as a sadist, but he was also a total goofball and a great hugger. He liked to joke that he was layered.

"Are you done with your shift?" Avery asked, patting the chair next to her since she already knew the answer. Curves packed into a corset, her dark blonde hair waved around her shoulders, and she tossed back the strands to get them out of her face.

"Yes." Iris groaned a little as she sat down, getting off her feet. "I don't know how you stand in the kitchen all day long. My feet are killing me after just a short shift."

"To be fair, I don't wear heels in the kitchen. I wear special shoes, and we have pads to stand on, which are supposed to help with the long hours," Avery pointed out. She was a sous chef for Marquis, a restaurant on its main floor, and served as a kinky sister club to Stronghold on its second. Right now, her boyfriend and Dom, Nick, would be finishing out *his* shift as the executive chef. "And my feet *are* killing me by the end of the day, even with all that."

"The heels might not have been the best idea." Some submissives

16

did bare feet while they were serving, but about half wore heels, and Iris had decided she was going to be part of that half. Her legs looked good in heels, and she wanted to look good.

Not just because Master Law was watching her all night.

She peeked over her shoulder. He'd gone back to talking to his friends, a seriously hot group of single Doms. It was no wonder the subbies were all drooling over them.

While she was pathetically still all warm and glowy inside from earning her 'good girl.'

Yup. Pathetic.

"Still drooling over Master Law?" Rae elbowed her in the side. Dressed in a pink and green tutu, which matched the two green braids amid the many long brown braids, and a pink bra, she looked as if she could be on her way to a rave right now. The bright neon colors were gorgeous against her brown skin, and Iris had a moment of stark envy. Neon colors like that always washed her out.

"I am not drooling," she responded indignantly. As if she would ever drool over a man. Salted caramel butter bars, sure. Men? No. Not even Jason Momoa. "I am lusting from afar on my completely inappropriate crush, with no drool involved."

Even as she joked, a niggle in her stomach made her squirm uncomfortably. While she might joke about it, she wondered if there was more beneath it than she wanted to admit. Like, yeah, she had a little crush.

It had turned out Law wasn't the unreasonable hardass he'd made himself out to be. When she'd put in the effort, he actually noticed. Praised her for it, even. It might be sad that something so little could make any kind of impact on her, but it did.

While he might have called her 'trouble' a month ago in Patrick's office, he'd been willing to let his perception change once he saw her trying. That was really rare in her world.

"He is hot," Avery said, glancing over. "I don't usually go for bald guys, but he pulls it off."

"Yeah, he does," Domi joined in, causing Mitch to frown. "He's like a sexy Filipino Mr. Clean, but with facial hair."

"Hey, I'm right here. I can hear you."

Giggling, Domi tipped her head back at her boyfriend with his full head of blond hair.

"That's what you get for insisting on coming to ladies' night."

"Nick will be here when he's done for the night," Avery said encouragingly, patting Mitch on the shoulder. He looked as though he was considering going all Dom on Domi's ass. It kept her on her toes that he could flip a switch, just like that, and suddenly, her bratty mouth was in trouble.

On the other hand, Iris had a feeling Domi liked to provoke it. She might look like a pixie, so petite and cute with a riot of dark brown curls, but she was a total brat when she wanted to be.

She exchanged a look with Rae, the other single in their group. They were happy for Domi and Avery, but Iris felt a bit of envy. She wasn't sure she would find what they had here at Stronghold. Even though she and Andrew had agreed to come on opposite nights when they wanted to scene, his friends were still always around. While she got that he didn't want her to go to clubs where she might not be as safe as she was at Stronghold, it was almost too safe at Stronghold.

Being a sub for the Dominance class had been nice because it had been at Marquis, and she hadn't been around her big brother's friends, who had a bad habit of coming over to talk to her when she was in discussions with a prospective Dom. Except, they didn't really come over to talk to her. They came over to talk to the Dom who had approached her, and it wasn't as though they were trying to chase him off, but that's what ended up happening every time.

It was a little demoralizing.

Rae's problem was she totally had a thing for Mitch's friend Brian but wasn't willing to admit it. Brian was one hundred percent a Daddy Dom, and Rae insisted she had no interest in a Daddy Dom, even if she dressed like a baby girl whenever she was at the club. It was too bad because Iris thought they'd make a good couple, but it wasn't her business.

"Are you two crazy kids planning on playing tonight?" she asked

Mitch, distracting him from his contemplation of whether to Dom out on Domi.

"Yes." He tugged one of Domi's curls, pulling it down and letting it go, so it sprang back into place. "I've reserved one of the rooms, but she doesn't know which one yet."

"It's the interrogation room," Domi said, a little smile curving one side of her lips.

"It's important to maintain an aura of mystery to keep the relationship interesting," Mitch said a little louder, acting like he hadn't heard her.

"It's the interrogation room."

Mitch got a little louder.

"Which is why I make sure to regularly surprise Domi."

"It's still the interrogation room."

"Are you two going to the interrogation room tonight?" A smiling face appeared behind Avery but not Nick—Brian quickly followed by Mitch's friends, Kincaid and Zach, who were holding hands. Though Iris noticed Zach glanced over at the Lounge area, where Amy was sitting and chatting with her friends Caroline and Morgan.

"No."

"Yes." Domi grinned when Mitch grabbed a fistful of her hair, bending her head back so she was forced to look up at him. The move also made her breasts move within her corset.

"It's not the interrogation room, little brat, and you'd better watch it, or you're going to get more than you bargained for tonight." The threat was made with a growl.

Rae and Iris sighed simultaneously. That was hot.

LAW

Glancing over to where the group around Iris had grown larger, Law's jaw clenched at the sight of her laughing up at something Kincaid had said. Where had Zach gone? It only took him a moment to find Kincaid's boyfriend—in the Lounge area, talking to Amy.

Were they looking for a poly arrangement? Kincaid and Zach together but each with their own girlfriends as well?

No, that couldn't be it. Everyone knew Amy was engaged. Maybe Kincaid was looking for someone to scene with when Zach was with Amy.

Why that didn't sit well in his gut, he didn't know, except... Iris deserved a Dom who was fully interested in her. Not someone who needed a placeholder while their boyfriend scened with someone else.

"Go ask her to scene with you once she's allowed to," Asad whispered in his ear, making Law jump.

Turning away from the sight of Kincaid and Iris talking, Law glared at his friend.

"Why must you insist on trying to push me and Iris together?" he asked.

"She's cute, and she looks at you like she likes you. She also melts when you call her a good girl. Aka, she's interested in you, and she's the first woman I've seen *you* interested in for ages." Asad picked up his drink, sipping and raising his eyebrows as he let those words sink in. "Whether or not you're willing to admit it, the chemistry there is undeniable."

Law looked at Connor to see what he thought, but Connor wasn't looking at him. He was looking at the next table over—in the opposite direction of Iris—where another newer Dom, who went by the nickname Q, was sitting by himself. A few minutes ago, he'd been with his friends, Adam and Angel, but they must have gone off to scene or home to their baby. Law hadn't noticed because he'd been so busy staring at Iris' table.

Talk about a humbling experience.

"Hey, Q, wanna come sit with us?" Connor asked, causing Asad and Law to look at each other in surprise. Connor was shy, though he had gotten to know Q during the class. Maybe the combination of knowing him a little and the confidence from the Dom class was breaking him out of his shell.

Law didn't have any objection to Q joining them. He'd enjoyed getting to know Q during the class and had a feeling Q and Asad would get along fabulously.

"Yeah, sure. Thanks," Q said, getting up and moving over to one of the empty stools at their table. "Apparently, the interrogation room has greater appeal than hanging out with me."

"That's a hard truth to deny," Asad said with a chuckle, holding out his hand. "Hi, I'm Asad, and clearly, you already know Law and Connor."

"Q. Nice to meet you." Q was about their age, in his early thirties, and a self-proclaimed nerd. In some ways, he reminded Law of a smaller version of Patrick, with the same bald head and dark skin, but while Patrick was big and broad, Q was slimly muscled like a swimmer or basketball player. "What are you all up to tonight?"

"Bothering Law about Iris." Asad grinned and tipped his head toward the woman in question, ignoring Law's groan.

"I thought we could move on from that topic."

"If you don't want to talk about Iris, stop looking at her."

"He has a point," Connor chimed in, and Law glared at him. Whose side was he on? Looking away, Connor shrugged one shoulder, but not before Law saw the smile on his face, even if it was partially obscured by his beard.

"I'm supposed to be keeping an eye on her. My responsibility doesn't end just because her shift did." He was pretty sure Patrick had meant it to, but Law couldn't just switch his feelings on and off.

"Iris is nice. She can take care of herself, though, and if she runs into anything here, I'm pretty sure Angel's entire group of friends will come down on them like a ton of bricks," Q said. "Even if she wasn't Andrew's little sister. They all adore her."

"Can we please talk about anything else?" Law did his best not to turn his head to look at Iris again, which is what he wanted to do, even as he demanded his friends change the topic. "She only has a few more days left of her punishment, then I won't have to watch her. Next Thursday is the final day for both of us. Okay?"

His friends and Q nodded solemnly. The truth was, Law wasn't sure he'd be able to switch it off even then since he'd been watching out for her for so long, but he was going to make an effort.

"So, did you want to scene tonight?" Asad asked Q, though his attention was on the Lounge area. "I think I might see if there are any subbies willing to play."

It was Asad, which meant there definitely would be. He was attractive, smooth, and damn good at what he did. Q, on the other hand, was a newer to the scene and could probably use some help. Asad was basically offering to be his wingman.

Law chuckled, taking a healthy swig of iced tea… then had to jerk his eyes away from Iris because they'd already drifted back.

Dammit.

CHAPTER THREE

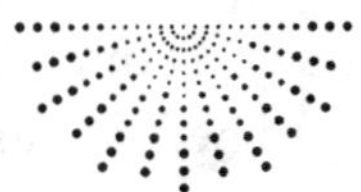

IRIS

Going home to her apartment was not the refuge Iris wished it was, especially after a night like tonight. Even as she approached the door, deep down, she hoped Noelle, her roommate and best friend, was asleep. She didn't really feel like dealing with her.

If she was being honest with herself, that was why she'd stayed at Stronghold later than she should on a Thursday night when she had to work the next morning.

The problem was, she felt guilty for not wanting to deal with Noelle. Noelle was her best friend, the one who had stood by her through thick and thin since high school, but sometimes, she acted as though they were still in high school. They had little in common anymore, and... well, being around Noelle had never been peaceful.

For a while, Iris had liked that.

Now, she wished she could come home and relax without having to worry about being pulled into whatever drama was swirling around Noelle this week. Granted, there wasn't *always* drama, but coming home felt like Russian roulette, never knowing if things in Noelle's life had exploded again while she was away.

Taking a deep breath, she stuck her keys in the door and pushed it open. The television was on, and she could see Noelle's dark blonde head over the back of the couch, twisting around.

"Hey." The brief greeting didn't give her much to go on, and Iris mentally crossed her fingers that it had been a good night.

"Hey." Coming in, she locked the door behind her, yawning exaggeratedly, so Noelle wouldn't protest when she went right to bed. "Long night."

"Ugh, you have no idea." Noelle sat up, twisting around on the couch, and Iris inwardly cursed. Dammit. She'd meant that to be a hint about why she was going to bed, not an invitation. "Do you know what Tyler did tonight?"

"Um, well, no, but..." Iris gestured vaguely toward the hallway. Of course, she didn't know what Noelle's boyfriend had done tonight since she'd been at Stronghold, and it wasn't like Noelle had texted her about it.

She didn't let Iris stop her, launching straight into the story right over Iris' 'but.' Sighing inwardly, Iris moved to the side of the couch so Noelle could see her easily. She was also a little closer to the hallway leading to the bedrooms, which would help her make her escape more easily. Hopefully, not sitting down would also give Noelle a hint she needed to get to bed.

"Well, we were supposed to go out, but then, like an hour before he was supposed to pick me up, he got called into work." Noelle crossed her arms across her chest and huffed. "He didn't even try to tell them he had plans tonight. He just went! I asked him if he could tell them he hadn't realized he'd double-booked himself and back out, but he said he'd already told them yes and didn't want to go back on his word. I guess going back on his word to me wasn't a big deal."

Ouch. Iris made a face. Yeah, that was pretty shitty. On the other hand, it wasn't like Noelle was a cheap date. Tyler seemed to be picking up an awful lot of extra shifts lately, and it was hard to tell if it was because he was trying to avoid his girlfriend or afford her.

"I'm sorry, that really sucks," Iris said, infusing sympathy into her voice. "Hopefully, he'll find a way to make it up to you."

"He'd better." Noelle tilted her head as Iris took a step back, starting to turn. "What are you doing home so late? Don't you have work tomorrow?"

"Yeah, I do. I should probably get to bed." Iris yawned again. She wasn't faking how tired she was. Starting to turn, she inwardly winced when Noelle's voice went a little shriller.

"So, why are you home so late? You were hanging out with those new girls, weren't you? You'd rather hang out with them than with me. That's why you're home so late."

Ugh. Guilt welled because there was enough truth in Noelle's accusation to make things uncomfortable.

"I just took a little extra time at the club to chill out before coming home, that's all, Noelle. You know you're my bestie." She turned back to her friend, knowing if she didn't soothe Noelle before she went to bed, it would be days of sulking and probably the silent treatment until Noelle felt Iris had begged for forgiveness enough.

Not how she wanted things to be around the apartment.

Noelle crossed her arms over her chest and pouted. Dressed in her pajamas, sulky expression on her face, she looked far younger than she actually was.

"You don't act like I'm your bestie. You stay late at the club to hang out with *other* people, then come home and don't want to talk to me, just like Tyler. Apparently, no one wants to be around me tonight." Big blue eyes filled with tears, hurt radiating off every inch of her. "Whatever... just go to bed. You don't have to stay out here pretending you care."

"I do care, Noelle." Iris dropped her purse on the armchair and moved to sit down next to Noelle on the couch, guilt still simmering. She hadn't realized Noelle had noticed Iris pulling away. Not that she'd meant to pull away exactly, but... well, she had more fun with Rae, Domi, and Avery. They had more in common.

She still loved Noelle, and they had their past in common, but living with her had become harder. They hadn't much time to hang out, and maybe Noelle was right. Maybe she was a shitty friend. And selfish. If she'd come home earlier, Noelle would have told her about Tyler then, and she could already be in bed.

So, really, tonight's late night was her own fault.

Wrapping her arm around Noelle's shoulders, she pulled her friend into a half hug.

"I'm sorry, you're right. Tell me about what's going on with you and Tyler. I'm here for you and always will be."

"Thank you, Iris. I don't know what I would do without you. Sometimes, I think you're the only reason I can hold myself together." Sniffling, Noelle leaned onto Iris' shoulder, unaware of how her words sank Iris' stomach like a lead weight. "I just don't know what to do about Tyler. I'm pretty sure he's working up to dumping me, and I don't know how I'll live without him."

"Okay, well, let's start there," Iris said soothingly, letting her head rest on top of Noelle's and pushing away her drowsiness. It was going to be a long night. She could consider this her penance for putting off coming home.

———

Law

Another late night at Stronghold, which wasn't necessarily a bad thing. Even though he was tired at the end of it, it sure as hell beat sitting alone at home with nothing to distract him from his thoughts.

Law sighed as he peeled off his leather pants, kicking them away across his bedroom floor as he headed for the shower. Another late night at Stronghold, another night of watching Iris, and another night of not scening. No wonder he was antsy.

It had been too long since he'd scened and he knew it. The Dom class was over, and the new submissives class wouldn't start till next month, which didn't help since it took away another of his outlets. The problem was, there wasn't anyone he wanted to scene with.

Liar.

He ignored the little voice whispering in his brain and turned on the hot water, giving it a few moments to warm up before he stepped in. The water beat on his shoulders and head, sliding over his skin, and he sighed as he relaxed under the spray. For a few moments, he allowed himself to enjoy the hot water and steam wafting up around him before he squirted soap into his hand and sudsed up.

Reaching down, he gripped his cock. This wasn't about pleasure so much as it was about stress relief. A physical need to be met. That was how it usually was. How it was supposed to be.

Closing his eyes, his hand pumping on his cock with fast, sure strokes, he didn't see the blankness he usually saw or the faceless female body that sometimes popped up in its place. This time, he saw a certain mouthy submissive on her knees in front of him, and he'd found the perfect way to keep her quiet.

Fuck.

His pulse pounded in his ears, hand tightening on his dick. Even as he tried to push the image of Iris' wide eyes out of his mind, lips wrapped around his cock, he knew it was already too late. The fantasy had taken off on its own, and it wasn't coming back.

Groaning, Law braced his forearm against the shower and leaned his head against it as his other hand moved harder and faster over his slick shaft. He wanted to finish as quickly as possible, as he always did, yet another part of him wanted to linger over the fantasy. That desire made him work his cock even more vigorously, rebelling against the strange urge. He panted as he came, shuddering from the intensity of his pleasure.

Dammit. She was even invading his brain at home now.

With how often he had to think about her at the club, maybe it wasn't a surprise. Especially after the way Asad had been teasing him about her all night.

No wonder the thought was stuck in his head.

Finishing his shower, Law got out and dried off, trying not to feel too disgusted with himself. It wasn't just that she was too young for him—though she was—or that she wasn't his type—she wasn't—he also knew deep down, his biggest problem was he knew he didn't deserve her.

He was pretty sure he didn't deserve anyone.

Because of that, masturbating hadn't brought the relief it usually did. It was supposed to be a release of tension. He couldn't remember the last time it had actually been about making himself feel good.

Feeling more tired than he had in years, Law put on a pair of boxers and flopped down on his bed. A moment later, there was a soft thump, then a purr as Whiskers jumped up beside him and rubbed her furry little face all over Law's bald head.

Cracking an eye open, Law glared at the tortoiseshell former alley cat.

"Why is it you're only affectionate when I'm not in the mood to pay attention to you?" he asked grumpily. Whiskers mewed and rubbed her face over Law's cheek. They both knew if Law had come home and actually tried to pet the cat, he would most likely have been met with a hiss and claws. It wasn't a certainty—Whiskers liked to be arbitrary—but it was always a possibility.

"Ornery beast," Law muttered, turning onto his back and pulling up the covers so Whiskers could settle on top of him and knead to her heart's content without digging her claws into Law's bare chest. The cat's purr was like a jet engine. Law yawned, and his eyes slowly closed. Because he wasn't really thinking, he reached up to rub his chin, and Whiskers clearly thought he meant to pet her and immediately hissed and clawed him.

"Ow!" He jerked upright, but the cat had already sprung away from his chest. As she swished her way out the door, Law glared at her, grumbling under his breath, "Damn cat."

When he'd found her in an alley, she'd been a pathetic little thing and clung to him when he'd picked her up. It had been the one and only time he'd been allowed to hold her without protest. Gratitude for being rescued? Yeah, not her.

Rolling over, Law turned out the light and closed his eyes again, willing himself to sink into sleep. The problem of Iris would have to be faced soon enough tomorrow. He needed all the rest he could get until then.

CHAPTER FOUR

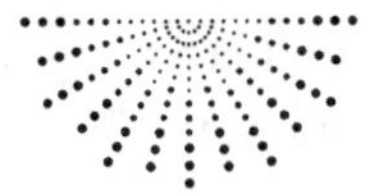

Talk about dragging. Iris' eyes felt like sandpaper as she forced herself through her morning routine, glaring balefully at Noelle's closed door. Noelle worked as a receptionist at a hair salon, which meant she didn't have to be up for another hour or two to make it to work on time.

Not like Iris, who needed to be at the Hill's house by eight to walk their dog. Working as a House Manager sounded like a cool job, but it wasn't the easy work Noelle sometimes teased her about. No, she didn't have to be on her feet all day like Noelle, but Noelle didn't have to be up at six in the morning, either. Iris had allowed Noelle to go on for far too long last night and hadn't gotten nearly enough sleep. Now, she was cranky as hell.

Thank God it was Friday, or she might have been even crankier.

She was also resolved to start coming home from Stronghold earlier, so Noelle wouldn't keep her up so late. Hopefully. It was worth a shot.

Coffee. Coffee was necessary.

Dressed, showered, and caffeinated, she managed to feel almost normal by the time she was out the door. Maybe she should see if

Patrick would let her off this evening. As much as she wanted to go to Stronghold, Noelle had still been mad at Tyler when she went to bed last night and hadn't been happy to hear that Iris was headed back to Stronghold both tonight and tomorrow.

It had made Iris realize how absent she'd been on the weekends, and even though Noelle spent a lot of time with Tyler, they hadn't hung out together in so long, which was pretty unusual. No wonder Noelle was feeling jealous of her new friends. To add to her guilt, she didn't really want to bring Noelle to hang out with them.

Noelle wasn't judgmental about the kinky stuff, exactly, but she didn't understand it, and some of the stuff she said could come off as judgmental. Iris didn't want to lose her new friends because Noelle said something that sounded bad. Plus… sometimes, she needed a break from Noelle.

Damn, I'm a shitty friend.

Pulling out her phone, she quickly tapped out a message to Patrick, asking him for the night off to help her roommate, who was having some personal issues. That done, she started a second pot of coffee and left it ready-to-go, so all Noelle would have to do was push the 'start' button when she woke up.

Feeling better, if still tired, Iris headed to her car.

"Today is going to be a good day," she murmured to herself. A little positive thinking never hurt anything, right?

---

*L*AW

Lunch out with clients was never one of Law's favorite things but was occasionally a necessity. Part of being a contract lawyer was schmoozing and keeping the clients happy. He wasn't great at schmoozing but did his best. Thankfully, most of them were happy to be taken out to lunch and talk while he listened. Sitting, eating, and listening were things he could manage.

Except today.

Halfway through lunch, Iris Baez had walked into Murphy's Meals and was shown to a corner booth for two. She'd ordered, then sat, reading something on an e-reader while she waited for her food. The table where he was sitting gave him a good view, but he wasn't sure she had noticed him.

It was incredibly distracting.

"Okay, we should get back to the office," Bryan Daniels said, getting to his feet. Law nodded, standing and holding out his hand. Daniels was one of the good ones. Ethical, generous, and easy to talk to, even if Law didn't do much talking. "I'll email you later with the contract."

"Sounds good. I'll keep an eye out for it." Law gave the other man a firm handshake before turning to his two associates and doing the same.

He should have then followed them out the door.

Normally, he *would* have followed them out the door, after pausing to take a last drink of water in order to give them time to go ahead of him.

But not today.

Instead, he took a sip of water, watching them walk out… then turned around and walked to the corner booth.

It had nothing to do with his fantasies from last night. He was just curious what Iris was doing eating lunch by herself. Not knowing anything about her outside of the club, he didn't know what she did for a living and was having a little trouble guessing based on the clues provided.

She was out at lunch on a Friday, but she looked like she had already been at work. Somehow, he didn't see Iris as the type to wear a white button-down shirt as her own choice, even if she was wearing jeans with it. With her hair pulled back in a bun, she came off as a tad more casual than business casual but far dressier than he guessed she would be if she wasn't working.

As he approached, she looked up, and her eyes widened almost comically. She snapped the e-reader case shut, putting it on the booth beside her, which, of course, made him wonder what she was reading.

He knew a lot of submissives at Stronghold liked reading racy romances. Was she one of them?

"Mas— I mean… um… Law, hi?"

Law grinned inwardly. It wasn't often he got to see her flounder. At the club, even as a submissive, she was usually completely in control of herself.

"Iris, hello. I hope I'm not interrupting. I saw you and…" His voice trailed off. And what? He'd seen her and wanted to say hi? *Great, tell her what a creeper you are.* Trying to hide his sudden discomfort, he shrugged a shoulder. "I figured I'd say hi." Yup, it sounded just as weird when he said it out loud as he'd thought it would.

"Oh, well, hi. Um… do you want to sit down?" She blinked, seeming as surprised she'd asked as he was.

"Sure." That definitely had not been what he'd meant to say. This was a terrible idea.

What are you doing?!

IRIS

Oh my God, what was she doing?

Master Law had probably come over to be polite, and now he felt like he had to sit with her because she'd asked him to. If she could have banged her head on the table, she would have.

Adjusting his jacket, he slid into the booth. Being a corner booth, meant to fit two people side by side, the arrangement was a lot more intimate than she'd realized.

"So, uh, what are you doing here?" she asked. They could chat a few minutes, then he'd probably leave once her food got there.

"Lunch with clients. What about you?" He actually sounded interested, which she wouldn't have expected.

"Lunch break. I'm a house manager, and they didn't have much for me to do today, so I figured I would give myself a treat." Hands in her lap, she fiddled with the edge of the napkin, folding it over itself and pressing down. It sprang right back as soon as she let it go, which allowed her to do it all over again... and again... and again...

"House manager?"

Iris took a deep breath. Explaining her job usually netted one of two reactions—the people who thought it wasn't a real job, like her father and brother, and the people who thought it sounded cool. Domi, Rae, and Avery had thought it sounded interesting. She'd been pretty nervous when she told them but not as nervous as she was to tell Master Law.

"Um, well, I was a nanny through an agency, then they got a posting for a house manager, and I thought I'd give it a try. Basically, the couple I work for isn't home often and needs someone to manage all their household stuff. Making appointments for repairs or anything around the house, walking their dog, running errands, getting groceries, decorating for the holidays, and cooking for them a couple times a week. Basically, any odd job they need done, I'm their go-to girl." About the only thing she didn't do was clean since they had a maid.

She loved her job—she really did—she just didn't love how some people reacted to her job. The Hills were nice, albeit a little crazy at times, but when you had as much money as they did, you could get away with being a little crazy—except it was called 'eccentric.'

"Oh, really? I could use someone to handle all that for me." To her surprise, Master Law looked more thoughtful than anything else.

"Really?"

"Yes. Well, not the dog walker since I don't have one." The little lift at the corner of his mouth was an almost smile, and Iris giggled. "But having someone at the house to make the appointment with the plumber, then meet them, or to get my groceries or whatever... who couldn't use that?"

Well, when he put it that way. Granted, Iris had to do all of those things for herself, but she didn't work eighty-hour weeks like the Hills did. They were both lawyers, like Law, although she didn't know what type of law he practiced.

"The family works pretty crazy hours. She's a defense attorney, and he's an attorney for a firm downtown. You're a lawyer too, right?" She knew he was—that was how he'd gotten his nickname at the club. She was pretty sure he knew that she knew, but he played along and told her about his work. They were still talking about what contract lawyers did when her food arrived... and he didn't leave.

Part of her wanted to ask him if he needed to get back to work. The other part of her was perfectly happy sitting there and talking. No one got to talk to Master Law like this at the club. She didn't know why he'd decided to come over and talk to her, but she liked it.

Law

What the hell was he still doing sitting here talking to Iris?

Yet he had no desire to get up and leave.

The impulse to say hi had turned into a surprisingly interesting conversation. Something he couldn't say about most people. Although he knew she was a hell of a brat as a sub, here at the restaurant, talking to her was easy. Enjoyable even.

"I should probably leave you to your lunch," he said, even though he didn't feel like getting up. He hadn't meant to sit here this long. "I'll see you tonight."

"Oh, no, actually." Iris made a face. "My roommate is having some, ah, personal issues, so I emailed Patrick and asked for the night off, so I can spend it with her. He said that would be fine, and he'd let you know."

"It's probably in my personal email. I check it first thing in the morning, then not again till the end of the day," he said automatically, the answer covering up how disappointed he was, knowing she wouldn't be there tonight.

That wasn't right, was it? Why would he be so disappointed? He finally had a night off to do what he wanted, which was supposed to be a good thing.

"I should be back tomorrow. I'm not trying to get out of my punishment." The way she said it was more than a little defensive.

Law blinked in surprise, focusing on her at the moment rather than thinking forward to tonight.

"I didn't think you were. You've been nothing but a model submissive this month."

"Even when I poured the drink on that Dom?"

Law felt his lips twitch. Hell, they weren't in the club, so he could smile. As he let his true feelings on the matter show, her reaction was worth it, eyes widening and jaw dropping open.

"He deserved it. That's why I barely punished you."

Recovering quickly from her surprise, Iris snorted.

"As if that's something new." There was a bitterness in her voice that dug under his skin like a thorn.

"What does that mean?"

"No one there ever punishes me. Not really. Not the way the other submissives get punished." Her gaze skittered away from his, and she stabbed at the macaroni and cheese on her plate with her fork. The bitterness hadn't gone away, and looking at her, Law suddenly wondered if he'd done the right thing by giving her the essay punishment instead of a real spanking.

She didn't look like a brat right now. She looked like a disappointed and frustrated submissive.

"Were you hoping to be spanked?" If she had been, giving her the essay had been the right move. He hadn't pegged it as a topping from the bottom, but at that moment, it had seemed like a true reaction.

"Not hoping, exactly. I wasn't trying to earn a spanking, but... I should have been spanked, right? If I'd been anyone else, I would have been."

"No." Law shook his head, throwing the word out there immediately because he could see how frustrated she was. "You weren't spanked because you had been good the days you worked before that and also because he deserved it."

"Oh." She still didn't quite meet his eyes, but some of the simmering tension he sensed dissipated. "I see. I guess that makes sense." But he could tell she was still disappointed.

"When was the last time you scened with someone?"

"During class." She looked even glummer. "I don't think I'm going to get a chance to really scene with someone again until the next Dom class… *if* I can convince Patrick to let me sub again." Her lower lip pouted, making her look even younger and making him feel like a dirty old man for finding it attractive. "No one wants to scene with Andrew's little sister."

Damn. She looked so sad, pushing her chicken and macaroni and cheese around her plate, it tugged something in his chest.

"I could scene with you." The words were out of his mouth before he thought them through, and the moment they were, he wanted to take them back… except she'd immediately perked up. Sat up straighter, met his gaze again, and her lips tipped up in a hopeful smile. Taking it back would be like kicking a puppy.

"Really?"

Fuck it. One scene wouldn't hurt anything, and maybe it would help him get his fantasies out of his head.

"Sure. Are you more comfortable at Stronghold or Marquis?"

She pulled her bottom lip with her teeth while she considered the question, and Law's dick twitched against his jeans. Yeah, it wasn't easy to look at her mouth without remembering that his fantasy of having his cock between her lips had taken over his masturbating session last night.

"Marquis probably…" she said slowly, though she looked uncertain. "If that's okay."

Law got it. A lot of the members treated Marquis as a special treat. He and Julie had access whenever they wanted since they were teaching the classes as a favor to Patrick and Olivia. He got one night a month as a Stronghold member, anyway, which he never used.

Normally, he wouldn't suggest taking a sub to Marquis, but Iris was different because of her brother and everyone else at Stronghold.

"Marquis is fine. Your last day of service for Patrick is Thursday. Are you free Friday or Saturday?"

"Both."

"Then let's do Friday." Feeling suddenly light, Law grinned. "I've got your number from the class, so I'll text you."

"Okay, great." She looked a little dazed, as though she couldn't believe the conversation was really happening. Truthfully, neither could Law, but now that it was, he couldn't find the wherewithal to stop it. Didn't really think he wanted to.

"Great." Getting to his feet, Law nodded down at her. "I'll talk to you later."

As he strode out of the restaurant, he felt like whistling.

CHAPTER FIVE

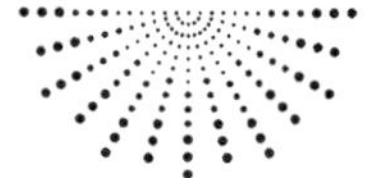

"So, he just left? No hug, no kiss, he just got up and left?" Rae sounded as though she was torn between being confused and insulted.

"Did he seem happy?" Domi wanted to know.

After an afternoon of running through the encounter in her head, Iris decided she needed to call reinforcements. Noelle hadn't come home yet, and Avery would already be at work, but she'd known Rae would definitely be available. She'd lucked out that Domi had been there, too, so she'd told them the whole story.

"He was smiling, so... yes?" Iris answered Domi instead of Rae's rhetorical question. He'd smiled a lot, actually. Iris hadn't expected that. Especially when he'd smiled about her pouring a drink on that Dom's lap. He sure as heck hadn't smiled when he'd been scolding her in the club.

Maybe that's because that was *Master* Law, and today, she'd met normal Law. Regular day Law. Lawyer Law. She was getting weird in her head because she'd been weirded out.

"Is it a date-date or just a scene-date?" Rae mused out loud.

Another rhetorical question. It was nice to hear she wasn't the only one wondering.

Master Law had confused the heck out of her today, there was no denying that.

"It sounds like a scene-date... right?" Iris asked. Master Law wouldn't want to go on a date-date with her. Even though he'd come over to sit with her today. And talked to her. Then offered to scene with her.

Lordy, she was brutally confused.

"Probably." Domi sounded sorry, but it was a relief to hear someone else say it. Yeah, her stomach dipped, and she wished the answer was different, but as long as she wasn't going into this, hoping it was one thing and it turned out it was another.

Hearing the door open behind her, Iris turned around from where she'd been pacing in the living room and waved as Noelle came in. Noelle opened her mouth, then closed it, frowning when she realized Iris was on the phone.

"Go with that," Rae said. "That way, if it *isn't* a date-date, you won't be disappointed, and if it is, it'll be a nice surprise. Assuming you'd want it to be a date-date. Um... am I assuming that correctly?"

"Yeah, I think you are." Even though it was kind of weird to say it out loud. "You're right, though. Keep my expectations low but allow myself to hope for more." That way, she wouldn't be hurt if he met her expectations, but if he wanted more, it would be a wonderful surprise. "Alrighty, I gotta go, but thank you so much."

"Of course! We're going to expect regular updates." They both giggled, and Iris grinned, though her expression faded when she caught the sour look on Noelle's face.

Dammit. She hated how jealous Noelle got about her new friendships, but she wasn't sure what she could do, short of avoiding talking to or about Domi, Rae, and Avery except when Noelle wasn't around. Iris knew that wasn't really reasonable, yet it didn't stop the guilt. Especially when Noelle looked at her like that.

Sighing inwardly, Iris looked away from Noelle so she didn't have to see her roommate while she was saying goodbye to Rae and Domi. As soon as she hung up, she pasted a smile on her face and turned back to where Noelle was getting a snack together in the kitchen. It might seem like she was behaving normally, but she was closing the cabinet doors a little harder than normal, putting the plate down harder than normal... the warning signs Iris had learned preceded a blowup.

If she was really lucky, she could head it off before Noelle got up a full head of steam.

"Hey, so good news," she said cheerfully, pretending she didn't notice Noelle's little signs. "I don't have to work at Stronghold tonight. I took it off so we could spend tonight together. Have some girl time. Maybe watch some chick flicks."

They'd used to do that all the time, and she was gratified to see Noelle's expression change immediately. Thank goodness. Blow up averted. Iris couldn't handle another late night of talking her friend down, but a night doing girl stuff would be fantastic.

"Oh, that sounds great. Can we order in Chinese?"

"Of course."

Tonight was about Noelle, and Iris had expected the question. Not like she would ever say no to Chinese delivery, even if she preferred Indian.

"How was today?" Iris asked, moving to stand on the other side of the peninsula counter and sitting on one of the barstools, so she could be comfortable while she watched Noelle get her snack together. Noelle liked to eat an apple when she got home, but she always sliced it up instead of eating the fruit whole.

"Not bad. Tyler messaged me to say he was sorry about last night." Noelle shook her head. "I haven't answered him yet. I guess I probably should, but I'm still mad."

"Yeah, but if you don't give him the chance to make it up to you, you'll never know how sorry he is," Iris pointed out. She wasn't sure if Tyler and Noelle were good for each other, but she'd never seen Noelle in a relationship that didn't have some drama, and Tyler seemed to really care about her and jumped through her hoops.

"Yeah, that's a good point." Noelle picked up a slice of apple, crunching on it thoughtfully. "Alright, I'll call him now."

"Awesome." Feeling as though she'd done her good deed for the day, Iris retreated to her room, so Noelle could have some privacy to eat and make her call. Settling on her bed, she opened the book she'd been reading when Law interrupted her at lunch. He would never know he'd been accorded an honor, considering she rarely reacted well to interruptions when she was in the middle of the newest Lexi Blake book. Hopefully, she'd be able to finish before Noelle was ready to hang out.

She was just in the middle of muttering curses under her breath at the bombshells being dropped on the page when there was a knock on her door. Stifling the much louder curse she wanted to utter, she swallowed it back and lifted her head. Damn. Normally, Noelle wanted more time to herself after getting home.

"What's up?"

The door opened, and Noelle peeked her head in, her eyes bright.

"Hey! So, Tyler was at work when I called, but he had a break, so he picked up and said he realized I was so upset last night and asked if I wanted him to take off tonight. I said, of course, so he asked one of his coworkers to cover for him, so we're going to hang out tonight!"

Wait, what?

"But..." Iris started, then stopped. Noelle seemed really excited, but... Iris had taken off tonight, so they could hang out.

"But what?" Noelle's expression had gone from thrilled and happy to annoyed so fast, Iris felt like she had whiplash.

"I just thought we were going to hang out tonight, that's all." Since she'd taken time off work.

Noelle sighed with exasperation, canting her hip to the side and putting her hand on it.

"You were the one who told me to call Tyler! Didn't you mean it?"

"No... I did, I mean..." Iris shook her head. "I'm sorry. You should definitely go out with him. I was excited about our girls' night, but we can do it some other time."

"Ugh, well, if you're going to make me feel guilty..."

"No!" Iris dropped her e-reader onto her lap, holding up her hands and shaking her head. "I swear, I mean it. Don't feel guilty. You and Tyler should go out. Have a good night. I didn't mean that to sound accusatory."

"Okay. As long as you're okay with it." Noelle eyed her.

"Yup. I'm good." Iris picked her e-reader up again and held it up. "Gonna finish reading my book and have a nice chill night."

"Okay, cool." Noelle grinned at her. "Don't wait up for me."

Iris snickered.

"Have lots of filthy make-up sex!" she called as Noelle closed the door behind her. She heard Noelle laugh on the other side.

Grinning, Iris snuggled back against her headboard and started reading again. Having a night to herself wasn't the worst thing in the world.

Law

Being at Stronghold felt… odd. He'd thought not having Iris there to watch over would be freeing, but instead, he was at loose ends.

Worse, he didn't even want to try to scene with anyone else, even though he could.

The realization grated.

He was looking forward to going to Marquis with Iris next week, probably more than he should be, but that didn't mean he couldn't scene with someone else tonight. He *should* scene with someone else tonight, if only to work off some of his built-up tension.

He didn't want to.

He also didn't want to sit alone at the bar, which was never a good spot for him, so he decided to do the rounds, even though he wasn't on Dungeon Monitor duty tonight. It was sad to realize he didn't know what else to do with himself.

Walking through the upstairs, he slowed as he looked through the open windows. Some scenes had spectators, some didn't. Friday night was always busy, though Saturday was the busiest, as was true at most places for socializing. As he passed by one of the Dungeon Monitors, he nodded his greeting before moving on and heading to the Dungeon on the lowest floor.

There were a lot more people in the Dungeon since it was mostly open space and had a lot more room to play, though there were three private rooms. The private rooms at Marquis were a lot *more* private, though, since they were set up like hotel rooms, albeit with security for the occupants that normal hotels didn't have.

"Hi, Master Law." Two of the submissives he passed as he headed back to the main floor broke out in giggles when they greeted him. Inwardly, Law sighed as he nodded to them. Why the subs got such joy out of the nickname they'd given him, he didn't know. Maybe because they felt as though they were getting away with something since he'd been the one to cave and give in on the nickname rather than continuing to fight what had clearly been a losing battle.

"Tori, Vicky." He kept moving after greeting them. While he'd scened with both, he still wasn't feeling the urge any more than when he first came in.

Walking into the main room, he looked around. No sign of Asad or Connor. He didn't see Q, either. As he was about to head out, a flash of red caught his eye on the far side of the room. There was only one submissive with that color hair and that much of it. Automatically, he turned his head to see who Morgan was talking to. If watching out for Iris over the past month was his responsibility, watching over Morgan's was *all* the Dominants' responsibility.

Interestingly, it looked like she was arguing with Brian. Arms crossed over her chest, chewing on her lower lip... arguing but uncertain. While Law knew Brian was a good Dom, he still veered over to see what was going on.

"I don't want anyone to hate me," Morgan was saying as he approached.

"No one is going to hate you."

Law's eyebrows shot up.

"Why would they hate you?" he asked, coming up alongside them. Both turned to him with expectant expressions, which made him want to step back. He'd been ready to intervene, but he hadn't expected to be welcomed.

"Morgan's roommate is moving out, and she can't afford her apartment on her own. I think she should move in with me," Brian explained.

"Um…" Of all the things he might have guessed they were talking about, that hadn't been on his list, and he didn't really know how to respond.

"Half the subs here already hate me. I don't want everyone to hate me." Morgan blinked, tears filling her hazel eyes.

"They don't hate you. They just don't know how to relate to you," Brian said soothingly. "You've made some friends."

She had. Morgan's social skills had gotten much better, although she still tended toward an almost abrasive bluntness and struggled with misconceptions she had about kink and people. However, she had been the object of envy from some of the other Stronghold subs, thanks to the special treatment and attention she received from the Dominants.

Moving in with the only currently single Daddy Dom might make for another point of jealousy, but it didn't mean everyone would hate her.

"So, this would be as friends, or…" He looked at Brian.

"As friends," Brian said firmly. He grinned and glanced at Morgan. "We have definitively determined that Morgan does not want a Daddy Dom."

"No, I don't," Morgan said as firmly as Brian had. Both men smiled encouragingly at her. Feeling secure enough to say there was something she didn't want was huge. "It would be purely platonic. Brian is my friend."

She hadn't called him Master Brian. Law felt like giving her a hug of congratulations, but he also didn't want to overdo it. They were all trying to wean Morgan off of doing things for approval and instead doing them for herself.

Maybe he should see if Iris and Morgan would get along. Morgan could use a little bit of Iris' 'I do what I want' influence.

"I think it sounds like a good idea," he said carefully. "If you don't want to, there are other options, and anyone who 'hates' you because of where you live or who you live with isn't worth your time. In fact, that would be a good way to determine what kind of person they are. Someone who is overly jealous or possessive will show it a lot sooner if you're living with Brian."

Morgan opened her mouth… closed it, and a thoughtful expression slid over her face. After a moment, she nodded and looked at Brian again.

"I'll think about it." She kept her voice firm, and Law felt like cheering, but he didn't want to make too big a deal of it. He could tell from Brian's expression, the other Dom felt the same way.

"Good. Thank you." Brian grinned. "I could use a roommate, too, you know. Cut down on costs. I used to have a roommate, and now I'm stuck paying for a two-bedroom condo on my own."

"Okay… oh, hey, there's Caroline." Morgan gave them both another smile as she waved. "I promise I'll think about it." She flounced off to her friend.

"She's making good progress," Law said.

"She is." Brian sighed. "I hope she takes me up on it, though. I'm a little worried about what kind of situation she might end up in on her own."

Weren't they all? It was a delicate balance, trying to give someone like Morgan the space she needed to make her own decisions while also keeping her safe as she learned to navigate her own life.

"Oh, hey, Kincaid and Zach are here. Want to join us?" The invitation seemed sincere, so Law nodded.

"Sure, thanks." It had been a while since Law had tried hanging out with anyone new, but Asad and Connor were still MIA, and it had been good getting to know Q the other night. Maybe he needed to relax and branch out a little.

Plus, conversation with people he didn't usually talk to would hopefully help him keep his mind off Iris and the unsettling realization of how much he was looking forward to scening with her next week.

CHAPTER SIX

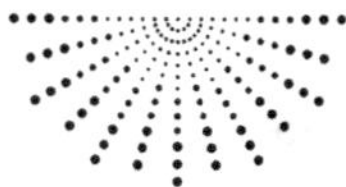

The one problem with reading e-books instead of paperbacks was she didn't dare throw her e-reader across the room, even when she really wanted to. Like when she finished a book that was just so damn good, but she needed the next one in the series *right now,* and it wasn't available.

It hadn't taken her long to finish the book because she'd been so focused on reading, she'd zipped right through it. Now, what was she supposed to do with the rest of her night?

No book. No Noelle. No Stronghold.

Sitting around alone didn't really appeal to her. She usually read when she had alone time, but now she was feeling antsy because she couldn't read the book she *wanted* to read since it wouldn't be available for months.

Maybe she should see what her other friends were doing tonight. Noelle might not like it, but she had been the one to ditch Iris. Besides, she should be out all night with Tyler, and as long as Iris never mentioned it, Noelle would never know.

Iris picked up her phone and tapped out a message in the group text she had with Rae, Domi, and Avery.

I don't have to go into Stronghold, but my plans got canceled for the night... are you all up to anything?

She'd barely gotten to her feet when her phone made a quacking noise and buzzed with a response from Rae. The duck's quack was the perfect text notification since she'd never met anyone else who used it.

Avery's at work. We're heading to Marquis in an hour to hang at the bar until she can join us. Wanna come?

Happiness lit up the inside of Iris' chest.

Sounds good. I'll see you there!

It was really nice having friends. Feeling a lot more excited about her evening, Iris hopped up to figure out what she was going to wear, then do her hair and makeup. She could use some in-person girl talk about Master Law if they didn't mind going through it all with her again. Of course, that made her wonder what Master Law was doing tonight.

Her hands stilled on the hanger she'd been about to shove aside to look through her clothes.

Was he at Stronghold? Or Marquis?

At lunch today, he'd asked her to scene with him, but she wasn't at Stronghold tonight, so he was free to do as he wanted while he was there.

Granted, he was free to do as he wanted regardless, but he'd only tried to scene with someone else once while he'd been keeping an eye on her during her Stronghold shifts. Not that she'd meant for him to keep from scening while he was watching over her, but deep down, she'd liked knowing he wouldn't be.

Ugh.

Well, if he was scening with someone else tonight, there was nothing she could do about it. In fact, if he did scene with someone else, that would be a pretty definitive indication of how he felt about their scene next week and whether it was a scene-date or a date-date.

Don't get your hopes up for a date-date.

Law

Unsurprisingly, at first, talk with Brian, Kincaid, and Zach centered around Morgan. Brian caught the other two men up to date, which allowed Law more insight into the conversation before he'd joined them. It appeared Brian really did need a roommate, even if he was okay living on his own for a bit, which made Law feel better about the situation. He'd be able to reassure Morgan on that front if she asked.

"Speaking of watching over cute subbies, Iris is done with her punishment stint next week, right?" Brian asked, turning to Law and surprising the answer from him.

"Yes." Something about Brian's thoughtful expression made Law's muscles clench. "Why?" Was the Daddy Dom interested in her? Would Iris want a Daddy Dom?

Maybe.

She'd been a lot less trouble since she'd had someone watching over her, but she'd been frustrated by the lack of play partners. Law knew if Brian was interested, he should step aside and let the other man have a try...

The very thought sent jealousy surging through his gut.

"I noticed no one really scenes with her." Brian shrugged. "I was thinking I might see if she's interested."

"Especially since she's never shown any interest in him," Kincaid said slyly, causing Law to raise his eyebrows as Brian scowled at the other man. Out of all of them, Kincaid was the tallest and most imposing, but clearly, Brian wasn't intimidated.

"That's not why."

"Sure, it's not," Zach chimed in. Unlike Brian and Kincaid, who were both in their leathers and vests, Zach looked as if he'd come by the club after work, wearing slacks and a button-up shirt with the top button undone and the sleeves rolled up. Although Law didn't ask, Zach explained anyway. "Brian prefers to scene with subbies who aren't interested in him because the subbie he's interested in doesn't want anything to do with him. So, rather than find someone who is, he tortures himself by waiting for her to become interested while trying to help the subbies who need a play partner but won't get attached."

"Sounds complicated," Law murmured, lifting his iced tea to his lips to take a sip. Though was it any more complicated than what he did? He preferred the submissives with no expectations of a relationship as well, even if he wasn't waiting for someone in particular.

He just didn't want a submissive who would get attached. He wasn't the relationship type. He wasn't a player type either, but that was safer than commitment.

"That's not what I'm doing," Brian complained, though he didn't provide evidence to the contrary. Crossing his arms over his chest, he glared at his friends as if the statement on its own should be enough.

Law had to chuckle. Though he didn't know these three very well, they reminded him a lot of himself, Connor, and Asad.

"I'm half an hour late, and you've replaced me?" The outraged whine belonged to Master Mitch, former club stud and now firmly attached to Iris' friend, Domi. Law choked on laughter at the outraged expression on the blonde's face and his hands on his hips. He wasn't glaring at Law but at the rest of his friends.

"You snooze, you lose," Kincaid replied, grinning. None of them took Mitch seriously at times like this. "Besides, we figured you'd be with your girlfriend. You were invited out of pure courtesy."

"Nah, Domi's having a ladies' night. She, Rae, and Iris are headed to Marquis to wait for Avery to get off work." Mitch rolled his eyes. "No boys allowed."

"Iris is going to Marquis?" Law asked, stilling. The others looked at him with surprise. His tone had come out a lot harsher than he'd meant, but... did that mean she'd flat out lied to him earlier today?

"Yeah, she texted the others right before I left. Apparently, she had other plans tonight that were canceled." Mitch eyed him a bit warily. "Was she supposed to be here?"

"Yes. I mean, no." Law floundered, with four pairs of eyes on him, waiting for an explanation... and he didn't really have one—not one he wanted to admit out loud. "Patrick let her off for tonight because she said her roommate needed her."

"Ah." The amusement in Mitch's blue eyes was matched by the interest glinting in them. "So, you thought maybe she'd lied. That would be fun if she'd been a naughty girl under your watch. She's been remarkably well-behaved the past month. It's been almost disappointing."

"Maybe for you," Zach cut in with a snort. "The rest of us appreciate a peaceful club."

"Says the sadist," Mitch muttered.

Law chuckled. As much as he wanted to leave Stronghold and text Iris to find out if she would tell him about her change in plans, he made himself relax. There would be enough time for that later.

Iris

Perched at the bar with Domi and Rae, wearing a cute sundress and her hair pulled back from her face, martini in hand, Iris was really glad she'd made the decision to text them. Making friends had never been her strong suit, but they'd made it so easy, and even though she knew they'd been besties for a really long time, they made sure to include her. Even when they had to explain their inside jokes, which mostly seemed to revolve around shows and movies they'd watched.

"You've never heard of Dr. Horrible's Sing-Along-Blog?" Rae asked, mock outraged. Tonight she was dressed in a super cute green tube dress that clung to her curves. As usual, she'd matched her outfit to the few colorful braids she had threaded through the mass of brown ones. Beside her, Domi was wearing a little black dress, but with heavy boots and a ton of makeup to complete her pixie-goth look. Even though she was tiny, several guys had already eyed her, then edged away, realizing that she was not to be messed with.

"Sorry?" Iris shrugged her shoulders, hands open wide.

"You don't have to apologize just... girl, we are going to have so much fun educating you."

"Cheers to that," Domi chimed in, raising her glass. Rae clinked it, then they held out their glasses to Iris. Giggling, she clinked their glasses with her own.

Whatever, if they wanted her to watch it so badly, she was down. Sounded like fun.

"How are we doing over here, ladies? Everyone behaving?" Shane, Iris' favorite bartender at Marquis, sidled up on the other side of the bar, smiling at them. He was a total sweetheart and pretty handsome for an older guy. In some ways, he reminded her a little of Master Law, except Shane was white and Master Law was Filipino, but they both had the same bald head and salt and pepper goatee.

"Misbehaving is more like it," Domi replied, winking at him.

"Hey, Shane, you're a guy," Rae said, leaning forward on her forearms and making him chuckle.

"Why yes, yes, I am."

"We have a situation here," Rae continued, pointing at Iris, who groaned as she realized where Rae was headed. They were a couple drinks in, but not enough to keep her from blushing hotly. "We need a man's opinion."

"Okay, hit me," Shane replied, leaning on the bar from the other side, his expression becoming much more serious.

"You're straight, right?"

"Right."

Great, this just kept getting better and better. Iris tipped her head back, taking the rest of her martini as a shot. Couldn't hurt, right?

"So, if you saw a woman you knew, having lunch by herself, and you went to speak with her, then ended up sitting down and talking to her for half an hour... then asked her to an event the following week... that's you asking her out on a date, right?" Rae didn't break eye contact once, and Iris groaned.

"It's more complicated than that," she said. "You forgot the part where he felt sorry for me because no one ever invites me to... events because of my brother."

"Ah... *ah.*" Shane's expression flickered with understanding, his second 'ah' making it clear he'd figured out what 'event' was code for. Considering that what happened on the second floor of Marquis was the worst kept secret among the first-floor staff, she wasn't surprised.

"It's not that complicated," Rae argued. "Right, Domi?"

"I mean... it's a bit more complicated than you made it sound," Domi said. Iris nodded her head firmly. "But I don't think it's as complicated as Iris thinks."

Just then, Iris' phone buzzed with a text message. Who would be texting her now? Crap... Noelle, but when she pulled it out of her handbag, it wasn't Noelle's name on the screen. It was Master Law's.

"Oooh, what did he say?" Domi and Rae were leaning toward her, trying to see more of her phone screen. Nosy bitches. Iris laughed, shaking her head.

"Well, give me a second to look at it."

On the other side of the bar, Shane straightened up, chuckling.

"Let me know if you need me for anything else, ladies."

"Hey, you never answered our question... oh, never mind." Rae sighed as Shane walked away, not looking back. Smart man.

"He just asked how my night is going." Iris chewed her lower lip, studying the simple text as if clues might suddenly pop out at her. She giggled when a thought occurred to her. "Maybe he feels weird not having to watch over me tonight."

"Or maybe he doesn't like not knowing what you're up to after watching over you for so long," Domi teased.

Iris laughed as she quickly typed her reply.

My roommate canceled our plans, so I'm at Marquis with Domi and Rae. I promise we're not causing any trouble =P What about you?

"This looks good, right?" she asked, tipping the phone toward them so they could give it a brief scan. Once she had approval, she hit send.

It only took a moment before her phone buzzed again, and she raised her eyebrows. Domi and Rae made encouraging noises, glee in their eyes.

Just got home from Stronghold. It was a pretty quiet night. Now I'm stuck on my couch with my cat on my lap, so who knows when I'll be able to go to bed.

"He has a cat!" She wouldn't have pictured Master Law with any kind of pet, but she supposed a cat was easier to imagine than a dog. It wasn't that he seemed like an animal-hater, but he wasn't the type to appreciate stray hairs all over the place.

"Oooh, tell him to send a picture," Domi said, poking her in the side. "Ana's still asking for a pet. I think Mitch is encouraging her behind my back." She scowled, though she wasn't actually angry. "If he gets her something for Christmas without consulting me, he's going to be in big trouble."

"Please," Rae snorted. "He's way too smart for that. He's much more likely to get *himself* a pet, then let Ana 'borrow' it as much as she wants."

The horrified expression on Domi's face was hilarious. Since she and Mitch hadn't officially moved in together, technically, he could do whatever he wanted pet-wise, but they spent just about every night together, so she would be affected by whatever he did.

"Oooh, look!" Iris held up her phone with the photo Law had just sent of the cat curled up on his lap. Her heart melted. What was it about men and cute animals? "Mast... I mean, Law says its name is Whiskers."

Had he named the cat? She had trouble seeing him coming up with such a cutesy name. Then again, she wouldn't have guessed he had a cat, either.

"Girl, you are in so much trouble," Domi murmured, peering at the phone, then glancing at Iris. "I hope you know what you're doing, scening with him next week. I'm living proof the whole 'bondage buddies' thing doesn't always work out the way you expect it to."

"Considering how cute you and Mitch are together, that's not exactly off-putting," Rae pointed out.

"No, but we got lucky. It could have blown up in our face multiple times. Heck, it almost did." Domi shook her head, though there was a little smile on her lips, as though she was remembering the way they'd worked it out, not the way the situation had almost exploded.

Iris mentally crossed her fingers.

If she ended up half as lucky in love as Domi and Mitch, she'd be thrilled. Maybe Master Law wasn't the one, but... heck, scening with him was a step in the right direction. Maybe once she got a few scenes in with someone, more Doms would follow.

Hopefully, by then, her crush would have run its course.

CHAPTER SEVEN

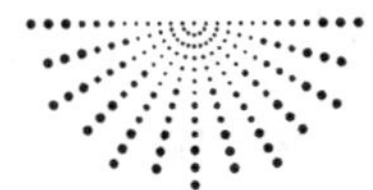

IRIS

Walking in through the front door, Iris yawned, stretching. The apartment was dark, the way she'd left it. When she flipped on the light, she screamed. Someone was sitting in the living room. When she realized it was Noelle, she sighed. Closing the door behind her, she winced as she glanced into the hallway, hoping no one had heard her scream. Her heart was still pounding.

Then she whirled around to face her roommate.

"What on earth are you doing sitting in the dark?" She pressed her hand to her chest, where she could feel her heart thudding against her palm as she willed herself to calm down. "You scared the shit out of me."

It wasn't until the words were out of her mouth, she registered the unhappy scowl on Noelle's face. She'd been too freaked out Noelle was there at all.

Inwardly she groaned. Crap.

"Oh, *you* were scared? Imagine how I felt when I came home, and you weren't here. You didn't text or call or anything to let me know you were going to be out."

She hadn't thought she'd need to, figuring Noelle wouldn't be here when she got home, that she'd be with Tyler for the night. Or she'd bring Tyler with her and wouldn't even notice Iris' absence. If Iris was completely honest, she'd been happy about both possible scenarios.

So, where was Tyler?

Iris got a sinking feeling in the pit of her stomach.

"What happened? Is everything okay?"

"You mean other than my so-called best friend lying to me about what she was doing tonight and sneaking around with her *new* friends?" Noelle spat out, resentment and betrayal emanating from every line of her body. Her eyes filled with fire as she leaned forward accusingly.

"I wasn't sneaking around! I didn't realize you'd be home. I thought you'd be with Tyler all night, and I didn't lie to you. I didn't make plans until after you left." Iris spread her hands wide, holding them up on either side of her in a gesture of surrender, hoping logic would calm Noelle down.

Unfortunately, it seemed to make her even angrier, and she got to her feet, her voice rising with everyone.

"Right, you waited until after I left so you could sneak around behind my back! Why didn't you just say you wanted to hang out with your other friends instead of pretending like you wanted to spend time with me?" Noelle shouted.

Iris made shushing noises. Between her scream when she'd come in and Noelle's shouting, there was no way they weren't disturbing at least one of their neighbors.

"Noelle, it's two in the morning!" Even though she was speaking vehemently, she still kept her voice lowered, giving Noelle a look.

"Then maybe next time don't stay out so late! And don't lie about it either!"

"I didn't—"

It didn't matter what she protested. Noelle stormed off to her room, slamming the door behind her. Iris winced.

There was no way in hell she would knock on Noelle's door now. It would have to wait until a decent hour in the morning because she didn't know if Noelle would keep shouting or calm down.

Granted, she might be even angrier tomorrow that Iris hadn't come begging for forgiveness, but... at least she would be yelling during daylight hours. To be perfectly honest, Iris didn't feel like begging for forgiveness. Yeah, she'd gone out with friends, but only after Noelle had ditched her for the evening.

She might have told Noelle she was staying in to read, but that really had been all she'd planned when Noelle had left. She hadn't realized she'd fly through the book the way she had. Rae and Domi might not have even been available. Maybe she could have come home earlier, but Avery hadn't been able to join them until close to midnight, and she hadn't wanted to leave immediately.

Besides, she should be able to go hang out with friends without Noelle freaking out. Especially since Noelle had been the one to ditch her.

Feeling justified indignation made things a little easier as she passed Noelle's door and heard her best friend make a hmphing noise from within. She knew she would eventually end up apologizing to keep the peace, but right now, she wouldn't give in. She wasn't in the wrong, dammit.

Hopefully, a good night's sleep would put them both on a more even keel. She could find out how things had gone with Tyler, which would probably explain why Noelle had been home and in such a bad mood.

———

LAW

"Take a step back!"

"I'm fine where I am." Asad lifted the axe over his head, stepped forward, and let it fly.

It thunked against the target and fell to the ground. Law smirked.

"I told you to take a step back."

"Yeah, yeah, yeah." Asad glared at the target before turning to glare at Law. Dressed in a tank top and jean shorts, he was at his most casual. Normally, he preferred to be a bit more dressed up, as did Law, but the summer's heat and humidity were brutal, even in the shade of Connor's yard. "Alright, Mr. Know-it-All, your turn."

Getting up from his seat, Law placed his can of sparkling water in its Stronghold koozie on the table while Connor chuckled and took a swig of his beer. Where Patrick had gotten the idea to make koozies with Stronghold's name on it, Law didn't know, but he had to admit they came in handy. Connor's had the Marquis logo.

Granted, looking at them, no one would immediately know that they were advertising kink clubs, especially since Marquis had become known for its restaurant on the first floor, but still. It felt a little surreal.

Still grumbling under his breath, Asad retrieved the two axes he'd thrown and put them back at the end of the run. He passed Law on his way back to the table, where he picked up his beer to take a large swig.

"Has it occurred to you the beer might not be helping your aim?" Law asked, calling over his shoulder.

Asad held up one hand, straight out in front of him, middle finger extended high to the sky, making both Law and Connor laugh.

"It doesn't affect Connor," Asad said a moment later.

"That's because Connor is basically a Viking."

"It's true," Connor said, shrugging one shoulder while Law got into position. He grinned at Asad, whose scowl deepened. Apparently, the reality of the situation—Connor towering over both of them in height and with the extra bulk to go with it—would not satisfy Asad.

Examining his distance from the target Connor had built, so they could throw axes during the Renn Fair off-season, Law nodded in satisfaction. He lifted the axe above his head, both hands wrapped around the base. Sometimes, they used the smaller one-handed ones, but Asad had wanted to practice with the larger ones today. Taking a deep breath, Law exhaled as he stepped forward, his arms swinging forward, carrying the weight of the axe with them.

"Heard you have a date with Iris on Friday."

He stumbled. The axe rotated twice and hit with a muted thunk, the head half-buried in the ground.

Growling under his breath, he turned and glared at Asad, planting his hands on his hips. Not that Asad cared. He and Connor were howling with laughter.

"Seriously?" Law asked, moving his glare back and forth between them. "That was cheap. I get a do-over on that one."

"Honestly, I didn't think it was true until you grounded the axe," Asad replied, holding one hand against his stomach, laughing through his answer. "Guess I was wrong, thinking maybe you meant it when you said you weren't interested in her."

"I'm not. It's not a date. It's a scene." Shaking his head in disgust, Law dropped his hands and went to retrieve the axe.

"Uh-huh." Out of the corner of his eye, he could see Asad and Connor exchange a glance, both still laughing, although it was finally dwindling. Despite the stark contrast in their appearances, they had the same annoying grin on their faces. "A scene you didn't tell either of *us* about."

"I knew you'd try to make more of it than it was." Law yanked the axe from the ground and made a face at the dirt covering its edge. He tapped it against his leg, knocking the worst of it off. "How did you find out, anyway?"

"Iris was at Marquis last night with Rae, Domi, and Avery, and they were talking about it. I also heard about it from Freddy, who got it from Luke, who heard it from Olivia, who had been talking to Shane, who was their bartender." Asad's grin widened even more. "So, you can understand why I was skeptical. I really thought it was a case of telephone gone wrong."

"Scening with her means nothing, huh?" Connor asked, raising an eyebrow. He might be the quietest out of them, but he had a talent for latching on to the thing his friends least wanted to talk about and choosing it as the topic for conversation.

Law scowled at him.

"She mentioned that no one scenes with her because of her

brother. I figured I could scene with her. You're the ones who were pushing me to do something with her."

"Which is why it's so interesting that you decided not to tell us about this scene… since it means *nothing*," Asad teased, leaning his hip against the table and grinning.

In hindsight, Law could see how not telling them made it seem like a bigger deal than it was, but he'd wanted to put off the teasing.

Shaking his head, he turned back to the target. Took a step. The axe flew. He frowned as it thunked into the target but not right in the center.

"Hmm, a little off your game there, are we?" Asad asked, taking another sip of his beer.

"Like you're one to talk," Law muttered. He picked up the second axe and let it fly. This time it hit dead center, filling him with satisfaction. Heading to the target, he yanked them both out and returned to the other end, where Connor was already waiting.

In Connor's hands, the axe looked more like a one-handed throwing axe, but the big man still chose to use both hands.

"Why not Stronghold?" Connor asked, loosely holding the first axe by his side, apparently more interested in questioning Law than in taking his turn. "Why Marquis?"

"That's where she wanted to go. I assume because she didn't want to risk running into her brother."

"Don't they usually go to the club on different nights? I mean, when she wasn't serving out her punishment." Asad tilted his head at Law, giving him a significant look. "Are you sure *she* knows this isn't a date?"

"I'm sure." He said it a lot more firmly than he felt, but giving it a moment's thought, he was pretty sure she did. He'd only offered after she'd told him about her trouble finding someone to scene with and was pretty sure she'd chosen Marquis for the privacy from her brother and his friends, not because she wanted to be alone with him.

If he felt a little disappointed about that, that was his problem and absolutely not something he would be sharing with Asad and Connor.

Asad and Connor exchanged another look, then the big man

shrugged and lifted the axe over his head to throw it. Back to business.

Law wondered what Iris was up to today... what she had told her friends... what she might think about next week. If Asad and Connor weren't watching him so closely, he would have texted her.

CHAPTER EIGHT

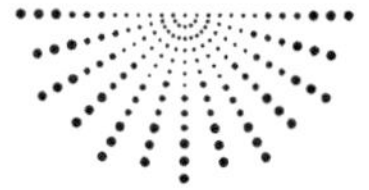

"What else do you need, Dad?" Iris dusted off her hands as she walked back inside. Even though it was hot as balls, she'd worn jeans because she knew she'd been kneeling in the dirt. Her dad loved his garden, but he was having more and more trouble keeping up with it and with the house, so she and Andrew made a point to spend at least one Saturday a month helping with the things he couldn't do so well on his own.

"You to take a break." Grinning, he turned and put a glass of cold water on the counter. "Here, hydrate."

Smiling, Iris sat down. Andrew and Kate would probably be inside in a minute, too. They were trimming the bushes in the backyard that had gotten a little overgrown.

"Thank you." Not much tasted better than cold water when she was hot and sweaty. She could practically feel the cells in her body cheering with relief. August was a bitch of a month in Maryland.

"How have you been doing? How's work?"

For the sake of peace, Iris decided to ignore the odd note in his voice when he asked about work. She knew he was trying. Doing someone else's busy work wasn't his idea of a job, but he couldn't exactly argue with the money. His prediction she would be miserable hadn't come true.

"Good and good. Mrs. Hill told me she wants to decorate the house for Halloween and Christmas this year. I get to go through all their decorations and decide where they go." Iris grinned, and her father smiled.

"You always did like decorating the house. You'll be good at that."

It was something she and her mom had done together before her mom passed. While it sometimes felt bittersweet, Iris always felt closer to her mom when she was putting up decorations.

"I'm looking forward to seeing what they have and if they'll let me add to it," Iris admitted. After their mom passed, things had been tighter financially, and buying decorations had not been on the list of priorities. Before her mom passed, they'd bought at least one new decoration every year.

Living in an apartment, Iris had some of her own decorations and bought a new one every year, but she had a long way to go before she'd have the collection she wanted. She bet the Hills had some epic decorations tucked away in their attic. Maybe even National Lampoon level.

There was every chance Mrs. Hill would give her permission to add to them. She'd already let Iris start ordering fresh flowers monthly for the vase in the entry hall. It was almost more fun spending someone else's money than spending her own.

Her father's lips quirked, but he didn't comment, which she appreciated.

"How is Noelle? You haven't brought her by in a while."

"Yeah…" Iris let out her breath on a long sigh. The answer to that question was so complicated. "We've been growing apart, I think."

That was true, but it was also true spending time with Noelle wasn't as fun as it used to be. Was it because she had new friends she had more in common with? Or was it because Noelle had become less fun? It was hard to figure out.

What she knew was she didn't enjoy hanging out with Noelle like she used to, but she felt guilty about not enjoying it and not doing it as often. That even her dad had noticed said she really had stepped back. She didn't feel like getting into the fact she and Noelle weren't talking since Iris still hadn't apologized for going out last night.

She hadn't had much of a chance. She and Noelle had barely seen each other for two minutes before she'd left this morning, but she also hadn't wanted to. She didn't feel like she should have to.

The back door slammed open, and Andrew held the door open for his fiancé as they came in from the backyard. They were even sweatier than Iris when she'd first walked in.

"Oh my God, air conditioning feels so good," Kate said with a little moan, using the back of her arm to wipe her brow. She used her other hand to lift her long blonde ponytail off her back.

"Sit, sit." Iris' dad was already hopping to his feet and hurrying over to get them glasses. "I'll get you some water."

"Thanks, Dad," Andrew said, going to the kitchen table and pulling out a chair for Kate before he plopped down on his own. Grasping the hem of his shirt, he pulled it up to wipe his face, flashing his stomach as he did so. Iris rolled her eyes.

There were plenty of women who would have appreciated the view, but she wasn't one of them. It never ceased to amaze her how her brother could be 'on' at all times. She was grateful Kate had come back into his life, and they'd gotten back together. Especially because she adored Kate.

"So, what were you guys talking about?" Andrew asked, letting his shirt drop, now wet and soggy at the bottom. Blech.

"I'm decorating the Hill's house for Halloween and Christmas this year," Iris said, pushing a cheerful smile onto her face. While her dad had been trying when it came to conversations about her job, Andrew still had no problem making his opinion known.

"I can't believe you get paid for that." He shook his head.

"Says the guy who makes decorations." Granted, with his carpentry skills, he made a lot more than decorations, but their dad didn't know Andrew also made BDSM equipment.

"And furniture." Andrew frowned at her. "I'm creating something."

"So is Iris. She's making a comfortable and beautiful home for someone else and allowing them to enjoy their free time when they manage to get it." Kate shot her an apologetic look before turning a much less pleasant look upon Andrew, but Iris didn't blame her for not being able to keep Andrew under control. There was only so much one could do when he was determined to be an ass. Besides, as her big brother, he felt morally obligated to give her a hard time, and she returned the favor. "I wish I could afford an Iris."

"We don't need an Iris." Andrew rolled his eyes. "We can do our own laundry."

Iris scowled at him. She did a hell of a lot more than laundry.

"Because we have the time, but think about everything we could do with our free time if we didn't have to do things like laundry, grocery shopping, and keeping everything in the house running smoothly. We could just spend our free time enjoying ourselves. Besides, you hate doing laundry. Think about how much nicer the house would be without you bitching through folding your laundry."

Andrew's mouth opened. Closed. He frowned. Kate winked at Iris, who desperately wished she could throw her arms around her brother's fiancé and hug the fuck out of her. Kate had been on her side from day one, and she so appreciated that. Out of the corner of her eye, she could see her dad nodding his head.

"I'm so glad you're back," she said fervently.

Sure, she'd said similar things before, but it didn't make its way through the men's heads until Kate was the one who said it. It had been the same way when she'd been growing up, so she'd long gotten over resenting it. Now, she was grateful they listened to *someone*, especially if they laid off the third degree afterward.

"Me, too." Kate grinned at her. Andrew made a grumpy noise, but that was nothing new. Since they'd exhausted the topic of her work, apparently, he moved on to the next thing he wanted to hassle her about.

"I hear you have a date next week."

"What?" Her dad sat up straighter, appearing interested but also wary.

"How did you hear about that?" she demanded. One of the cardinal rules of being siblings who were both into kink—thou shalt not mention kink in front of the parents. At least, that was the unspoken rule in their household. Andrew had gotten around it by calling it a 'date,' but that just made things more complicated.

"You were at Marquis' bar last night. Shane told Olivia, who told Lexie, who told me. And Lexie told Patrick, who told Andrew." Kate shrugged, sending Iris an apologetic look.

"Who is Shane?" her dad asked, obviously confused but also amused. He was used to playing catch-up to their conversations.

"The bartender," Andrew replied.

"Oh my God… do you all not have anything better to do than gossip? It's worse than high school," Iris complained, rubbing her hands over her face. She would never get used to how fast gossip spread like wildfire through the clubs. She wouldn't have pegged Shane as gossipy, but then again, even if he only told Olivia, who was his boss, that was enough to get the whole train started.

"So, does that mean you have a date? What's his name? What does he do?" Her dad was ready with the third degree.

Before she could answer, Andrew was already jumping in with his version of events—which would have pissed her off, even if it hadn't included his opinion.

"His name is Lawrence, he's a lawyer, and he's too old for her."

"He's like maybe ten years older than me." She glared at Andrew. "And it is none of your business. It's not even a real date… it's a hang-out date. You know, we're hanging out together since I struggle to get any *real* dates thanks to my overprotective big brother."

Andrew scowled but said nothing, probably because he couldn't think of anything to say since it was one hundred percent true.

"Ten years isn't too bad," her father said slowly. "So, he's in his early thirties."

"Yes." Iris stuck her tongue out at Andrew.

"It's not a question of years but maturity," Andrew muttered.

She flipped him off when their dad wasn't looking. Who cared if Law was too mature for her? Maturity was overrated.

Law

The week was dragging by. Law knew it was because he was looking forward to the end of the week and scening with Iris, but that didn't help. If anything, it made him more anxious about scening with her.

When was the last time he had actually looked forward to scening with a submissive? A particular submissive?

Easy answer? He hadn't.

Ever.

That wasn't how he operated.

He was having trouble focusing, so he'd decided to take some work home. Whiskers stated his objection to Law's at-home hours by walking across his keyboard as much as possible, which didn't help, either. Dammit. When he'd called Iris trouble, he hadn't meant for him personally.

"Get down from there." He picked up Whiskers, ignoring the cat's angry hiss, and set her on the floor. She tried to swipe at him, but he'd learned his lesson from the past and easily got his hand out of the way. "Now, stay there. I have work to do."

Glaring at him, Whiskers sat completely motionless, exactly where he'd set her down. It was a little freaky, but he did his best to ignore her.

Ten minutes later, his phone buzzed, and it was a text message from Iris. The little jump his heart did wasn't something he wanted to think about too hard. He felt like a teenager, excited about getting a text from a girl. That was bad.

For the first time, he felt pulled in two different directions. What he wanted and what he thought he needed usually aligned. Now, what he wanted was Iris, and he was pretty sure she was the opposite of what he needed. Even if he'd wanted a relationship, she was too unpredictable. Too wild. Too impulsive.

But under my eye, she's been a good girl. She's kept out of trouble.

Maybe I'm what she *needs.*

That thought tugged at a part of him he'd thought long dead and made him want to run even faster, but he wasn't sure if he wanted to run away from or to her.

Pushing aside his conflicting emotions, he checked the text.

Just wanted to give you a heads-up. My brother knows about Friday night, in case you want to back out while you can. =P

The silly face emoji didn't take away from the resignation in her words. She was expecting him to back out because of her brother, just like every other Dom at Stronghold and Marquis had backed away from her outside of the class, where they'd been required to scene with her.

Shit.

She needed this. Deserved it, even.

Something Law couldn't ignore, no matter how conflicted his emotions were about the situation. Other people came first. He'd been selfish in the past—there was no way he was going to put his needs before hers. Especially not when he'd been the one to make the original offer.

Nope, not going to back out. The only way we're not scening on Friday is if you cancel on me.

That would leave things open on her end in case she got cold feet. Part of him almost hoped she would, but it would disappoint as hell the rest of him if she did.

The message she sent back made his chest hurt for her.

Thank you.

Yup, Law kind of hoped Andrew said something to him because he would love a good excuse to give Iris' big brother an earful. Although he wasn't sure, Iris would want him to do that.

Sighing, he looked down at Whiskers, who was still glaring up at him.

"What?"

Sniffing haughtily, she stood and stalked away, tail high in the air, as though she couldn't believe he'd even asked the question. Watching her go, Law chuckled, then turned to get back to work.

Oddly, it was a lot easier to concentrate, as if not backing out had settled something inside him. Hell, maybe it had.

CHAPTER NINE

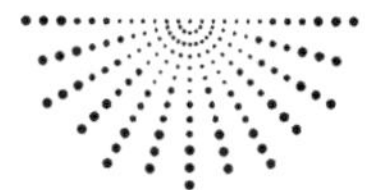

Thursday night. His last night on Iris Watch and her brother wasn't working at the club. Probably a good thing, all things considered. Law was having trouble keeping his eyes off her, though she was dressed almost modestly compared to some outfits she'd worn to Stronghold.

A corset pushed her breasts up but covered most of her upper body. The flirty skirt fluttered around the tops of her thighs but didn't cling to her ass the way some of her skirts did.

She was giving him little sidelong glances, too. The biggest difference was instead of pretending they weren't looking at each other, their gazes kept catching... and holding.

"This is almost painful to watch," Asad said after Iris nearly tripped over one of the subs kneeling on the carpet in the Lounge, and Law hastily looked away. "Maybe you two should just go grab a room here tonight and get rid of some of the sexual tension filling the air."

Law scowled at him.

"I'm just keeping an eye on her. The way I'm supposed to, remember?"

"Pretty sure Patrick did not know what he was asking when he set you up with that job," Asad murmured, taking a sip of his beer. Connor chuckled but thankfully, didn't add to the running commentary.

Glancing around, Law caught Q's eye as he was making his way toward the bar. Gratefully latching onto the distraction, he greeted the other man and asked if he wanted to join them.

"Here alone tonight?" Law asked after everyone said hello. Q sat down with them at Asad's invitation. The question was fairly rhetorical since he wouldn't have joined them otherwise, but Law was feeling somewhat desperate to keep the conversation off him and Iris. He didn't want his friends looking too closely at them because—if he was being honest—he didn't want to look too closely at his own motivations.

"Yeah, figured I might try doing a scene with someone. Maybe." Q glanced at the Lounge area where the subs congregated.

When Law followed the other man's gaze, he was surprised to see Q was looking at Samantha. A switch, she'd been in the dominants class at the same time as Q, and they had not gotten along. Mostly, they'd avoided each other, but there had been definite friction. Apparently, she was feeling subby today since she was hanging out in the Lounge, chatting with Morgan. Law wondered if Morgan had given Brian an answer yet.

"The curvy blonde?" Asad asked, also following Q's gaze. "I wouldn't mind a scene with Morgan. She's fun to play with, and she knows the score. I can wingman you."

"I'm pretty sure she'd murder me," Q said drily. "We knew each other in high school, and we didn't exactly get along."

"Then why do you keep staring at her?" Asad enjoyed uncomfortable questions, and it was a relief he'd found a new victim for it.

"Because I think she post-it noted my car the last time I was here."

"What?"

Q explained that the last time he'd been at Stronghold, someone had covered his entire car in post-it notes. The doors, the windows, the top, the sides. The frustration was clear in his voice, but it was also one of the funniest things Law had ever heard.

"It took me almost an hour to take them all off." Q's gaze flicked back to where Samantha was sitting. As far as Law could tell, she hadn't looked over at him.

"What makes you think it was her? Did you check the security footage?"

"Apparently, there was an hour-and-a-half-long blackout right before she left the club with Angel and Lexie." Q pressed his lips together. "The cameras came back online right after Lexie returned. Alone."

Law coughed to cover his chuckle, and Asad looked as if he was about to lose it, trying to hold his laughter in. Connor was flat-out grinning, but he was using his mug to hide his expression.

Yeah, Q was probably right. Lexie had a bit of a reputation for pranks at Stronghold. Being the owner's girlfriend, she could get away with things other subs couldn't—people still talked about the pink glitter incident. Patrick always made sure she paid a price, but that wasn't enough to stop her. She'd just gotten a lot better about not getting caught.

"Okay, but why would Samantha do that?" Law asked, genuinely curious. He'd gotten to know all the Dominants who'd gone through the class with Q and had to admit, while Angel and Lexie were known pranksters, Samantha had always seemed more serious. If he'd had to assign her a stereotype, he would have guessed top of her class, never got into trouble, too smart to be popular, and high school vale-dictorian.

Even at the club, she'd struggled a little to make friends, though not in the same way as Morgan. It was more she was shy, always holding herself back from engaging with people. He had trouble seeing her pulling a prank, much less roping Angel and Lexie into one.

"Ah... well." Q's gaze found its way to the ceiling as though he thought he might find a suitable answer written there. Though his dark skin and the dim lighting made it hard to tell, Law was pretty sure he was blushing. "It's possible, on the last day of Dominant class, someone got a hold of her phone and changed all her ringtones to Lord of the Rings soundtrack songs."

Law felt his eyebrows rising up.

Well, that was unexpected.

"So, you're saying she had a reason," Connor said thoughtfully, still grinning as he rubbed his fingers over his beard. Q scowled, dropping his gaze, so the baleful glare landed on Connor.

"She can't prove it was me."

Oh, but it definitely had been.

"And you can't prove this was her." Asad grinned, his attention returning to the Lounge. "I like her. She's a switch, right? It looks like she's interested in subbing tonight."

"I wouldn't if I were you," Q muttered.

Iris

Last night with a Watch Dom... and he *was* watching. Iris could feel his gaze on her everywhere she went. Not that he was being subtle about it. Almost every time she'd looked up, his eyes were on her. The few times they hadn't been, she hadn't looked at him for longer than thirty seconds before he'd met her gaze.

Was he thinking about tomorrow?

Regretting his decision?

She hoped not. Iris knew it was a pity scene, despite the attraction between them, but right now, she'd take what she could get. She was wound up, sexually frustrated, and desperately in need of getting out of her head for a bit.

The last week at home had been increasingly uncomfortable. The first few days of Noelle's cold shoulder had been a relief, despite the guilt that piled on whenever she had the thought, but now it was getting stressful. She hated the dark looks, the exaggerated sighs and derisive sniffs, and the feeling of being unwelcome in her own home. She was going to apologize soon just to get over the hump, even though she still didn't feel as though she'd really done anything wrong.

Hopefully, she'd feel more like apologizing to Noelle after she'd worked out some of her tension with Master Law.

"Hello, would either of you like a drink?" she asked as Samantha and Morgan paused in their conversation when she walked up.

"Water for me, please. I'm hoping to play tonight," Morgan replied brightly before looking at Samantha.

"I'll have a Sprite, thanks." Samantha smiled up at her. Nodding, Iris went to get their drinks. She glanced at Master Law and his friends on the way and noticed they were all looking over at Samantha and Morgan. Maybe Morgan was going to get her wish.

When she returned, she handed the drinks over with a smile and jolted. Instead of pausing, they continued their conversation, and she wasn't sure she'd heard what she thought she'd just heard.

"Sorry, I couldn't help but overhear… did you just say you're moving in with Master Brian?" Iris kept her tone as apologetic as she could, even though inside, she was freaking out a little. If she *had* heard correctly, she was pretty sure she knew someone who would *totally* freak out.

Rae might pretend she didn't have any interest in the Daddy Dom, but Iris wasn't buying it and didn't think anyone else was. Not only that, but she was nearly one hundred percent sure Brian had a thing for Rae as well.

What the hell was he thinking, letting another woman move in with him? Especially Morgan. Iris didn't know her very well, but she hadn't pegged her as the type who wanted a Daddy Dom.

"Yes," Morgan replied, though her brow furrowed, and she looked up at Iris. "You're friends with… a lot of people here. Do you think everyone will hate me if we do?"

Iris blinked. One of the things she liked about Morgan was how blunt the other woman could be. She might say the wrong thing at the wrong time on a regular basis and have some very odd ideas about kink and people that weren't great stereotypes, but every word out of her mouth was authentic. And she had no problem being corrected.

"Why would they hate you?" Iris asked, even though she knew, but she was frantically trying to think of how to answer in a way that wouldn't be hurtful.

Rae was totally going to hate her. She and Domi had never said anything out loud, but it was clear Morgan had rubbed both of them the wrong way, and neither of them was interested in hanging out with her. Once Rae knew Morgan and Brian were a thing, she was totally going to hate her, which meant Domi probably would on principle.

Shit, did that mean Iris would have to hate her? Noelle would never stand for Iris being friends with someone she hated. Would Rae be the same way?

She didn't hate Morgan. Morgan was very naïve and sometimes mean without intending to be, but she did try, and Iris identified with how hard she tried.

"Because I'm moving in with the only single Daddy Dom. I mean, he'll still be single." Morgan wrinkled her nose, not in disgust, more confused. "People keep thinking there's something going on between us, but he's like… like a brother or what I think having a brother might be like."

"He does watch out for you like a big brother." Samantha appeared amused. The impression Iris had of the two of them during class was they were friendly but had little in common. "If someone hates you, that's their problem, not yours."

Morgan chewed her lower lip, unconvinced. Sometimes, she was the oddest mix of complete confidence and crippling insecurities. Totally confident in her looks, sex appeal, and ability to be the perfect submissive but cripplingly insecure whenever she had to make a decision.

"Why did he ask you to move in?" Iris had a feeling the 'why' would be more important than the act. At least, she hoped so.

"My lease is coming up, and my current roommate is moving in with her boyfriend," Morgan explained. "I can't afford a place on my own yet, at least not one anyone seems to approve of. Brian said he needs a roommate and suggested I move in with him." She sighed, rubbing her left wrist in a soothing gesture.

"Do you not want to live with him?"

"No, I do, but that's why I think maybe I shouldn't." Morgan frowned. "I'm supposed to be learning how to do things on my own. How am I going to do that when I'm living with another Dom?"

"I have a feeling your biggest problem is going to be him pushing you to do everything on your own," Sam replied, one side of her mouth curving up in a smile.

"Me, too," Iris agreed, hoping she wasn't ruining her friendship with Rae by encouraging this. "I sincerely doubt he'll take charge if he knows you're working on learning to do things on your own."

"You're right." Morgan wrinkled his nose. "I guess I'm going to say yes." She didn't sound one hundred percent sure, but Iris had no doubt she would come around. She wasn't sure what was going on with Morgan and the Doms but recognized a group effort when she saw it.

She'd have to give Rae a heads up, though. That should be fun.

Law

"Do you have your scene for tomorrow planned out?" Asad asked, watching Iris talking to Morgan and Samantha. He didn't seem convinced to stay away from them, but he wasn't making a big deal out of it.

"Yes. Will and Gina are onstage, and I've reserved the Dungeon Room for myself and Iris." He was so distracted watching her, he didn't think twice before sharing that information—and he really should have.

"Wait, you're spending the whole night?" Asad's head whipped around, his eyes wide as he pinned Law with a stare. Q and Connor were both staring at him as well. Knowing him better than Q, Asad and Connor were far more flabbergasted, but even Q looked surprised.

Shit.

Now they would be all up in his business.

"No, but I wanted to have a place to scene with her after the show." His voice came out clipped. He really wasn't planning on spending the night there with her. Hadn't even thought about it.

So sure about that?

He shook his head as if he could shake away the thought.

"It's easier. I have to go to Marquis straight from work for a meeting with Olivia and Julie about the next submissives class. That way, I have somewhere I can change before the show. It just made sense." On multiple levels.

Asad's dark eyes were lit with amusement, and Connor wasn't bothering to hide his grin. Even Q's eyebrows had risen, and his expression was skeptical.

Listening to himself, Law couldn't blame them. He sounded like a twit.

"Uh-huh. You keep telling yourself that," Asad said, raising his glass and toasting Law.

"I'm not a relationship guy." Law scowled. "You know why." Asad and Connor were the only two friends he had left from that time in his life. They exchanged a glance while Q looked on in confusion.

"We know why you haven't been, but you aren't the same man anymore." Connor reached out, clapping his hand on Law's shoulder in a gesture of support. "You know, if you want a relationship, you deserve to have one."

No, he didn't. Not anymore. He didn't want to put another woman in that position ever again. Especially not one so much younger, like Iris, who still had her whole life ahead of her and deserved far more than a cynical old bastard like him.

Tomorrow's scene would be it for them.

CHAPTER TEN

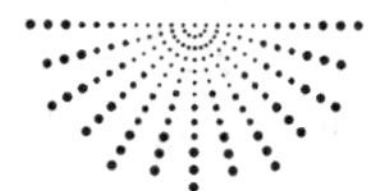

For the first time since her fight with Noelle, Iris practically bounced into their apartment. It didn't matter what had been going on between them—nothing was going to get her down today.

Last night, she'd gotten her final 'good girl' from Master Law while serving out her punishment, and tonight, she would finally have a scene with a real Dom. She'd ignored all the texts her brother had sent today. She'd check them tomorrow, but she could guess what they said and would not let him ruin this for her, either.

Not him, not Noelle... nobody was messing with her good mood today.

Which apparently startled the heck out of her roommate since Noelle was in the kitchen when Iris came in. Noelle actually looked at her, making eye contact for the first time all week, and her eyes widened.

"Why are you so smiley?" she asked, curious instead of antagonistic, so Iris answered her.

"I have a... sorta date tonight." She'd explained about 'scening' to Noelle, and her friend didn't entirely understand but had mostly taken it well. Regardless, Iris didn't want to deal with Noelle if she decided to make a thing of it.

To her surprise, Noelle's face lit up.

"Oh, that's great! It's been forever since you've had a guy interested in you. It's about time you put yourself out there. Do you want some help with your hair and makeup?"

That was classic Noelle—saying something she didn't realize sounded incredibly insulting, then offering her help.

"*I* haven't been interested in any of the guys I was meeting," Iris pointed out drily. Noelle's offer was an olive branch, and Iris would be a fool not to take her up on it. Things around the apartment would be a lot more comfortable if they had a détente. "And sure, I'd love some help."

"Awesome, let me get my things." Noelle took a last sip of water, then rushed to her bedroom, leaving Iris standing there, shaking her head.

She knew Noelle didn't mean anything by it and didn't even notice Iris' small correction, but sometimes, the things she said could really burrow under Iris' skin. Good thing she was in such a good mood. She would not let a little thing like miscommunication bother her. Especially since that little exchange amounted to her and Noelle making up.

Dropping off her stuff, Iris went into the bathroom and pulled her hair out of its bun, giving it a good brush out. She'd taken a shower that morning, so all she had to do was make it look nicer.

"Up or down?" Noelle asked as she entered the bathroom. Of the two of them, she had the better makeup kit and loved to play 'Barbie doll' with Iris, dressing her up and doing her hair. It had been a long time since they'd done this. Iris realized Noelle's words might have stung because of the truth in them.

Not so much the whole guys not being interested in Iris, but that it had been so long since she'd wanted a specific man to be interested in her. She really wanted a guy who was into kink, and the guys at the club definitely hadn't shown an interest in her, even if they felt it.

Thanks, big brother.

Yup, going into tonight, she would need to make sure she didn't have expectations from Master Law. It would be way too easy to start wanting him because he was the only Dom willing to go toe to toe with her brother. Fingers crossed, he would start a trend, but it was hard not to judge other Doms for holding back until they saw someone else go for it.

"Earth to Iris, hair up or down?" Noelle's blue eyes sparkled in the mirror, a smirk on her lips. "Distracted much?"

"Maybe a little. Let's do up, please." Iris smiled at her in the mirror, and Noelle grinned back. It was as though they'd never fought and hadn't been avoiding each other all week. Noelle expertly curled Iris' hair and pulled it back, using a single clip from which the curls all spilled out. The clip was long and vertical, making it look as if they were pulled into an updo when in actuality, it would be very easy to take out the clip and let her hair loose.

Noelle had Iris flip around on the toilet, so she could do her makeup, updating Iris on everything that had happened with Tyler while they weren't talking. Not that Noelle said it that way. She just told Iris what had been going on without mentioning why she needed to catch Iris up on a week's worth of gossip.

"I don't know if we're going to last much longer. He blows hot and cold... I think his friends all hate me, and they're influencing him." Noelle made a face as she brushed some blush over Iris' cheekbones. "Not that he says they hate me, but they used to be a lot nicer to me."

"They're mean to you?" Iris frowned.

"Not outright, but like... they're always trying to get Tyler to hang out and have guy time without me. When we do all get together, nobody makes an effort to include me." Noelle made another face. "Close your eyes. Do you want them smoky?"

"Yes, please," Iris replied, grateful Noelle had changed the subject. She would have had to bite her tongue against the obvious question since she had to wonder how much *Noelle* was trying to get along with Tyler's friends.

From what Noelle said in the past, she hadn't liked Tyler's friends all that much. If they were sensing that, it wouldn't be surprising that they weren't into hanging out with her.

"So, tell me about the guy," Noelle said as she did Iris' eyes.

"He's a lawyer, a little older but hot. Filipino. Bald. He has a beard and is pretty bossy."

"Ooh, an older guy, that *is* hot. How much older?"

"Ten years."

"Mm, so not too much older, but still hot." Noelle giggled. "Where'd you meet him? Did you use an app?"

"No, I met him at Marquis." Iris opened her eyes when Noelle moved back. The expression on her roommate's face wasn't happy, but she didn't appear to want to pick a fight.

"Is this like one of those sex dates you told me about?" Noelle asked.

"Well, we haven't talked about if we'll be having sex yet. He's taking me out to dinner." At a sex club, but Noelle didn't need to know that.

"Hmm. Well, I hope you have fun. If he's older, that probably means he's looking to settle down." Again, it was unclear from Noelle's tone whether or not she thought that was a good thing.

"Maybe." Iris stood up to get her mascara. That was the only part of her makeup, Noelle didn't do. When she saw herself in the mirror, she had to smile and pose. "Damn, I look hot."

"Of course, you do," Noelle replied smugly, squeezing in so she could see herself next to Iris. Her eyes swept critically over Iris' reflection. "I do good work."

"I'm gonna get changed. Thank you." Iris reached her arm around Noelle to give her a hug, relieved they were back on an even keel. Still grinning, Noelle hugged her back.

"Have a great night!"

Iris definitely planned to.

Law

The Marquis manager's office was decorated in a distinctly femi-nine way despite the heavy wooden furniture and red and black color scheme. Unlike the office at Stronghold, which was far more mini-malist and designed more for function than visual appeal. Not that Marquis' office wouldn't function as effectively—Olivia, the manager, had made it both functional and beautiful.

She was the Mistress of Marquis, overseeing the second-floor operations and acting as the liaison to the restaurant beneath on the first floor. Not a job Law envied. Her boyfriend and submissive was one of the silent backers of the business and was sitting in a chair in the back corner of the office, seemingly engrossed with a book.

Despite being an owner, Luke never involved himself in the day-to-day running of the club. Probably for the best, since Law didn't think Olivia would take that well.

Sitting behind the large desk, wearing one of her signature red suits, with her red hair pulled back into a tight bun, she exuded both an air of inherent sexuality and professionalism. She gave off a kind of naughty-librarian vibe that was extremely appealing.

"So, next month we have the class for newer submissives to the clubs, but we have a small problem, which is why I've asked you both to join me today. I want to talk through it and get your thoughts." Olivia's gaze passed back and forth between Law and Mistress Julie, the Domme who also taught the classes.

Mistress Julie was the shortest and least physically imposing of the three of them, but Law would also classify her as the scariest when she wanted to be. Especially since Olivia had softened after becoming involved with Luke. Not that he'd ever tell *Olivia* that. He liked his balls right where they were, thank you.

"What's wrong?" Frowning, Julie leaned forward with interest. Like Law, she was still dressed for work, though she wore a pair of jeans and a polo shirt with the company logo. She liked to joke it constituted business casual for tech geeks like herself.

"Well, we have another switch. Possibly." Olivia's lips quirked, which meant she had an opinion on the subject but wouldn't share in the interests of not influencing anyone else's thoughts. "Q would like to sign up for the submissive class and explore that option as well."

Law and Julie took a moment to absorb that statement.

"Interesting. He definitely has dominant qualities, but I could see where he might enjoy the other side," Law said thoughtfully.

"Where's the problem?" Julie frowned. "Unless you think he has an underlying motive for signing up?"

"No, I think he's genuine in his desire to explore both sides." Olivia sighed. "The problem is he's indicated a strong desire to work with a female dominant, and since he's straight, that probably would help give him the best indicator whether or not he has a submissive side, but the only female top who signed up to work with the class this session is Samantha."

Oh. *Oh.*

Law and Julie exchanged grimaces. Even if Law hadn't talked to Q recently about what seemed to be an escalating prank war between the two of them, it had been obvious in the Dominance class they had some kind of issue with each other. On the other hand, if Q wanted to explore his submissive side with a woman, the club would do their best to honor that, and if Samantha wanted more practice as a top, they would do their best to help her as well. He could understand why Olivia found it to be a quandary.

"Law, I need you to talk to Q, and if he's onboard, then Julie, I would like you to talk to Samantha." Olivia made a face. "I would do it, but at this point, I think both of them would be more comfortable with each of you and more likely to be truthful. I can call in some favors if we need another Domme to step in and help with Q, so it's not entirely on Julie's shoulders."

"I can do that," Julie said, and Law nodded after a moment.

His initial instinct said Q would balk, but he deserved the right to make the decision for himself. Not to mention, even though he'd been annoyed about his car being covered in post-its, he really hadn't wanted Asad scening with Samantha.

In some ways, it reminded Law of the way kids teased each other because they didn't know how to deal with a crush.

"I'll talk with him."

Before anyone could say anything else, there was a knock at the door, causing all three of them to frown. Olivia looked past them at her boyfriend, and Law turned his head to see Luke's reaction, but he looked as puzzled as the rest of them.

"Were you expecting someone?" she asked.

"No," Luke replied as he got to his feet and headed to open the door. He swung it open, standing far enough to the side, they could all see who was there.

All of them were taken aback when they saw one of the bartenders from downstairs, Shane, standing awkwardly, holding a vase full of a dozen red roses.

"Shane?" Olivia blinked, taking in him and the roses.

"Um, this was delivered downstairs for Julie Kim." Shane met Julie's eyes. "I knew you were having the meeting up here, so I figured..."

"Right, of course." The obvious question of how someone would know Julie was here had them glancing at each other. Olivia got to her feet, making a sweeping motion with her hand. "Bring them in."

"Is there a card?" Law asked, also getting to his feet. Julie followed more slowly, her expression blank.

"Yes." Shane set the vase down on the center of Olivia's desk, Luke close behind him, so they were all crowded in. He pointed, and Julie paused for only a moment before plucking the card from among the roses.

The office was silent as she opened it, all of them staring at her. Law didn't know why it felt ominous. Maybe because Julie didn't work here. So, how did someone know to have flowers delivered to her here at exactly this time?

"What does it say?" Olivia asked, too impatient to wait for more than a minute.

"It says, 'I think you're beautiful.'"

"That's it?" Law frowned, leaning sideways to see it. Wordlessly, Julie handed him the card.

That was it. No name, no signature, and the message was printed rather than handwritten, so no clues there, either.

"Huh. Looks like I have a secret admirer." Julie leaned forward and gave the flowers a sniff. Whether she was pleased was impossible to tell. "I wonder how they knew I was here." There was some skepticism in her voice, which made Law feel even more justified in his own unease.

"Please, it's Stronghold and Marquis." Luke snorted. "It's amazing anyone can get anything done without everyone knowing about it. Like Law and Iris' date tonight."

"You and Iris have a date tonight?" Julie asked, turning to him in surprise.

"Ah, I'd better get back to work." Shane zipped out the door, which reminded Law that the bartender was the reason everyone knew about his date. Well, Iris was the real reason since she'd been talking about it in front of Shane, which she'd only done because Law had texted her while she was at Marquis. So, it wasn't really anyone's 'fault,' but he could still blame Shane for being part of the gossip train.

"It's not a date. She needs someone willing to scene with her who isn't intimidated by her big brother."

"Uh-huh." The others exchanged a glance, and Law scowled at them. This club was full of nosy gossips.

"I'll talk to Q. In the meantime, I have a scene with a submissive I need to get ready for." He stressed the word 'scene.' Not that it mattered. The other three were whispering to each other before the door closed behind him.

Hopefully, tonight didn't end up being more trouble than it was worth.

CHAPTER ELEVEN

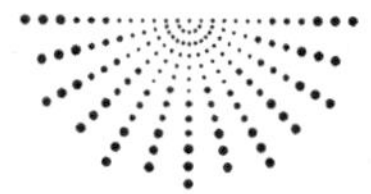

IRIS

There were two ways to reach the second floor of Marquis, three if she counted the emergency exit. Tonight, Iris used the back door. The front would have taken her through the Marquis restaurant, and even though she was wearing a little black dress that would have fit in just fine, she'd already sparked enough gossip by running her mouth at the bar last week.

The more circumspect she could be tonight, the better.

Was she second-guessing tonight?

Yeah. Maybe.

This was her first time at Marquis for something other than class.

She was honest enough to admit she had a crush on the Dom she was scening with and realized she did not know how *he* felt about *her*.

As much as she tried not to think about this as a 'pity scene' because beggars couldn't be choosers, the thought still floated around in the back of her head. She was pretty sure she'd felt a spark of mutual attraction between them... and hoped she wasn't fooling herself.

Even if nothing came of tonight but a great scene, she would be happy. She'd be a lot happier if it meant she got to start scening more regularly, even if it was with Doms, who'd previously been too intimidated.

Slipping in the back door, she could hear the buzz of the restaurant down the hallway. Only the staff and the upstairs club members used the back entrance, so it was designed not to be seen by anyone in the restaurant. Heading around the hall to where she could just see inside the dining room—past the stairwell and bathrooms—she smiled with relief that no one was there.

The sounds of people talking and eating dropped away as she headed up the stairs to the lobby of Marquis' second floor. It was a lot like Stronghold, just fancier. There was a door to the manager's office, as well as a desk next to the door to the main stage where the performances were held, and standing beside that door was a Dom who also served as a bouncer.

A lot of Doms and subs chose to take positions at Stronghold and Marquis to get discounts on their memberships—unlike Iris, who had ended up being a server at Stronghold because she'd gotten into trouble. She was hardly the only subbie it had happened to. It was a pretty common punishment, especially for brats who were trying to top from the bottom.

Sometimes, she wondered if that described her or if she just had an issue with authority she couldn't quite seem to let go of.

"Hey, Iris!" Freddy, who ran the front desk at Marquis and often manned it, perked up when he saw her appear. Next to him, one of the other club subs, Tori, let out a low whistle. "Damn girl, you look good. Going to give Master Law a run for his money, huh?"

"Is that something you think I need?" The dry question came from behind her, and Iris jumped, cheeks flaming. Thankfully, despite her stiletto heels, she didn't stumble as she turned around.

Master Law had apparently just come from the hallway that skirted around the 'show' area and went straight back to the hotel portion of the operation. Marquis not only boasted theme rooms like Stronghold but each theme room was attached to a regular hotel room so guests could spend the night without having to worry about going home after an intense scene.

That was why a lot of the members used a visit to Marquis as something special since they could stay overnight. Though, not everyone did.

"Hi," Iris said, hands smoothing nervously over her skirt as she tried to push down her jangling nerves. Wearing his usual leathers, he also wore a button-down white shirt with the top button undone—a fancier version of what he often wore at Stronghold.

When he smiled at her, it was all she could do not to melt into a little puddle on the floor.

"You look beautiful," he said, coming forward and holding out his hand. Iris took it, blushing even hotter as she felt his fingers against hers.

Yes, sometimes, he'd used her for demonstrations during class, but that had been different. That had been impersonal... in front of a bunch of people. He'd barely looked at her.

Not like he was looking at her right now, with heat in his eyes as they scanned her body. The spark of attraction? Yeah, that lit up her fingers where their hands were touching, making her entire arm feel tingly.

Girl, you have got it bad.

Lower your expectations, lower your expectations, lower your expectations...

Just because he was attracted to her didn't mean he would want more than a scene. In fact, he probably *wouldn't* want more.

The mental reminder helped her get her heart rate under control as they approached the desk. Freddy was still grinning. The light blue suit he was wearing matched his blue eyes perfectly, and his hair had been gelled and was sticking up in a messy bedroom look. Iris thought he was adorable. He was a submissive, but he could also be bossy as hell and was a mother hen to all the other submissives.

"We have your table all ready for you," Freddy said smoothly, accepting the menus Tori held up. The pretty brunette winked at Iris when Master Law wasn't looking. "Right this way."

Master Law nodded to the Dom outside the door—Iris was pretty sure his name was Victor, but she only knew him by sight—then they were in a room she had walked into probably a hundred times, but this time it felt different. Because it *was* different.

This was the first time she was here as a real sub.

Law

Fuck, he needed to get his head on straight. Freddy hadn't been wrong. Seeing Iris in that dress, as if she was here for a real date, was making him want things he didn't have any right to want. The little black dress wouldn't have turned any heads at Stronghold, where half of the attendees were wearing nothing at all, but it looked fantastic on her.

Like something she would wear on a real date.

Which made it feel more like a real date, despite his leather pants, which he only wore to the club. He hadn't realized he'd picked them out for tonight specifically to make it feel less like an actual date until this moment. He'd donned them like armor and still took a direct hit right to the groin the moment he saw her.

It was going to be a struggle to keep his head on straight and treat this like a scene.

It was not helped by the fact they were having dinner together before the show started.

"Here you go," Freddy said, turning and gesturing at the booth he'd led them to. The stage in the center of the room was surrounded by booths. They could seat up to six people comfortably, and there were plenty of bolts and rings that didn't normally adorn restaurant tables and booths.

The booths themselves were curved around the circular tables, backed by walls that went to the ceiling, and had two sets of curtains that could be drawn across their openings. Basically, they were set up for maximum privacy. It was possible to hear what was going on in the other booths, but you couldn't see beside you, and most of the sounds were muffled.

With the stage lights off and the booth lights on, they could see into the booths across from them, but that would change when the house lights went down, and the stage lights were turned on. For those who wanted a little more privacy and retain the ability to still watch the show, they could draw the sheer curtains across the booth opening. The heavy brocade curtains were for those who wanted complete privacy.

"Thanks, Freddy." Iris smiled as she let go of Law's hand and sat down, scooting her way along the booth to the back, where she would have the best view of the stage.

"Yes, thank you." Law took a deep breath and followed her. Dammit. It really felt like a date as Freddy handed their menus over.

Law didn't think about the last time he'd been on a date. He really didn't want to. It had been with Elaine, and he was doing everything in his power not to think about Elaine. It would put him in a foul mood, and he needed to focus on Iris tonight.

Iris and their not-date.

Focus and control. That's what he needed. How he'd ended up being drawn to BDSM. Once he'd discovered the lifestyle, he'd realized how much he truly enjoyed it. Almost a little too much, but it had also given him the tools he needed to keep *himself* under control, and he did what he could to give back to the community that had helped him so much.

Do you think it's possible your friends are right, and it's time to stop punishing yourself for the past?

Maybe.

Not exactly something he could think about right now, and considering where he was, he wasn't sure he should be listening to that voice because his motivations were highly suspect.

"So, ah, come here often?" Iris joked.

Law looked up, chuckling despite the conflicting emotions and thoughts swirling within him.

"Not for the shows," he admitted. "I've heard Will and Gina put on a good one, though."

"I'll admit, I don't know if I could have come here if the couple performing were friends with my brother." She shuddered delicately, still smiling but completely serious. Law didn't blame her. He enjoyed being a voyeur, but he couldn't imagine doing so with one of his sisters' friends, especially not one of the ones she'd grown up with.

"I have wondered how much having them around inhibits you." Mentor-mode was a place where he was comfortable. Although, as a mentor, he usually tried to avoid looking at his mentee's breasts, even when she was wearing a very low-cut dress and taking a deep breath.

"I think it's more they inhibit the others around me. I mean, I wouldn't stop to watch them if they were doing a scene in the Dungeon, but other than Andrew and Kate, I wouldn't walk out of the Dungeon, either. It's more their reaction to my presence I find inhibiting, especially how their presence affects the others around me." She made a face. "By the way, if I haven't expressed how grateful I am that you were willing to scene with me, please know that I am."

The gratitude made him uncomfortable, as though she was saying she didn't think he would have scened with her if he didn't feel sorry for her and her lack of scening partners. While part of him was tempted to let that notion stand since it felt safer, he didn't want her believing she was undesirable or unattractive. Nothing could be farther from the truth.

"You don't need to be grateful. I asked you to scene tonight because I want to scene with you. If I didn't want to, there's nothing in the world that could make me."

The truth made him feel a little more raw and exposed than he was comfortable with, but it was worth it to see the way Iris lit up in response and the relief in her expression. He also needed to change the subject as quickly as possible while he tried to regain his equilibrium.

"So, you've eaten here recently. What's good?"

Iris wrinkled her nose, obviously picking up on his teasing jab about how her time at the bar had spread the word they'd be here together tonight.

"I don't know if I'd call drinking at the bar 'eating,'" she muttered before pushing her voice back to its normal volume. "The sirloin is excellent... or the crab cakes if you don't like steak."

"I like crab cakes, but I'm not a huge fan of Old Bay," Law replied, looking down at the menu, then jerking his head back up again when Iris gasped. Her hand was pressed against her chest, eyes wide, and her expression as though she couldn't believe what she'd just heard.

"We are in *Maryland*," she whispered. "You can't just say things like that out loud."

Law's grin stretched wider. She wasn't wrong, but he enjoyed her reaction.

Movement out of the corner of his eye had him looking up. Mark, dressed in Marquis' uniform of black shorts, a tight dark red shirt, and a black server's apron, stepped up to their table. His Dom was Victor, who had been standing guard at the door to the theater, so it wasn't too surprising to find him working tonight as well.

"Hello, welcome to Marquis." Mark grinned widely, his dark eyes sparkling with anticipation, thrilled to have them at his table. The gossip about Law and Iris must have really been flying. "What would you two like to drink tonight?"

"Just water for me," Law said, glancing at Iris. Her eyes widened.

"Oh... I... should I not?"

The rule was a two-drink maximum for both Stronghold and Marquis—and the liquor drinks were always watered down unless you confirmed you had no intention of scening that evening.

"Get whatever you like. You won't be having more than two." Law smiled at her. Over the years, he'd gotten used to being the odd man out. That didn't bother him much anymore. It was people's reactions to why he didn't drink that bothered him, which was why he usually didn't give an explanation.

Thankfully, both Mark and Iris seemed to take at face value he wanted to be clearheaded tonight. It was one of the nice things about the clubs. While there were plenty of people who went there to hang out or get a drink before or after a scene, there were just as many who didn't.

"I'll have the hard cider." Iris glanced at him as if trying to gauge his reaction. Law had to wonder if she really wanted the cider or if she was just testing to see whether he'd really meant it. Maybe both.

"Great! I'll be right back with your drinks and give you a chance to look over the menu." Mark smiled at them and whisked away.

"How much do you want to bet he's going to repeat everything word for word to the other subs on duty tonight?" Iris asked with amusement. The look she gave Law made his chest tighten in an odd way.

"I'm absolutely not going to take that bet." He was sure everyone who saw them would be hoping for some kind of a show, but they would be disappointed. Law was looking forward to watching the show, then taking Iris back to the Dungeon room where he could play with her to his heart's content.

No, not his heart, his cock. Dammit. His heart was going to have nothing to do with it.

CHAPTER TWELVE

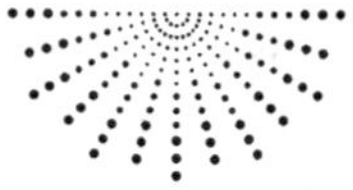

Dinner with Master Law felt a little awkward at the beginning, but by the time the lights dimmed, they were deep in conversation about their love for *Schitt's Creek,* and Iris had almost forgotten what they were actually there for. She was almost disappointed they had to stop talking.

During class, Master Law had always held himself apart from the students. Not tonight. She made a joke—he laughed. She told a story —he listened. And he had his own stories and jokes, too. Iris cracked up when he told her about the time he accidentally clotheslined himself on a tree in his front yard when he was chasing after his sister, Joanne. Turned out, he'd grown faster than the tree and tried to run under a branch that he'd run under the previous summer... but the branch had no longer been above his head.

He and Joanne sounded a lot like her and Andrew, in some ways—protective big brother, wild younger sister—but she could hear the caring, even when he sounded exasperated. It made her wonder if she tuned out the caring in Andrew's voice. When she talked to her brother, she mostly heard the exasperation.

Not that she was comparing Master Law to her brother.

She'd never had less brotherly feelings for anyone in her life.

Although their conversation was completely innocuous, and he didn't make a single move on her while they were eating, there was a simmering tension bubbling just below the surface. Iris could feel it every time their gazes caught and could see the heat in his eyes. The way his gaze dropped to her lips and her breasts when he thought she wasn't looking. And the way her body reacted to all of it.

It was flirting without actually flirting. She was attuned to his every move. Which was why she saw the way his head jerked up, nostrils flaring slightly, as the lights changed. Anticipation thrummed through her immediately.

Their meals were long gone, and Mark quickly came by to scoop up their dessert plates, tipping them a wink as he did so. Iris smiled at him, the expression hiding the sudden increase in her pulse. Her heart felt as though it was beating twice as fast, and all the nerves that had previously settled surged upwards.

What was she supposed to do now? Did she move closer to him? Stay where she was? What did she do with her hands?

"Iris." Master Law's voice was low, almost husky. "Scoot a little closer to me."

Oh, right.

Him, Dom. Her, sub.

She didn't have to worry about what to do—he would *tell* her what he wanted her to do.

Not that it stopped her heart from pounding, but she was able to relax a smidge as she followed his instruction. She scooted closer, and he lifted his arm, so she could move right next to him, the outside of their thighs pressed together. The heat of his body seemed to flow into her, adding to the warmth already curling through her core.

"Relax," he murmured as the room went entirely dark.

Easy for him to say. How was she supposed to relax when he was pressed up against her, his fingers stroking the top of her arm where his hand was resting? It wasn't sexual, exactly, but it was sensual, and the soft strokes sent little shivers through her. The darkness created a cocoon, only for them… but it didn't last long.

The lights came up on stage.

A large wooden frame had been added to the stage, with chains hanging from the top crossbeam and cuffs dangling at their ends. The very sight made Iris' insides clench.

This was completely different from being at Marquis for a class. Far more intimate than she'd realized it would be.

Squirming in the seat next to Master Law, she didn't dare look at him. Not that she'd be able to see much in the shadows of the booth, but it felt achingly intimate for what was supposed to be a simple scene. A pity scene. This felt more and more like a real date with a Dom who was actually interested in her.

Stop thinking. Just go with it.

Going with the flow wasn't Iris' natural state—she usually asked questions the whole way, trying to find out which way the flow was going and what would happen when it got there—but right now, she didn't have much of a choice. This was not the time to make conversation. She'd missed her chance during dinner, but well, she'd been enjoying herself.

Movement caught her eye as Will and Gina stepped onto the stage. Will, was wearing jeans, chaps, and a cowboy hat, looking right at home in them, showing off his shirtless physique—a very nice physique. Gina was outfitted in full pony play gear. Long blonde hair was pulled back into a ponytail, which flowed down her back, and she had a matching tail between her legs.

Iris' cheeks clenched together as she realized it must be a plug tail because there was nothing else that might be keeping it wedged between Gina's buttocks. Thigh-high boots with odd platforms on the sole made to look like hooves, a leather harness made of straps around her body, and a gag that looked like a horse's bit was wrapped around her head and holding her lips open completed the look.

Iris stared in fascination. She'd never seen anything like it in person, though she'd seen photos. Marquis had a pony playroom, but it hadn't interested her. Now, she had to admit Gina looked surprisingly sexy as a kinky pony, and Cowboy Will was seriously hot.

When they reached the edge of the stage, Gina balked, and Will's hand reached out and slapped her bottom, leaving a bright red print. Iris jumped at the sound of flesh cracking against flesh. As if that had been a cue, a low, throbbing beat began to fill the room, tickling the edges of her hearing.

"Naughty pony, up on the stage." Will had even added a bit of a southern drawl to his voice. Damn. That was hot. Lucky Gina.

Lucky me.

Master Law's hold on her tightened a little, and Iris' breath hitched as Gina pranced away from Will. He grabbed the bridle of her bit, his other hand going to his belt where a small flogger was attached. It was made of black leather and blended so well with his pants, Iris hadn't noticed it.

Law

Seated next to a squirming aroused Iris was pure erotic torture. He couldn't just hear the hitches in her breath—he could *feel* them. He was attuned to her every movement, every tiny quiver, every little change in breathing. His cock was achingly hard, more from her presence beside him than the erotic tableau in front of him.

Watching scenes was always enjoyable, but it was hardly anything new. Watching with someone, with her tucked under his arm and sides against each other?

That was very new.

Using the small flogger, Will managed to 'drive' Gina up on stage and get her into position, so he could cuff her wrists to the chains hanging from the frame. She stamped her foot, smiling around the bit in her mouth as Will walked around her as though he was inspecting her. Despite her show of reluctance, she was having a good time.

"Hold still, girl," Will ordered, swishing the flogger again, catching the underside of her breast and making Gina jerk before she settled back into place. Seated at the side of the frame, he and Iris had a pretty good view of everything Will did.

Moving his hand, Law curved his fingers around Iris' ribcage to tease the side of her breast, feeling her quick intake of breath. He turned his head, watching her profile as his hand moved over her breast, waiting to see if she showed any sign of hesitation.

She bit her lip as he caressed the soft mound of flesh, his fingers seeking the hard nub of her nipple beneath the fabric.

"Oh..." She started to turn her head, and Law pinched her nipple through the dress, which took away some of the sting but not all of it.

"Keep watching the show," he murmured, shifting so he could pull her onto his lap. It was a bit of a tight squeeze to get her atop his thighs with the table in front of them, which forced her to open her legs and drape them on the outside of his. Perfect.

While the new position obscured most of his view of the show, since her curls got in the way, he didn't mind at all. He was far more focused on how she felt atop him than he was on watching the show. It would be easier for him to maintain his self-control if he didn't have to deal with extra distractions.

Having the curves of her ass pressed against his aching erection was distracting enough.

Law slid his hands up her stomach to her breasts, cupping them, and heard her soft moan. She squirmed again on his lap, and one of her hands reached up to cover his. That wouldn't do.

"Put your hands on the table in front of you," he murmured in her ear. The music for the scene was getting louder, but she would still be able to hear him easily enough. "Flat. Don't move them."

Another hitch in her breath, and this time, he was certain it was because of his command rather than the scene. His cock throbbed against her backside as he tightened his grip on her breasts. The soft handfuls filled his fingers, spilling out between them. Deliberately arranging them so her nipples were caught between his middle and forefinger, when he squeezed, the tiny buds were pinched.

Her squirming increased, especially now that she could no longer press her thighs together to put pressure on her pussy. Instead, she was squeezing her legs against his and wriggling more and more as her arousal heightened. Fuck, he wanted to sink inside her. His arousal made him rougher with her breasts, which made her squirm even more.

It was like a self-perpetuating cycle of erotic torture.

Iris

Master Law was touching her breasts.

Not just touching them, but full-on kneading them, fingers pinching and rolling her nipples, squeezing to his heart's content. She could feel the throbbing press of his erection between the cheeks of her ass. The empty ache in her pussy made it even more frustrating to feel him so close, yet not where she wanted him.

Her clit was screaming with the need to be touched, especially now that she couldn't put any pressure on it by squeezing her legs together.

Whimpering, she squirmed against Master Law, hoping her movements would inspire him to move things a little faster. This wasn't all that kinky; all he was doing was playing with her breasts.

Playing with your breasts while you have your hands flat on the table in front of you, and you're watching a woman dressed as a horse being whipped. Sure, not kinky at all.

It was possible her idea of what was and wasn't kinky needed to be readjusted.

Gina threw her head back as Master Will flicked the whip up between her spread legs, hitting her inner thighs, dangerously close to her pussy. He followed it up with the small flogger in his left hand, and the many leather strands *did* hit squarely against her labia. She cried out, and Iris felt like crying out with her, her own pussy throbbing in sympathy and envy.

She might not be as much of a masochist as Gina, but she still liked that bite of pain. Craved it. It made the pleasure sharper, hotter.

As if sensing her need, Law shifted his grip on her breasts, pinching her nipples between the pads of his fingers, pulling and twisting, before releasing them and leaving her panting. The twin spots of pain throbbed, sending electric sparks through her body, straight to her pussy.

"Please, please, please, please..." She realized she was whispering the word over and over again while she squirmed against him.

Feeling his hand moving down her body to her thigh and between her legs, she thought she might combust on the spot. Onstage, Master Will was still whipping Gina's thighs, with the occasional stroke for her pussy, circling around her like a predator ready to pounce. Master Law's fingers encountered the tiny scrap of fabric that was Iris' thong.

She felt his chuckle.

His fingers moved past it, pressing right against her clit... and stopped.

"Get yourself off, Iris."

Iris blinked. Did he mean?

She shifted experimentally, rolling her hips forward, rubbing against his fingers. Fuck, it felt so good. She moaned.

"That's it. Good girl."

Despite the many times she'd now earned the accolade from him, none had felt as good as this one.

Iris rolled her hips forward again. Master Law's fingers stayed on her clit, but he didn't move them with her body. He made her work for it. His other hand moved up to fondle her breast again, squeezing the soft flesh, then yanked the top of her dress down, so she could finally feel his calloused palm against her skin.

She writhed on his lap, moving her hips, rubbing against his fingers. He was motionless beneath her, making her do all the work to get herself off using him... for some reason, that turned her on even more.

Rubbing, rubbing, rubbing as she watched Will lift Gina's legs, draping them over his arms and lining his cock up with her abused pussy. Gina's scream of passion as he thrust into her made Iris move even more frantically. She whimpered, trying to rub herself harder against Law's fingers, trying to get a reaction from him.

Pinching her nipple, he tugged and twisted, and the sharp bite of pain sent Iris reeling. She reached down between her legs, putting her hand over his and pressing him farther into her pussy, giving her exactly what she needed. The pressure was perfect. Iris cried out as her orgasm finally peaked, but her voice was drowned out by the music and Gina's enraptured cries.

Writhing against Law's hand, she shuddered and gasped as the sensations rolled through her. The waves of pleasure pushed her about until she finally slumped, panting, her hand still over his.

Onstage, the music crescendoed as Will thrust into Gina hard one last time, the two of them crying out in unison as he shuddered between her thighs. The lights slowly began to dim.

Iris felt Master Law shift beneath her. His cock was still pressing into her backside, thick and insistent, and despite her orgasm, she felt an ache of emptiness in her pussy.

Then she felt his lips brush against her shoulder.

"Naughty girl. You were supposed to keep your hands on the table."

The erotic menace in his voice slid through her, and Iris shivered, snatching her hand away and putting it back in place on the table, knowing it was already too late.

CHAPTER THIRTEEN

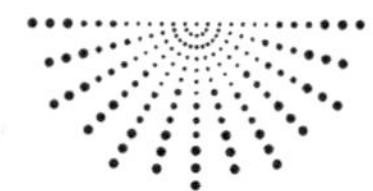

Law

Every impulse screamed at Law to take Iris by the hair, drag her back to the Dungeon, and fuck her senseless. Whoever had the idea for a hotel for the guests to retreat to following the show was fucking brilliant.

The panting, shivering submissive on his lap made wrestling with his control far more difficult than it should be. This was exactly why he didn't scene with submissives he actually *wanted*. His attraction to Iris was more than physical, no matter that he'd tried to tell himself that it wasn't.

Can't back out now.

If he were being truly honest with himself, he didn't really want to… which was exactly why he should. It was too late, though. Backing out now would not only be hurtful, it would be harmful.

It was his responsibility to see the evening through.

Which, coincidentally, happens to give you exactly what you want. Interesting argument there, counselor.

Time to shut off the voice in his head and be the Dom Iris needed him to be. There would be plenty of time for self-recrimination later.

"Let's go," he growled, patting her hip as he finally released her breast and tugged the neckline of her dress over it. She slid off his lap, smoothing down her skirt as she went, and scooted through the booth.

The booth scoot might have been the unsexiest thing he'd ever done, but somehow, it did nothing to dampen the sexual tension still simmering between them. From the sounds coming from some of the booths, not all the occupants were done with their own amorous pursuits. A few others were moving out of their seats and also heading toward the door leading to the hotel portion.

There were more booths than there were rooms in the back, so there would always be stragglers after the show. Marquis was prepared for it.

Wrapping his fingers around the back of Iris' neck, Law propelled her forward. A quick glance down at her expression was all he needed to reassure himself she was perfectly happy being moved about in this manner. If there was something possessive about his grip on her, she didn't seem to mind.

"Which room?" As they walked into the hall, her eyes darted back and forth. The flirty skirt she was wearing rippled around her thighs, and he could see her nipples were still pebbled through her dress.

"The Dungeon."

He felt her shiver, and he smiled.

What he had planned was a fairly basic scene, but they should both find it mutually satisfying. He wanted to give Iris what she'd been missing out on—a good, solid scene with a Dom… and likely, sex at the end.

When they got to the door, he reluctantly released her, so he could get the key card out of his wallet. Opening the door, he let her precede him into the room.

It was hardly a new room to either of them. During both her Introduction class and the Dominance class she'd helped with as a submissive, she'd spent time in each of Marquis' rooms. The Dungeon was always a favorite since it had just about everything anyone could possibly need for a standard BDSM scene.

Knowing ahead of time what Will and Gina had planned for

tonight, Law had set up the square frame in the center of the room. Chains dangled from it with leather cuffs waiting for delicate wrists. Iris ground to a halt, sucking in a breath as she realized what was waiting for her.

She spun around with a faintly accusatory look in her eyes.

"Did you know what they were going to be doing ahead of time?"

"Yes." Law grinned. "Don't worry, we're not doing pony play, but I thought you might enjoy recreating some of what we watched."

Going by the way her eyes lit up, yes, yes, she would.

"Do you want to add anything to your limits before we begin?" Thanks to the classes, he was well aware of all her limits.

Sex wasn't one of them.

"Nope, nothing to add."

His cock throbbed.

"Good. Put your purse down by the door over there, then come back here."

<hr>

Iris

Holy shit, holy shit, holy shit.

Despite all the classes, Iris was suddenly feeling very unprepared.

Her relationships with the other students had always been friendly. Sometimes, they had sex. Sometimes, they hadn't. She'd even been mildly attracted to a few of them—Q was pretty hot.

She'd never felt like *this* with any of them.

Uncertain. Vulnerable. Wary.

None of them had ever looked at her quite like he was, even when there had been a spark of mutual attraction. The way he was looking at her wasn't a spark—it was an inferno.

Pretty sure I'm gonna get burned.

With her purse in place, she returned to where she'd been standing. Master Law hadn't moved, but now he prowled toward her. With her heels on, he was only about an inch taller, so when he stopped right in front of her, their lips were mere centimeters apart. Iris felt as though she was barely breathing.

She waited for him to say something, but he reached up to the straps of her dress. Her mind went blank. Holding her gaze, he tugged the straps down over her shoulders, then pulled them off and down her arms. The dress wasn't skintight, although it was formfitting to her hips, so he pulled it down easily enough.

The skirt was fairly loose, so as soon as he got it over her hips, the fabric dropped to the floor in a puddle, leaving her in nothing but her heels and a thong. Master Law barely blinked as he'd undressed her in less than five seconds, and Iris felt like her lungs had seized up. She'd never had anyone, not a regular boyfriend or another Dom, undress her. Normally, they liked to watch while she did it. Having Master Law take control this way... she felt stripped of more than her clothing.

"Are you a good girl, Iris?" he asked, his voice low, demanding. All the little hairs at the nape of her neck and along her arms stood up.

"Yes, Sir." Her voice sounded higher than normal, almost squeaky. If she wasn't caught in his gaze, a mouse under the hypnotic stare of a predator, she would have been embarrassed, but she was too frozen with arousal to feel anything else. Her lips were slightly parted, waiting for a kiss she wasn't sure was coming.

It was a good thing her expectations weren't very high.

"Good. Then spread your legs apart and bend over. You'll need to keep your balance, so make sure you spread them wide enough." With that instruction given, he moved away, and Iris finally felt like she could breathe again.

Carefully stepping out of the little circle of fabric around her feet, she spread her legs wide and bent over. In heels, there was no way she could touch the floor, so she gripped her ankles instead.

The position left her horribly exposed.

Breasts hanging down, ass up in the air, pussy vulnerable and spread, the blood rushing to her head—she took in as deep a breath as the position would allow, then let it out slowly. At some point, her heart would *have* to stop pounding so hard, wouldn't it?

Behind her, Master Law was moving to one of the cabinets and taking out a toy. With her head between her legs, she could see everything he was doing, and every one of her nerves was buzzing and humming in anticipation.

Law

Fuck, he needed to get a grip on himself.

For a second, he thought he was actually going to kiss her.

Which wasn't a huge problem. It wasn't like they were re-enacting *Pretty Woman*. Law had kissed submissives he'd scened with in the past, but he knew it would be different with Iris. It already felt different. He felt more out of control than normal, more affected.

It was his attraction to her. The pull he felt toward her. The effect she had on his body was far stronger than any other submissive he'd allowed himself to scene with.

Turning around, he opened the packaging around the plug he'd picked out for her, a basic plug, about an inch around the thickest part and four inches long. Nothing substantial, but enough for her to feel it and give him something to play with.

He wanted to make sure she felt she had the full experience with him. Impulsively, he picked up a pair of nipple clamps and slid them into his pocket. He wouldn't put them on her until he finished flogging her breasts. He didn't want any of the strands to catch on them, but they would be a good addition to the scene he planned.

Clamps pocketed, plug in one hand, he picked up a tube of lube in the other and walked back toward her. She was holding perfectly still, her hands wrapped around her ankles, ass in the air, with all of her most vulnerable parts open and displayed. Nothing he hadn't seen in class before, but... it didn't feel the same.

This wasn't for a class or for another student... it was for him.

She was holding herself in position for him.

Obeying his commands.

It was fucking hot as hell.

"Good girl," he said, just because he could. He didn't need to see her expression to know it affected her. With the lube and plug in one hand, he patted her ass with the other. "Very pretty."

The brownish-pink lips of her pussy were splayed open, revealing the glistening interior, slick with her arousal. His cock throbbed. Exercising his self-control was torturous, yet it felt good. Law enjoyed teasing subbies with orgasm denial, but it was something he practiced on himself as well.

Above her pussy, the little star of her anus appeared impossibly small as he lubed up the plug. He knew she was no stranger to the plug but didn't know how recently she'd had one used on her. As he covered the plug in the slick lubricant, he heard her mutter something, although he couldn't quite make out the words.

Reaching out, he gave her ass a hard smack, making her yelp and rock forward, but she managed to maintain her balance. The skin of her bottom was several shades lighter than her legs and torso, same with her breasts, a testament to the amount of time she'd spent in a bikini this summer. The spot where his hand had landed pinked up rather nicely.

"What was that, Iris?" he asked mildly. "I couldn't hear you."

"I was just wondering what was taking so long, Sir." Despite how respectful she'd made her tone, there was no sugarcoating the words. At least she was honest. On the other hand, he was pretty sure she was looking for a reaction. Poking at the bear, as it were.

"I'm making sure the plug is properly lubed. I was going to use my fingers to stretch you out a little, but since you're in such a hurry..." Law pressed the tip of the plug to her anus and pushed, enjoying the sound of her gasp as he smoothly pressed the plug through the resisting muscle of her sphincter. "Relax, Iris. This will be as hard on you as you make it."

Iris

Easy for him to say, he wasn't the one having something shoved up his ass.

At the same time, she knew he was speaking the truth. She did her best to relax her muscles, but they burned as the plug pushed inside of her. She hadn't scened since the class, which had been over a month ago, and hadn't kept up with inserting a plug herself. She hadn't seen the point. Having fingers stretch her out first would have made the insertion easier.

On the other hand, a part of her reveled in the burn and in that he'd made her punishment fit the crime.

Mouthing off had always been a problem, especially when she was feeling vulnerable. She felt especially exposed with him standing right beside her while she was bent at the waist. He could see *everything*.

The punishment fit the crime, but it also didn't really feel like punishment. Iris moaned as the fattest part of the plug stretched her open. The stinging burn flashed for only a moment before it was fully seated, her sphincter snapping shut around the thinner part between the bulb and the base.

The plug hadn't looked all that big, but it felt big inside her. She burned from the initial stretch, though the sensation was subsiding. Hopefully, it was a precursor to how good *he* would feel inside her.

Whether they'd actually be having sex tonight, she still didn't know, but she really hoped so. *All signs point to yes.* The bulge at the front of his pants was a clear sign he wasn't unaffected, even if she thought he could ignore the chemistry sizzling between them.

"Good girl." Despite the accolade, he smacked her other cheek as hard as he had with the first swat and Iris groaned as she rocked forward again. It hurt. It felt good. The contrariness of kink was something she related to. "You may stand up now."

The head rush was real, but Master Law was there, arm steadying her behind her back until the wave of dizziness passed. Iris shook her head to clear it, squirming as the new position made the plug feel even more intrusive. The flat rectangular base was snuggled between her cheeks, and she could feel it a lot more now that her cheeks and legs weren't spread apart.

"Better?" he asked, and Iris nodded, lifting her head to meet his gaze. The heat in his dark eyes made her sway toward him, tilting her head slightly. She wanted a kiss.

It felt as if they were supposed to kiss.

Instead, he looked away, turning his attention to the frame.

Dammit.

"Let's get you in position."

"Yes, Sir." Even if she was disappointed, her body was ready for whatever he wanted to do, though she had a new goal—get a kiss from Master Law before the end of the night.

CHAPTER FOURTEEN

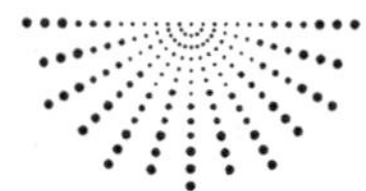

Leather wrapped around her wrists, legs spread apart and cuffed to the bottom of the wooden frame, Iris was relieved Master Law had ultimately decided to take her shoes off. Standing this way was a lot easier without heels.

The inability to move didn't bother her. Iris enjoyed being bound. She felt freer. The ultimate dichotomy. She didn't have to worry about what choice to make or whether she was making the right or wrong one. She just had to wait to see what deliciously deviant pleasure was going to happen.

This position was a little daunting since it gave her Dom completely unfettered access to her body. Not just her ass but also her breasts and pussy. She could only imagine how Gina had felt in this position.

The memory of watching the scene while Master Law's hands played with her breasts made her breath hitch. Now she would experience some of it. Her skin tingled in anticipation, and she could feel her inner muscles clenching, gripping the plug more tightly while her pussy ached with emptiness.

Would it have killed him to fill her pussy with something, too?

Circling around her with the flogger in his hand, his gaze met hers, and his lips tipped up.

"What's your safeword, Iris?"

"Foliage."

That stopped him in his tracks.

Iris pressed her lips together to keep from smiling. Master Law blinked, staring at her, then his gaze narrowed.

"Is that from *The Office?*"

"Yes."

He shook his head, but he couldn't entirely hide his smile.

"I thought you used 'red.'"

"I did for the classes. I was saving my real safeword for a real scene." She'd considered it a test—did the Dom recognize where it came from? Did he find it funny?

Master Law had just passed on both counts.

She'd liked the idea of doing something that differentiated a real scene from the scenes she'd done in class. At the time, she hadn't realized her safeword would hardly be a blip in the number of differences during the evening. She hadn't needed it to make the evening special. She already knew she'd remember this night for the rest of her life, regardless of what happened between them afterward.

Shaking his head, he swung the flogger around in a little loop, keeping it close enough to his side, it didn't actually hit her. She flinched when she felt the air rushing past her hips, and his smile grew.

Sadist.

"Foliage it is then." Moving again, circling around behind her so she couldn't see him anymore. Her anxiety ramped up, and she debated if she should turn her head. She had a feeling she wasn't supposed to, but having him behind her, being unable to see where he was standing and what he was doing. Her entire back tingled, muscles tensing in anticipation until she forced them to relax, then knotted up again when she heard him make the smallest movement.

Yet it was still a shock when the leather strands of the logger slapped against her upper back. The stinging patter made her suck in a breath and quiver before relaxing again. Almost the moment she did, the flogger landed again on the other side of her upper back.

Then on the right side of her ass.

Then the left.

Master Law wielded the flogger with precision, the strands falling against her skin in a stinging pattern that was hypnotic. Moaning, Iris rocked forward slightly as the surface of her skin became more and more sensitive.

When he stepped forward to run a warm hand over that skin, she shivered.

"How are you doing, Iris?"

"Good." She practically sang the word. So good. So relaxed, yet so aroused.

A little smack to her ass made her sigh, then the flogging started up again... except Master Law was moving around her. She gasped, straining against her bonds as the flogger fell against her sensitive sides, the outside of her thighs, then her breasts.

Her nipples, already budded, stiffened further under the assault, and Iris' head fell back, thrusting her chest forward as if her body was begging for more.

Because it was.

More sensation.

More pain.

More pleasure.

More, more, more.

She was greedy for it.

When the flogger snapped between her legs, the same way Will had done to Gina, she cried out, rocking against the restraints. It hurt a lot more than her back, her buttocks, or her breasts, but it felt better too.

The pattering sting kissed her skin, traveling over her, then back between her legs.

More!

It wasn't enough. She whimpered, clenching around the plug, moving her hips forward. The brief spark of leather against flesh didn't give her what she needed to push herself over. The flogging was a tease. A taster.

And Iris wanted it all.

***

LAW

Fuck, she was beautiful. Straining. Whimpering. The sights and sounds of Iris' responses to the flogger went straight to his dick, adding to his own torment.

He'd turned the lighter parts of her body a pretty pink while adding reddish color to her limbs and back despite her tan. He rather enjoyed trying to decorate within the tan lines. It was a fun challenge.

This might be a fairly basic scene, but Iris made it special.

The way she went up on her toes when he swept the flogger up between her legs, the ends of the strands snapping against her pussy. The way she thrust her breasts out when he flicked the flogger over them. The way her lips parted as she cried out in pained pleasure. The puffy lips between her legs were more swollen, and the traces of her arousal glistened on the end of the flogger.

Fuck.

Law's mouth watered.

He wanted a taste.

Reaching into his pocket, he pulled out the clamps he'd stored there earlier. Setting the flogger down, he moved closer to Iris. She lifted her head, arousal and need glazing her dark eyes, and her lips slightly parted. Tilting her head as he came closer, her expression lightened with anticipation.

Cupping her breast with one hand, he ran his thumb over her nipple, and she moaned, arching her back in encouragement.

"Trying to tempt me, naughty girl?" Whether or not she was trying was irrelevant. Iris was temptation personified. She didn't have to do anything extra.

"That depends." Her eyelashes fluttered as her pink tongue flicked her lower lip. She twisted slightly, rubbing her breast against his hand. "Is it working?"

Law chuckled.

"Naughty girl." He said it in the same tone he usually called her a 'good girl' and enjoyed the flash of happiness in her eyes. "Hold still for me."

Iris hummed under her breath as he squeezed her breast, lifting it so he could apply one of the clamps. The soft flesh spilled out around his fingers, dark pink and so pretty against his brown skin. Fuck, he wanted to taste her so bad, he couldn't resist dipping his head down to lick his tongue over one pert, brown nipple.

Her shudder and sigh were delicious.

Opening the clamp, he closed it around that same nipple, savoring her shriek as the tiny bud was pinched. The tight grip was merciless. Iris panted as she worked her way through the pain while Law cradled her breast in his hand, watching her expressions as she worked her way through pain to acceptance and pleasure.

When her gaze finally refocused on him, he grinned and applied the second clamp.

"Sadist!" she gasped out, then whined with the pain of having the second clamp applied.

Law chuckled, brushing his fingertips over the exposed tips of her nipples. Iris writhed in her restraints, gasping from the sensation.

"Exactly."

Iris

The fascination with which Master Law was watching her was arousing all on its own, even if she wasn't tingling and throbbing all over. It felt like he was completely in control while she was completely out of it. Her nipples throbbed, pulsing against the tight confines of the clamps. The initial pain had subsided quickly, and her body was confused if she was still hurting or if she was enjoying it.

Both. Definitely both.

When Master Law dropped to his knees, it was as if all the air had been sucked out of her lungs.

This hadn't happened in Will and Gina's scene.

Strong arms wrapped around the backs of her legs, fingers digging into her thighs, and she felt his hot breath against her pussy lips a moment before she felt his tongue.

"Fuck!" Iris' hips jerked forward, rubbing more of her sensitive flesh against his mouth—and in the wake of the flogging, it felt extra sensitive. She whimpered at the hot jolt of pleasure, her body clenching and squeezing the plug in her bottom.

Looking down, she could see the top of Master Law's bald head as he tipped it back to get his mouth fully on her pussy. His tongue slid between the lips, teasing her tender folds. Tasting her. Circling her clit. Then he sucked the little nubbin between his lips, pulling hard. It felt as if there was a line of electricity between her breasts and her pussy, the throbbing pulse of pleasure running counterpoint to each other.

"Please... oh, fuck... please..." If the flogger's touch hadn't been nearly enough, this intense stimulation was almost too much. Her thighs squeezed, trying to press together, but even without the restraints, his broad shoulders would have never let her. His fingers found the base of the plug between her cheeks and pressed on it, pushing it inside her, then pulling back, fucking her ass with the toy while his tongue laved her pussy. "Oh, fuck!"

Iris jerked against the restraints, but they were far too strong to break. They held her up when her knees trembled, threatening to give as the sensations washed over her. The plug twisted, adding to the intense stimulation as Master Law returned his attention to her clit, making her throb, clench, and squirm atop his face.

Then his tongue did something that made her toes curl, and she cried out again, going upward to escape the intense pleasure, but there was no escape. She was pinioned in place, her limbs restrained, body held in place by his grip, and the suction of his mouth was relentless.

"Law!" She screamed his name, writhing against his lips, as ecstasy blossomed over her, starting in her core and unfurling along her nerve endings.

The pressure on her lower body increased as his arms tightened, holding her against his mouth, and the throbbing suction sent wave after wave of erotic bliss crashing through her. Iris threw her head back and cried out as she rode his face, shuddering as the rapturous explosions of passion wracked her body.

The waves gentled, slowed, and she sagged against the restraints. His hands were at her ankles, releasing them. Before she could bring her legs together or even try to stand, they were being lifted into the air. Iris shook her head, trying to focus again, and realized he was picking her up and putting her in position—the same position Gina had been in at the end of the show.

Their eyes met. Held.

She felt his cock pressing against the entrance of her pussy, realizing she didn't know when he'd taken his pants off. Thrusting forward, he pulled her toward him. Iris moaned, clenching as his cock pushed into her, jostling with the plug in her bottom for space. Her breasts bounced, sending another wave of pleasured pain through her nipples, especially where the protruding tips rubbed against his chest.

Heat flicked through every inch of her body, every point where they touched, setting her aflame.

Even if she'd wanted to maintain the almost disturbingly intimate eye contact, she couldn't. Her eyelashes fluttered closed in reaction to the sensations erupting through her. The swollen tissues of her pussy were exquisitely sensitive in the wake of her orgasm, and the feel of his cock sliding into her, then pulling part way out before thrusting back in made her feel as if she was going through a series of rapid mini orgasms with every stroke.

Law

Sinking into Iris had felt unlike anything else.

It didn't matter that he'd put on a condom as he always did. The rubber felt thinner than ever, her heat engulfing him. Usually, it provided more than a physical barrier, but with her, it didn't feel like it was making any difference at all.

"Law… oh, fuck… *Law!*" Her body tightened around him again, her back arching as her eyelashes fluttered in passion.

Every one of his muscles tightened.

Fuck.

Just let go… for once. It'll be fine.

There was no reason he had to maintain his iron control right now.

He wouldn't hurt her if he let go.

So, he did.

Groaning, Law pounded into her, giving over to the sensations, giving over to the need driving him. Iris writhed against him, her breasts bouncing, and he could feel the metal nipple clamps scrape against his chest as they moved. Driving into her as deeply as he could, he could feel her hot cream coating his groin as she came around him, muscles clenching and squeezing his cock. His balls tightened, body tensing as his orgasm reached the tipping point.

"*Fuck.*"

Bending his head, Law uttered the word in a hoarse voice, thrusting deep and burying himself inside her as his cock swelled and pulsed. Her body throbbed around him, milking him of each jet of cum. The pleasure was so intense, for a moment, he thought his knees might give out, and he clung to her to stay upright.

At that moment, nothing else mattered—it was just the two of them, alone in a room, with the rest of the world and all its myriad problems shut out.

It was the best moment Law had had in a long, long time.

She lifted her head, and there was nothing to stop her, not enough space between them, and he was too weak to pull away... he didn't want to. Their lips met, and Law stopped resisting. He gave in. His hands squeezed her legs, holding her close as he devoured her the way he'd wanted to all night, the way he'd craved.

It was everything he'd wanted and everything he'd worked so hard to deny himself.

CHAPTER FIFTEEN

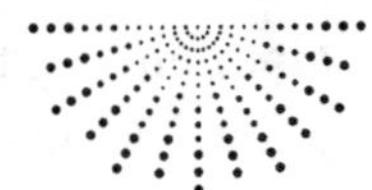

Kissing Master Law was even better than she'd imagined... and gave her the closeness she was craving. He wasn't just kissing her. He was kissing her as if he couldn't get enough of her. If he'd kissed her like this before the scene, she'd probably have melted into a little pile of Iris goo.

Of course, almost as soon as she had the thought, he pulled away. There was an odd expression on his face and an almost bewildered look in his eyes.

"I... I don't do relationships."

Iris blinked. He was still inside her, though his dick was slowly softening, his hands gripping her legs, while her nipples throbbed in the clamps he'd put on them—which were really hurting now that the scene was over—and that's what he had to say?

On the other hand, she didn't think she'd ever seen him so at a loss, so that was something. Iris knew when she'd gotten under someone's skin since she'd spent a lifetime doing it.

"Okay?" She tilted her head to the side. "Pretty sure I didn't ask for one, but if I said something while you were fucking me, I was under the influence of a good cock."

That made his mouth twitch, though she didn't get the full-out laugh she was going for. Nope, he was reverting to stick-in-the-mud Master Law. She'd seen a hint of the man beneath, though, and was curious.

"We need to get you down," he said, clearly looking for a diversion.

Since her arms were getting tired, Iris didn't fight him as he slid out of her. He undid her wrist restraints, then removed the plug, which made her sigh with relief. The nipple clamps came off next, accompanied by her hiss of pain. Bending forward, Master Law took each unhappy bud in his mouth, sucking gently and soothing the sting as feeling returned to the turgid nubs.

It also made Iris laugh.

"Kisses… no. Sucking my nipples… yes. Got it," she murmured. Master Law straightened with a scowl, but that didn't bother her. She knew when someone was actually upset with her, and he wasn't. He liked her bratty mouth, even if he didn't want to admit it.

"Kisses give the wrong impression."

"Ah, but fucking me till I scream, doesn't?" Iris batted her eyes at him and tried to take a step—tried, being the operative word. Her legs were still pretty wobbly, and she stumbled, but he caught her. "Whoops. I'm a little shaky."

He swept her up into his arms. Yup. Totally not giving off mixed signals.

"Come on, we can go rest in the other room."

Leaning her head against his chest, an arm wrapped around the back of his neck, Iris sighed happily. Being carried like this, she felt as though she was in a movie. A really romantic one.

Leaving the equipment behind, Master Law took her to the back room, the hotel portion of Marquis. Iris perked up and looked around. During class, they hadn't had access to these rooms, and she was curious. Unfortunately, it looked exactly like a regular hotel room.

Big king-size bed, dresser, television, couch, mini-fridge, closet, and a door that led to what she presumed was the bathroom. The walls were plain beige, and all the furniture was medium brown. The sheets and comforter were a nice, crisp, bright white, and there was a big black bag resting on the foot of the bed. All in all, everything about the room was super neutral and soothing.

"What's with the bag?" she asked. Was he planning on spending the night? Should she have brought stuff with her? She'd assumed they were only scening, and his 'I don't do relationships' thing backed that up. If kissing said 'relationship,' actually sleeping together *screamed* it.

"I came here straight from work for a meeting with Olivia and Julie. I needed a change of clothes for tonight since I didn't want to do this in my suit." Carrying her over to the bed, he set her down on the edge rather than laying on it, his gaze not quite meeting hers. "How are you feeling?"

"Very, very good." Iris grinned as her answer and purring tone caught his attention, and his eyes met hers. "So, is there any particular reason you jumped straight from kissing to a relationship? I promise I've kissed lots of guys without thinking we were going to get married and have babies." She kept her tone teasing, but she had to wonder if he jumped there with everyone or if she was a special case.

"I just don't want to accidentally hurt anyone," he replied quietly, turning as he did so. She could see him removing the condom, still barely clinging to his cock, and she admired the backside view as he went to throw it away in the trashcan next to the mini-fridge.

"I get that, but... I mean, most people don't immediately jump into a relationship after a first date. There are multiple dates before they do a relationship." Iris squirmed on top of the bed, trying to get comfortable and also make herself look a little more seductive. Seductive was good, right? She leaned back on her elbows so she was propped up and hoped it didn't look stupid.

"This isn't a date." He said the words so quickly, Iris had to roll her eyes.

"Are you trying to convince yourself or me?" Before he could answer, she quickly went on. "Why can't we just go with the flow? This was a fun night. I'd love to do it again with you sometime, with no expectation of a relationship. Though I'll be honest, I'd rather not close that door entirely. It would be nice to know there's a chance we could go on a real date in the future."

He finally turned around, coming to sit at the end of the bed before he answered.

"I'm too old for you."

That wasn't a no.

"How old are you?" She was pretty sure he was around her brother's age, maybe a little older, but she wasn't sure.

"Thirty-four."

"A whole nine years… oh, no…" Iris flopped back onto the bed, throwing her arms out wide. "You're right, Grandpa. I can't believe I let you put your wrinkled, old— eek!"

Do not poke the cranky Dom too much.

On the other hand, poking at him got him to put his hands on her again, even if it was to turn her over on the bed. Since her butt had been right on the edge, that put her in the perfect position for him to spank—and he did exactly that, right on top of her already tender-from-being-flogged cheeks.

Iris yelped and wriggled, trying to escape his hand, even as she enjoyed the sensation of being pinned down and spanked.

"You were saying?" Despite the sternness in his voice, she could hear his amusement. Iris turned her head to look over her shoulder and pouted at him.

"I said the same thing you did. I don't see why I should be punished for agreeing with you."

Law

She was an incredible brat, and he didn't know why he liked that so much. He shouldn't.

He also didn't know why he was pulling her up from her position, so he could settle her on his lap. He knew he shouldn't, yet he did it, anyway. It felt good. It felt right. She was seriously messing with his self-control, and he was on the highway toward destruction.

Once she was on his lap, she snuggled in and rubbed her face against his shoulder, sighing happily as she settled.

"I'm not really a go-with-the-flow kind of person," he said finally. "I'm… I'm the person with a plan. The responsible person. The one everyone can count on to know what the next step is, the one who won't let anyone down. That's who I've chosen to be."

He hadn't always been that person, and he never wanted to go back to being the person he had been. He'd let down the people most important to him and had vowed *never again.*

"I can't imagine you being anything else. Will keeping the future open to possible dating change all that?" Iris rubbed her face against his chest and yawned.

No.

Maybe not.

I don't know.

It was the *not* knowing for sure that stymied him—not knowing whether he'd be able to keep control of himself, not wanting another woman to become collateral damage if he fell off the wagon.

I've been sober for nine years. What makes me think I'll fall off the wagon?

The little voice in his head sounded an awful lot like Asad. As usual. Law scowled.

But it had a point.

He'd had strict rules in place because he'd needed to prove something to himself. He'd never put a time limit on those rules, but maybe he should have. Did he really believe he needed to keep everyone at a distance forever? That he couldn't have a relationship with someone ever again?

Also maybe.

He still felt bad about how he'd treated Elaine until she'd finally left him, but… he'd been younger. Iris was now the same age as Elaine was when she'd walked. At twenty-five, Elaine had known what she'd deserved and that she'd deserved better than him.

So, maybe he should trust Iris to know what she deserved. At the very least, she was right. He could keep himself open to the possibilities instead of shutting them down immediately.

Maybe they'd keep scening together, and everything would fizzle out on its own.

Yeah, right.

Unlikely, but possible.

"What are you suggesting?" He was uneasy because he was normally the one who came up with a plan but couldn't do that until he knew more about what she was asking for. What she wanted from him.

Her head tilted, so she could smile up at him. The lids of her eyes were getting heavy. While she wasn't in subspace, she looked happy and fizzy, the way a sub should look during aftercare. Clearly, she liked the cuddling, which he'd known from seeing her in the classes, but he was surprised how much he liked it, too.

He'd never minded cuddling during aftercare, but he hadn't enjoyed it quite this much either. Something about having her snuggled up safely against him, leaning on his strength so trustingly, added to his satisfaction.

"Well, that was a pretty basic scene." Iris walked her fingers up his chest, over his pecs. Not in a sexual way, more like she was exploring. "Is there any kink you're particularly into? I've heard you do stuff with the violet wand."

Electricity was one of his kinks. What could he say? He liked to play with his toys, and his sadistic side adored the myriad ways he could play with electricity and a willing subbie's body. Iris was definitely masochistic enough to enjoy it.

The thought of doing a scene with her more aligned with his favorite interests...

Fuck.

His cock was stirring again.

"Maybe we could agree to be scening partners for a while," he found himself saying. "Have a club contract."

"Ah yes, because that always wards off developing feelings for each other," she responded drily. "Just look at how well it worked out for Mitch and Domi."

Law opened his mouth. Closed it again.

She had a point.

He was already far more interested in her than he wanted to be. Suggesting they scene and nothing else? That was coming from his need to delude himself, this wasn't a big deal.

"Tell you what, though, we can do that." Iris yawned again, leaning her head on his shoulder and snuggling in. "As long as you don't shut down the idea of changing things up in the future. If you run the moment you catch feelings, I'm gonna be pissed. I want that option open."

Her bossy tone was ruined by how sleepy she sounded.

Swinging around, so he was no longer sitting on the edge of the bed, he rested his feet down and let her fall the few inches to the surface. Her legs were still across his torso and her head still snuggled into his shoulder, but now they were technically lying on the bed.

Law hadn't planned to sleep here tonight. He really hadn't.

Uh-huh. Keep telling yourself that. That's why you reserved the room for the whole night.

He'd reserved the room; he always liked to have a backup plan for unexpected contingencies. Like Iris falling asleep after their scene in the middle of aftercare. Not entirely unexpected.

Though he knew damn well from experience, he didn't hesitate to wake up a subbie after half an hour or so and send her on her way. He knew that he wouldn't do that with Iris.

Whether or not he wanted to admit it, he wanted this.

CHAPTER SIXTEEN

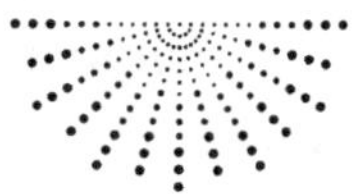

IRIS

This is not my bed. This is not my house.

And whose shoulder is that?

Oh, yeah...

Oh, yeah!

Holy shit!

Talk about coming awake in a rush. The events of the previous night flooded her mind. Iris froze. Peeked upward to see the face of the man whose shoulder her head was resting on.

Master Law was still asleep.

She should probably start calling him 'Law' in her head, even though it felt weird. She'd thought of him as 'Master Law' since the moment they'd been introduced. If they were going to date—and they *were* going to date—she needed to start thinking of him as Law.

Also, since she wanted to date, she shouldn't follow her first impulse and sneak out.

What had woken her up?

A duck quacked, and she froze.

Whoops. Someone was texting her.

"Is it the quack of dawn?" Law's deep voice rumbled, and Iris squeaked, realizing he was awake, even though his eyes were still closed... then she cracked up.

"You did not just make that joke."

"What joke?" A little smile curved the edges of his lips.

Shaking her head, she propped herself up on her elbow to look down at him. Her phone quacked again, and he cracked one eyelid open.

"Seriously, where's the duck?"

"It's my text notifications. They seem to be blowing up." Iris glanced at the clock on the nightstand and made a face. "Probably because I didn't plan to be out *all* night. Why did you let me fall asleep?"

"Why is it my fault you fell asleep?" Law raised an eyebrow. Other than that, he hadn't moved, though his arm was still around her. As if the thought sparked the action, she felt one of his fingertips drawing little patterns on her bicep. The sensation was distracting.

"You're the Dom. You're the one in charge," she said, innocently blinking at him.

He snorted. "Oh, I am, am I?"

Just like that, Iris found herself rolled onto her back with Master Law above her. Yup, Master Law now. He'd flipped his Dom switch, and the man settling himself between her legs, his thick erection pressing against her mound, was definitely in charge.

Her breathing hitched as she stared up at him, her heart pounding.

The lazy lion who hadn't bothered to move more than an eyebrow and a finger had morphed into a threatening predator who wanted to eat her for breakfast. Her insides were turning into heated mush, and her arousal had gone from vaguely interested to a lightning strike of need.

"Um... yes, Sir?" Her voice was breathy, reminding her she probably had epic morning breath.

On the other hand, he did, too.

Chuckling, he leaned down and brushed his lips over hers but thankfully, didn't go for the deep kiss.

Her phone quacked again, and Iris giggled. Talk about ruining the moment. Law cursed under his breath and pushed away from her. She pouted, and he chuckled, patting her thigh as he got off the bed, erection bobbing in front of him.

"Answer your friends, then come meet me in the shower." Turning, he gave her a nice view of his ass as he headed to the bathroom.

Grinning, Iris slid off the bed to get her phone. At some point, Law had moved her purse from the playroom into this room. He must have gotten up during the night when she was sleeping.

As she opened her phone, which was down to thirty percent battery now, she heard the shower come on in the bathroom.

Quickly, she checked her messages.

One from Noelle. *I assume you're not coming home tonight, but can you just text me back so I know you're not dead?*

Yup, should have let her roommate know. Not that *she'd* known at the time, but she would have been pissed if Noelle had gone out with a new guy and hadn't given her a heads-up she wasn't coming home. Safety first.

Sorry! Fell asleep right after the amazingly hot sex, which I will tell you all about later, and just woke up. I'll be doing the walk of shame soon.

Two from Kate, one telling her to have fun, the other telling her to ignore anything her brother said.

The texts that had woken her up were from her group chat, of course. Avery, Rae, and Domi were speculating why they hadn't heard from her yet and that some theories were getting really out there.

Maybe he has her tied up in his Dungeon.

Maybe she's agreed to be his 24/7 slave, and he's taken away her phone.

Maybe she did something super embarrassing and has had to run away and take on a new identity, so she'll never have to face him or anyone else who might hear about it again.

What could she do that's so embarrassing?

Fart while they're spooning.

Fart while he's eating her out.

What's with all the farting suggestions?

It's embarrassing.

It's a bodily function!

What's more embarrassing than farting on him or in his face?

Confessing her love for him.

Okay, that might be worse.

We're all in agreement that they definitely fucked last night, right?

Probably fucked her into oblivion since she's not texting us back. Has anyone seen him scene before? How big do you think his dick is?

It's not about the size. It's about the motion of the ride. Size Queen.

Hey, what's wrong with liking a nice girthy cock?

Ew, I hate that word.

What word? Cock?

No, dumbass, girthy.

But it's such a good word!

Agreed, it's a good word. You're outvoted, Domi.

That doesn't make me wrong!

So, when do you think she's going to answer us?

Maybe we should stop texting. Doesn't her phone quack when we text?

OMG... do you think they're trying to have morning sex, and all they can hear is quaking?

Poke.

Poke.

Poke.

Poke.

Poke.

Domi, stop it! She's gonna murder you!

Her friends were insane.

Iris was laughing so hard by the time she got to the end of the texts. Law came out of the bathroom and raised his eyebrow. The shower was still going, which meant he'd heard her over that.

"Sorry. I'll show you later."

Quickly she tapped out a message back.

Yes, he fucked me into oblivion, and yes, you interrupted morning sex with the quacking. Now we're going to take a shower. I'll update you all later!

"Come on." Law held out his hand.

Iris put her phone down, giggling as it started quacking again.

Even he looked amused, though he shook his head as he pulled her into the bathroom. The heat curled around them as steam filled the room. Her phone was quickly forgotten as he pulled her into the shower with him.

LAW

It had been the best Saturday morning he'd had in a long time, which of course, meant his friends had to come over that afternoon and invade his house. They'd texted him about two minutes before they arrived, giving him basically no choice but to let them in. Whiskers, already grumpy from having been left alone overnight and missing her morning breakfast, crouched on top of the fridge and hissed at everyone who came to get a beverage.

Asad hissed back at her.

"Demon cat."

"If you think she's a demon, why are you antagonizing her?" Connor asked, reaching in to grab one of the sparkling waters Law kept there. Whiskers eyed him balefully but didn't hiss.

"You can't show your fear to demons," Asad glared back up at Whiskers as he was getting his can of sparkling water.

"Or you could have not invaded my house and stayed away from the demon cat entirely," Law pointed out dryly. Seated next to him on the couch, Q chuckled. Law eyed him. "How did these assholes convince you to come along?"

He definitely didn't think this invasion had been Q's idea. Q was sitting with his legs together, straight up, as if he was trying not to touch anything.

"I thought we were having a BBQ at Asad's, and next thing I knew, we were here." Q shrugged, giving Law a sheepish grin.

Figured. Once Asad and Connor both wanted to do something, resisting was like trying to stop a force of nature, and Q was the newest friend.

A BBQ sounded pretty good, though Law had his doubts about if it was anything but an excuse since he hadn't heard about it before now. Though they were all dressed for it. Everyone except Law was wearing jean shorts. He'd opted for linen pants and a Cuban short-sleeve shirt. Q was wearing a Hulk Smash t-shirt, Connor had on a plain green shirt, and Asad was wearing a linen button-down.

"Once I found out you had actually spent the night at Marquis with the delightful Iris?" Asad shook his head, coming to sit down in one of Law's chairs. "You should have expected us to show up today."

Yes, he probably should have. Law didn't regret it, although he was still having trouble wrapping his head around the idea of dating her.

It had been a damn good morning. Once he got her in the shower, he had a good time making sure she was thoroughly clean before having her press her hands against the wall so he could fuck her from behind. He'd soaped her breasts while he did, playing with nipples still sore from the clamps…

Well, he needed to stop thinking about it, or his cock was going to react, and he didn't need that with his friends around.

"How did you know we spent the night?"

"Uh, duh, the security cameras?" Asad shook his head. "They always know who stays overnight. I got texts from three different people this morning, asking if you and Iris were a thing. So, are you a thing? I need to know how to answer them."

"That's no one's business." Law scowled. He knew it couldn't work that way, but he didn't need the pressure of the whole club member-ship watching them to see what was going to happen next.

This was supposed to have been an easy 'scene and be done with it' thing. It still could be. He could tell Iris he'd changed his mind. No more scenes. No chance at a date.

Everything in his body rebelled at the idea.

Fuck.

He wanted her—for more than last night and this morning.

"Good luck with that." Asad grinned. "I'll back you up for as long as you want to make it work. Are you going to tell us what's going on, though?"

"We're… seeing each other, I guess." Law took a deep breath giving

Q a sidelong glance. This would have been easier without him there, but hey, at least it gave him practice telling someone new. "I'm not sure I'll be good for her."

As expected, Asad and Connor nodded, while Q looked bewildered. It was heartening to know Q couldn't think of a reason Law would be bad for Iris. It showed that he'd overcome some of his past... for the people who hadn't known him then.

Facing Q head-on, Law rolled his shoulders back.

"Most of the people at the club don't know this, or they know I don't drink but don't know why. I'm a recovering alcoholic." He never said he was recovered—ever—because it never felt like he was. The worst relapse was when he'd thought he'd 'fixed' himself and could drink just one beer, no big deal. That was when he'd discovered how little self-control he had.

He hadn't been recovered at all, and it had sent him right back down the path he'd thought he'd escaped. Except he'd been even worse than he had the first time around. Meaner too. That was when Elaine had finally walked.

Q blinked. Nodded.

"Okay. What does that have to do with Iris?"

The question took Law aback. He glanced at Asad and Connor, who both looked smug.

"I... I wasn't very good to my now ex-wife when I was drinking. She left me because of it."

"And you've punished yourself for what happened with Elaine for long enough," Asad said firmly. Q's brow had wrinkled, and he was looking at Law as if he didn't quite know what to make of his statement. "She wanted you to get better and be happy. So far, all you've accomplished is the first part."

Better.

Yes, he was better, but he knew he was one step away from backsliding again. All it had taken was one drink. On the other hand, he hadn't had a drink in nine years and didn't plan on having another one ever again. Did he think dating Iris would suddenly change that?

"I like Iris. I think she could be good for you. She doesn't take life too seriously."

Law made a face at Connor's pointed comment. Like Connor was one to talk about taking life seriously. He was even more slow and deliberate than Law when it came to making decisions.

"Clearly, I've known you the least amount of time, but I don't see why what you used to do should get to dictate what you do now." Q shrugged, appearing uncomfortable, but he was getting his word in, anyway. Law had to respect that. "You can't change the past. All you can do is live your best life in the present and work toward the future you want."

Well, shit.

When he put it that way…

"We did agree to continue scening and keep things open for the future," he admitted gruffly, omitting the fact he'd already had second thoughts. It was time to put those to bed. His friends were right. Iris was right.

"Great. So, you'll invite her to go to Renn Fair with us?" Asad grinned.

Law scowled. "I'll think about it."

If she'd want to go… well, they'd see. It hadn't come up in conversation.

"Do you Renn Fair, Q?" Asad asked when Q chuckled at Law's response.

"I used to. Angel from Stronghold used to live with me and a couple of our friends before she met Adam, and we all went together every year. I even have my own garb she made for me." A pensive expression crossed his face. "I haven't been in a few years. After Angel moved out, we didn't feel as motivated to go, then the other guys moved away…" He shrugged. "I wouldn't mind going again. It's more fun with people I know."

"Good, it's settled. Now, let's talk about what we're doing for dinner tonight." Asad clapped his hands together, grinning.

CHAPTER SEVENTEEN

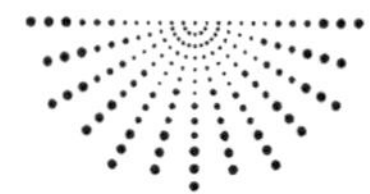

Iris

"So, is he like your booooyfriend now?" Noelle drawled the word teasingly.

"Well, he's definitely not a boy," Iris smirked, moving around the kitchen in her comfiest shorts and tank top. "He's *all* man."

Noelle groaned and made a gagging noise. They both dissolved into giggles. Having her friend back was such a huge relief, though Noelle's expression twitched for the umpteenth time when Iris' phone quacked. She felt her own muscles tense. She probably should have turned it on silent since the group chat was still going strong.

Or maybe she should have changed the notification sound for the group chat. Part of her balked at having to make that change. She should be able to get texts from other friends without Noelle getting mad at her.

Noelle hefted a big sigh.

"Why don't you invite them over?" Noelle asked. There was an edge to her voice, but she mostly sounded sincere.

"Invite who over?" Iris responded as if she didn't know who Noelle was talking about. Obviously, she did, but her first response was to pretend otherwise.

Noelle rolled her eyes.

"Your friends who are texting you non-stop. Invite them over. We can all hang out, then you don't have to keep bouncing back and forth between talking to me and texting to them." Yup, there was a definite edge to Noelle's voice. Still, it was a reasonable suggestion.

Yet... Iris didn't want to. She didn't want to introduce Noelle to the others. Which was kind of... fucked up. She couldn't articulate why, just a kind of general 'I don't wanna.' Maybe it was the edge to Noelle's voice, maybe Noelle hadn't been a fan of Iris' other friends in the past. On the other hand, Noelle was trying.

Maybe Iris should try as well.

"Okay, if you're sure."

"Of course, I'm sure, that's why I suggested it. Text them. I'm gonna go to the bathroom."

Blowing out her breath after Noelle left the room, Iris gave herself a little shake and texted the invite to the others. Who probably had better things to do.

As it turned out, they didn't. Not even Avery, who would be working tonight but not this afternoon.

Woo-hoo! You can't avoid dick-size questions in person!

Iris snorted. *Watch me.*

Though she thought it was funny that they were obsessed with finding out how big Law's penis was, although it made sense. There was a lot of casual nudity at Stronghold and plenty of exhibitionist fucking, but she had never seen him having sex. She'd seen a few of his scenes before he'd been assigned as her Watch Dom, and none of them had ended in sex.

Something that she hadn't considered until now.

Her scene with him had ended in sex.

It was totally possible he just didn't have sex in public. Some club members preferred to keep things at home or behind the closed doors of the private rooms with the curtains drawn.

"So, are they coming over?" Noelle asked, coming back out of the bathroom.

"Yup, they'll be here in about an hour." Iris glanced at the clock.

That would put their arrival time at around two. Maybe she should put out some snacks.

"Great. It'll be nice to finally meet your friends."

Was it Iris' imagination, or had Noelle stressed 'finally'? It sounded as though she had, but it wasn't as if she'd wanted to meet them before. Given the fact they'd just made up, Iris decided to let it go. She might have imagined it, and even if she hadn't, it wasn't worth pursuing.

"So, how are things going with you and Tyler?" Iris asked, changing the subject.

"Ugh." Noelle flopped down on the couch. "It's hard to tell. He's so hot and cold with me. One day he wants to hang out, then the next day, he wants nothing to do with me." She made a face. "I'm pretty sure his friends are trying to break us up. I think they want him to date Laura."

Iris wracked her brain, trying to remember what Noelle had told her about Tyler's friends. Something seemed very wrong with that statement.

"Isn't Laura engaged?"

"Yeah, but they don't like her fiancé, either." Noelle made a face. "He's a douche, so I can't blame them for that, but trying to break me and Tyler up so he can date Laura instead is fucked up."

Yes, it would be if it was true, but it sounded a little far-fetched. On the other hand, weirder things had happened.

"I hope Law's friends aren't jerks to you." Noelle shook her head, a scowl forming. "It's the worst when their friends don't like you. I wish he'd stop hanging out with them."

Iris bit her tongue against advising Noelle to learn how to get along with Tyler's friends since him ditching them completely didn't seem likely. He and Noelle had been dating for a while, and she'd been complaining about his friends long enough, if he was going to choose her over them, he probably would have already done it.

She wondered what Law was doing this afternoon. He'd said he was having a relaxing day at home and possibly doing some work before going to Stronghold tonight for a shift as Dungeon Monitor.

The urge to text him made her fingers twitch, but she didn't want Noelle to think she wasn't paying attention.

It was her own darn fault for starting this line of questioning.

Law

While Connor and Asad were messing around with the grill, Law sidled up to Q.

"Olivia talked to Julie and me yesterday. You want to sign up for the submissive class?" He kept his voice low and neutral. Being a switch was not something to be ashamed of, but not everyone wanted their private business bandied about where others could hear. A lot of people struggled when they realized they had a submissive side and didn't want other people to know at first. They'd find out eventually, but he wanted to let Q tell Asad and Connor, and anyone else at Stronghold, on his own terms, which meant not blurting it out where the other two could hear.

Q tensed, then relaxed, confirming Law had been right to approach him privately. He'd planned to do it at Stronghold, but it was even easier here since they only had Asad and Connor for company, and they were busy getting the BBQ ready that they'd promised.

"Yeah, I guess."

"I think you're smart to explore both sides." Clearly surprised, Q jerked his head up, and his gaze met Law's. Law smiled at him, doing his best to convey his understanding. "Kink is a spectrum, just like sexuality. There are some people who are 'all' one thing, but everyone else falls somewhere within the spectrum." He grinned. "It might surprise you to know I've enjoyed being tied up and restrained." Granted, that was about as far as it went since he didn't enjoy punishment or anything like that.

A masochist, he was not.

Occasionally being restrained and letting someone else take the lead? He'd only done it a couple times, mostly with newer Dommes or switches, who were feeling adventurous, as long as they kept things sensual and not painful. That still left plenty of opportunities open.

"Really?"

"Really. There are also some people who go back and forth, with years between being one or the other. We use terms like Dom, sub, and switch to help us define what we are, but sometimes a label is just a box we put ourselves into. You don't have to confine yourself to that box. If you want to occasionally expand your box or step out of it entirely, then go back in, that's what being a member at Stronghold is all about."

While there was such a thing as "one-true-way" kinksters who believed in very strict adherence to the boxes, Stronghold wasn't like that, nor was Marquis. Patrick, the owner of Stronghold, had wanted to create a place where people could be themselves, whatever that meant to them. His two partners for Marquis were in total agreement.

Patrick had no problem tossing people out the door, something Law heartily approved of.

Q nodded thoughtfully, squaring his shoulders when he realized Law wasn't judging him for his desire to explore the other side of things. He still didn't look as confident as he had at times during the Dominance class, but this was new territory for him. A lot of men struggled with the idea of submitting, especially straight men. Society raised them to be in charge, and that handing over control to someone else was a weakness.

"Yes... I want to explore. The Dominance class... I enjoyed a lot of the stuff we did on the submissive side, a lot more than others seemed to... especially when Mistress Julie was partnered with me. Sometimes, I feel like I fit with the Dom thing, and sometimes, I don't. I know Zach is a switch..."

His voice trailed off, but Law knew exactly who he was talking about. Zach was a Dom and a wicked sadist, especially with women, but he was also submissive to his boyfriend. Q cleared his throat.

"I'm straight, though."

Which was likely why he enjoyed having Mistress Julie as his partner.

"There are straight switches, too. That does bring up the point I wanted to talk to you about." That got Q's attention, and he turned his head to fully face Law for the first time, curiosity in his eyes. "Only one woman has signed up to be a dominant volunteer for the submissives class… Samantha."

Q's expression went blank, his eyes unfocused, and his mouth dropped open a bit. Leaning against the wooden bench that wrapped around part of Law's back porch, Q let out a long breath of air.

"Fuck."

"You don't have to answer immediately, and Olivia is going to ask around to see if we can find another volunteer, but your other option would be to work with a male dominant."

"Right." Q closed his eyes, putting his hand up to his head, and groaned.

"Everything okay over there?" Asad called out. Looking up, Law scowled and waved his hand, gesturing for him to put his attention back on the grill. Sensing Law was serious, Asad turned around and said something to Connor, which made the other man chuckle.

"Do you want to talk about it?" Law asked, opening the door, but he would not make Q step through it unless he was ready.

"It was just high school bullshit." Q scrubbed his hand over his face, his expression twisting into a grimace. "It shouldn't even be a thing now."

"High school bullshit… like playing pranks on each other?"

"No, that's mostly new." Was it Law's imagination, or did Q's lips twitch in a smile? "We were competitive, always competing for… well, just about everything. Top of the class, first seat in the clarinet section, president of the computer club, valedictorian."

"Who won?" Law's interest was piqued. Of all the scenarios he'd imagined, high school rivals for top of the class hadn't been one of them. There had to be something more to the story.

"It was pretty evenly split."

"And that's it?" Since Q was already talking, he didn't feel bad about trying to pry a little.

"Uh... well..." Q turned his head, no longer meeting his gaze. Law was beginning to interpret that as Q's indication he wasn't comfortable with what he was saying. "I asked her to prom, and she said yes, then the next day she told me she couldn't go with me."

"Did she say why?"

"No." Q shrugged. "Didn't really matter in the end. Made the competition for who was going to be valedictorian pretty fierce." A little smile appeared on his lips. "I won that one."

But he didn't get the girl. Interesting.

"You know what?" Q sat up a little straighter. "I'm fine with it if she is. I've never backed out of a challenge with her, and I won't now. If she doesn't want to be paired with me, she can say so. I don't have a problem with her as long as she keeps her post-it notes away from my car."

"Uh-huh." Law wasn't sure exactly how this would go down, but it would probably be entertaining to watch.

Unfortunately, he had a feeling his friends felt the same way about him and Iris.

CHAPTER EIGHTEEN

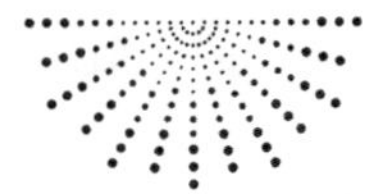

IRIS

Things were going far better than she could have hoped. Everyone was seated in the main room around the food and getting along well. She hadn't talked much about Noelle to the others, and so far, her roommate was on her best behavior and definitely working to impress them, which was a relief. Part of her had been worried Noelle would try to antagonize them since she'd been so annoyed about Iris spending time with them.

"So, the next thing I know, she has me as Mirabel, Mitch as Isabella, and herself as Luisa." Domi cackled as she recounted her six-year-old daughter's latest antics. "I'm pretty sure I know what she'll want to be for Halloween."

"Why didn't Mitch get to be Camilo?" Iris asked, amused as she sat back down after handing Avery another glass of water. She'd gotten up to get herself a drink and had offered to grab a refill for anyone else who needed it.

"It was more important we have the three sisters, of course." Domi's headshake made her curls dance, and Iris could have sighed with envy. With her long, straight hair, she'd make a good Isabella, but sometimes, she wished for curls. Domi was Puerto Rican, and her hair literally spiraled. She was perfect for Mirabel.

"No surprise she wanted to be the strong one," Rae said, grinning. "The girl is smart."

"She sounds adorable. I bet she makes the perfect Luisa," Noelle enthused, which was kind of funny because Iris knew Noelle only had a vague idea of what they were talking about. She hadn't been interested in watching Encanto when Iris had suggested it. It showed how hard she was trying, and Iris wouldn't take that away from her.

"She does." Domi grinned. There was no faster way to her heart than complimenting her daughter. "And watching Mitch with her always melts my heart."

"And your panties," Rae muttered, then squawked when Domi launched a throw pillow at her, making the rest of them laugh as she batted it away. "I'm just saying! Any time Mitch is playing with Ana, you get little hearts dancing around your head, then as soon as she's asleep or gone, you drag him off to the bedroom. There's a connection between the two."

"A man who is good with kids is hot," Avery agreed, looking a little dreamy-eyed.

"Uh oh, someone has baby fever," Rae teased.

Avery made a face, shaking off the dreamy expression.

"Not yet... definitely not yet, but I can still appreciate how sexy it is."

Was Law good with kids? Iris wasn't sure she wanted to have kids. On the other hand, even if she didn't want kids, she had a feeling she'd find it hot if he was good with kids. Maybe it was a biological thing.

She shouldn't think about that yet. He was barely open to the possibility of dating.

Maybe she was setting herself up for heartbreak.

"Iris? You okay over there?" Avery asked.

Iris realized the conversation had kept going on around her, and she hadn't been paying attention. Oops.

"Oh, she spaces out like that all the time." Noelle flipped her hand. "Off in her own little world, don't mind her."

"Sorry. I was just thinking that I am nowhere near thinking about that with Law." Iris blushed. Even saying it out loud felt weird. It was way too soon.

"Not necessarily. At a certain point, you gotta figure out if you're looking for something long-term, in which case why waste time with someone who won't suit you, or if you're still enjoying yourself without having to worry about the long-term."

"Oh, she's definitely not looking for long-term," Noelle said, shooting an amused glance at Iris as though she was sharing an inside joke. While it was true, Noelle had always been more interested in serious relationships than Iris, that didn't mean it was still true.

"I don't know that I'm not." Iris crossed her arms over her chest. She knew she sounded defensive, but… well, she was feeling defensive. "I told Law I didn't want to keep doing anything with him unless there was at least a possibility of eventually becoming serious."

"That's smart. That way, you can let it develop naturally or not," Domi jumped in. Noelle closed her mouth on whatever she'd been about to say, frowning at Iris.

"Here's hoping, although he did say he's not really a go with the flow kind of guy." Iris wouldn't tell them everything he'd told her, but she figured that much was okay. It wasn't as though anyone who had met him would think otherwise. As if to prove that thought, Domi, Rae, and Avery snickered.

"That's an understatement." Rae giggled, tossing several lengths of her long braids back over her shoulder. Her dark eyes sparkled with mirth. "He is the *Law*!" All of them cracked up at the way she'd deepened her voice to make it sound like she was introducing an episode of *Law and Order*. "In the BDSM lifestyle, inexperienced subs are considered especially dangerous. At Club Marquis, Master Law is the dedicated Dom assigned to babysit brats before they are formally expelled. This is his story…"

"Dun-dun," Domi and Iris gasped between hysterical giggles. Avery was done, holding her hand to her stomach and laughing so hard, she was crying. Tears filled Iris' eyes, too, realizing she couldn't stop laughing, and Rae was laughing now. Their eyes met, which just made Iris laugh even harder.

She waved her hand in front of her.

"Don't look at me... we can't look at each other... oh God, it hurts..." She pressed her hand over the aching muscles of her stomach.

When they finally managed to stop giggling—which meant avoiding each other's gaze for about five minutes—Domi cleared her throat and sat up.

"So, does that mean you've made plans to see each other again?"

"No. He'll be at Stronghold tonight as a Dungeon Monitor, so he's busy." Iris shrugged. She'd hoped they might make *some* kind of plan, but she'd been the one to say, 'go with the flow.' She'd sensed he needed some time to get used to the idea. At least, she was pretty sure that's what she'd sensed.

"Does being a Dungeon Monitor mean he can't talk to you?" Noelle asked, her forehead wrinkling. Iris wasn't surprised. Noelle wouldn't like that at all. She expected her boyfriends to be available to her at pretty much all times.

"Not exactly, but it means he can't talk to me much. I shouldn't distract him." Iris could only imagine what her brother would have to say about that. "Besides, Saturdays are Andrew's night at Stronghold."

"Yeah, but as long as you stay out of the play areas, you're fine," Rae pointed out. "It's not like much happens at the bar, and I don't think he and Kate have ever used the dance floor for anything except dancing."

That was a good point. Iris wanted to see him, but she didn't want to abandon Noelle. She looked over at her roommate, who had a slightly pinched expression. Iris wouldn't ask, not while the others were around. Noelle didn't mean to be judgmental, but she didn't get the kink scene, and Iris didn't want to risk her inadvertently insulting the others.

"Did you want to do something tonight?" she asked Noelle. "I just saw him last night. I don't need to go see him again tonight. Or you could come with us."

"No, go ahead." Noelle waved her hands at Iris flippantly. "I don't need a babysitter. I'll see if Tyler can hang out. I want to have a talk with him, anyway."

Iris bit her lip against protesting that she didn't think Noelle needed a babysitter. No point. That would lead to a circular argument, and she didn't feel like getting trapped in one of those right now. She also wouldn't ask if Noelle wanted to talk to him about his friends since her opinion was Noelle probably shouldn't, and she didn't think Noelle wanted to hear it right now.

"Okay, cool." Then Iris frowned. "Do you think I should text him and let him know I'm coming?"

"Oh, where's the fun in that?" Rae asked, her eyes sparkling. "Aren't surprises more fun?"

"Oh, good, a brat encouraging another brat. That won't end terribly," Avery quipped, making them all giggle.

She had a point, but so did Rae.

"I think surprising him sounds fun." Iris grinned.

"This is one of those times when I wish Stronghold allowed cell phones in the club, so you could take a picture of his face when he sees you there." Avery shook her head. "I'm sorry I'm going to miss it."

Law

Since he had the second shift of DM duty, Law kicked his friends out right after dinner, promising he'd see them at Stronghold. It was Saturday night, so there was no way Asad wouldn't be there. Connor had been coming every weekend, even though he hadn't shown much interest in scening so far, despite Asad's encouragement. Law wondered if Connor *really* hadn't been interested or if he'd wanted to make sure Law didn't end up sitting alone while watching over Iris.

He supposed now that his duties with her had ended, he'd find out since he was free to walk the floor. If Connor had been holding back to keep Law company, now he would be free as well.

Arriving at the club, he tried not to scowl when the two submissives at the front desk grinned widely at him. They were likely just being friendly, but of course, his brain insisted they were grinning that way because they'd already heard about him and Iris.

Paranoid much?

Not really, considering the way gossip moved through the club. It seemed arrogant to assume everyone would care, yet he couldn't shake the feeling.

"Have a good night!" they chorused after checking him in. Unusual? No, yet his instincts were insisting there was more meaning behind it than usual.

As soon as he walked through the door between the lobby and the club, he knew he'd been right to be paranoid. The two submissives had known what he hadn't—Iris was already here. Law spotted her immediately, seated at one of the bar tables with Mitch, Domi, Rae, and Asad.

Law growled under his breath as he strode toward them. What was Iris doing here tonight? Why hadn't she let him know she was coming? She'd better not be here to play with someone *else* tonight.

The only thing that helped cool his temper was she wasn't in the Lounge area. Submissives in the bar area were there to hang out, while submissives in the Lounge area were there to play. Not all of them, of course, but they tended to use the location to show their intent.

The logical part of his brain said she wouldn't scene with him one night and say she wanted him to keep an open mind to something more between them, then scene with someone else the next night... but sometimes it was hard to listen to the logical part of his brain. Like right now, when he felt blindsided. He hadn't been kidding when he said he wasn't great at going with the flow.

Tonight, he'd expected to come here, serve his Dungeon Monitor shift, then go home and maybe text or call her. He hadn't expected to find her here, looking far too tempting in a corset, skirt, and fishnets, all set to distract him. This was not how he'd seen his evening going.

Try not to be a dick.

Asad leaned over and said something to Iris, gesturing at Law, and she perked up as her eyes lifted to his. Their gazes caught, and he could see her reaction at the sight of him, which helped settle his emotions even more. She was happy and excited to see him. He definitely needed to do his best not to be a dick.

"Hello there, I didn't expect to see you tonight," he said as he came up beside her. There, that didn't sound too accusatory, right? He'd managed to inject some of his pleasure at seeing her into his tone.

Over her head, Asad gave him an approving nod, so he couldn't have done too badly. Law came to a stop beside her, his arm curling around her waist... then floundered. Was he supposed to lean down and kiss her?

You're the Dom. Do what you want. She'll follow your lead.

Too late. Iris had leaned into his side, resting her head against his shoulder in a way that made it impossible for him to kiss her without awkward maneuvering.

"I wasn't originally planning to come, but Domi and Rae were and invited me along, so..." She shrugged. "Figured I'd surprise you. And as long as I stay out of the play areas, Andrew can't complain."

"He's not here yet, anyway," Rae interjected, grinning as she spun her straw around her drink.

Law chuckled as he greeted each of them before turning his attention back to Iris. She was still leaning against him as though she was perfectly happy to be there. He was also aware of everyone at the nearby tables watching them. No one was looking directly at him and Iris, but he could tell. The gossip train had left the station.

With her leaning against him, they looked like a couple ... and he liked it. Didn't want her to stop. Catching Asad's eye, he had to turn away from his smug expression. Law hated it when his friend was right.

"I have to go start making the rounds." Normally, he was all business on nights when he was a DM, but with Iris there, he realized he was feeling reluctant to get started.

A big part of him wanted to sit down and join them.

"I'm just gonna hang out here with Rae," Iris responded, grinning up at him.

"I'll hang out with you, too," Asad chimed in, ignoring the glare Law sent his way. Great, just what he needed. Connor and Q would likely join them once they arrived.

Usually, it didn't bother Law that he might be missing out on something while he was doing his rounds. Tonight, it was definitely going to bother him.

On the other hand, there was something satisfying about knowing exactly where Iris was and what she was doing instead of spending the evening wondering what she was up to. He probably needed to take what he could get and be satisfied.

"I'll stop by when I can." Throwing all caution to the wind, Law bent down to give Iris a very thorough kiss before taking off. The kiss he'd been craving from the moment he'd wrapped his arm around her.

The kiss that declared to the entire club—*mine*.

CHAPTER NINETEEN

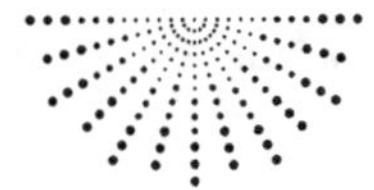

Iris

"Be a good girl," Law said, lifting his lips from hers. Iris stared up at him in shock. That had been the last thing she'd expected. She couldn't come up with a response, which was kind of a moot point since she'd lost her voice. Was it possible for a kiss to cause temporary loss of speech? Because it felt like that's what had just happened.

"Okay, well, that was hot as fuck," Rae said, fanning herself as Law walked away.

The hot kiss he'd just planted still burning on Iris' lips, she was a little swoony as she stared after him. How did his ass look just as good clad in leather as it did when he was naked?

She was pretty sure, as the woman, she was supposed to be the one walking away, having her butt stared at by him, but he'd turned that around on her. Not that she was complaining. It was a very nice view.

Hate to see him go, but love to watch him leave.

"Has he ever done that before?" Mitch asked.

It took Iris a moment to realize that he was asking Master Asad, not her.

Master Asad was one of Law's friends. The two of them were complete opposites in a lot of ways. Master Asad was taller with muscles that were less bulky and always quick with a joke, though not in the same way Mitch was. Asad seemed more serious—and he definitely took his scenes seriously, even if he didn't do serious relationships.

As far as she could tell, he was intent on working his way through every submissive in the club, unlike Law, who had seemed intent on scening as little as possible. Master Asad reminded her of her brother after he and Kate had broken up. Not that she'd been at Stronghold to witness his manwhore days, but she'd heard about it plenty since joining the club.

Blech.

Why people were so intent on talking to her about it, she didn't know. Though to be fair, it wasn't everyone, but still, more than she would have liked.

"I've never seen him publicly claim a submissive like that, no, if that's what you're asking," Master Asad answered Mitch's question, but he was looking at her, studying her as if he was trying to figure out what made her so special. Joke was on him—the answer was nothing—though she could understand his interest.

She was curious why she'd brought out that response in Law. After their discussion last night, she'd been pleased when he'd stood next to her and put his arm around her, but she hadn't expected anything more.

"It was just a kiss," she said, downplaying it, even though it had felt like so much more than a mere kiss.

"Law has never kissed a submissive outside of a scene that I can remember," Asad answered quickly. "Hell, he rarely does it within one."

Iris pressed her lips together to keep from grinning as widely. Why she felt the need to pretend as if it wasn't a big deal, she wasn't sure. Maybe because she was still afraid he'd change his mind.

Next to Iris, Rae made an unhappy noise. It kind of sounded like she growled.

Frowning, Iris turned to see Rae glaring across the room. When she followed Rae's gaze, she winced. Master Brian had just come in, and Morgan was running from the Lounge to meet him as he entered. His expression brightened as she approached, though Iris noted he kept his gaze on her face and not on her barely-there black teddy.

While she was trying to decide if she should say something, there was a quick exchange of words between Master Brian and Morgan, then he grinned widely, pulling her in for a hug. Rae made another growling noise. When the pair broke apart, Brian kept his arm around Morgan's shoulder and escorted her toward the bar.

Across the table from Iris and Rae, Domi spun back around, looking at Rae with sympathy. Mitch looked as uncomfortable as Iris felt, and she had a feeling he knew what was going on.

"Why is she always throwing herself at him?" Rae seethed, pulling the label off of her beer bottle. It wasn't coming off easily, but that didn't stop her. There was a little pile of paper flakes already on the table, and she kept adding to it with every bit she managed to scratch off.

"Um... well..." Iris shifted uncomfortably on her seat, but she didn't feel right, leaving Rae in the dark. She was also aware of Master Asad's confusion as he looked around, trying to figure out what had just happened. "I heard Master Brian asked her to move in with him... as friends. It looks like she might have just said yes."

"They're moving in together?" Rae's voice was rising to a shriek. Domi reached across the table to put her hand over Rae's, hushing her. Several people at nearby tables looked over at them, frowning, but turned away again when they saw nothing interesting was happening. Rae was frozen in her seat, breathing heavily, obviously trying to get a hold of herself. Unfortunately, Domi's movement seemed to have drawn her attention to Mitch. "Did *you* know about this? You had to have known."

"I knew he'd asked her," Mitch said calmly, his blue eyes steady, his demeanor more serious than Iris had ever witnessed outside of a scene. There was sympathy in them, but his tone was firm. "I decided not to tell you in case she said no. There was no point upsetting you if it wasn't going to happen."

"Wait, *you* knew?" Domi's gasp was outraged as she twisted in her seat to look up at her boyfriend.

Crap, this was such a shit show. Master Asad was frowning as he took in the conversation. Apparently, he hadn't been in the know about whatever weird not-thing was going on between Rae and Master Brian.

"I knew." Despite the glares coming from both his girlfriend and her best friend, Mitch seemed unfazed. He slid his hand up to the back of Domi's neck as if he was taking control of an unruly puppy— an observation that Iris would never, never make out loud. "It wasn't either of your business."

Domi opened her mouth. Closed it. Looked at Rae. Iris looked down at the table, not wanting to catch either of their eyes. She'd known and was relieved neither of them seemed angry at her, but she also felt incredibly guilty. Should she have told Rae sooner? On the other hand, Mitch was right.

It wasn't really her business. There would have been no point in upsetting her if Morgan had said no. Mitch wasn't wrong about that.

"What is the problem exactly?" Master Asad interjected. His tone was perfectly pleasant, but there was a bit of an edge as though he wasn't happy about what he was hearing.

Iris, Rae, and Domi exchanged a glance. Iris didn't have a problem with Morgan, but she knew Rae and Domi weren't huge fans.

"Nothing," they said in unison. Mitch rolled his eyes.

"Rae wants Brian, but she doesn't want to admit it. Brian wants Rae, but he can only handle so much rejection. Rae and Domi didn't get along with Morgan during their introduction class, and now Rae is convinced Morgan wants Brian."

"Mitch!" Domi elbowed him in the side, causing him to use his grip on her neck to tilt her head back. Whoops. *Master* Mitch had entered the building.

"Domi darling, you and Rae are making yourselves look bad. You need to get over whatever this thing you have against Morgan is."

"She was rude in class… and mean." Rae crossed her arms over her chest, scowling. "She didn't think Luke could be a submissive because he 'looks like a Dom.' She *said that* out loud. She was bitchy to Sam about her weight."

Ouch. Iris winced. She hadn't known that. Definitely not a great first impression.

The two Doms exchanged a glance across the table.

"There's a reason Morgan is… the way she is. You two need to be kinder."

"Maybe if someone would tell us *why*." Rae glared at him. She didn't quite glare at Master Asad, but she shot him a look, too. "*You* know. All the Doms know. You expect us to act as if we're in the know, too, but all we can go by is her behavior. Which isn't always very nice, especially toward other submissives. She's perfectly nice to all the Doms, and sometimes, I think that's all you see."

"It's not *our* business either," Master Asad said, though he didn't seem as stern as he had a few moments ago, as if what Rae said had struck a nerve. "Master Patrick got Morgan's permission before he told us about her. She didn't want the submissives to know. It's not a nice back story, and it's hers to tell when *she* feels comfortable." His voice got a little sterner.

"What I will say is you have been told there are reasons for you to think twice before making judgments about her, and even if you don't get to know those reasons, you should appreciate we're not throwing her personal business around the club. Just like we wouldn't with yours."

"Other than Mitch throwing his theories about Brian and me out there," Rae muttered.

"Which I wouldn't have done if you and Domi weren't making fools out of yourselves in front of Master Asad. And it's hardly a secret." Mitch shook his head. "I know it's hard feeling as though you're in the dark, but you shouldn't have to know every detail of someone's pain in order to respect it. If and when Morgan decides to share what her life was like before coming here, I can guarantee you two are going to feel really bad if you keep on acting the way you do toward her."

Until that moment, Iris hadn't been curious about Morgan, but now she was *wildly* curious. Dammit. Domi and Rae looked as if they felt the same way.

"Okay, fine." Rae blew out her breath, slumping slightly as she glanced over to the table where Master Brian and Morgan were sitting, talking with their heads together. She made a face and turned to Master Asad. "Master Asad, were you planning on playing this evening?"

Master Asad raised one dark eyebrow, but he didn't look disinterested. If anything, he looked intrigued.

"Are you trying to use me, sweetheart?" There was no judgment in his voice.

"Yup." Rae met his gaze head-on with no hint of shame. "I've heard the Persian Excursion is one of Stronghold's best tours."

The Dom grinned and sat up, his eyes sparkling with interest and none of the stern censure he'd had a few moments before.

"Then absolutely."

Oh, good grief. Law's friends were as crazy as hers.

<hr>

Law

Walking through the Dungeon, Law was doing his best not to think about Iris being upstairs. He needed to focus on his duties.

Though truth be told, most of the time, things were not particularly eventful at Stronghold, which was exactly the way he liked it. Patrick had a thorough screening process, which kept out a lot of the assholes who tried to use BDSM as an excuse or a cover for abuse. Keeping the vast majority of them out—and kicking out the ones who made it through and crossed the line inside the club—helped keep incidents down to a minimum.

They still happened, of course. No process was perfect, but thankfully, it was rare.

Unfortunately, that meant there wasn't a lot to distract him.

He paused to watch scenes, focusing on the submissives and checking on the Dominants to see how everyone was feeling. There could be mismatches on both sides. He'd once intervened in a scene with a Dominant who thought they could handle a heavy masochist. It turned out the Dom couldn't, but he'd been trying so hard to give the sub what she needed, he'd been on the way to doing emotional damage to himself before Law had intervened.

Doing a slow circuit around the Dungeon, he glanced over at the table where Iris was still sitting when he headed upstairs to walk through the second floor but only allowed himself that one glance.

When he went back down to the Dungeon, he scowled when he saw Asad setting up a scene at one of the spanking benches with Rae standing to the side, obviously watching him. They were supposed to be with Iris. What were they doing down here?

Reining in his emotions, Law headed over. Asad saw him coming and grinned, turning to gesture at Rae.

"Over the bench, lovely girl, and flip up that skirt for me," he ordered before turning back to Law.

"What do you think you're doing?" Law asked in a low voice, crossing his arms over his chest.

"Being used like the stud I am." The reply was so far from what Law expected that confusion sank him for a moment, and Asad chuckled. "Iris is fine. Connor and Q are at the table. They came in while Rae and I were negotiating. Mitch and Domi are waiting for one of the private rooms upstairs, so they'll be there a while longer as well. Rae needed a distraction, and I'm happy to be used."

"I see." Law sighed. He did see but didn't particularly like it. Connor and Q were good buffers for Iris, but it itched that his friends were keeping an eye on her instead of him.

"Why don't you go get your lady if it's going to bother you that much?" Asad asked. "There's nothing to say she can't walk around with you as long as you don't drag her off to scene while you're on duty as a Dungeon Monitor."

He started to respond, then closed his mouth. Asad was right. Other Dungeon Monitors had done the same on occasion when they had their partner at the club with them. Patrick didn't mind as long as they fulfilled their duties. He'd even joked it was getting two for the price of one—not that Law was being paid in anything other than reduced membership fees.

It wasn't something Law would have ever considered before, but then, he was already doing a lot of things with Iris he wouldn't have considered doing with anyone else.

"Have fun. Don't... mess with her." Law's eyes dropped to where Rae had draped herself over the spanking bench and had turned to peer at them curiously.

"Don't worry. She doesn't want me." Asad grinned. "No sex, but we're going to have some fun. You know me. I'm always happy to be used."

Yeah, Law would have to ask Iris about that.

Feeling more cheerful than he had a moment ago, he headed to the stairs.

CHAPTER TWENTY

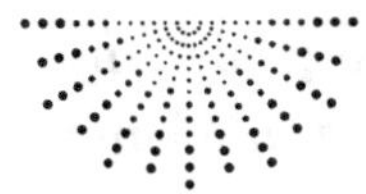

LAW

Everyone was at the table when Law returned to the main floor, just as Asad had said. A few tables past them, Law happened to glimpse Morgan's red hair and realized she was talking to Master Brian. The two of them looked awfully cozy, and he had a sneaking suspicion of what Asad had meant when he said he was being used by Rae.

Not that he was going to get involved. If Rae wanted to scene with someone who would give her a good time, be perfectly fine foregoing sex, and absolutely not get involved emotionally, Asad was a great choice.

Making his way to the table, he grinned and greeted Connor and Q, who had drinks in hand and were happily chatting with Mitch, Domi, and Iris. Connor grinned when he saw Law approaching.

"Shouldn't you be working?" he teased as Law stepped up to the table.

"Yes, I should," Law replied, refusing to be baited. He looked down at Iris. "Want to do rounds with me?"

"Sure!" Iris' eyes brightened with interest, and she hopped up from the barstool, tugging at her skirt to pull it down from where it had ridden up. Then she paused. "Um, if my brother and Kate show up, I'll have to come back to this floor. Or at least stay away from whatever floor he's on."

"Understood." Did it make him a bad person that he hoped her brother and fiancé stayed home tonight? It wasn't like they were going to scene, but now that he had her to walk around with, he didn't want to have that taken away.

Go with the flow.

Inwardly he sighed, but it made sense. Not everything could have a plan. This whole evening was unplanned, other than showing up for his shift. Might as well go with it.

Taking her hand, he ignored the startled looks they received—including one from Iris herself before she grinned and went with it—as they headed to the Dungeon. If they were going to give Stronghold something to talk about, they might as well go all in. Not everyone had seen the kiss earlier, but they couldn't miss him walking through the club, holding Iris' hand.

Hopefully, confirming everyone's suppositions would result in less interest around them. Mysteries were interesting. Full disclosure, much less so.

"Want to tell me what's going on with Rae and Asad?" Even though he had his suspicions, he wanted to know if he was right.

Mysteries.

Iris groaned, shaking her head.

"Yeah, so I'm pretty sure Morgan is going to move in with Master Brian, and Rae just found out." She made a face. "She didn't handle it very well. Not that Master Asad seems to mind being used for his body."

"I'm pretty sure that's one of his goals in life." Law chuckled. "As long as Rae won't be looking for a relationship with him, they'll be fine."

"I don't think we have to worry about that."

Iris

Walking around the club with Law was a revelation. Not only were people looking at them, a lot of the Doms were looking at her with sudden interest. Doms who hadn't looked twice at her before.

It was all Iris could do to keep from sticking her tongue out at them. They'd shown no interest, but now that she had a Dom clearly interested in her, despite her brother, they were taking a second look? Yeah. Screw them.

She was relieved Law seemed open to exploring whatever this was between them. She didn't think she'd be able to reciprocate interest with any of the Doms who were checking her out when they hadn't before she'd scened with Law. A lot of the subs were looking at her with envy and awe. She gripped Law's hand a little tighter.

Yup, he's all mine. Not sure why, but not going to let go.

He wasn't really all hers, but he was for tonight. Master Asad had said he'd never seen Law kiss a submissive outside of a scene. She didn't think he often walked around holding a submissive's hand, either, especially while he was on duty. His words about being the responsible one flittered through her mind.

Taking her around with him wasn't irresponsible, but it sure as hell wasn't something she had expected.

She did her best not to get in his way, following his lead through the club as he picked out a path, making the rounds between the second floor and the Dungeon. They chatted, but she tried not to take up too much of his attention, and when he paused to observe a scene, she fell silent so she didn't distract him.

Seeing him in action was fun, especially because she got the feeling, he was watching *her* for reactions.

Though the most interesting part of the night was when Master Brian came downstairs and saw Rae being spanked by Master Asad. He immediately headed across the Dungeon, well away from them, but Iris noticed he didn't stop *looking*.

At some point, that situation was going to blow up. That or maybe they'd get over each other. She was sorely tempted to lock them in a room and tell them they could come out when they figured out their shit.

As the night was coming to a close and they did their last round, Iris' feet were hurting like a bitch, but she didn't want to complain. She was enjoying hanging out with Law too much.

"How would you feel about doing another scene next weekend?"

The question came as they were climbing back the stairs from the Dungeon. Iris' head jerked up in surprise, though she shouldn't be too surprised. Law liked his plans.

"It depends." She grinned at him. "What kind of scene? Another basic scene?"

"Brat." He let go of her fingers to land a hard swat on her butt before recapturing her hand, all before she took a breath. *Hot.* "You said you wanted to play with electricity."

Interest shivered through her. Yes, she did. It was both scary and exciting. It felt dangerous, but she trusted Law to know what he was doing and to make it pleasurable.

"Yes, please." Funny how her voice went all breathless and soft when she was with him. That definitely hadn't happened with any other Dom.

The grin that Law flashed her way warmed her insides. She knew exactly how little he smiled, yet he was smiling an awful lot at her, especially tonight. It gave her hope, she wasn't sure she should have.

That didn't stop her from having them, particularly as he walked her out to her car and gave her a thorough kiss goodnight.

"Text me when you get home."

As much as she wanted to suggest their night didn't have to end, she didn't want to push him. So, she nodded and waved to him before she pulled out of her space and headed home. The whole way home, she kept going through the events of the evening. By the time she walked into her apartment, she felt as though she was walking on air.

"Oh. You're back." Noelle's tart tones caught Iris' attention as she set down her purse, and she blinked.

"Hey, how was your night?" Iris asked, turning her attention to Noelle in the kitchen. The expression on her roommate's face was not promising, and neither were her slightly jerky movements. *Danger.* Iris knew the signs well enough to know when Noelle was in a mood.

"Like you care."

Oh, good, it was going to be one of those nights. Taking a deep breath, Iris closed her eyes for a moment and gathered her patience.

"Of course, I care. If I didn't care, I wouldn't have asked." Iris wouldn't play that game tonight. She'd had too good a night to let Noelle ruin it.

"You mean like you cared when you went out tonight without me? So, you could go hang out with your new friends and your new boyfriend, and just leave me on my own. The way you always do lately."

Iris stared at her. This was a familiar tune, and normally, she would apologize and placate, thinking that maybe she'd misread the situation earlier, but this time, she had witnesses. If Noelle had shown any reluctance or unhappiness over Iris going out, Domi, Rae, and Avery would *never* have encouraged it.

They would have insisted Iris stayed home or even tried to figure out a way to get Noelle into the club with them, despite how difficult that would be on such short notice. None of them had mentioned a worry that Noelle was upset when they'd left earlier, which meant Noelle had definitely not indicated in any way that she was unhappy about Iris going out. She knew for sure she hadn't imagined it.

"I asked you if you wanted me to stay and hang out with you."

"You put me on the spot! What was I supposed to do, say no?" Noelle glared at her, putting her hands on her hips, but this time, Iris wasn't having any of it. If Noelle had wanted her to stay home, she should have said so, but she not only hadn't, she'd encouraged Iris to go out.

This was not her fault.

"Yes, Noelle, that was exactly what you should have done. I can't read your mind. I don't know what you're thinking. You *encouraged* me to go out and said you were getting together with Tyler. There is literally no way I could have known you wanted me to stay and hang out with you." Iris crossed her arms over her chest and felt her heart pounding against her arm. "Heck, you were invited to come with us if you wanted to!"

Confrontations like this sucked, and usually, she would do anything she could to get out of it, but this one wasn't fair, and she knew it.

"I encouraged you, so you and your *new* friends didn't pity me! Oh, poor Noelle, left all alone. No one wants to hang out with her, but you don't care about that." Noelle snatched the plate she'd made for herself and stormed down the hallway. "The only person you care about is yourself."

"Then why did I invite you to go with us?"

"You wanted to make yourself look good! That's why I said no. I knew you didn't actually want me coming with you. That or you wanted me to come, so you could leave me out again, and show me how little I mean to you!"

The blatant untruth made Iris want to scream. She didn't know what to say, had no idea what she wanted to say because literally none of what Noelle was saying made sense. Noelle's bedroom door slammed behind her, and the silence in its wake was resounding.

Iris let out a long breath. Definitely not how she'd wanted to end her night.

Law

Frowning at his phone, Law hesitated. Iris should be home by now. She'd said she lived only twenty minutes from Stronghold, and it was forty minutes since she'd left.

Should he start to worry?

Should he text to remind her?

While he didn't like the idea that she'd forgotten about him, he also didn't want to *not* check in on her if something had happened.

Dammit.

Yeah, that was what did it. He couldn't go to bed not knowing.

Quickly, he tapped out 'Home?' and hit send before he could

second-guess himself. No, it didn't look desperate. Or overly controlling. He just wanted to make sure she *had* arrived home safely since he'd told her to text when she was there, or he wouldn't be able to sleep tonight. It was self-preservation as much as anything.

When his phone vibrated a moment later, every muscle in his body relaxed.

I'm so sorry. I got home, and my roommate picked a fight with me, and I completely forgot. I'm home safe, though.

Law frowned.

He didn't know much about Iris' roommate, though she'd talked about the other woman a little yesterday during dinner. From what she'd said, they'd been friends for years.

Now what? It was late, and he needed to get to bed, but it didn't feel right to leave their conversation like this. While it had been a long time since he'd been in a relationship, he thought he was supposed to see if she wanted to talk about it. Sure, they weren't officially in a relationship yet, but... He quickly sent back his reply.

Do you want to talk about it? You can call me.

The wait for a response was almost painful. The phone rang a few minutes later when he'd finally given up and had started getting ready for bed. Hastily spitting his toothpaste into the sink and giving his mouth a quick rinse, he snatched the phone.

"Hello?"

"Hey. I'm sorry, I probably shouldn't have called." Iris sounded down, almost defeated, a far cry from her demeanor when they'd parted. Law scowled.

"I wouldn't have offered if I hadn't meant it. I wanted you to call if you needed to talk."

"Funny, I said something very similar to my roommate." Iris sighed. "Sometimes, she just makes me so angry. I got home, and she was mad I'd gone out tonight, even though before I left, I asked her if it was okay or if she wanted to come, and she encouraged me to go out and said she was going to hang out with her boyfriend tonight." She made a noise of aggravation. "I would have stayed home if I thought she was in any way upset since I'd already gone out last night."

"Right." Law wasn't sure what else to say, but she seemed to want some kind of response, so he threw that out there. He couldn't picture Iris as the type to leave her roommate to her own devices unless she thought her roommate would be fine with it.

"Domi and Rae and Avery were all here, too. They saw everything. If they thought Noelle was upset, they would have said something. Anyway, I got home, and Noelle immediately got on my case for going out. She said I put her on the spot, asking if she was okay with me going and that I didn't care about anyone other than myself."

"Well, that's definitely not true." Law could feel his anger rising. Though he hadn't actually met Noelle, so far, he wasn't impressed. He could hear the uncertainty in Iris' voice as if she was worried about what her roommate was merited. "If you asked her if she wanted you to stay home tonight and she didn't want you to go, she needed to say something. Or she could have come out with you."

"That's how I feel, but now I'm second-guessing myself." Iris sighed. "Sometimes, I feel like I'm walking on eggshells around her because I never know what's going to set her off. And when I try to see things from her point of view, I feel like maybe she has a point? Like, she didn't want to seem like a spoilsport if she told me she wanted me to stay when Rae, Domi, and Avery were all there."

"Okay, but even if that was true, she could have told you that when you got home instead of being angry."

"That's true." Iris sounded thoughtful.

"Did she try to talk to you about it first?"

There was a pause.

"No, she was mad when I got home and jumped right into accusing me of ditching her."

"You can ask Rae, Domi, and Avery if they thought she seemed upset when you went out. Though I feel like they would have said something before you left if they'd thought she was."

Iris laughed. "I had the same thought." She paused again. "Thank you. I feel better now."

"Good, you should." Law grinned. Surprisingly, he did, too. Being there for her when she'd needed him felt good. "Tomorrow, I'm just getting things done around the house, so if you need to text or call at any point, feel free."

"Thank you." She yawned. "Oh my God, it's so late. I need to go to bed."

"Go. Goodnight."

"Night."

Law laid down on his bed, feeling supremely satisfied. He didn't even mind when Whiskers jumped up on his chest, doing her best to crush him or work her claws through the comforter to reach his bare skin.

CHAPTER TWENTY-ONE

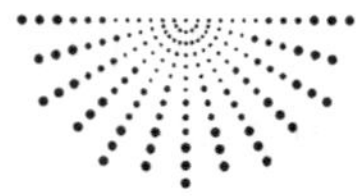

Was this what it felt like when a friendship was ending? Day of stomach twisting nausea every time she was home, doing her best to avoid Noelle in the common spaces, and cold silence accompanied by cold stares every time they did. Although she wasn't the one doing the cold silence and stares, she wasn't trying to make it better, either.

She had nothing to apologize for.

I will not apologize, I will not apologize, I will not apologize.

She kept repeating it to herself in her head. Though she was finding it was making her angrier and more resentful, which made her wonder if she was helping things by digging in her heels.

Domi and Rae were all for it. They were pissed Noelle had picked a fight with her when she'd encouraged Iris to go out and were very clear Noelle hadn't shown the slightest bit of hesitation or unhappiness that Iris was going out or in coming with her. Avery was more inclined to try to understand where Noelle was coming from, but Avery also agreed that Noelle had behaved unreasonably, even if her feelings had been hurt.

Mostly, Iris talked to Law about it. He listened and didn't offer much in the way of opinion, but the questions he asked her really clarified how *she* felt about all of it.

Which was both sad and angry.

She didn't want to live like this, but she also didn't want to apologize and smooth things over when she'd done nothing wrong. Besides, going by their past, if she held out long enough, Noelle would just pretend as if nothing had happened. Again.

Though she wasn't sure she felt like that was okay, either because she thought Noelle owed her an apology for picking an undeserved fight, at this point, she would take any kind of truce, so their living situation wasn't so damn unpleasant. When Law asked her how often she did that, she was uncomfortably aware it was pretty much all the time. When he asked her when the last time Noelle had apologized for something she'd done, Iris literally couldn't remember.

Between her other friends and Law, it was a little easier to hold her ground, even if it didn't make the living situation pleasant.

Friday night, she was in the bathroom getting ready to meet Law at Marquis while Noelle had taken over the main room. She was reading on the couch, making very loud, pointed sniffing noises every few minutes. Not as if she was sniffling or she had a stuffy nose. She was huffing her breath out her nose as loudly as possible to show her displeasure.

It was incredibly distracting. It was also a stark contrast to the last time Iris had been getting ready to go to Marquis, and Noelle had jumped in to help with her hair and makeup.

This time, she didn't offer that olive branch, trying to pretend like nothing had happened.

Which probably meant she expected Iris to apologize

When Hell freezes over.

Yup, that was Rae's voice in her head, but Iris wholeheartedly agreed. Last time, Noelle had offered the olive branch, pretending everything was fine—even though it hadn't included an apology or fixed anything. They'd gone right back to the norm of Noelle doing what she wanted while Iris tried to work around her.

It had taken other people pointing it out for her to really notice, but now that she had, she refused to do it again.

Her phone quacked.

Noelle sniffed.

Iris ignored her and checked the message. Andrew. She sighed as she opened the phone to her brother's text.

I heard you're going to Marquis with Law again tonight. You sure this is what you want?

Typical Andrew. No contact until he wanted to interfere in her life.

Would you prefer we came to Stronghold?

Iris smiled wickedly as she sent her text. She already knew Andrew's answer would be no, but if he was going to be an interfering butthead, she wouldn't take the opportunity to taunt him. She hadn't heard from him all week and wondered if someone had told him about her and Law being at Stronghold last Saturday or if people were keeping it from him. Whatever. He didn't get a say about what she did or who she did, no matter how much he wished he did.

You would think by now, he'd have learned that lesson, but apparently not.

A moment later, her phone quacked again. Noelle sniffed again. Iris gritted her teeth. Between her roommate and her brother, her mood wasn't where she wanted it to be before her date with Law. She checked her text from Andrew.

You know that's not what I meant.

Even over text, she could feel his censure as if he was her dad or something. She rolled her eyes.

Ask stupid questions, get stupid answers. Try paying attention to your own life instead of mine.

This time when her phone quacked, she waited until she was done applying her eyeliner to look at it. Her stomach was a tight knot. She didn't like fighting with her brother, but sometimes he drove her nuts. The only times he seemed to really care about what she was doing was when he didn't like what she was doing.

She'd gone weeks without texts or calls from him, and even now, he wasn't checking on her to see how she was doing but because he disapproved of something she was doing. Iris knew he loved her, but sometimes, she wanted to kick him.

Like when she checked the message.

I'm asking because I care.

No, you're asking because you don't like a choice I made. If you cared, you would have asked how I was doing and told me to go have fun, the way Kate did when she texted me earlier today.

And Send.

Iris pressed her lips together. If he texted back, she wasn't sure she wanted to look at it. Of course, she did when her phone quacked again.

Have a good evening then. Stay safe.

She shook her head, but her stomach settled a little.

At least he was trying… unlike someone. Noelle sniffed again.

"Do you need a tissue?" Iris asked, keeping her voice sugary-sweet. If Noelle could end a fight, pretending like nothing was wrong, she could, too. A moment passed.

"No."

"Okay." Iris shrugged and went back to finishing her makeup. Noelle was waiting for her to say something more, but she'd be damned. Nope, she was going out tonight to have fun with Master Law and forget about everything else.

Law

"More roommate troubles?" Law asked when Iris appeared at the top of the stairs to the second floor of Marquis. There was something about how she was holding herself stiffly that made him think she wasn't happy, and considering the week she'd been having with her roommate, that seemed the most likely culprit.

She looked incredible, which was probably what he should have started with, but it was too late. Her little red dress was skintight, and he was pretty sure she wasn't wearing a bra or panties under it. He would definitely have to make sure he expressed the proper appreciation before the evening was over.

"She's still giving me the silent treatment," Iris responded, reaching out to take the hand he offered her.

The moment their fingers touched, she seemed to relax, which was more than a little gratifying. He liked that being around him eased some of her burdens.

"Mostly. I feel as if she wants my attention and for me to apologize, but there's no way I'm doing that. I don't think she'll apologize, so we're at an impasse."

She sighed and leaned into him, so Law let go of her hand and ran his fingers up her back to her neck, massaging the tense muscles. Sighing again, she nuzzled against him.

Out of the corner of his eye, he could see Freddy and Tori behind the desk, watching them and whispering. The smiles on their faces made it clear they supported what was going on, but he was sure the gossip mill would be running rampant this weekend. He shot them a stern look, which made Tori glance away, but Freddy just grinned back at him.

"Why don't we go in and talk about it over dinner?" That way, they'd have the privacy of the booth. Not that Freddy and Tori could hear them from this distance, but they were watching closely, which made him antsy.

"Sounds good. I'm starving." Iris smiled up at him. He wasn't sure if she'd noticed their invested observers. At least Mistress Julie, standing at the side of the door to Marquis as the bouncer, wasn't staring at them.

As Freddy led them past her, Law paused.

"Have you received any more odd flower deliveries?"

"No, why?" Julie laughed. "Do you know who they're from?"

"No, just curious." Curious. Worried. It amounted to the same thing as far as he was concerned.

"Let me know if someone says something to you." Julie's smile was devilish. "I would love to know who to thank." Whether that was a threat or sincere was a little hard to tell.

Iris shot him a curious look but walked into the main dining area as Law used his hand on the small of her back to guide her forward. Ahead of them, Freddy was also looking at them curiously. For a moment, Law had the thought that Freddy might be Julie's secret admirer… but that wouldn't make sense because Freddy knew when she was at Marquis.

He ran the front desk, but he also knew everyone else's schedules when the classes were, and Olivia relied on him to help keep track of her meetings. If he'd sent the initial batch of flowers, it would have been easy for him to send another set. Besides, while he knew about a lot of the meetings, the flowers had been delivered during an impromptu meeting.

He couldn't imagine Freddy being so shy as to send something as a secret admirer rather than a more hands-on show of interest. In the club, submissives were supposed to wait to be approached by a Dominant, but if they wanted a particular dominant to approach them, they knew how to make that clear.

But it was definitely a thought.

"What was that about with Mistress Julie?" Iris asked once they were settled at their table. Law glanced over to see if Freddy had heard her, but there was no sign he had as he walked away.

"A secret admirer sent her flowers to a meeting she had here with Olivia and me. I was just wondering if she'd gotten any more."

"Aw, that's really sweet." Iris grinned, and it took him a moment to realize she was talking about the flowers and not about him checking in with Julie. "What kind of flowers?"

"Red roses."

"Classic." Iris' eyes widened. "Wow. And she has no idea who they're from?"

"Nope. It was odd because it was an impromptu meeting, so it wasn't on the schedule." Law rubbed his hand along his jaw against his beard. There was something about the whole thing that was really bothering him—he just couldn't put his finger on what. Julie could take care of herself, of course, but his instincts were trying to tell him something.

Iris seemed to sense it and tilted her head.

"You're worried about it?"

"I don't particularly like mysteries," he admitted. "I also don't like that she received flowers from a mystery admirer at a time when most people wouldn't have known where she was."

"Do you think the person who sent them might be dangerous?" Iris sounded more curious than worried, and he couldn't blame her since it seemed unlikely so far.

"Since there hasn't been follow-up or anything else weird going on with her, I would say no." Law shrugged. Hopefully, he'd figure out why it bothered him. He smiled at Iris. "Sorry, I didn't mean to derail the conversation."

"That's okay. What's your favorite kind of flower?" She rested her hand on her chin as she watched his reaction.

Law was taken aback. He couldn't remember the last time anyone had asked him what his favorite flower was—*if* anyone had ever asked him.

"Uh, well, I always liked gardenias." A little smile curved the edges of his lips. "Though irises are nice, too."

"I like irises, but I get a little tired of them. I've always loved lilies and orchids." Iris smiled back at him.

The conversation was interrupted when the server appeared to greet them, but Law tucked the information away—lilies and orchids, not irises. She'd probably received a lot of irises over the years, thanks to her name. He'd much rather give her the flowers she wanted.

CHAPTER TWENTY-TWO

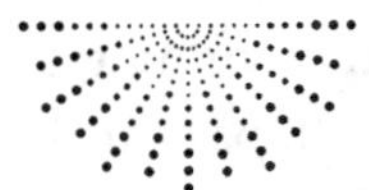

Waiting for their food, the conversation flowed, and Iris slowly relaxed. Being with Law was easy, even fun, though that was not a word she would have used to describe him when they'd first met. It turned out, when he wasn't in charge of a class, he had a lot of funny stories, a wicked sense of humor, and was only a little bossy.

Hell, Iris liked it when a man was a little bossy. They were so much easier to annoy.

Not that she was trying to annoy Law tonight. That wouldn't be a smart move since they were scening right after dinner. But in general. She'd once heard Andrew's friend, Angel, say she'd married her husband because he was the person she wanted to annoy for the rest of her life, and that had resonated with Iris. She remembered her mom teasing her dad a lot, and Kate definitely did that with Andrew, although when he was growing up, he hadn't been as serious as he was now.

A lot of things changed after her mom died.

Still, Law was the serious one, so she would be the annoying one. It worked for her and would give him an excuse to spank her now and then. Not that he needed an excuse. If he wanted to spank her, he would, but Iris liked to think she was earning it.

Underneath the table, she slipped her heels off and found his foot. Law turned his head, raising his eyebrows as he met her gaze. Iris smiled serenely as if she wasn't exploring his ankles with her toes. The leather of his shoes was hard, but the fabric of the pants he was wearing was far softer. There were socks, too.

Playing footsie wasn't exactly erotic, but it was fun. She could see him trying to decide whether or not to stop her. When her foot skated up the inside of his calf, past his knee to his thigh, he stopped mid-sentence to pin her with a look. Iris blinked innocently.

Finished eating, she wasn't bored, but she couldn't help wanting to tease him.

"Is this your way of telling me you'd like to go straight to the dungeon and miss the show?"

Iris blinked. "Is that an option?"

It wasn't that she wasn't interested in the show, but she'd seen plenty of scenes during the month she was 'volunteering' her services at Stronghold. Sure, the scenes at Marquis were more elaborate with a lot more pageantry, but right now, she was far more interested *doing* than watching.

"Keep up what you're doing, and it will become one."

Iris contemplated the threat for all of thirty seconds while Law took the last bite of his steak and put his fork down. She slid her foot along his thigh right up to the... oh my. Yup. The very hard bulge at the front of his pants.

Maybe playing footsie had been a little more erotic than she realized.

Quick as a whip, Law reached down and grabbed her ankle, making her shriek in surprise. There was no way to yank it back and pretend she hadn't been doing anything. Her foot was now pressed against his thigh, her toes still touching the hard ridge of his cock.

And the expression on his face was pure Dom.
Oops.

Maybe she'd miscalculated. Not scared, though definitely apprehensive, she hadn't meant to piss him off.

"Okay, naughty girl, if that's how you want to play."

Iris shrieked again when Master Law scooted to the edge of the booth, dragging her with him. The hem of her skirt slid up to her waist, and she didn't have time to drag it down before she found herself upended over his shoulder.

"My shoes!"

"Someone will bring them to our room." Master Law held out the hand that wasn't holding her in place over his shoulder and gestured to someone, although she couldn't see what the gesture was or who he directed it to. Iris whimpered when he reached up to smack her upturned ass.

A few chuckles from around the room made it clear they were drawing attention.

"Is the show starting early?" someone called out. From their tone, they were teasing, but it drew another laugh. Iris felt her cheeks burning, but not her bottom cheeks—her face cheeks.

She couldn't remember the last time she'd blushed this hard.

Not only could everyone see Master Law carrying her off over his shoulder like a sack of potatoes, they could see her ass and pussy since she hadn't been able to pull her skirt down, and she wasn't wearing any underwear. Knowing she'd probably seen most of them naked at Stronghold didn't help her. That was then; this was now.

And throughout the entire display, all she could think about was how turned on she was.

---

*L*AW

Who are you, and what have you done with Lawrence?

Yeah, if any of his friends had seen him, they probably wouldn't have recognized him, either. This wasn't his norm, but something about Iris made him want to do new things. He hadn't thought much, just reacted to what she was doing.

He wasn't entirely sure that was a good thing. Reacting rather than thinking through his actions didn't feel very in control. On the other hand, so far, he wasn't out of control, so maybe it wasn't a bad thing. He could be a little spontaneous and maintain control.

Once they reached the Dungeon room, he had everything set up and meticulously planned out, as always. They were just getting to the room a little sooner and in a manner slightly different than expected. Knowing that helped make him feel a little better about acting so impulsively.

He'd also really enjoyed surprising Iris.

When her hands crept down to cup his butt as he strode through the hallway, he had to laugh. She was irrepressible.

Law gave her upturned ass another hefty swat.

"You just can't help yourself, can you?"

"I'm sure I could if I wanted to." Her voice sounded a little odd, breathless, and far away, which made sense, considering her current position. His shoulder pressing against her stomach and being upside down didn't create an optimal speaking state. Her response made him laugh.

Yes, she could control herself when she wanted to. He'd seen proof over the month he'd watched over her. Of course, sometimes, she'd acted as impulsively as he'd originally thought her to be, but overall, she'd behaved.

Shaking his head, Law opened the door to the Dungeon room and walked in. Iris twisted around on his shoulder, trying to see. Chuckling, he set her on her feet and spun her around, so she could see the setup.

It was very different from the last time.

She'd asked for electricity, and she was going to get it.

Instead of a wooden frame in the middle of the room, there was a massage table, though modified with places to attach restraints. The legs were wood, but that was about the only similarity to the frame. Around the table, Law had laid down rubber floor mats to walk on as he moved around Iris. Next to the table, on one of the mats, was a cart with his violet wand and quite a few attachments he enjoyed using.

Not all of them since this was Iris' first time playing with electricity.

They'd just eaten dinner, so he knew she wouldn't be dehydrated. He'd made sure she drank plenty of water during the meal but had put a few bottles of water on the cart, just in case.

All the other furniture—especially anything with metal bits—had been moved away from the play area to the edges of the room.

"Oh..." Iris stepped forward, then paused, glancing over her shoulder at him with an apprehensive expression.

"Go ahead and look." Law put his hands in his pockets, watching as she crept forward and inspected the items on the cart. While many of them would be familiar in appearance, he was fairly certain she wouldn't truly understand what they did. Not until he used them on her.

"Woah..." she whispered under her breath as her fingers hovered over some of the attachments.

"You can touch them," Law said, moving closer. "They won't feel like much right now, but if you want to know the difference..."

Her fingers skimmed over the glass electrodes he'd laid out.

"These look like fairy wands." Her smile was more than a little cheeky. She touched the one with a star shape. "Especially this one. Growing up, I'm pretty sure I had a wand like this."

"Probably not exactly like that." Law grinned when she snuck a look at him. Lately, his face hurt from how much he'd been smiling since his first scene with Iris. "Ready to start? You need to get completely naked."

He rested his hand on her back and felt the little shiver of apprehension, which he reveled in. There was nothing better than having a slightly anxious and very aroused submissive to play with. He enjoyed it with Iris because she was so confident all the time.

"Yes, Sir." She looked up at him, and her eyelashes fluttered. "I might need a little help, though."

His erection, which had already begun to swell at the table when she'd been teasing him, surged to full mast as blood rushed to his groin.

"Then, by all means, let me help." Law wouldn't object to having the chance to have his hands all over her.

———

IRIS

Stripped out of her clothes, her nerves humming from Law's teasing caresses while he was helping her undress, Iris bit her lip as she glanced at the cart set up next to the massage table again. She didn't know what to expect. Electricity wasn't covered in the newbie classes unless someone expressed real interest, and she hadn't been all that interested until she'd become interested in Master Law.

She'd heard from the other submissives it could be a lot of fun, could be exquisitely painful, and Master Law loved to play with it.

It was also dangerous.

Iris had done a little research at home this past week, then decided she wanted to be surprised by what he might do. Most of the research had started off with warnings about what *not* to do and all the nasty consequences of unsafe electrical play. She didn't have arrhythmia—one worry eliminated—but there were still plenty of other pitfalls of playing with electricity.

The nice thing about scening with Master Law was she absolutely trusted he knew what he was doing, or else he wouldn't be doing it.

But nothing was one hundred percent safe.

That I find that even more exciting shows I might have more work to do with my therapist...

She was hardly the only one who found dangerous sex exciting, though. The bit of scary added to her arousal, which was pretty common among kinksters. The idea of actually being hurt or dying wasn't exciting, but knowing she was doing something that could have dangerous consequences gave her an adrenaline rush like bungee jumping or skydiving.

Except with an orgasm at the end.

To her surprise, rather than getting her immediately on the table, Master Law stepped in front of her, cupped her chin with one hand,

and tilted her head back. Out of her heels, the difference in their height made it necessary for their gazes to meet.

He was still fully dressed, and—as always—the dichotomy made her feel all fluttery and hot inside.

Looking deep into her eyes, his serious expression made her body perk up and take notice.

Time to be a good girl and pay attention.

"Do you trust me?"

"Yes." She answered without thinking, too caught up in the intensity of his gaze to prevaricate. Not that she would have wanted to. She could tell how much this meant to him. He'd needed a real answer, and she'd given it to him. She did trust him—completely.

"Good girl. Your safeword is 'red' or 'foliage,' but if you say stop, I'll pause to check in with you." He spoke calmly, steady, yet her anxiety ramped up a little more with every word. That he was taking this so seriously hammered home that it wasn't the average kink play. "Understood?"

"Yes, Sir." Excitement fizzed and popped through her body, arousal coiling in her core as she stared into his dark brown eyes. He was rock steady, calm, and entirely in control, while she felt as if she was going to go off like a rocket at any moment. Yet his presence soothed her to keep her feet on the ground.

They stared at each other for a long moment, then he moved, using his hand on her chin to hold her in place while his other arm wrapped around her back, and his lips descended on hers. There was something about the suddenness that made her think he hadn't planned to kiss her, and everything in her body thrilled with the impulsiveness of the move.

Iris' hands went to his chest, her palms flat against him, not pushing him away but exploring the hard contours of his chest and shoulders as she was pressed against him. The fabric of his shirt rubbed against her nipples, stimulating them, as the hand cupping her chin slid around to the back of her neck, holding her in place as he deepened the kiss.

She whimpered against his lips as their tongues danced together, heat sliding through her. Pressing her thighs together, she wriggled, feeling the hard bulge of his erection digging into her stomach. Her pussy ached, clenching emptily in anticipation.

He pulled away, his face a mere inch away.

"Alright, sweetheart. Up on the table."

CHAPTER TWENTY-THREE

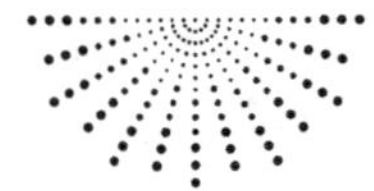

Iris

Lying on her back on the padded table, Iris was surprised by the looseness of the restraints Master Law was securing her with. She turned her head, pulling on the leather around her wrist and raising her eyebrows at him at the amount of give she had.

"Not to question your technique, but is it supposed to be this loose?"

"Yes. Electricity can cause muscle spasms, so I want you restrained so you can't jerk around too much, but on the other hand, restraints can cause muscle strain if your body is trying to move and can't." With her wrists now immobile, Master Law reached down to tweak her nipple, making her squeak, before he palmed her breast, squeezing it gently.

"That wasn't a very reassuring answer," she muttered, making him chuckle.

"It wasn't meant to be." He pinched her nipple again before moving down the massage table to her ankles, pulling them apart and restraining them in the same manner. Her nipple throbbed from the pinches, her other breast feeling almost itchy with its need for the same attention.

Iris looked at her wrist again, tugging. She was still pretty secure, even though they had more give than she was used to. Knowing the reason behind the give amped up her arousal. Law ran his hands over her legs, pressing his thumbs into the sensitive insides of her thighs as he moved them almost all the way up to her pussy, making Iris' back arch. She tried to bend her knees, but they didn't go very far.

"Ready? We're going to start out small," Law said, releasing her and moving to the cart.

Her heart pounded in her chest when she heard the hum of the machine once he turned it on. He was holding the little wand with the star on the end, which was now glowing purple.

Nope, definitely not like the wands she'd grown up with.

"Are you ready, Iris?" he repeated, and she realized she hadn't answered him.

"Yes, Sir."

Hopefully.

With a small smile, which wasn't as reassuring as she might have liked, Law stepped up to the table. He quickly ran the wand up the inside of her leg—not quite touching her skin but getting incredibly close—following the same path as his thumbs. Iris gasped, writhing at the sensation.

It didn't hurt, other than an initial sting when it was first set on her skin, like static electricity, but she could definitely feel it. It was almost ticklish, like small champagne bubbles fizzing against her inner thigh. The path traced up her inner thigh, almost to her pussy, then was pulled away again. Iris didn't know if she was relieved or disappointed that he hadn't gone all the way to more sensitive areas.

"How was that?"

"Tickly… not nearly as scary as I thought it would be." Iris made a face. She didn't want to jump right into the deep end, but she didn't need a bunch of handholding.

Law just laughed.

"Okay, sassy girl, let's see how ticklish you are."

Iris squealed as he ran the wand over her ribcage. Her hands jerked in the restraints and pulled on them as she tried to twist away, giggling the whole time. That was definitely not what she'd expected Law to do.

Law

What are you doing? This wasn't part of the plan!

The alarm bells ringing in the back of his head as he went with his impulse rather than his plan were easily ignored. He hadn't planned to tickle her, but the best plans were flexible, right? Watching her squirm was highly enjoyable as her breasts jiggled, her cheeks flushed, and her body twisted. Knowing he'd managed to surprise her, again, was even more satisfying.

Law moved the wand over one side of her ribs, then the other, doing his damndest to keep his smile under wraps.

"Is this supposed to be a turn-on?" she gasped out, shrieking again as the wand went down the center of her body, from between her breasts to the top of her pussy, though he didn't quite touch her clit.

"Why don't you tell me?" he asked, using his free hand to slide his fingers up her leg. Iris moaned as his fingers brushed against her swollen pussy lips. He didn't need to touch her to know she was aroused. He could see it.

As he slid one finger between her soaked folds, he moved the tip of the wand over her erect nipples, making her gasp and arch her back. His finger pushed into her pussy, the muscles clenching around the digit, while he kept a close watch on her reaction.

Playing with electricity above the waist could be dangerous, though the risks were lower with her because she was in good health and young, but he was still going to be careful. A wand like this should be safe. She certainly enjoyed it from the way her pussy spasmed around his fingers.

Iris

Ouchy stingy hot pleasure. The wand moving over her nipples didn't feel like bubbles, more like a static shock to two of her most sensitive bits. It was crazy how Law had managed to go from torturing her with tickles to flipping the switch to something sexy. His finger pumped inside her, and the heel of his palm brushed against her clit as the wand made a second pass over her nipples.

She sucked in air at the sensation, which hurt but felt good and didn't last nearly long enough.

"Law!"

"You wanted me to stop tickling you." Chuckling, he drew the wand down her side. It didn't feel ticklish with his finger inside her pussy. Bubbles fizzed and popped over the skin of her stomach, and when he drew the wand over her mound, he didn't stop until it sparked against her clit.

Iris cried out, limbs pulling at the restraints at the sensation on her sensitive nub. It was stingy and hot and made her body spasm like she was having an orgasm, and yet she wasn't. At the same time, Law's finger pumped in and out of her pussy as she clenched around it, shuddering with the overwhelming assault on her senses.

Then the wand moved over her thigh, taking the fizzy popping sensation with it. Iris whimpered, wriggling against the confines of her restraints.

"Breathe, Iris." At his command, she sucked in a deep breath. She hadn't realized she'd *stopped*. "Are you ready for another one?"

Was she? That was a good question. The sensation wasn't like anything she might have imagined, and it was a little terrifying how lost she'd become… but yes. She wanted more.

"Yes, Sir."

The wand he picked up looked like a rake. Iris squealed when he moved the little tines over her thigh. It still felt like fizzing, popping bubbles but much more intense since the sensations were localized at the end of the tines instead of being spread out over the wand.

"Fuck!" Iris writhed as he literally raked her body with electricity, concentrating on her thighs but pulling it briefly over her breasts and nipples. Had he turned up the intensity, or was it just the change in the wand?

"Too much?" he asked, lifting the rake for a moment while Iris panted for breath. Her entire body felt like it was buzzing.

"No, just... different... but fun." Iris grinned up at him, causing him to smile back, which felt like a win. "What else can you do?"

He laughed out loud, which made her smile even wider.

"Well, if the wands aren't satisfying you..."

"Oh no, they are," Iris said quickly. They were fun, but she knew there was more. "But I want to know if there's more."

"Mm-hmm." Law chuckled as he moved away, switching the wand for what *looked* like another wand, except this one looked more metal, and it didn't glow. He also didn't touch her with it. Instead, he reached out and ran his fingers down her thigh, and Iris shrieked with surprise as the fizzy bubbles ran from his fingers to the surface of her body.

Again, it didn't hurt exactly, but she wasn't expecting it.

She hadn't known he could be a conduit.

He had a lot more flexibility with what he could do with his fingers than he had with the wand.

"Oh!" Her head fell back, body arching as he moved the tips of his fingers up her legs to her pussy, the hot, pulsing fizzy sensation tickling the sensitive folds. Law swirled his finger, and Iris moaned, her hips moving in reaction to the stinging pleasure.

Law

Watching Iris writhe for him as he played with the electricity was well worth the little shocks he received through his fingers. She was enjoying herself more than he had expected. Maybe next time they played with electricity, he would have to get some insertables.

For now, he enjoyed moving his fingers over her thighs and pussy, watching as she shuddered and moaned. This had been part of the original plan, and her reaction was exactly what he'd hoped.

Taking a shock to his own tongue was never fun in and of itself, but he had mentally added it to his plan as an option if Iris was into it. Considering how aroused she was, he couldn't help himself.

Moving his hand away, he leaned down to give her pussy a long lick. His tongue tingled from the unpleasant shock before his tongue connected with her flesh, but it was more than worth Iris' reaction when she jerked against her restraints—not because of the current but from the sensation the lick provided. Moving from touching to not touching, he was able to alternate between little shocks and the pleasure of tasting her, making her writhe and moan at the back-and-forth sensations.

His cock was hard as a rock watching her, playing with her. Being able to tease and torment her exactly the way he wanted. Seeing how she responded with eagerness.

There were so many things he could do, and he wanted to explore every single one with her, but right now, he knew they'd been playing with electricity long enough. This was her first scene with it.

First, of many, a little voice whispered in his head.

Law knew he was getting in deeper than he'd intended, much faster than he would have thought. There was just something about Iris that called to him in a way he couldn't ignore.

Turning off the wand and setting the body contact wand on the cart, Law quickly stripped off his clothes and climbed onto the table with Iris. She opened her eyes as he moved atop her as though she'd lost track of time and hadn't been paying attention to what he was doing.

She shivered when he ran his hands up her sides, cupping her breasts, her arms automatically pulling at her restraints to reach for him. Law smiled at her expression when she came up short and realized she couldn't move.

"You did incredible, sweetheart." Bending his head, he kissed one pert nipple. Iris moaned again, sighing in pleasure as he took the little bud into his mouth and sucked. It would soothe any of the remaining sting left from the electricity, though there shouldn't be much. He'd been very careful on her chest, keeping the voltage lower than when he'd moved the wands below her waist.

"Law…" She squirmed beneath him, and the wet folds of her pussy rubbed against the head of his cock, teasing them both deliciously.

He ignored her plea as he moved his mouth to her other nipple, teasing it with the tip of his tongue before sucking it into his mouth. Feeling her undulating beneath him, knowing she couldn't move, thanks to the restraints, was hot as hell. He was going to enjoy slowly taking his time with her body at his mercy.

"Law, please!"

Releasing her nipple, he shifted his hips so his cock rubbed along the seam of her pussy.

"Please what, sweetheart?"

CHAPTER TWENTY-FOUR

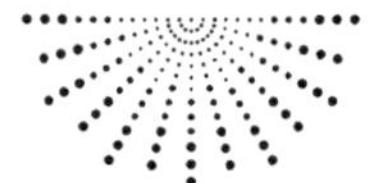

IRIS

Holy crap, who knew Master Law could be such a clit tease?

"Please fuck me," She didn't care that she was begging. There were some situations where begging was appropriate, and this was one of them.

"Soon," he answered, like the sadist he was. Iris moaned, her limbs jerking.

The bit of give she had in her restraints was more frustrating than anything else, giving the illusion she could move before they pulled her up short. God, she wanted to touch him.

Yet wanting to touch him but not being able to turned her on even more. She couldn't even wrap her legs around him like last week. She was effectively pinned to the table, entirely at his mercy.

Every part of her clenched.

His hot mouth sucked at her nipple while his other hand moved up to cup her breasts, kneading and massaging before taking that nipple between his fingers and giving it a sharp pinch. It stung in an entirely different way than the electricity had but felt even more sensitive than before because of how he'd used the electricity on her.

Iris whimpered as she strained against the cuffs on her wrists and ankles, then fell back to the table, accepting that she couldn't hurry him, couldn't do anything to tempt him… all she could do was lay there and let him have his way with her. *Which is way sexier than it has any right to be.*

She shivered as his tongue began to trace little circles on her skin, making a path from her breasts, over to her stomach to her pussy. The lick wasn't electrified anymore, but she felt it through her clenching core all the same.

Law settled between her thighs, his hands moving under her legs, then up her sides to cup her breasts as he feasted on her pussy. His tongue laved between her pussy lips, stroking her sensitive folds as his hands closed over her breasts. The gentle touch of his mouth contrasted with the rough way he gripped her breasts, squeezing and pinching, sending little shocks of pain to compete with the pleasure his tongue was bringing her.

With his shoulders under her legs, the lower half of her body had even less give. Squirming against his mouth, she gasped at the hot flashes of pleasure that surged through her. When he sucked her clit into his mouth and pinched her nipples, pain and pleasure clashed inside her body in a euphoria of sensation.

"Law! Please!" The words came out as a shriek as her back arched and her hips tried to move against his mouth. Her orgasm was cresting… then he pulled away.

At least, he pulled his mouth and tongue away, and she could have sobbed at the loss of the hot suction against her clit. His fingers remained where they were, pinching even harder and giving her nipples a little twist. Iris writhed, right on the edge of bliss but unable to cross over.

"Fuck!" She jerked even harder at the restraints, working out some of her anger on them, but nothing happened.

Law released her breasts.

Opening her eyes, she glared up at him, only to find him getting into position above her, his cock pushing against her pussy, right where she needed him. Being denied her climax when she'd been so close was painful, but she bit her lip against complaining since he was finally putting his cock in her. No sense risking him changing his mind and returning to torturing her.

And she knew he would do just that.

Braced above her, Law thrust in with exquisite slowness that had her body clamoring for more. She tilted her hips as much as she could, meeting his thrust. His eyes burned into hers as he retreated just as slowly before thrusting in again. Hard. Firm. And so damn slow.

"Law..." She knew she was whining but couldn't seem to stop. "Faster... please..."

He chuckled as he thrust again, burying himself inside her, even as he expressed his amusement about her whining.

"Oh no, sweetheart. We're doing things at my pace tonight." The smile on his face grew to a wicked grin, his voice becoming a near purr. "Though if you want to beg me, I won't object."

What she wanted to do was curse him out as he kept up the slow, steady pace of his thrusts, taking the time to rub his groin against her clit, then pulling away before the friction could give her what she needed.

After his comment about begging, she didn't want to give in, but as he took his time with every thrust, enjoying himself thoroughly with no urge to pick up the pace, her willpower was crumbling. She'd never had anyone fuck her with such controlled, slow thrusts, savoring every single one, taking the time to feel every inch of her as he sank into her pussy.

It was mind-bogglingly hot and incredibly frustrating.

Even though she'd begged and hadn't minded, for some reason, she was holding off out of pure stubbornness.

Law was taking his sweet time with fucking her, happy to keep up the slow, steady thrusts, savoring each one of them until the end of time.

Whimpering low in her throat, she moved underneath him as much as she could, feeling like a sacrificial victim to his pleasure. And, apparently, his pleasure was driving her mad with need.

Each slow thrust in and out of her pussy made her clench around him, her clit buzzing with the sensation of his body rasping against hers, then he was pulling away again. The pleasure slid through her like molasses, leaving her aching, tingling, and needy all over.

Lowering his lips, he kissed her deeply and thoroughly, still moving over her and within her. Her nipples rubbed against his lowered chest, increasing the teasing stimulation. Iris kissed him back desperately, her lips clinging to his, putting all her pent-up frustration into the kiss since it was the only way she *could* touch him right now.

It worked.

She felt his response.

Felt him move harder, faster.

Not a lot, but that little bit encouraged her.

She lifted her hips to meet his thrusts as her body hummed and buzzed. Worry that he might suddenly slow, or even stop, rose in her, making her even more desperate as she writhed beneath him.

Wanting him.

Needing him.

"Law!" His name came out as a strangled cry when he tore his lips away from hers, finally moving too fast to kiss her. The sudden onslaught of passion, the hard, fast strokes of his cock filling her over and over again, sent her soaring. She cried out as her orgasm slammed into her, the waves of bliss pummeling her body. Clenching around him, her muscles spasmed in relief.

But he wasn't coming with her. He kept fucking her, riding her through her orgasm. Iris struggled against the restraints for a new reason as he kept going, and going, and going. The exquisite bliss began to twist and turn into overstimulation, the pleasure becoming painful in its intensity.

Law

"Please..." The plea was different, and Law looked down at Iris' face. Her lips were slightly parted, tears gathering at the corners of her eyes. "I can't... I can't..."

"Yes, you can, sweetheart... and you will." He knew exactly what she was talking about. Her orgasm had been hellishly pleasurable for him, the squeezing muscles of her pussy nearly bringing him to his own completion, and he'd had to focus to keep moving through it. "You're going to cum all over my cock again."

"I can't... I can't..." Shaking her head back and forth, her expression scrunched up, and he knew she would be getting close again.

Good, so was he, and he was determined she would cum again—with him this time.

Thrusting in deep, he circled his hips, rubbing his body against her overstimulated clit, and she let out a choked cry, squirming beneath him as the onslaught of sensations overwhelmed her.

"Cum for me, Iris. Or I'm going to turn you over, fuck your ass, and play with your clit until you cum again, begging me to stop." Increasing the speed of his thrusts as he spoke, his lust rose, and his balls tightened as his body moved to its pinnacle.

"*Fuck!*" Iris shuddered beneath him. "Law!"

Her pussy spasmed around him as she came again, her body jerking against the restraints. The tears spilled from her eyes and ran down her cheeks at the intensity of her climax. That was all he needed. His long-withheld desires surged through him, and he finally let loose the tightly held tethers of his self-control.

"Iris..." He breathed out her name as his climax peaked and buried himself fully inside her. The clenching muscles around his cock massaged its length as though she was sucking the hot jets of fluid from his balls into her body, milking him of every last drop.

Thank God they were lying down. Slumping on top of her, completely breathless, muscles going lax, he emptied himself inside her. When she whimpered, he pushed up on his elbows, so he wasn't crushing her.

"Holy shit." She sighed and shuddered as another, smaller orgasm gripped her.

Now, it was his turn to grit his teeth as pleasure turned slightly painful. Her pussy squeezed his sensitive cock, still semi-hard though slowly softening. The extra stimulation was intense to the point of hurting. Just as he'd done to her.

Though perhaps not on the same scale.

"Good girl," he murmured, enjoying the way her lips tipped into a smile. Pressing a kiss to her lips, he gathered his strength and made himself get up so he could undo her restraints. Iris was half-aware when he lifted her up from the table, nuzzling against his neck as he carried her through the other room to the bathroom.

A bath would do them both good.

Cuddled against him in the warm water, she slowly roused, coming back to herself. It probably helped that he was washing her with a washcloth. She winced when he got to her pussy. He was gentle, knowing he'd been rough on that particular area—and as a sadist, enjoyed knowing she'd be feeling it for a few days.

"Too much?" he asked wickedly, whispering in her ear as he moved the cloth in a slow, circular motion over her tender flesh.

"I don't know," she answered after a moment, still shuddering. With one arm wrapped around her ribs, he felt her unsteady breathing and the increase in her pulse. "I think I might die if you try to make me cum again, though."

Chuckling, he gave her pussy one last slow wipe, then moved to wash over her hip and upper thigh. The tension slowly releasing from her frame confirmed it had been the right choice. She was nearing her limits, and Law had no desire to push these particular ones.

Especially after such a successful scene.

"So, if you held onto that wand thing and fucked me, would your dick be electrified?"

Choking on his laughter, he buried his face in her hair as he laughed harder than he could ever remember laughing. It only took a moment before Iris giggled, which made him laugh even harder. His sides and cheeks actually hurt because he couldn't stop grinning.

The things she did to him.

"No," he finally said when his laugh slowly died down, though he had to laugh again when she made a noise of disappointment. "If I held on tightly to you, the current would run through you, and you wouldn't be able to feel it, though you could shock someone else. We could actually create a human chain, though the amount of shock the final person could conduct would be less with each addition. My dick being inside you would have the same effect. You wouldn't be able to feel it anymore if I could get my dick close enough to get inside you. I feel the same shock you do and having my dick shocked is not something I'm interested in."

There were Dominants who enjoyed playing with electricity as much as he did and definitely male subs who enjoyed having their dick and balls zapped. The very thought made him shudder. He admired their strength and courage but had no desire to emulate them.

"Oh." From her tone, Law couldn't tell whether she was disappointed or relieved. Then she giggled again. "So, it would be a cock block shock?"

He laughed so hard, he snorted.

Which made her laugh so hard, she started to sink in the water. He had to hold her up as his cheeks turned red from mortification.

Since when had he *ever* snorted when he laughed? Maybe when he was a teenager.

Maybe that was it. Iris made him feel like he had during the *before* times.

It felt dangerous, but he also didn't want to let go of that feeling. Especially right now when she was warm, giggling, wriggly, and pressed against him in the tub, leaning trustingly on him, laughing with him, and making him laugh. He felt light. Like his past wasn't weighing down on him anymore. As though he could be who he wanted to be with her.

CHAPTER TWENTY-FIVE

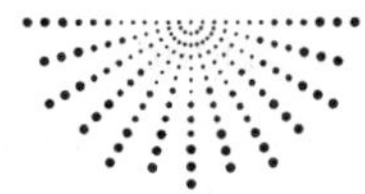

Iris

Waking up next to Law was fast becoming one of Iris' favorite things. After brunch at Marquis, it was finally time for her to head home, which she was not looking forward to.

"Let me know if your roommate gives you any trouble," he said before closing her car door behind her. "You can always come over to my place."

"Thank you, but honestly, I'm hoping that won't be necessary. Not because I wouldn't enjoy seeing you before going to Stronghold tonight, but because that's how I want my home life to be."

Law's grin flashed, making her feel all warm and melty inside. She really loved making him smile.

"Understood."

He leaned in for another kiss, then closed the door and stepped back so he could watch her drive away. Iris may have glanced in her rearview mirror a few more times than necessary. Driving away from him sucked, especially since she didn't know what she was going home to.

She hadn't lied when she said this wasn't how she wanted her home life to be. Dreading going home wasn't pleasant. On the other hand, she wasn't sure what other option she had. Maybe Rae would be interested in moving in together. Domi and Mitch had said a few things that indicated they might be heading that way, which would leave Rae out in the cold.

With her long friendship with Noelle disintegrating under the weight of living together, Iris wasn't sure she wanted to take that risk again. Being friends and being roommates could be two very different things, and with things between her and Noelle falling apart, she didn't want to lose her new friends.

Maybe she could find an apartment on her own, though she didn't think so. The Hills paid her well, but that would really strain her budget. A room might be more manageable, but if she did that, she might as well move back in with her dad for a while rather than renting a room from strangers.

Iris made a face.

Definitely did not sound appealing, but it seemed like the lesser evil between this and living with Noelle for much longer. Unless things changed at home. She was so tired of walking around on eggshells. At least when her dad disapproved of something, he just said so and didn't give her the silent treatment.

That living with her dad sounded more appealing than living with Noelle right now was pretty telling.

When she arrived home, she got to the front door before taking a deep breath and putting the key in the lock. From the muffled sounds coming through the door, she was pretty sure Noelle was home and watching television. The minute she walked through the door, she almost sighed with relief when she saw Tyler's blond head over the back of the couch.

We're not alone!

Thank goodness.

The television was on to some cooking show, which wasn't surprising since both Tyler and Noelle enjoyed them, but as soon as Iris stepped in, Noelle cleared her throat and started talking.

"So, like I was *saying*, I'm just *so* glad you were able to come spend the night with me last night, so I wasn't all alone." Noelle's voice was a little louder than it probably needed to be for Tyler to hear.

"Sure, babe," Tyler said.

Iris pressed her lips together. She might not be able to see his face, but she was pretty sure his eyes were glued to the screen, and he hadn't heard her come in. He probably wasn't paying attention to what Noelle was saying, either.

"Hey, Tyler." Sure enough, Tyler jumped and twisted his head around, then smiled vaguely when he caught sight of her. He was a cute guy, even if he didn't have the presence Law did. Tyler was more surfer boy, despite living on the east coast.

"Hey, Iris, nice to see you." He gave her a wave and turned around to face the television. Iris held back a snicker. Very cute, very nice for the most part, and completely uninterested in making friends with her, which was fine with Iris.

"Yes, it is nice for you to see Iris, isn't it?" Noelle asked, rather than sitting up to say hi to Iris. "It's been a while."

"Sure has, babe." Unlike Noelle, Tyler didn't sound at all bothered. He just agreed with her, the way he always did—the way Iris usually did—because it was just easier.

Yikes.

Shaking her head, Iris walked past them as Noelle kept talking, doing her best to ignore her roommate's pointed statements.

"It's so hard when someone who used to be a good friend just stops being around. Ditching her old friends for bright, shiny new ones and forgetting about the people who have always been there for her. I can't—"

Iris shut her bedroom door firmly behind her before she had to hear whatever it was Noelle 'couldn't.' She pressed her hand to her churning stomach. These weren't anxiety butterflies, more like someone had swirled a bunch of saltwater, then shoved it down her throat. She felt sick and nauseous.

She definitely needed to find a new living situation if this shit with Noelle kept up.

Even now, the urge to go out there and apologize, to sit and hang out with Noelle and Tyler until Noelle was satisfied, was still prodding her. That's what would keep the peace, but why was it always her job to keep the peace? Why didn't Noelle ever have to be the one to bend?

Yeah, that was Rae's voice in her head again, but it was right.

Rae wasn't the only one who felt that way. Domi did. Avery did. Law did. Iris hadn't realized how bad things were between her and Noelle until she talked about it and saw their expressions and reactions to the things Noelle said to her.

Tyler didn't see anything wrong with it, but she wondered if the reason Tyler had lasted so long as Noelle's boyfriend was because he didn't pay attention to much of anything, *and* he always tried to please her.

Iris had always tried to please Noelle, too, but now that she had new friends and new activities that didn't revolve around Noelle, it seemed like nothing she did was good enough.

Still, it was getting under her skin.

She opened up her group text.

Tell me I shouldn't feel guilty for going out last night.

It took less than thirty seconds for the first response to come through from Rae.

What? Is the roommate who has chosen not to talk to you mad you dared not be there for her to not talk to?

Iris snorted, which reminded her of how she'd made Law snort last night, which made her giggle, her mood already lifting. By the time she'd changed out of her dress from the walk of shame and put on comfortable yoga pants and a t-shirt, her phone had been quacking almost non-stop.

Avery: *You should definitely not feel guilty for going out last night.*

Domi: *Why should you feel guilty? Like Rae said, it's not like she was talking to you, anyway.*

Rae: *She probably wanted Iris there, so she could ignore her. You can't ignore someone who's not there.*

Avery: *Maybe she really felt lonely? Not that I'm saying it's okay that she took it out on Iris.*

Domi: *Mitch says you shouldn't feel guilty.*

Rae: *Maybe she's a cunt rag.*

Domi: *Rae!*

Rae: *I'm just saying.*

Avery: *She seems like a very unhappy person, but that doesn't mean you should let her make you unhappy as well.*

Now Iris felt bad. Maybe she'd been overplaying how Noelle had been. Did she really deserve to be called a cunt rag?

Yes.

Iris ignored the little voice in her head that sounded far too much like Rae for comfort. Part of Rae's biggest problem with Noelle was she didn't like the things Iris had said about Noelle. But Noelle had been a really good friend, too, even if she'd been difficult recently. Rae and the others had only seen and heard a lot about a small part of that of her relationship with Noelle.

Iris: *She's not really unhappy most of the time*

Staring at the text, Iris deleted it before sending it. That wasn't really the truth, was it? Maybe it had been at one point, but lately, Noelle never seemed happy. She tried again.

Iris: *I think she's having trouble adjusting to me making new friends and feeling left behind. I think I've given you all the wrong impression of her, and that's my fault.*

Even though her stomach twisted, she sent it. She didn't want them to think badly about her, but she didn't think Noelle was *that* bad.

Rae: *Nice try, hun, but I think you're blinded by your long friendship with her. I think we have the right impression.*

Avery: *It was weird that she encouraged you to go out, then turned down the invitation to join us and picked a fight about it.*

Domi: *I don't know if you noticed, hun, but even when we were all hanging out together, she kept saying things to make herself look good and you... not bad, but not as good as her. It was off-putting.*

Iris had noticed but thought it was all in her head. Domi now saying it, too, meant she hadn't imagined it this time. Maybe she hadn't imagined it in the past, either, when Noelle had accused her of being too sensitive.

Rae: *You're still coming to Stronghold tonight to hang out with us, right? Avery got the night off! You can't miss that.*

Iris: *Holy crap, Avery got the night off? No, I definitely can't miss that.*

She didn't want to, either. Despite what she'd told Law about not coming over today, she felt trapped in her room. She didn't want to bug him, so she was going to deal with it, but only because she had Stronghold to look forward to tonight.

Law

When he got home, Law started second-guessing himself. Last night had gone well. Really well. Iris was everything he wanted.

But was she everything he deserved? It sure didn't feel as if he deserved her.

Did she deserve to be saddled with someone like him?

The doubt creeping in was hard to ignore, no matter how distracting Whiskers was, demanding attention after being left alone for another night. Every time he stopped petting her, as his thoughts distracted him, she head-butted his face. That helped a little.

"Sorry, Miss Princess," he murmured, scratching under her chin and warily watching in case she suddenly decided she was done with him. Chin scratches were particularly risky, but when she was in the mood, she loved them more than anything. "Maybe I'll see if Iris wants to sleep over here next time."

The moment the words were out in the world, panic tightened in his chest.

He hadn't had a woman sleep over—*ever*.

It was easier to keep anything romantic out of his space. To keep anything intimate out of his space.

"Mrow." Whiskers head-butted him, rubbing her whiskered cheek against his cheekbone, so her whiskers poked him in the eye. Talk about bringing him back to himself.

"Thanks, Miss Princess." True to form, Whiskers went from little princess to demon in the blink of an eye. She hissed at him and jumped away, chin and tail high in the air as she pranced toward the kitchen.

At least she hadn't clawed him.

Shaking his head, Law was about to get up and clean something instead of sitting around all afternoon overthinking when his phone rang. He picked it up without looking at it, thinking it might be Iris needing him.

"Hello?"

"You picked up!" His mother's delighted tone made him groan inwardly.

It's not that he didn't like talking to his mother, she just talked too much, and what she wanted to talk about was usually whatever he *didn't* want to talk about. Voicemails he could eventually respond to tended to be easier. She would tell him what she actually wanted instead of making him wait through twenty minutes of stories about her friends' single daughters before getting to the point.

"Hi, Mom." He kept the resignation out of his voice. It wasn't her fault, really. She just wanted him to have a certain life, the life she'd thought he would have when he'd married Elaine. Instead, she'd been deprived of both a daughter-in-law and grandchildren when he fucked up. Even though his two sisters had provided her with the latter, he was the only boy and the only child who didn't live across the country.

Sometimes, he wondered if she would move to be closer to her grandchildren. So far, she didn't seem to want to leave Delaware, and his dad would do whatever made her happy. So, they stayed on the east coast even though two of their three children and all of their grandchildren were on the west.

"Oh, it's so nice to hear your voice." Cue the guilt for not taking more time to talk to her. That was inevitable. "How are you doing?"

"I'm good. How are you and Dad?"

"Good, good, we're both good. Have you heard about Elaine?" The question was asked with a bit of disapproval, though he knew the disapproval wasn't for him. His parents were staunch Catholics, and Elaine had the gall to divorce their only son. It still stuck in his mother's craw, no matter how many times Law explained it was exactly what Elaine should have done.

"No, I haven't." This was why it was easier to bear the guilt of not answering his mom's calls than picking up. Elaine was definitely a subject he didn't want to talk about. "Is she okay?" That was all he really cared about. He wasn't in love with her anymore. He just wanted her to live a good, happy life and get everything she deserved after everything he'd put her through.

His mother made a hmphing noise.

"She's engaged." The words sounded almost like an accusation.

"Good for her." Relief filled his chest, even though he knew it would rile his mom. That was exactly what he wanted for Elaine.

"Not good for her. She swore to live with you, for better or for worse." The anger in his mother's voice was real, as was the sorrow.

Law felt bad because he knew his mom had loved Elaine as if she were blood but knew she also needed to let this go.

"It was definitely for worse, Mom, and it wouldn't have gotten better. Her leaving me was what finally made me hit rock bottom and admit I needed help."

"She should have come back to you."

"No, she shouldn't have. She should have done exactly what she did and moved on." Law closed his eyes, pinching the bridge of his nose. He was about to throw himself on the sacrificial altar for Elaine. His mom and her mom were still part of the same social circle, and Elaine didn't need his mom's drama. He was pretty sure his mom would leave Elaine and her mom alone, but this was the only way to be one hundred percent certain. "Besides, I've met someone, too."

"You have?!" The utter joy that filled his mom's voice made him smile and shake his head.

She'd loved Elaine and thought Elaine should have stayed by his side, but at the end of the day, she wouldn't complain if Elaine wasn't who he ended up with. The quickness with which she pivoted made him laugh.

"We just started seeing each other," he said in a warning tone.

"Yes, but you're telling me about her, which means she's special."

She was. Maybe too special for him. He was glad to hear Elaine was getting the happily-ever-after she deserved but did he have it in him to try again for himself?

He didn't know.

CHAPTER TWENTY-SIX

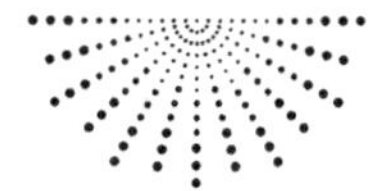

"I'm glad everyone got the memo," Domi said mock-seriously as Iris walked up, gesturing at Iris' outfit. Looking at all of them, Iris had to laugh. She'd decided to forego the usual clubwear and stay comfortable in a purple negligee.

Apparently, she hadn't been alone feeling that way. Avery, Domi, and Rae were all also wearing lingerie rather than corsets, PVC, or leather.

"I guess everyone wanted to feel comfortable?" she asked teasingly. Even though they were in lingerie, they looked completely different. Iris had opted for sheer purple with lace, whereas Domi was wearing a black all-lace teddy. Rae was wearing a soft pink baby doll with a furry hem and bra, while Avery was in red silk with embroidery.

"Nick's not here, so why stuff myself into a corset?" Avery grinned. "Besides, he'll be tired when he gets home. This will be much easier for him to work with than trying to get me out of a corset."

"Rae didn't feel like dressing up, so I got lazy, too," Domi said, her eyes twinkling with mischief. Rae snorted, tossing her long braids over her shoulder.

"I wanted to do something different." Her gaze skittered across the room, and Iris had to work not to turn around to wherever Rae was looking, but she would bet Morgan, Master Brian, or both were over there. Poor Rae. Though maybe this was a good thing if it brought Rae to a tipping point, and she finally made a move or got over Brian.

"Where's Mitch?" Iris asked, settling herself on a barstool.

"Bathroom," Domi answered, lifting her drink to her lips for a sip. "What time is Master Law supposed to be arriving?"

"In about half an hour." Iris grinned. "So, we have some time to hang out."

"Perfect." Rae elbowed her. "Now that we're all here, update us on the roommate situation."

Groaning, she gave them the rundown of everything Noelle had said, only pausing to order some water when the server came by. Rae listened expressionlessly while Domi and Avery nodded several times.

"It's possible I'm reading way too much into it," she finished up. "I mean, I could be taking it the wrong way. It sounds a lot worse than it is when I say it out loud."

"Actually, if anything, I'm pretty sure you're downplaying how bad it is," Rae said, glancing at the other two. "Look, we weren't sure if we should say anything because you two have been friends for a long time and live together, but a few of the things she said about you when you were out of the room were kinda fucked up."

Blinking in surprise, Iris turned to look at Domi and Avery, who nodded in confirmation. The expression on Avery's face was one of pure sympathy, while Domi's lips were pressed together in disapproval. The disapproval wasn't directed at Rae, which meant it was for whatever Noelle had said.

"Like what?"

"She made a 'joke' about how needy you are," Rae said bluntly. "And how you think you're so much better than everyone. It was all 'joking,' which was why we weren't sure we should say anything, but it didn't feel like she was actually joking."

"More like she was waiting for us to agree," Domi muttered.

"Oh. I mean… that's just how she is." Though it hurt to hear Noelle had been saying things like that. "She doesn't realize how she sounds."

"I think she does, hun," Avery said, reaching over to take Iris' hand. "She's like the epitome of a mean girl. She does it in a way that makes it hard for anyone to say anything, so she can hide behind it being 'just a joke,' but that doesn't make what she says okay."

"Just… think about how she's making you feel. We don't want to mess with your friendship, but we don't like seeing her mess with your head." Domi nodded firmly before looking past Iris and rolling her eyes. "I was wondering what was taking Mitch so long."

Twisting in her seat, Iris looked over her shoulder. Mitch had stopped to talk to Brian and Morgan, confirming her guess about who Rae had been looking for.

"Anybody want to take a walkabout?" Rae asked as Mitch and Brian both lifted their heads, as though they sensed the eyes on them, and looked over at their table.

"Sure," Iris said, glancing at the clock. Her brother and Kate hadn't come in, so it would be safe. "I have about fifteen minutes before Law gets here."

"I'll hang out here with Domi." Avery smiled as Domi relaxed. Clearly, she'd wanted to wait for Mitch to return but didn't want to make Rae interact with Brian when she didn't want to. "You two stay out of trouble."

Rae and Iris snorted in unison.

"What kind of trouble could we possibly get into here?" Rae asked as she got up from her seat. Iris nodded.

"We'll be back soon." Iris linked her arm with Rae, and they headed for the Dungeon. Taking a look around the Dungeon was nothing new since it had been her homework for a month. Even if her Watch Dom wasn't here to keep an eye on her, it wasn't as if she needed it anymore.

Law

If it wasn't for Iris' plans to be at Stronghold tonight, Law wouldn't go. He wasn't in the right headspace. At least she wouldn't expect to scene tonight. She just wanted to hang out with her friends and him, and he could do that.

He was hoping that seeing her would ease some of the unsettled feelings that had been niggling at him since talking to his mom earlier in the afternoon. Going with the flow had sounded like a possibility, but now he was feeling in over his head. His mom's excitement hearing he had a girlfriend—her word, not his—had felt like moving into even deeper waters.

When he'd been with Iris last night, everything had felt right. He hadn't questioned everything and was able to just be in the moment and enjoy it. He really needed that back.

"Hi, Master Law… are you okay?" Lexie, wife and submissive of Stronghold's owner, was at the front desk. She was a cute little pixie of a woman, with bright blue eyes and black hair cut short, and in her current outfit, she looked like a goth Tinker Bell. As Master Patrick's life partner, she got away with a lot of things other submissives wouldn't dare—like nosy questions. It didn't hurt that she genuinely cared.

"Fine, just distracted. Is Iris here yet?" He knew the question would divert her attention, and he was right. Lexie brightened up. She was good friends with Iris' older brother, which meant she was interested in what was going on with Iris, even beyond the usual club gossip.

"She is. She got here a while ago. Are you meeting her here tonight? Do you need a room?" Her eagerness almost made him laugh. She clearly approved of Iris dating him, even if Andrew didn't, which was nice to know. Maybe some of her attitude would rub off on him.

"Yes and no. We don't need a room for tonight, but thank you." Law passed her his phone to be stored and waved as he headed to the main floor entrance. Master Will nodded a greeting from his position as a bouncer as Law passed to go through the door to the bar.

As always, the sounds of conversation and the smell of leather washed over Law as he walked inside, soothing his inner turmoil. Walking into Stronghold, he was in a space where he was at his most comfortable. Looking around for Iris, he frowned when he didn't see her but caught sight of Master Mitch's blond head among the bar tables and headed that way.

He turned out to be at a table with Domi, Avery, and Master Brian. Law's eyebrows rose as he approached. This was where he would have expected to find Iris and Rae as well. Perhaps they were in the bathroom.

"Hello," he said as he approached, feeling a sense of relieved satisfaction as he was welcomed to the table. Knowing Iris' friends welcomed him, even when she wasn't there, was a nice feeling. After he'd greeted everyone, he asked the obvious question. "Where's Iris?"

"She and Rae went to walk around the Dungeon," Avery said. "They should be back soon." Domi glanced at Brian, but only for a moment before her eyes darted away. Law thought he knew why Rae and Iris had chosen to do a walk around, just from that one look.

He didn't mind that she'd gone with her friend instead of waiting for him. It was a very Iris thing to do, taking care of the person right in front of her. She had a generous heart. But he was antsy to see her, so he didn't care if it might be a little rude to immediately leave the table. He wasn't here for her friends—he was here for her.

He needed her to make him feel the way he had last night. Standing around with her friends, who all had a drink in front of them, wasn't helping his mental state.

"If you'll excuse me, I'm going to hunt her down." He smiled, hoping it would take the sting out from him barely stopping by to say hello. Thankfully, none of them seemed to think it was odd.

"I'm sure we'll see you later." Domi grinned as they all waved him off with understanding.

Relieved, Law headed for the Dungeon... and Iris.

IRIS

The dungeon was as busy as ever, with a scene at almost every station. Dungeon monitors were roaming, along with everyone else. Some scenes had small audiences; some didn't. When it came to watching scenes, Iris disliked Saturday nights. There was just so *much* going on, it was hard to focus on any one scene.

Rae didn't seem to mind as much, though she might be trying to distract herself, going from scene to scene with intense focus. That or she really was that focused and was taking notes for her book. She was working on her third book, and Iris knew it was a kinky romance.

"Hey." Iris elbowed Rae, curious now that she'd had the thought. "Are you planning on using this for inspiration?"

"Huh?" Rae tore her gaze away from the admittedly fascinating sight of Master Victor using a flogger in each hand while he worked over his submissive, Mark. "What?"

"Inspiration for your book." Iris grinned. "Or are you just having fun?"

"A bit of both?" Rae giggled, her gaze moving on to the next scene, where a man was applying clothespins all over the submissive he had tied to the St. Andrew's cross. It looked both painful and fun, and from the submissive's expression, she definitely agreed. "It's hard not to get ideas when I'm here."

Iris laughed. "I find that easy to believe." Heck, if she thought she could write something, she'd be inspired, too. She was still inspired, just in a different way.

Inspired in my panties.

As Rae watched the clothespin scene, Iris' gaze skipped to the next one, which didn't seem to have an audience. The submissive already had a few dark wheals across her breasts, and tears were streaming down her cheeks from pain-filled hazel eyes. She didn't look like she was sighing in masochistic pleasure… and her Dom was picking up another cane.

Where were the DMs? Usually, when there was a more intense scene going on, they made sure to be nearby. Iris turned her head, looking back and forth. The DMs wore leather vests with bright orange or yellow trim to make sure they stood out. Unfortunately, the dungeon was so crowded, she didn't spot any immediately.

The sound of the cane hitting flesh didn't stand out in the room, and neither did the submissive's yelp, but her soft cry of "Red" did.

Iris' head whipped around, relief flooding her that the submissive wouldn't be taking anymore.

Except... the Dom was raising his arm again. Had someone else safe worded?

The submissive's eyes darted back and forth, wide and panicked, and her gaze met Iris'.

"Red!" she said again, her voice strangled. Out of the corner of her eye, Iris could see Rae looking over, frowning as if she was trying to figure out what was going on. Iris was already moving because so was the Dom.

His arm was coming back, ready to flip the cane forward again, even though the safeword had been called.

Iris couldn't see his face, so she didn't know what he was thinking. All she knew was someone had to do something, and right now, but the only one who seemed to have noticed what was going on was her. She didn't think. She *moved*.

"Red!" She screamed the word as she surged forward, hands stretching up to grab the cane. "She said red!"

The Dom faltered as her hands wrapped around the cane. He tried to pull it forward and was strong enough to drag Iris partway with it. As he realized someone had grabbed it, he turned, bringing his arm down, and Iris jerked back, letting go of the cane and barely managing to dodge the elbow that almost hit her in the face.

She didn't recognize the Dom, but she could see his expression clearly enough to know he was pissed.

"What the hell?" He jerked the cane away from her.

Iris took the moment to dart around him to stand between him and the bound sub, protecting the woman with her own body.

"My question exactly," Iris snapped, hands fisted by her side. How fucking *dare* he. "She called her safeword, you fucking dickhead, and you were ignoring it!"

Though his face was bright red with fury, she could tell he was probably a pretty attractive guy, maybe in his mid to late thirties, with blond hair and dark brown eyes that were spitting fire. Clearly, he hadn't expected anyone to intervene, even though he'd ignored a safe word.

All around them, conversations and scenes were coming to a halt, but Iris kept her focus on the asshole, who looked as if he was about to have a coronary.

"You little bitch!" He raised the cane, but they would never know what his intention was. Suddenly, Law appeared and grabbed the man's wrist, like something out of a movie. She hadn't even known he was there. The so-called Dom—he was no Dom as far as Iris was concerned—cried out and dropped the cane, reaching for his wrist with his other hand.

Iris didn't know what Law was doing with his grip, but it must have hurt.

Suddenly, DMs were shoving through the crowd surrounding them.

"What happened?" Master Jared, a friend of her brother, glanced at Iris, his brow furrowing as he recognized her. His expression when he looked beyond her at the submissive still bound to the St. Andrew's cross turned him from the normal giant teddy bear of a man she knew to a terrifying predator. He shifted so he was partially in front of Iris, crossing his arms over his chest.

The dumb-dumb Dom had managed to snatch his arm away from Law and was cradling his wrist in front of him.

"That little bitch interrupted my scene! I want her fucking kicked out of here!"

CHAPTER TWENTY-SEVEN

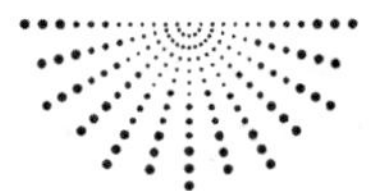

LAW

This was not how he'd seen his night going. Law's heart felt as if it was going to pound right out of his chest as his blood pumped through him in pure rage. It was as though he'd left his vaunted self-control in the Dungeon, along with any patience he had.

When he'd finally found Iris, right as she'd screamed 'Red,' he had been too late to do anything but stop the unknown from lashing out at her. He was still shaking from the adrenaline dump and had nowhere for the energy to go. Plowing his fist into the man's face seemed appropriate.

Jared and Kincaid, both on DM duty, decided to take everyone up to Patrick's office rather than continuing the confrontation in the Dungeon. Iris and Rae, who had been allowed to come along as a witness, were standing on one side of Patrick's desk, glaring at the asshole Dom while Kincaid stood next to the man.

Behind the desk, Patrick had his arms crossed over his chest as he listened to the 'Dom' finish up his version of events. Truthfully, the submissives didn't even need to talk for everyone to know the man was a self-important jerk.

"I demand some kind of punishment for the interruption of my scene." The man glared at Iris, raking his hand arrogantly through his hair. "And an apology from your Dungeon Monitors for indulging this nonsense."

"It's not nonsense," Master Kincaid said before Law could speak up, which was probably for the best.

His infamous self-control hanging by a thread, Law clenched his jaw even tighter to keep from unloading on the asshole.

"You were about to hit Iris with your cane. Regardless of whether or not she interrupted her scene, that is a clear infraction of the club rules. You do *not* strike a submissive you have not negotiated a scene with, no matter what they've done."

"And you don't hit a submissive after they've safe worded, which your submissive did," Iris shot out, rather than keeping her mouth shut. Unlike Law, she didn't have a problem speaking impulsively. He shot her a look. It was better if the Dom hung himself with his own rope, but she wasn't looking at him. "You *ignored her safeword.*"

"My sub doesn't have a safeword. She doesn't need one."

Red clouded Law's vision, and if it wasn't for the door opening to allow Master Jared and the submissive in question to come in, Law wasn't sure what he would have done. The asshole didn't realize it, but he was definitely out of the club. He was clearly taking Patrick's silence as encouragement to keep talking, not as the judgment it was.

Everyone turned to look at the woman, who was tucked under Master Jared's arm. Despite being one of the tallest and most muscular Doms in the club, subs were instinctively drawn to Jared, as though they could sense he was a protector at heart, and this sub was no exception. Wrapped in a blanket that covered her completely except for her bare feet, she was clinging to his side, her head down, staring at the ground.

From the way Jared glared at the wannabe Dom as they stepped inside, this would be over with quickly.

Thank God.

Because Law felt…

There weren't words for how he felt.

Out of control was the least of it.

About to crash headfirst into something he didn't want to.

If he held his hands out in front of him, he was sure they'd be shaking. A need had risen inside him, as if a demon he'd shoved in a deep, dark cave had gotten loose and was moving up from his stomach to his throat, demanding to be let out.

Demanding to be appeased.

This is why I never say I'm recovered.

He couldn't think about that right now.

Focus. Focus. Focus.

Once they got this over with, he could get out of here and take Iris with him. Get her away from the asshole and reassure himself she was all right. Then, hopefully, he'd feel more like himself. The 'him' he wanted to be.

Master Jared maneuvered the submissive around the jerk Dom, keeping his body between them. The man actually moved toward her before Master Jared's glare drove him back. He faltered, understanding dawning on his face as he finally realized he didn't have a single ally in the room.

"Hey, I didn't do anything wrong! She agreed to no safeword. It's in our contract."

The submissive sniffled. Law couldn't see her around Master Jared, but he was pretty sure she was crying by the way Rae and Iris moved to the side not taken by the big Dom, both of them speaking in low, comforting voices. Asshole glared, but he didn't intervene.

Master Patrick got to his feet.

The asshole was smart enough to realize he'd fucked up. Paling, he took a step back as Master Patrick crossed his arms over his chest. Both Patrick and Jared were over six feet tall, and while Law wasn't intimidated by their greater height, the asshole definitely was. Something Patrick took immediate advantage of, looming over dickhead.

"There is a *club* safeword, Don." Master Patrick's voice was low, lethal. He'd deliberately left off 'Master.' "One which you agreed to honor when you signed the contract to join the club. Not only that, but while agreeing not to have a safeword is a perfectly legitimate choice, someone who does it in order to push their submissive beyond what they can take is not a Dom. They are an abuser."

"No, I—"

"Wouldn't you agree, Detective Kincaid?"

Asshole Don's head snapped around so fast, it was a wonder he didn't crack his neck as his eyes widened in horror.

"D-D-Detective?"

Kincaid nodded as Patrick continued.

"That's right, and one of my lawyers. Master Law, are BDSM contracts legally binding in court?"

Law snorted. Seeing how freaked out Asshole Don was helped soothe his swirling emotions. It wasn't near what the jerk deserved, but it was something.

"No, no, they're not. In addition, a personal contract would not supersede the membership contract he signed with Stronghold, which actually *is* legally binding. As you said, a true Dom, whose submissive doesn't have a safeword, would carefully watch that submissive to ensure they weren't pushed beyond their limits. Abusers, such as Don here, use it as an excuse to abuse."

Iris

Holy shit, Master Law was hot when he was lawyering. If it wasn't for how serious the situation was and how pissed off she was on behalf of the woman whose shoulder she was rubbing as comfortingly as she could, she would be totally turned on watching Master Law take down Douchebag Don.

Granted, he wasn't the only one, but he was still the hottest one. There was no way Douchebag Don was getting off the hook, but what made it even better was the Doms were letting him have it, in no uncertain terms, so even if the message didn't get through, both he and his submissive heard it.

"Now, Master Kincaid will escort you out. You are not welcome back here. Your membership fees will be refunded." Master Patrick bit off the end of his words, his glare hot.

Douchebag Don seemed to rally a little, his chin lifting in belligerent defiance.

"Fine. Cassidy, come here." He snapped his fingers.

Snapped. His. Fingers.

Iris clamped her hand around Cassidy's shoulder. No fucking way was she letting the woman go off with him. She didn't care what the Doms had to say about it.

Thankfully, they weren't having any of it, either. Master Jared had already shifted his body, so he was between Cassidy and Douchebag Don.

"Cassidy is going to stay here for a chat with me," Master Patrick said. He paused, turning to look at her. She shivered against Iris, and Iris and Rae squeezed her a little tighter. Master Patrick's gaze softened, as did his voice. "Unless there's something at his house you need to retrieve? We can send someone with him."

"N-No…" For the first time since she'd cried 'red,' Cassidy seemed to have found her voice, shaky but present. Her hand found Iris' and squeezed, hanging on for dear life. "There's nothing there, and I don't want to go with him."

"You—"

Iris peeked around Master Jared to see Douchebag cut off as Master Kincaid's hand landed on his shoulder in a very different grip than Iris' and Rae's on Cassidy. Douchebag's face was turning red again.

"Trust me, you want to leave her alone." Master Jared's voice was colder than Iris had ever heard it. "Do not contact her again… or you will regret it."

"Let's go," Kincaid said, pushing Douchebag toward the exit, keeping a firm grip on his shoulder.

The man glanced back but didn't say anything else. His jaw seemed to have locked into place. Apparently, he'd finally decided to show some sense and keep his mouth shut. Too little, too late, but Iris didn't mind that he'd talked himself into a corner.

She hadn't even had to say anything. He'd obviously thought he had the right to do whatever he wanted, and neither she nor anyone else should have stopped him. Fucking dickweed. He was an abuser, pure and simple, hiding under the banner of kink and thinking that made him safe.

Iris had heard about it, though this was her first time encountering it. Guys like him were why Andrew had insisted she come to Stronghold, even though it was uncomfortable as siblings belonging to the same kink club. He'd been worried she'd encounter an asshole like this.

Even here at Stronghold, a few slipped through now and then.

Cassidy kept her head down as the door closed behind Douchebag and Kincaid, her long, dark hair falling to either side of her head to keep her face hidden. As soon as the door shut, she sighed with relief.

Master Patrick picked up the phone on his desk and pushed a button.

"Lexie, I need you back here, please." He hung up as soon as he finished speaking, without waiting for her to reply. "Cassidy, please have a seat. Law, Iris, Rae... thank you all so much for helping her out. Iris, I know I told you not to interfere... in this case, I will eat my words and say you weren't wrong. Lexie and I will take it from here. Oh, and if you see Morgan, can you send her in here?"

The abrupt dismissal chafed, but Cassidy was the priority, and as Lexie came bursting in the door, Iris nodded. She got it. Patrick telling her she wasn't wrong to interfere meant more than he could know.

"What's going on?" Lexie asked, hurrying over to the desk. Clearly, she'd figured out something was wrong—it wasn't often Patrick was abrupt when talking with her. That he had been so short on the phone had been a major sign something big was up. Plus, she'd been at the front desk when Kincaid escorted Douchebag from the building.

"Come on, ladies," Law said, gesturing to Rae and Iris. Cassidy had already moved away from them and sat down, clutching the blanket around her, head still down. As much as Iris wanted to stay, it didn't seem as though Cassidy cared if she did. When she looked at Law, she didn't argue.

There was an odd expression on his face, and his jaw was clenched, similar to how Douchebag's had been. Now that Cassidy was in good hands, Iris should find out what was going on to make him look that way. Coming in to find her in the middle of an altercation with a Dom was definitely not how she'd wanted him to first see her tonight.

She knew he wouldn't blame her, Douchebag was clearly at fault, but Law looked as if he was struggling with someone.

So, while Rae grumbled as they were led out of Patrick's office—Iris was pretty sure she heard her say something about Morgan—Iris didn't argue. She was curious why Patrick wanted Morgan there, but she was more worried about whatever was going on with Law.

LAW

Going back to the bar wasn't the best move for Law's current state, but on the other hand, it was the only move unless he was going to go out the front door on the heels of the asshole. Not something he wanted to do. Besides, he still needed to talk to Iris and find Morgan if he could.

He knew why Patrick wanted Morgan's presence while talking to Cassidy and inwardly agreed she'd likely be able to help a great deal.

What he really wanted to do was get the fuck out of Stronghold until he could get control of himself again.

Thankfully, Morgan was sitting in the Lounge area with some of her friends. Keeping Iris' hand in his, he pulled her over to send Morgan to Patrick's office. Rae was already moving toward where Domi and the others still were, a bit of a flounce in her step.

"Excuse me, ladies. Morgan, Patrick needs you in his office... please." Law knew his voice was brusque, sharper than he wanted it to be, but he couldn't soften it anymore. He felt as though he was holding onto himself by his fingernails, and they were going to break at any moment. He didn't know what would happen then but doubted it would be good.

He needed to get out of here.

"Of course, Master Law." Morgan hopped up, giving her friends a wave before hurrying along. Her friends looked curious, but they didn't get the chance to ask what was going on.

Law was already moving, still holding Iris' hand—except she was pulling back against him.

"Woah, Master Law, wait. Where are we going?"

Coming to a halt, he turned to face her. He could see the worry in her eyes but couldn't do anything about his expression. It felt tight on his face as though his skin was stretched over his skull.

"Hey, it's okay—let's go over to the bar and talk about it." Iris' expression turned comforting, her tone soothing, dark eyes filled with sympathy. She put her free hand on the outside of his, so she was holding his hand with both of hers as her fingers gently stroked his skin. "We can have a drink, hang out, and talk things over."

Have a drink.

She didn't know how badly he wanted to.

No idea.

Because he hadn't told her the full truth about his past.

The words wouldn't come now, either.

It felt as if someone had wired his jaw shut, and there was a roaring in his ears, drowning out all the other sounds around them.

He couldn't think.

He couldn't breathe.

Bands were tightening around his chest, locking on and squeezing the air out of his lungs.

Get out. Get out now.

It wasn't a thought; it was an impulse.

He jerked his hand away from hers, seeing only a flash of her shocked expression as he turned and rushed from the room without her.

CHAPTER TWENTY-EIGHT

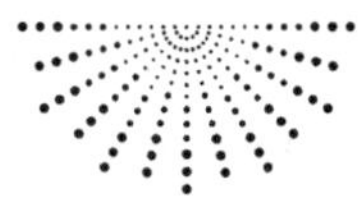

IRIS

Frozen in place, Iris' gaped as Law ran away from her. Well, he wasn't actually running, but he was moving fast enough he might as well be. Before she'd recovered, he was already through the door into the lobby. The sight of the door swinging shut was what finally got her moving—except someone grabbed her arm.

"What just happened?" Master Asad's voice was harsher than she'd ever heard before, and he had a grip like a steel cage. Iris tried to jerk away as she answered him, but it wasn't an easy hold to break.

"I don't know!" She turned, purposefully jerking her arm to where his fingers and thumb met, the weakest part of his grip. Three cheers for Angel's self-defense class because it worked, and she took off after Law. She could hear Master Asad's low curse behind her, but she ignored him as she darted for the door.

Blowing through the lobby, she ran outside—straight into Master Kincaid. He grabbed her upper arms, both of them, to steady her but didn't let go. Damn these interfering Doms. Iris tried to look around him, trying to figure out where Law had gone.

"What is going on? Where is Law going?" Master Kincaid's questions were drowned out by the sound of Master Asad coming through the door behind her and cursing as he came to an abrupt halt. She actually felt the air move behind her as he managed not to run into her, but he came damn close.

Before she could answer, she heard the sound of a car starting.

"Shit! Where's he going?" she wailed, yanking away from Master Kincaid. It didn't work quite as well as it had with Master Asad since he was holding both her hands, but she got to the side of him. Enough that she saw Master Law's car back up, then peel out of the parking lot.

"Law!" She screamed his name at the back of his car, anger rising inside her as she realized he was just driving away without saying anything to her, without explaining. What the fuck was going on?

A blur of movement aimed at Law's car.

The sound of metal crunching against metal.

The front of Law's car went sideways, spinning as the other car slammed into it.

Someone was screaming.

Iris was moving, Master Kincaid only a step or two ahead of her as he bolted for the cars, before she realized the scream had come from her.

Behind her, she heard shouts, but it was as though they were very far away as she dashed through the parking lot, dodging around cars, running for the one Law was in. She could see him through the windows, slumped sideways.

The car that had hit him had hit the driver's side.

A sob bubbled up in her throat, but she pushed it back.

The other car pulled back and turned, speeding away down the road. Iris gaped, her head snapping to look after it.

What the fuck?! A hit and run?

She didn't stop moving. The important thing was Law.

"Law!" she screamed again as she got to the passenger side and saw the blood trickling down his head. He wasn't moving. Fear fueled her panic, and she didn't come to a stop so much as she slammed into the side of his car, using it to stop her.

Master Kincaid was more graceful, using his hand to vault himself to slide across the trunk and landing on the other side. He pivoted the moment he touched down.

"Fuck! That asshole." Master Kincaid's head snapped up, looking at her. "Iris, can you get in on that side? The door is warped. It'll never open."

Panting for breath, Iris grabbed the handle and pulled. A sob rose in her throat again, panic clawing at her from the inside—but Law needed her to be calm. She took a deep breath.

"Locked. We can break the window?"

"Got it." Master Asad joined her at the side of the car. "Move back."

He slammed something hard into the window, and it shattered. Iris would have darted forward to open it, but someone else was already holding on to her—she hadn't even noticed the rest of the people who had come out of the club. Master Asad was the one to reach through the window and unlock it.

"Law!" she cried out as she saw him move, his head turning slightly but not lifting.

"They have him, Iris. It's okay." The familiar voice took a moment to recognize. The same voice that had been there for her, over and over, throughout the years, no matter how much of a pain she was.

Her brother was wrong, though. It wasn't okay.

Still, she turned and pressed her face to his broad chest, crying because there wasn't anything she could do. All she could do was step back and wait while Master Mitch crawled onto the passenger seat to check Law over. He was a nurse and could actually help. Then she stood there when the ambulance and firetruck arrived, and they finally got Law's car door open and got him out of the car.

With a brace wrapped around his neck, strapped to a wooden board they lifted onto the stretcher, he looked small. Vulnerable. Utterly unlike himself. And it terrified her even more.

"I have to go with him." She pulled away from Andrew, running to where they were loading Law into the back of the ambulance. Master Asad stood there, talking to one of the EMTs. She grabbed onto his arm. "I should go with him."

She didn't need to turn to know her brother was behind her, his presence supporting her.

"And you are?" The EMT asked, looking up. She had shoulder-length brown hair and bangs that wisped in the slight breeze. Her eyes scanned over Iris, though she'd clearly seen enough of the surrounding crowd not to be shocked by Iris' outfit. The expression on her face was blank, but at least it wasn't judgmental.

"She's his fiancée," Andrew said. Master Asad's eyes widened, and Iris' jaw clamped shut, but neither of them refuted Andrew's lie. Whatever it took to get her in the back of the ambulance with him.

"It's new, she's not his emergency contact, but I'll follow," Master Asad said. "If he wakes up, he'll want her with him."

Would he?

He ran from her in the club. Right out the door and got into the car, which was the whole reason for this mess.

Iris clenched her jaw. Maybe it would be better to let Master Asad go with him. She didn't know if he'd want her there.

"Here." Kate's voice sounded in her ear as something wrapped around her. Dimly, Iris realized Kate had just put a mid-thigh light coat on her, covering her outfit. Right now, she didn't care what she looked like or what people thought of her, but when she got to the hospital, she might.

"Get in. We'll meet you there." Andrew held out his hand to give her a leg up. The EMT nodded and gestured, so rather than hold everyone up even longer, Iris got in. The doors closed behind her as she sat on a little bench, reaching out to hold his hand. His fingers were limp in hers, without the reassurance she was looking for, and she had to bite her lip to keep from crying.

"Hi, I'm Jenn," the EMT said, tucking her hair behind her ear. "Does your fiancé have any health conditions that we should know about? Allergies?" If she noticed the lack of a ring on Iris' finger, she didn't say anything.

"No, not that I know of," Iris said tensely, but then, why would she? She felt like an impostor, but she didn't want to let go of his hand.

"We'll go over it again at the hospital," Jenn said reassuringly. The other EMT ignored Iris, cleaning the wound on Law's head. "If you want to talk to him, it might help him wake up a little faster."

If that was true, Iris had no idea, but at least it gave her something useful to do. She just hoped if—when—he woke up, he was happy to see her. She still didn't know what had happened at Stronghold or why he'd run out the way he had. Run from her.

Leaning down, she whispered in his ear, promising she'd be a good girl—the best girl—if he'd just wake up.

***

Law

Everything hurt. Law groaned as a kind of throbbing ache pulled him slowly into the waking world, despite how badly he wanted to stay asleep.

Fuck, why do I hurt so much? I feel like I got hit by a truck.

"Oh, I think he's coming around." Iris' voice slipped into his consciousness, and he felt something tighten around his hand. They were holding hands, but it was an odd position. He didn't think she was lying next to him, even though he was in bed. "Law, can you open your eyes?"

Of course, he could open his eyes... except that he couldn't. He tried. They didn't move.

"Give him a minute." Asad's voice was calm, measured.

It struck him how stressed Iris sounded by comparison.

"It was a hard knock to the head."

It was?

Law tried, but he didn't remember getting knocked on the head. He remembered being in Stronghold... in Master Patrick's office after he'd stopped some asshole from assaulting Iris. Had the asshole hit him?

No, that didn't track.

Groaning, Law forced his eyes open.

Holy shit. He was in a hospital.

"Law!" Iris' face swam before his eyes as she bent over him. Squinting up at her, he tried to talk, but his mouth didn't feel like it was working. "Oh, thank goodness, he's awake."

"What happened?" This time the words made it out, his diction a little fuzzy but understandable. Iris and Asad tried to answer him at the same time. Almost immediately, Iris bit her lip and stopped talking, so Asad could fill him in.

Apparently, after the asshole Dom had been escorted from the club, Law and Iris had gone into the main area. He'd cut and run out the door as if his ass was on fire— Asad's colorful commentary—then Asad and Iris had run after him. Unfortunately, they'd been too slow to keep Law from getting into his car and driving off, which was when 'that asshole Don' had done a hit and run while Law was on his way out of the parking lot.

"The cops already have him." Asad shook his head. "Fucking idiot. The cameras caught everything. The only thing I don't understand is why you ran out of the club like that."

"I don't remember." Law frowned. Everything was very fuzzy and far away. He knew he'd been in Master Patrick's office and why and remembered he'd been pissed to all hell, but he couldn't think of why he'd run. Had he been running after the man?

"We walked back into the club, and you freaked out. I mean, for you," Iris tacked on hastily. "You were… odd. I suggested we go to the bar and get a couple drinks to decompress, and you just started running."

"Oh, yeah, well, that would do it," Asad said before Law could respond. He blamed the accident for making him slow on the uptake.

"What? Why?"

"He's an alcoholic."

Iris

Staring at Master Asad, Iris tried to make the words make sense in her head. Little clues started clicking into place—the things she'd seen, things Law had said.

Oh. *Oh.*

"Asad." Law growled the other man's name. Like… like, actually *growled*.

"A recovering alcoholic," Master Asad corrected, giving Law a look.

Law glared back at him.

"So that's why you don't drink." Iris shook her head. "I thought you just wanted to maintain control before scening. Why didn't you tell me?"

"It hadn't come up yet." Law avoided her gaze, which wasn't easy to do since he was pretty much immobile. He winced as he moved his head. Yeah, she bet that hurt. He had a head wound that required two stitches and a hairline fracture on his clavicle. Pretty much any head movement was guaranteed to hurt.

Iris pressed her lips together and swallowed her words. He was avoiding the topic, which wasn't like him, but it wasn't hard to figure out he was doing so because he was ashamed. It was all over his expression and in his voice. If he hadn't been in a car accident, she might have gotten butthurt over the fact he hadn't trusted her with the information yet, but as it was, she was going to give him a pass.

"Oh good, he's awake!" Nurse Rhonda, a no-nonsense woman in her fifties, bustled in. Iris had been a little worried about the hospital staff's reaction to the leather, silk, and lace worn by her, Master Asad, and all their friends in the waiting room, but most of them had taken it in stride. Rhonda had assured Iris she loved "those kinds of books" and had asked several questions about whether they belonged to a "real club." She'd also promised to bring Iris some homemade penis candies. Iris kind of loved her.

She was tempted to talk to Master Patrick about hooking Rhonda up with some information about Stronghold and maybe a membership or at least a tour.

Especially when she bossed around a very reluctant Law, actually getting results and answers from him. Brusquely checking him over, Rhonda finally nodded her head in satisfaction.

"We'll get the doctor in here soon enough, but I think you'll be cleared to go as long as you have someone who can keep an eye on you." Rhonda smiled. "Now, no strenuous aerobics or odd positions, and since it's his right arm, if he likes to use a whip or a flogger, he should definitely wait at least six to eight weeks."

The slightly horrified, slightly awed expression on Law's face as he listened to Rhonda's at-home healthcare advice made Iris' sides ache as she forced down her laughter.

Glancing at Law, then back at Iris, Rhonda lowered her voice.

"Does he like to use a whip?"

"He favors electricity," Iris whispered, though, from Law's groan, he still heard her. Master Asad was grinning widely, not bothering to hide his amusement. "But he's not bad with a whip."

"You are in so much trouble, Iris," Law growled.

Rhonda's eyes lit up.

"Oh, that was very good. Damn, I wish I'd been recording that. Okay, I'll go get the doctor. I'll be back." She whisked out of the room, leaving Iris and Asad cracking up while Law's grumpy expression got even grumpier.

If some of Iris' laughter was a little hysterical because she was so relieved he was okay, no one else seemed to notice.

CHAPTER TWENTY-NINE

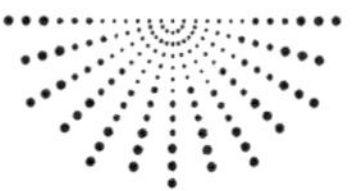

Being wheeled out to the hospital exit by a grinning Master Mitch wasn't among the highlights of Law's life, but on the other hand, he was touched by the number of people in the waiting room who cheered as they exited. It seemed as if half the club had turned out to wait for him.

His friends, Iris' friends, her brother and his friends, and a bunch of students who had gone through his classes. The hospital waiting room looked like a leather convention, though some people had found something to wear over their fetwear or had changed before their arrival. Iris was wearing the light trench coat-type jacket that went down mid-thigh and belted around her waist, which she'd had on when he'd first woken up. She wasn't the only one wearing some kind of long, light jacket. They still stood out because it was way too hot for a jacket outside, but not as much as if they'd been walking around in their underwear.

Everyone cheered when he was wheeled into the waiting room, getting up from their seats, relief on their faces. Even Iris' brother, Andrew, looked happy to see him, despite Iris' hand being firmly in Law's as she walked next to the wheelchair. They had a lot to talk about when they got some privacy, but right now, he was holding on tight to the fact she hadn't deserted him.

He still didn't remember running out of the club, though from the way she'd sounded when she'd talked about it, he was pretty sure he'd hurt her. It seemed he had a lot to make up for, even though he didn't remember it and wasn't sure how to make it up to her.

"So, everything's okay?" Connor was one of the first to approach, with Q right on his heels.

"He'll be alright, though he needs to rest that arm," Mitch said.

Law couldn't see Mitch since the nurse was behind him, but since his left arm was in a sling, it was pretty clear which one he needed to rest. What was confusing was his clavicle hurt almost as much when he moved his right arm as when his left was jostled. There really wasn't any winning.

"The fracture should heal pretty much on its own as long as he rests and doesn't use it too much. He'll need to follow up with his GP. He'll also probably need some help around the house to keep from overusing it."

"Iris has that," Asad said, coming up beside Law on the other side before anyone else could say anything. "We'll help, too."

Law scowled and turned to look up at Asad, though he didn't let go of Iris' hand.

"Don't put that on her. I'll be fine on my own."

"Nope, you'll need help," Mitch countered cheerfully. "Doctor's orders. And Dom's."

Iris giggled.

"Iris is going to spend tonight with grumpy pants here," Asad said, making Iris giggle again. Law scowled even harder. He hated feeling like they were talking over his head, and Asad knew it. With friends like these, who needed enemies?

"I can come over tomorrow," Connor said.

"Any updates on Douchebag Don?" Iris asked. More people were crowding around, though plenty hung back to give them space. Her brother and his fiancée Kate were two of the ones who had come up, and Andrew's scowl matched Law's.

"He's been arrested," Andrew said immediately. "Kincaid and Patrick are taking care of it. Patrick has the video feed of the parking lot, and one of the cameras has a view of the exit, so we can see that asshole plowing into Law's car. He was trying to claim it was an accident and that he panicked, which is why he drove away. Patrick said it looks pretty fucking deliberate, and following the confrontation in the club, there's definitely motive."

"Yeah, but that will mean having to go into club business," Law grumbled. He shook his head, then winced. Iris made a cooing sound as though she was trying to soothe him, her free hand going to his shoulder. "Not something I think any of us want to do."

"Well, he can't just get away with it," Iris said, squeezing his hand, a scowl forming on her face to match his.

"No, he can't. I have to think about it. Sometime soon when I can think." Which was not right now. His brain was still fuzzy, and with all the people around, it was far too loud.

Concern lit up Iris' features.

"Let's get you home, so you can rest," she said, looking around anxiously. Asad and Connor agreed, and things moved quickly after that, with Law having to do very little.

In fact, no one would let him do much of anything, which was extremely annoying. He wasn't a complete invalid, though hissing in pain every time he tried to do something normal, like getting into the car and putting on his seat belt, was no fun.

The seatbelt, in particular, hurt like a bitch until he settled back and stayed absolutely still, even though he was on the passenger side, and it wasn't going over his cracked clavicle. Thankfully. He couldn't imagine how much more painful that would be. Sighing, Law's eyes closed, almost of their own accord.

Despite the fact he'd spent about half an hour unconscious, he still felt tired. It appeared he had plenty of helpers heading home with him. They would be watching him closely. Scratch that—Iris would be watching him closely, at least for now.

Law still wasn't sure how he felt about that. He wanted her close, yet it chafed. Asad had spilled his secret before Law had had to chance to talk about his past with her himself, which was not how he'd wanted her to find out.

The door to the driver's side opened, and the air moved as Iris slid into the driver's seat beside him.

"Law, you have to stay awake."

The concern in her voice was clear, but like a coward, Law wasn't sure he could face her right now.

"I'm awake. Just resting my eyes."

"Well, open them, so I know you're awake. Or start talking… it's up to you. But if you're already drowsy, we should probably call Mitch or the doctor since you swore you were wide awake in the hospital." There was a no-nonsense tone to her voice Law had never heard before. It was kind of hot.

Not that he'd let her get away with bossing him around too much, but there was something enjoyable about seeing this other side of her. He hadn't known she had a bossy side. It made him want to wait for her to finish bossing him around, then flip her over his knee for a spanking.

Not that he could do that right now. He winced inwardly at the idea. The nurse hadn't been wrong when she'd said he shouldn't be wielding a whip for a bit. Something like picking Iris up would be well beyond him right now.

Dammit.

He hated feeling helpless. Another reason he shouldn't let her go home with him. He was an absolutely shit patient, and he knew it.

Law cleared his throat. "You know, I really will be okay. You don't have to—"

"I know you're not about to do something silly like tell me you don't need someone to stay with you," Iris interrupted, her tone conversational, but she gripped the steering wheel harder. "Not after your doctor, the nurse, *and* Master Mitch, who is *also* a nurse, all told you otherwise. Unless, of course, you don't want it to be me looking after you because you're dumping me, in which case you'd better spell that out clearly."

IRIS

To Iris' relief, Law did not immediately dump her, though she wasn't sure 'dump' was the right word. She wasn't even sure if they were boyfriend and girlfriend. Hell, she'd had to get his address from Master Asad because she hadn't been to his house.

He didn't start talking, but when she glanced over at him, his eyes were open, and he was looking out the window alertly, so she had to be satisfied with that.

Maybe she shouldn't have given him the option.

Start talking about all the things you haven't told me.

Right, she was sure that would have gone over well with a Dom.

Besides, the silence wasn't the worst thing in the world, giving her a chance to calm down. She finally felt like her heart was beating at a normal rate rather than being about to burst out of her chest. Everything had been a whirlwind, even after they'd arrived at the hospital.

Thank goodness for Asad, who had taken control of the paperwork, so she could cling to Law's hand while he was checked over. Obviously not during his x-rays. And thank goodness the emergency room hadn't been particularly busy. She was sure Master Mitch's presence hadn't hurt getting Law in to be seen quickly.

Now, it was just past midnight, and the caravan of cars behind her said tonight wasn't over yet, although they'd lost some of the entourage after leaving the hospital. She was pretty sure those following were Law's friends, though her brother and Kate shouldn't be too far behind them. They were stopping off at her apartment first to grab some things for her. The relief she felt at not having to deal with Noelle tonight was only tinged with a little guilt. Mitch, Domi, Avery, and Rae had all said goodbye to her at the hospital, along with hugs and the demand she contact them if she needed anything. Domi had said something about bringing food over to Law's tomorrow, which Iris would happily accept.

She didn't know how much help Law would need getting around the house, but she was sure, however much it was, he was going to fight it. Not having to make every meal would be helpful. It wouldn't be her cooking for him but him accepting the generosity of their friends.

Which was exactly how she planned to pose it to him if he tried to fight food donations. People liked to feel like they were helping.

Her included.

The GPS took her straight to his house. It was a very nice house for a guy living on his own. Then again, he was a lawyer. No garage, but there was a carport. Iris decided to park there, so he wouldn't have to walk far. It wasn't like his car was going to be arriving any time soon—it had already been towed to a shop. She wasn't an expert, but she was pretty sure it was going to qualify as totaled.

"Alright, stay there until I can come around and help you out."

"I don't need help." Growly Law was back. He was like a lion with a thorn in its paw. A really painful thorn, he discovered when he tried to undo his seatbelt with his right hand, and he needed to twist.

Shaking her head, Iris didn't comment as she got out of the car and walked around it. By the time she got to his door, he'd gone ashen under his regular skin tone, and little beads of sweat had appeared on his head.

"There's nothing wrong with needing a bit of help," she scolded as she leaned over to undo his seatbelt. Was it her imagination, or had she caught an odd glint in his eye when she'd said that? Iris straightened and stepped back but was ready to lend a hand if he needed it.

"Is he being a big baby?" Asad was stepping out of his car as well, shutting it with a small bang, before moving up the driveway toward her. On the street, Connor was parking his car. "I hope you know what you're in for. He's the worst when he's sick or injured."

"Asshole," Law grumbled as he let Asad help him out of the car. Iris tried not to be insulted that her help wasn't good enough. She knew Asad was the better choice when it came to pure muscle. "Like you're any better."

"True, but I'm self-aware," Asad teased. "Let's get you inside. You look exhausted, and so does Iris."

Law's mouth, which had started to open, snapped shut as he looked at Iris.

Wisely, she kept her mouth shut as well. She thought he looked a lot worse off than she felt, but she knew he'd also do for her what he wouldn't do for himself.

Doms.

So much easier to manipulate than they often realized.

CHAPTER THIRTY

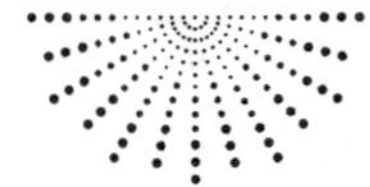

Iris

Waking up in Law's bed to a cat in her face was a bit unnerving. The whiskers brushing against her cheek had actually woken her. She knew Law had the cat, but the animal in question had been somewhere last night, probably because of the number of people. Asad claimed it was a demon cat, but Connor and Law had snorted, so she wasn't sure he was a reliable witness.

On the other hand, waking up to a cat, inches from her face, made her wonder if Asad had a point.

"Hello there," she murmured.

The cat—her name was Whiskers, Iris was pretty sure she remembered that correctly—head-butted her and meowed.

"Be careful. She can go from friendly to scratching in the blink of an eye, though she usually won't go for your face. Just your hands. Or chest." Law's eyes weren't open when Iris looked at him, and he didn't have a smile on his face, so she wasn't sure if he was kidding or not.

"Really?"

"Really. I've learned how to dodge. That's assuming she'll let you pet her. She won't with most new people." Law cracked an eye open, turning his head slightly. Whiskers meowed again. "I'm actually surprised she came out to say hello."

"Maybe I'm special," Iris said, gathering her courage to pet the cat. Whiskers purred, her back arched, followed by her butt, the way a cat normally did when someone ran their hand along its back. So far, so good.

"Oh, you're definitely spe— Fuck!" Law's murmured compliment, which would have been pretty hot, was cut off as he apparently forgot about his injuries and tried to roll toward her. Iris sat up so fast, Whiskers yowled and jumped off the bed, making her feel bad, but there was nothing to be done about that.

"Are you okay? What hurts? Oh my God, stop moving!" Iris' hands hovered over his chest. She didn't want to actually push him down because she was worried about hurting him, but she didn't want him trying to get up.

Dark eyes glittered at her.

"Iris, I am fine."

"All evidence to the contrary," she retorted. "You're making it worse by moving around."

His arm snaked around her, hand grabbing an ass cheek, and it was her turn to narrow her eyes.

"I am *fine.* I moved without thinking, but now that I'm more awake, I won't do it again. Relax." He squeezed her ass.

Iris let out a long, slow breath. She did need to relax. He was fine. Mostly. The injury had happened, and the lingering pain would not kill him even if she didn't like to see it.

"Okay… okay, but the doctor said you needed to rest, not grope me." She swatted at his arm. Law's eyebrows rose in that Dom way.

"You need to be careful, sweetheart," he said in a lethally quiet voice. "Just because I'm injured doesn't mean I can't find creative ways to keep you in line."

And boom, just like that, whatever morning-lady-wood would be called, Iris had it. Regardless of what Law said, there was no way they were doing *that* this morning, which meant she needed to get out of bed and away from temptation.

"Yes, Sir," she said, only a little cheeky. His eye narrowed as if he was trying to figure out if she was being sassy. "Um, what would you like for breakfast?"

Distract, distract, distract.

She had no doubt if pressed, he would make good on his word.

Law

His chest hurt more than it had yesterday, which made him cranky. Especially because he couldn't even help with breakfast. Iris made him pancakes and bacon, which smelled amazing and tasted even better, but he still hated being waited on in his own house. Breakfast conversation didn't improve his mood much, though she waited until he'd had half a cup of coffee before broaching the sensitive subjects.

"So... you were an alcoholic?"

Law appreciated that she didn't pussyfoot around the topic. She was watching his expression, eyes clear but nonjudgmental, and she didn't sound like she was upset.

"I was. Am. I'm recovering. Some days are harder than others. That's what happened last night. I was already feeling... off. Then everything with that asshole happened, and you suggested going to the bar, and I wanted to. I wanted to so badly, I had to get out of there." Huh. Law blinked. He hadn't remembered that until he'd started talking, and it wasn't so much a memory, but more that he'd started speaking, and the words kept coming, but he knew they were true.

"I'm so sorry. If I'd known..."

"You don't have to apologize. You couldn't have known. I didn't tell you." Law looked down at the syrup soaking into his pancakes. "I was also married before. We got divorced because she finally realized I wouldn't change. I went to rehab and got better, thinking that meant I was cured, that I could handle one drink... but things got even worse after that until she left. That was what finally made me realize how far gone I was."

Even now, the memory carried both relief and guilt, along with a healthy dose of gratitude.

There was a short moment of silence before Iris finally spoke.

"That must have been hard," she said cautiously.

"It was," he said grimly, raising his gaze to meet hers again. "Elaine took her marriage vows seriously. She stayed far too long, really, giving me a chance after chance after chance. Until she left, I really didn't understand how much I'd been hurting her. Hurting everyone I cared about. I knew she'd never leave me over anything trivial, and… truthfully, I'd started thinking she would never leave me at all."

"So, you quit then?"

Law smiled grimly. He didn't want Iris to have any illusions, but his chest tightened in fear. It wasn't only his clavicle hurting, but he was also worried about what she would say.

How she would react.

"I did… for a while. Got to the point where I thought I might win Elaine back. Then I went out with coworkers and thought, 'just one drink, what's the harm' because I hadn't learned my lesson the first time. One drink turned into another and another, and I was almost right back to where I started. That time I got help faster." He rubbed his chest where it felt the tightest, trying to massage the tension away, but it wasn't going anywhere. "I learned my lesson, though. I'm only a drink away from falling down the rabbit hole again."

Compassion filled Iris' eyes… and sympathy.

"What happened to Elaine?"

"She's moved on. Apparently, she's engaged now." Some of the heaviness tugging at him lightened.

"So you never tried to win her back?"

"No. Honestly, I'm not sure I wanted to. I was a different person by then, and she was as well." He turned his head away. "Mostly, I wanted to do right by her when I hadn't before. Then I realized doing right by her meant letting her go to find her happiness without the weight and baggage of our relationship. I don't know if I could have been happy, either. I would have spent my life trying to make everything up to her, and while she might have deserved that, she didn't deserve to be saddled with a husband who was there out of guilt as much as love. I wasn't *in* love with her anymore, either. We hadn't been together in years at that point. I still loved her, which meant letting her have what was best for her."

Iris nodded slowly, looking thoughtful.

Law wondered if she regretted asking. Regretted coming over last night. Regretted starting anything with him.

"So, still wanna go with the flow?" His smile was a little off, but he managed one all the same.

To his surprise, Iris laughed, which broke a lot of the tension.

"Yes, yes, I do. As long as you want to." She grinned at him.

Oh, he definitely wanted to.

IRIS

"I think we have two very different ideas of what 'go with the flow' means," Iris grumbled, panting for breath as Law shoved a plug in her ass.

Okay, so he wasn't exactly shoving, more like thrusting it back and forth as he worked it into her ass, but this was not how she'd expected her morning to go. The man had been injured in a car accident, had a hairline fracture and a head wound, and what did he want to do this morning?

Plug her.

Freaking Doms.

She hadn't argued. How was she supposed to argue with a guy who had been in a car accident the day before? He'd promised to stop trying to do things for himself if she'd wear a plug for the day.

A plug he controlled.

Offering myself for sexual torture to keep the Dom entertained, so he doesn't injure himself further and lets me handle everything he shouldn't.

Talk about using the tools she had.

"I think this is an excellent example of going with the flow," Law replied, sounding far too cheerful as he twisted the plug, eliciting a mewl. Iris wasn't an anal virgin. She had been plugged plenty of times during classes, but it had been a while since class, and she hadn't been doing it herself. "Besides, I want to fuck your ass, eventually, and I'm bigger than this plug."

Iris bit her lip as his words made her pussy clench. Yes, she knew he wanted to fuck her ass, and she wanted him to as well. Anal sex wasn't something she'd done in years because it was incredibly intimate. She hadn't wanted that intimacy with her recent dates or even her last boyfriend, but with Law… oh, yes. Yes, please.

The thickest part of the plug stretched her wide, then as it settled inside her, she gasped with relief as her ring of muscle closed around the thin part between the bulb and the base. The plug wasn't huge, but it made its presence known, especially when Law let her get back to her feet. Flushed and hot, she squirmed with the feeling of being so full.

It turned her on. Her ass was full, but her pussy was empty because he was prepping her for anal sex.

Who needs foreplay when you have intention and a plug?

"Good girl." Law patted her butt under the skirt she was wearing before his hand fell away. He'd insisted on the skirt once he'd seen it, and Iris had silently cursed Kate for bringing it. Giving a Dom easy access was hardly a good idea.

"So, what else are we doing today?" she asked brightly, trying to hide that she felt odd wearing a skirt and a plug outside of the club. Sure, she wore skirts, though rarely unless she was going on a date, but definitely not a plug. It made it impossible to forget the dynamic between them. "What were your plans?"

"Connor, Asad, and Q are coming over this afternoon," he reminded her, one corner of his lip tipping into a smile when she blushed. Yes, she remembered and knew Law would enjoy keeping her plugged while they were here. "Is there anything you need to do today?"

"I'm free as a bird."

Free and fairly relieved to be here, knowing she didn't have to go home to Noelle and that whole situation. Despite the plug up her ass and that she was incredibly aroused and didn't know when/if Law planned to relieve that need, she felt more relaxed than she had in days. Weeks. Maybe even months.

Which told her something important, but she would have to figure out that situation later. She didn't have time for it right now.

"Great. How about we sit and watch something? Movie, tv show… I can't do much else, according to the doctor." Law's expression soured for a moment, then cleared, and Iris was pretty sure she'd caught a hint of mischief.

Yeah, sure, plug the subbie, then make her sit. On the other hand, he was right. He was supposed to be resting today. They could go for a walk, but she didn't want to tire him out.

"What movie?" she asked suspiciously.

"Your choice." He pointed at the cabinet under his television. "I have some DVDs and also streaming."

Curious, Iris went to check out his DVD collection to get a hint of what he liked to watch. They'd talked about recent popular movies, but there was a difference between what someone was willing to talk about and what they actually invested money to purchase.

The biggest surprise in Law's collection was the Planet Earth collection. Otherwise, it was about what she'd expected from their conversations—superhero movies, Kung-fu movies, and a bunch of thrillers with one or two horror movies in the mix. All of which Iris enjoyed. She liked lots of different genres of movies.

However, she did feel like she owed Law a bit of payback. Sitting there all smug, happy to have her plugged and then waiting for her orgasm. Sure, sex was a no-go for a few days, but it's not like they had to have sex for her to get off.

Looking over her shoulder at him, she smiled.

"Have you heard of a show called Bridgerton?"

CHAPTER THIRTY-ONE

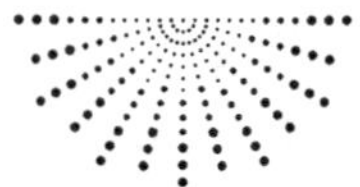

Law

Other than being unable to bend Iris over whenever he wanted, the first day of living with her was a lot of fun. Not that they were living together, but it felt a little like a test run.

All this, and more, could be yours...

Having a woman in his space again didn't feel nearly as odd as he'd worried it would. Iris fit. Whiskers seemed to think so, too. She'd spent most of the afternoon on Iris' lap, protesting vociferously whenever Iris had to get up. The only time she tried to claw Iris was when Iris *stopped* petting her.

The cat had good taste.

Law wanted Iris to pet him, too.

Maybe in a day or two when he was more recovered and not as sore all over... and he *was* sore. He knew she'd been trying to be bratty when she'd chosen Bridgerton for their viewing pleasure, but he'd meant it when he'd told her to choose whatever she wanted. She was spending her day off taking care of him, which deserved some recompense.

The show was more interesting than he thought it would be. They were about halfway through the first episode when Connor and Asad

"

showed up. They had to go back to the beginning so Law's friends could see the whole thing. Q had come a little later, but apparently, he'd already seen the whole thing and happily settled in to watch it again.

Iris seemed vaguely amused but happy, tucked under his arm for the duration of the binge-watch. About halfway through the afternoon, he let her take the plug out. He could tell by the way she was squirming that she was aroused, even after the plug came out and her television show choice had backfired. He was enjoying her self-inflicted torture and had a feeling he was having an easier time of it than she was.

After dinner, Law realized he probably needed to call his parents and let them know he'd been in an accident. He'd made the 'fun' conversation in his room. His mom had needed a lot of reassurance that she didn't need to come out and take care of him. Hearing that Iris was the one doing so seemed to help the most. She was thrilled to know his girlfriend was staying with him while he recovered.

Law realized that was probably the only reason she wouldn't show up on his doorstep—she wouldn't want to interfere now that he was finally moving on. It still amused him that his mom had replaced Elaine with Iris so quickly in her head when they hadn't even met.

It was satisfying yet worrisome. It felt as if things were moving really fast between him and Iris, as fast as his mom thought they were. He wasn't sure that was for the best, but he wasn't sure he wanted them to slow down. It might be fast, but it also felt right. Yet he couldn't get rid of the anxiety niggling him.

He wasn't sure he was prepared for everything a real relationship would bring—except he was kind of already in one, and it felt great. He felt as though he was waiting for the other shoe to drop, but if getting hit by a car didn't count as the other shoe, then what did?

Of course, there were still things to do about that. One of the first things his friends wanted to talk about was what he was going to do about Don.

"I won't press charges yet," he said when the topic came up.

"What?" Iris was clearly furious he would even consider letting the douche get away with deliberately ramming his car. Law hadn't been finished and shot her a look with one raised eyebrow. She quickly subsided, but her expression made it clear whatever he was going to say next, it better be good.

"I won't press charges if he'll promise to stay away from Cassidy." Law shook his head. "He was stupid enough to purposefully ram me, minutes after leaving Stronghold, in a place where he knew there were cameras. I don't trust common sense to keep him away from Cassidy."

"But not pressing charges will?" Iris looked dubious, and Law couldn't blame her. None of his friends appeared to be a fan of the idea, either.

"For at least a year. I can change my mind any time between now and then about criminal charges. I have friends in the state prosecutor's office. If I talk to them, they'll follow my lead. That'll give her a whole year without having to worry about him, and hopefully, by then, he'll have moved on and forgotten about her."

"Hmm." Asad sat back, letting his head fall back against the chair.

Law knew his friend was thinking over the implications. Like Law, he liked to see things from all angles. Though, it usually took him a lot less time to reach the conclusions Law did.

Iris was quiet for a long moment, then nodded.

"Especially if you do press charges or the prosecutor's office decides to, there will be a lot of explanations about Cassidy, Stronghold, and what preceded the crash, which wouldn't be good for anyone. Although he might not care about that if he's angry enough." Iris made a face. "I still can't believe he rammed you. I don't understand people like that. In what world did he think that was going to be at all helpful?"

"Anger management issues coupled with entitlement," Connor said. "Sadly, there's a lot of people in the world who fit that description. He probably thinks he's totally safe and that Law won't want to say anything about what led to the altercation or drag the club into it."

"I don't want to, but I will if I have to. I would do my best to keep

Stronghold and its members out of it. It's some protection for Cassidy, though." That would be difficult since all the events had occurred on club grounds, which was why Law had thought of his unusual proposal. Thankfully, he didn't have to worry about what his firm would think if they found out—they were all aware he was into kink. They didn't care, nor would they throw him out if the knowledge became public.

The world had changed a lot, and these days, it seemed like everyone was a little kinky. He doubted they would lose any clients over it. Hell, they'd probably gain some. That wasn't why he wanted people to come to him, though he had taken on some clients specifically because they were kinky—like Patrick and Stronghold.

Iris tilted her head as she looked up at him, snuggling in a little closer.

"You're such a good guy."

"Hey, hey, you two." Asad wagged his finger. "He's supposed to be resting. No taking advantage of the injured Dom and using him for your own nefarious pleasures."

Iris giggled.

"I doubt he'd mind," Q muttered, flashing a cheeky grin when Asad wagged a finger at him, too.

"The doctor might," Connor pointed out, then glanced at his watch. "We should get going. Is there anything you need before we head out?"

Warmth washed over Law as his friends got to their feet. Iris hadn't had to do much today because they'd shown up to lend their support. She'd spent most of the day relaxing next to him—exactly where he wanted her.

"We're good. Thanks for coming over."

"Of course. No, no, don't get up. We can see ourselves out." Asad wagged his finger again.

Iris burst into another fit of giggles, and Law shook his head.

"I hurt my clavicle, not my legs," he muttered but didn't mind settling back against Iris. Movement in general hurt and the longer the day had gone on, the more his shoulder around the fractured bone was hurting. He kept delaying taking his pills—he didn't want to trade one addiction for another—and it was definitely aching.

Iris

When her alarm went off, Iris yawned and stretched, bumping into Law before she remembered where she was. Quickly, she rolled over to turn it off. He made a grumbly noise, but it didn't seem like the sound had woken him. Good. He was sleeping hard, and he needed it.

Last night, he'd made sure she got what she needed. He had enjoyed watching her play with herself, following his directions, until she'd brought herself to orgasm, but he hadn't wanted a blowjob afterward. All he'd wanted was his pain pill—which showed just how bad of shape he'd been in. Iris had noticed he'd been pushing himself to the limits before taking one—and going to bed.

She'd felt a little guilty until he'd caught her expression. He told her to cut it out, or he'd prove he could punish her without a spanking or whip. If he'd wanted a blow job, he would have ordered her to give him one.

One of the things that had appealed to her about kink was there were no guessing games or trying to figure out what her partner wanted from her. He would tell her. Law would not deprive himself of anything he wanted when it came to her, so if he didn't want to get off last night, it was because he actually didn't want to get off.

Iris got herself together as quietly as she could. She still had to go in to the Hills today, but Law would stay home and rest. Tomorrow, he'd be back to work, though he'd told her he was planning to work from home this week, other than a meeting or two with clients, to make sure he was able to properly rest.

When she approached the bed again, dressed and ready for the day, she smiled. Law was still sleeping, but Whiskers had joined him, curling up in the depression Iris' head had left in the pillow. Goofy cat. That warm spot had been way too tempting.

Law's eyes opened as she leaned over him, and he blinked sleepily.

"You're up?" His voice was husky.

"Yes, go back to sleep. You have the day off. Olivia will bring you lunch and check on you."

Law groaned, which made her laugh. She gave him a quick kiss, careful not to put pressure anywhere but his lips, and scooted away.

"I'll see you later."

"See you later," he murmured, but Iris understood.

The rest of the day was spent taking care of the Hills' needs and answering text messages from her friends and others from Stronghold. Asad had wanted to know how Law was doing when she left that morning. Connor checked in to find out if she needed anything, Q offered to stop by with help for dinner, and that was just Law's friends. She told Q that Avery, Domi, and Rae were already planning to bring over what amounted to a feast and sent him the link to the meal schedule sign-up Julie had set up and texted to her.

It was already pretty full. Law was a popular guy, and apparently, no one wanted him to go without a meal because of his injury.

Her brother also checked in to make sure she was doing okay, and Kate texted to wish her luck living in sin with Law, making Iris crack up. She loved her soon-to-be sister-in-law so much. Not that they were living together, exactly, but she supposed they sort of would be for a bit. This week at least.

She really needed to let Noelle know she wouldn't be home for a while.

Call or text... that was the question. Swinging by the apartment didn't guarantee Noelle would be there, and just thinking about having to face Noelle in person right now made her stomach twist. Maybe that made her a bad person, but it was true.

The bit of guilt from not wanting to see Noelle in person was what compelled her to call since calling felt less impersonal than texting.

Her relief was visceral when Noelle didn't pick up, and it went to voicemail.

"Hey, it's me, Iris. Law was in a car accident yesterday, so I'll be spending this week at his house to help take care of him. He's okay, but he hurt his shoulder and needs some help. I might stop by home at some point to grab more clothes." She paused for a moment because even though she and Noelle were fighting, she didn't want to sound antagonistic. "Have a good week."

There. That was friendly enough without making it sound as though she was giving in.

Eventually, she would have to deal with Noelle, but right now, it was easier to stay away. Hopefully, doing so would help her take a step back and give her some perspective.

Her phone went off, and she tensed before she recognized her brother's ringtone. Strangely, she didn't feel the same tension she used to when he called. She didn't wonder what she'd done wrong or what he was going to hassle her about now. She was actually happy that he was calling her.

Maybe she was growing up.

"Hello?"

"Hey, flower. I just wanted to check in and see how you and Law are doing." Her brother's warm tone made her smile, and she hadn't forgotten how he'd lied about Law being her fiancé.

If only she'd known that all Law needed to do was get hit by a car to be welcomed…

"We're good. He's been in a little bit of pain, and he keeps trying to do things that he probably shouldn't, but for the most part, he's been good."

Andrew chuckled.

"Yeah, I can relate to that. I'm not the best patient. I'm sure you and Kate can get together sometime soon and commiserate."

"What? Something you're not perfect at?" Iris teased. "Say it isn't so."

Her brother snorted. "Don't tell Kate."

"Pretty sure she already knows," Iris drawled, rolling her eyes. "I need to get back to work, but thanks for calling."

"Have a good day. Let me know if you need anything, okay?"

There was her big brother, looking out for her as always. Iris didn't feel any of the resentment that sometimes popped up, only gratitude. Her brother was a good guy, even if they didn't always get along, which was normal for siblings. Sure, sometimes he treated her like a *much* younger sister, but for a while, she'd been acting out and relying on him to bail her out of everything.

Now, for the first time, it felt like he really saw her and that she'd grown up. He wasn't trying to take over the situation or tell her she should let someone else handle it. He was just offering help if she needed it. That felt pretty good.

"Thanks, I will."

Hanging up, Iris' lips curved in a smile. Despite everything, it was feeling like a pretty good day.

CHAPTER THIRTY-TWO

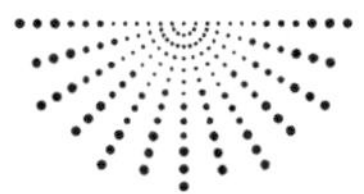

Since Olivia had taken over managing Marquis, which was closed on Mondays, she was the perfect person to keep him company. Especially if everyone wanted to make sure he wasn't doing anything he shouldn't be. They would all trust her to make sure he didn't.

It was definitely tempting. He had a feeling reaching into the upper cabinets to get himself a coffee cup was on the 'no-no' list, even though he was using his right hand. Thankfully, it was his dominant hand, but no one seemed to care about that. And it did hurt.

Fucking everything hurt.

Without Iris to distract him, it seemed to hurt even more.

By the time Olivia showed up with lunch for him, so he didn't have to prepare anything one-handed, he was actually relieved to hear the knock on his door. He wasn't prepared to open it and find her *and* Julie on the other side of it—not one Dominatrix, but two.

"How did I get so lucky to merit a visit from both of you?" he asked as he stepped back to let them in, eyes narrowing in suspicion. "I'm not that bad of a patient."

They laughed as Olivia set the bag she was carrying down on his kitchen table, and Julie sat on one of the chairs. Outside of Stronghold and Marquis, they were both more relaxed in dress and demeanor.

Olivia's red hair was pulled back in a loose ponytail, and she was wearing jean shorts with a green shirt that was fitted but not too tight.

Next to her, Julie looked even less imposing, and not just because she was so much shorter than Olivia. Her hair was in two low ponytails resting on her shoulders, and she was wearing a black sundress with bright sunflowers decorating it. If she walked into Stronghold like that, the Daddy Doms would come running before they realized their mistake.

"I didn't have any clients scheduled for today and wanted to talk to you about Cassidy," Julie explained, grinning. "And to see how you're doing, of course."

"Ah, I see where your real priorities are," he replied, laughing. He didn't take offense—Cassidy was where his priorities were as well. He'd already called the prosecutor's office and talked to Diego, who had been happy to do him the favor of not immediately pressing charges. He wasn't surprised Julie had been apprised of the situation —it was likely Cassidy would end up as one of her clients. He didn't know what the woman's situation was, but if Patrick didn't end up paying for her therapy, he knew Julie would move earth and heaven to get an abused sub the help they needed. "How is she?"

If anyone knew, it would be these two.

"She's doing pretty well, all things considered. We spent a good chunk of yesterday with her," Olivia said. Of course, they had. Law wasn't the least bit surprised. "Thankfully, they hadn't moved in together yet, though apparently, he'd been pushing her to."

Law whistled low and shook his head as he sat at the table with Julie. It was odd to be sitting and watching Olivia getting out dishes and utensils, but he knew she wouldn't accept his help. Heck, attempting to help would probably get him her best Domme look and an order to sit his ass down.

As much as sitting by his own choice grated, being scolded would be way worse.

"Was he abusing her before?"

"Emotionally, I believe, and some verbal, but according to her, Saturday night was the first time he'd really stepped out of line," Julie said. "I'm surprised he escalated so quickly and in public. I think he might have been pushing her to see how far she would let him go."

"Fucking shitgibbon," Olivia muttered, setting a dish down with a little too much force and a loud clang. She winced and glanced apologetically at Law. He just shook his head. He'd probably have done the same thing.

"Had they been to the club before?"

"Yes, and trust me, Patrick is shitting ferrets over how Douchebag Don managed to fly under the radar."

Despite the seriousness of the situation, Law had to smile at Olivia's use of Iris' insult for the asshole. It looked like that one was probably going to stick.

"I pointed out it's not like abusers show their true colors right away. They're good at fooling people. If they weren't, life would be a lot easier. Plus, they joined as an experienced couple, which meant he had them under the observation of a Dungeon Monitor the first few times they played."

Standard operating procedures for those in an experienced kink relationship who joined Stronghold was they didn't plan on scening with anyone outside of the relationship. Law didn't blame Patrick. They had plenty of safeguards in place, and every once in a while, an asshole would make it through, but he had every faith they wouldn't last long. Just like Don hadn't.

Patrick didn't hold back on kicking an abuser to the curb, though he was also invested in educating those who were intent on being good dominants but made a mistake here and there. If Don hadn't been so belligerent, if he had shown any remorse or understanding, he might have been given a second chance, though he would have definitely had to go through the Dominance class before he was allowed to play on the floor again.

They couldn't save everyone but did the best they could. He knew it would be cold comfort to Patrick, who was even more of a control freak than Law was. He anticipated there would be some changes made to how those with experience and in a relationship were vetted when they applied.

They chatted over lunch. Julie wanted to know what Law knew about Cassidy and the altercation. He was able to give her a good rundown on what happened from both his and Iris' perspectives, which should help her when talking to Cassidy.

Eventually, Olivia leaned back in her chair and pinned him with her gaze.

"How are things going with you and Iris?" She wasn't the only one curious. Julie leaned her chin on her hands, staring at him just as intently.

Law made a face at them, but he knew Olivia was asking with good intentions. She was a mother hen to the single submissives in the club, and even more so with Iris because she was good friends with Andrew.

"Good." He popped the last bite of his sandwich in his mouth.

The two women stared at him as if he might crack if they stayed silent long enough. Finally, Olivia tilted her head questioningly.

"Just good? No issues. No problems. You're in love and ready to sail off into the sunset and live happily ever after? Congratulations, this might be the first time this has happened to me." Her tone was more amused than anything else, but Law still found himself bristling.

"I didn't say I was in love or that I was ready for… that."

"For what? Happily-ever-after?" Olivia's gaze sharpened. "So, you're starting a serious relationship with Iris, but you haven't thought about where it might lead? She wants marriage, babies…"

"She doesn't know that she wants kids." He snapped out the words in reaction. Iris had said something to him in passing, but he hadn't realized it was a test until Olivia grinned at him.

"Ah, so you have talked about it."

"Well… I… we… not seriously. We're going with the flow." He knew he sounded defensive. He felt defensive. It wasn't often someone got under his skin, but Olivia made an art out of needling people and getting them to admit things they didn't want to.

Julie and Olivia burst out laughing.

Law crossed his arms over his chest, trying not to scowl or feel like they were laughing *at* him. Except they were, but he wouldn't take it personally because even as he'd said the words out loud, he'd known how ludicrous it sounded.

"Since when,"—Julie was laughing so hard, she had to gasp out the words through her laughter—"have you ever… gone with the… flow?" Her voice actually cracked on the last word, which made Olivia laugh even harder and lean sideways as though her muscles could no longer hold her up, putting her in serious danger of tipping over onto the floor.

Law almost wanted to see it happen but didn't want to encourage them.

"I can go with the flow if I want to. It's working."

"Oh… oh, honey…" Olivia wiped away the tears that gathering under her eyes. "Law. Seriously. You are completely incapable of going with the flow. You're letting Iris stay here with you indefinitely. Whether you've admitted it to yourself, your brain has already done a risk assessment and decided it was worth it. You're halfway in love if you're not already there, and I would be willing to bet, within a year, you'll be engaged." She looked at Julie, who was nodding. "Don't suppose you'd want to take that bet."

"Hell, no, I'm not giving my money to you that easily," Julie scoffed.

Law opened his mouth to tell them he wasn't in love with Iris, he wasn't anywhere near falling in love with her because it was far too soon, and he didn't have those feelings for her.

He closed his mouth because… well… shit.

***

Iris

The difference between heading home to Law versus heading

home to Noelle was stark. There was no unhappy churning in her gut, no bracing for what might be thrown at her when she opened the door, no mentally preparing herself for an encounter. She hadn't realized she did all that before going home until she didn't have to.

She was actually excited about the end of the day, eager to rush from her job to her car and head out instead of dreading it. She hadn't realized how much she'd dreaded it until, again, she didn't have to.

She was so high on anticipation and happiness, when she opened the door, she called out in true 'I love Lucy' fashion.

"Honey, I'm home!"

Looking up from his spot on the couch, Law laughed, and Whiskers hissed from her spot on his lap. She looked as if she'd been enjoying being petted, but since her peace had been disturbed, she jumped up and stalked off down the hallway with her tail in the air.

"Oops," Iris said sheepishly as she watched the cat stalk off. She set down her purse on the table by the door.

"Don't mind her. She'll be back in five minutes to say hello." Law was grinning, so Iris figured he wasn't too upset about Whiskers' abrupt departure.

Unable to contain her joy to end her day in a place where someone was happy to see her, and she didn't have to pick apart words for hidden meanings, Iris bounced over to say hello. Law winced but pulled her onto his lap.

"Law!" Iris squirmed but was afraid to move around too much because she didn't want to accidentally hurt him. She wasn't pressed against his arm in the sling, but she was definitely brushing against it with every move she made. "I'm going to hurt you."

"It's worth the pain." He used a deep, gruff voice that wasn't his own as though he was trying to sound extra manly, and Iris cracked up.

Playful Law was still a surprise each and every time, and she didn't think she would ever get tired of seeing him. Now that she knew more about him, she had to wonder if this was who he used to be. It didn't matter, though. She liked him as he was—stern and bossy most of the time with a hidden playful side.

Like a grumpy cinnamon roll.

The thought made her giggle again.

"Kiss me."

Huffing, Iris shook her head and gingerly bent to kiss him. Was it awkward? Yes. Would it have been easier if she'd been standing instead of on his lap? Absolutely.

That didn't stop Law from running his hand up her back to her neck and holding her in place, so he could kiss her the way *he* wanted instead of delicately as she was trying to kiss him. Which was pretty freaking hot, even if it made her worry she was hurting him.

Slowly, she relaxed into it since he didn't seem to be in pain. The hard bulge forming against her side indicated that at least one part of him was feeling just fine.

When he flinched, Iris tried to jump up and pull away, but his hand was still wrapped around the back of her neck, so he ended up coming with her before resisting. She fell back against him, and he groaned before gritting his teeth against the clear pain he was in. Iris squeaked as she was dropped to the floor, immediately getting on her knees, her hands on his thighs as she peered up at him in horror.

"Shit! I'm sorry… Shit. Are you okay?"

"Yeah, just give me a sec," Law gritted out between his teeth. He was panting for breath but otherwise seemed okay. Iris' hands moved of their own accord, rubbing up and down his thighs, trying to soothe him. The steady motion soothed her as well, and her racing heart began to slow as she watched him relax.

He opened his eyes and looked at her, leaning back against the chair.

"Better?" she asked, peering up at him worriedly. He didn't look too ashen, but that had clearly hurt.

"Better." Nodding and letting out a long, slow breath seemed to relax him even more. A smile quirking the side of his mouth, he tilted his head and lifted an eyebrow. "You know, if you really want to make it better while you're down there…"

Despite everything, Iris laughed again. If he was making jokes, hopefully, that meant he wasn't in too much pain.

Though, it turned out he wasn't joking so much.

It was the first time Iris had to be careful giving a blowjob. She didn't want him moving around too much, so it took a little longer than usual, but he didn't seem to mind. Neither did she. When he took her back to his room afterward, he plugged her and used a vibrator to bring her to her own exuberant orgasm.

CHAPTER THIRTY-THREE

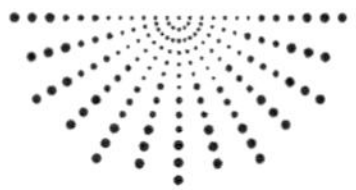

As much fun as Iris was having, staying with Law, she knew she would eventually have to go home. The first week passed way, way too quickly. It felt way too natural to be living with him.

Every night she went to his house, which felt more like coming home than going to her apartment had for a while. They always greeted each other with a kiss, even on days when he was grumpy from the pain or from something that had happened at work. On his worst day, she still felt more welcomed and at home than she did with Noelle. At least he had good reasons for being out of sorts.

She loved getting him back to a good mood by teasing him or going full-on service-sub and making him comfortable until he finally relaxed.

They spent the evenings watching tv, playing board games, or just sitting next to each other and reading. One night, he was working while she read, but it amounted to the same thing. It was comfortable. Safe. The kind of life she'd always imagined living when she'd imagined living with a boyfriend.

She never wanted to leave.

A few times, she caught Law looking at her a little funny and worried she was overstaying her welcome. When she brought it up, he shut it down immediately. He liked having her there, and she was making his life easier by being there, and that was that. He wanted her to stay another week.

Whether he actually needed her to—he was moving much better, they didn't need to be worried about his head wound anymore, and he was grumpy about having things done for him at the moment—was unclear.

So, she wasn't sure what was going on in his head and was a little afraid to ask. All she thought about was how much she wanted to stay.

Did he have quirks about how he wanted things kept in the house?

Yes.

Was she still more comfortable being in his house than she was in her own apartment, where all her stuff was?

Yup.

Granted, he'd made room for her. He had a whole closet he hadn't used for anything other than a few boxes of clothes he hadn't gotten around to donating yet—Q and Connor had taken care of that for him. Her stuff was strewn around his bathroom, in his shower, and across the counter, and he didn't seem to mind. She was pretty tidy but had a lot more stuff than him in general

Friday was the day. She'd go home, switch out her clothes, do a few things around the apartment, then head straight back to Law's. Even knowing she would not stay there, her chest knotted up at the idea of having to go back to the apartment at all.

I really need to find a new living situation.

It was so much worse now that she'd had a taste of doing something else.

This week had been great, but it was way too soon to suggest something as big as moving in with Law. She would hate for him to think she only wanted him for his house, which was far, far from the truth. Moving into the apartment in her dad's basement sounded pretty good by comparison to continuing to live with Noelle, but she would rather move into the apartment in her dad's basement than make Law feel she was using him for a place to live.

Driving into the parking lot, Iris' tension ratcheted up another notch when she saw Noelle's car. It didn't necessarily mean she was home since she relied on Tyler a lot for rides.

Pressing her ear to the apartment door, Iris bit her lip as she listened and waited. She didn't hear anything, no television or conversation. Mentally crossing her fingers, Iris let out a long, deep breath and put the key in the lock. The door opened to an empty apartment, and she sighed in relief, the knot untwisting in her stomach.

Crap. Too soon.

The unraveled knot pulled tight when she heard a door in the back of the apartment open, then Noelle appeared in the hallway. She'd been in her room, but Iris hadn't heard a thing.

"Oh, finally checking in, are you?" Noelle asked sarcastically, putting her hands on her hips. "A little late, don't you think?"

"What are you talking about?" The question popped out of Iris' mouth before she could think. Dammit. That was an open invitation for Noelle to unload, and her friend took immediate advantage.

"I'm talking about the fact you've been gone *all week* and haven't called or texted me once to see how I'm doing." Still standing in the middle of the hallway, Noelle didn't look as if she would be moving any time soon, which meant Iris had to deal with her since she couldn't get past her.

She was barely two steps inside the apartment, and Noelle was already pissing her off.

She *was* getting mad instead of wallowing in guilt, which was what she would have done in the past and what she was pretty sure Noelle intended. There was still a little part of her that felt bad she hadn't checked in on Noelle, that she'd been relieved to be away from her, but a part of her that worried she was a bad friend... a really tiny part.

"I've been taking care of Law. You got my message, right? About how he was in a car accident?"

Noelle rolled her eyes. *Rolled. Her. Eyes.*

Iris' nails dug into her palms as her hands turned into fists, her jaw aching from how hard she was clenching her jaw shut.

"He isn't even actually your boyfriend, and he was fine, right? Did he really need you all week? And what happened to chicks before dicks?"

"We're in a relationship, even if we haven't put a label on it yet, and yes, he needed me."

"What, he has no friends to help him out?" Noelle snorted. "Well, at least he and I have something in common."

It was a verbal jab that would have once hit Iris right in the solar plexus, but it didn't have the same weight. It didn't sting the same way. She was no longer afraid Noelle would end their friendship. There was no driving need to fix things because she'd reached the end of her rope.

She just wanted Noelle to leave her alone. Iris wasn't a bad friend, and she knew it. Not only that, but being away so much had ripped the blinders from her eyes. All the little comments, Iris always brushed them off as Noelle not realizing how they sounded…

No. She was pretty sure now Noelle knew exactly how they sounded. Even if she didn't, that didn't make it okay. Especially since when Iris pointed out how it sounded and how Noelle's words made her feel, Noelle was never willing to change her perspective or apologize. She always brushed it off or turned it back around on Iris.

Iris tested it, just in case.

"That's really hurtful. We've been friends for a long time, and not being around for one week while I was taking care of… of someone I care about after they were in a car accident does not negate that. You didn't check in with me to see how I was doing, and I'm not mad." Iris kept her tone reasonable, taking deep breaths to stay calm.

Realizing she didn't have to put up with this, that she was going back to Law's tonight, really helped. She wasn't trapped anymore and didn't particularly care if Noelle was mad at her. Well, mostly. At least, she didn't care enough to stick around and grovel when she knew she wasn't in the wrong so that Noelle wouldn't be mad at her.

"I didn't check on you because you made it clear you didn't want to hear from me when you left me that voicemail, then never contacted me again." Noelle huffed. "Well, guess what, you won't have to put up with me any longer. The lease is up in two months. I contacted building management yesterday with our sixty-day notice that we'll be moving out. So, I hope you're happy."

Iris gaped. Of all the things Noelle could have said, she hadn't expected *that.*

"What? You can't just... we didn't even... what the hell, Noelle?" She didn't want to keep living with Noelle, but she wouldn't have contacted the management office without at least talking it through first.

"Oh, now you care. Maybe you should have thought about that before you treated me like shit." Noelle was looking for all the world like the injured party, hurt, anger, and betrayal clear in her expression. She meant it, and that was the thing that messed with Iris' head the most.

She could feel the waves of emotion coming off of Noelle and knew they weren't fake. Noelle was visibly, palpably upset.

That was why Iris ended up questioning herself all the time.

Not this time.

She was done.

She was so, so done. Noelle wasn't acting rationally—twisting the truth, making it into something it wasn't, making Iris out to be something she wasn't. She was truly upset, but she didn't have to be.

"I'm not treating you like shit. You are the one making decisions that affect both of us without talking to me. You are the one who didn't bother to reach out to see how I'm doing while accusing me of doing that. You are the one twisting things around." Iris was holding her ground and not giving in this time. Not again.

"Great, and now you're gaslighting me! I can't wait till the end of this lease!" Throwing her hands in the air, Noelle whirled around and stalked into her room, slamming the door behind her.

Tears formed in Iris' eyes, but she quickly wiped them away. She wouldn't shed one tear over this stupid fight. She wouldn't. This wasn't her fault.

Right?

LAW

The moment Iris returned, Law knew something was wrong. She'd been a little off that morning before leaving for work, but nothing compared to how she was now. She was jittery, and the smile on her face wasn't anywhere close to being genuine.

It was all Law could do to keep from frowning the moment he saw her, but he didn't want to add to her upset by having her misinterpret the expression on *his* face.

She set the bag in her hand on the floor, which made it even harder not to frown. It was a reminder she'd gone back to her apartment. Whatever the problem was, he would bet good money it had to do with her roommate.

"Hey, how was your day?" If she didn't want to talk about it right away, he didn't want to push her. Moving toward her, he put his hands on her hips. She tilted her head back for a kiss, sighing before his lips even touched hers. Not an unhappy sigh, more a sigh of relief —as though she was happy to be there, as if his mere presence made her feel better.

Talk about an aphrodisiac. Having that kind of effect on her was like catnip to his ego. He loved knowing that just being in his presence could calm her.

Sliding his hands around her waist, he pressed them flat against the small of her back, keeping her trapped against him as he kissed her. Iris kissed him back, careful where she placed her hands and arms. She'd been diligent all week about making sure not to put pressure anywhere that might hurt him.

Ending the kiss, he enjoyed the feel of her leaning against him—on his right shoulder, definitely not the left. The sling between them was still uncomfortable, but at this point, he'd gotten used to it.

"Are you gonna answer my question?" he asked gently.

"What was the question again?"

Law snorted softly. "I asked how your day was."

He felt, as much as heard, her sigh. She rubbed her nose against the side of his neck, and with tiny movements of their bodies, he swayed them. Not rocking her, exactly... but sort of.

"It started off pretty well, but when I went to the apartment to switch out my clothes for the next week, Noelle was there." As Iris told him about the confrontation, Law found it more and more difficult to hold his tongue, but he did because Iris clearly needed to get it all out.

Though she sounded defeated when she started, she got angrier as she spoke, and he sure as hell didn't want to stop that. He hated the way Noelle treated Iris—and no, he didn't need to meet the woman to feel that way. Iris self-examined everything she had said to Noelle, and he could see her doubt that she remembered the events correctly, despite how self-aware she was.

Law could feel her distress growing along with her anger. When she got to the part about Noelle ending their lease, he had to hold back a sigh of relief and joy. Even though he didn't want her to live in that toxic situation anymore, Noelle going behind her was fucked up. Unfortunately, there wasn't much she could do about it.

Turning her head, she pressed her forehead against his shoulder, letting out another long sigh.

"Now, I have to live another two months with her while I find a new place, and just thinking about being in the same apartment makes my skin crawl."

"So, move in here." The thought had been in his head almost from the first moment she'd started talking, and it hadn't gone away. It was a crazy thought—definitely, a thought unlike him—but it hadn't gone away. In fact, it had only gotten stronger.

They'd fallen into a routine almost immediately. A good one. He loved spending his evenings with her, whether they were sitting side by side on the couch, doing separate things, watching something together, or at the table playing a game. He didn't want her to leave.

"What?" Iris jerked backward, staring up at him in shock, but didn't look horrified by the idea. More disbelieving, as though she couldn't believe he had suggested it but hoped she hadn't heard him wrong. "I… isn't it too soon?"

Maybe, but it was also too soon for him to have fallen in love with her, and look how that had turned out.

"It doesn't have to be permanent. You could move in here while you're looking for a new place to live when the lease is up. That way, you can keep paying for the apartment. I don't need a roommate financially, so you wouldn't have double expenses." The more he spoke, the more he liked the idea… a trial run living together.

If it worked, he'd make sure the trial run went on forever.

Iris blinked. Her lips firmed.

"I would want to help pay for utilities and food," she said.

"Not while you're helping me as I heal," he countered. "Really, you're doing me a favor. It's just an extension of what you're already doing, but after that, you can pay." When she opened her mouth to argue, he shook his head. "Go with the flow, remember?"

A little light appeared in her eyes, and as the tension melted away from her body, he could feel her relax against him.

"Live here while I look for a new place… I could do that… if you're sure." She searched his gaze, worried he might change his mind at any moment.

Fat chance.

If they lived together for a bit, maybe wanting to tell her he loved her wouldn't feel too soon.

"I wouldn't have offered if I wasn't sure."

The smile that lit up her face was the best one yet.

CHAPTER THIRTY-FOUR

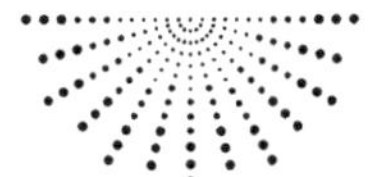

Moving Iris out of her place into his had been almost anticlimactic. He'd been looking forward to meeting Noelle face to face and seeing what she was like, but she'd made herself scarce when he and the rest of Iris' friends and family had shown up to move her stuff out. She and Iris had been communicating solely by text, and he was pretty sure Iris preferred it that way, but he'd wanted to see the woman in person.

It was for the best that she wasn't there. Iris was relaxed and having fun, though she kept looking around, expecting Noelle to pop up out of nowhere. The relief on Iris' face when she didn't see her was worth missing out on meeting the now ex-roommate.

"Hey. So, I hear you're the man who's going to be living in sin with my daughter." The deep voice jolted Law out of his reverie, and he actually jumped as someone appeared at his side.

Turning, an older man, who looked an awful lot like Andrew, was standing next to him. Andrew grinned at him, clearly enjoying Law's discomfort.

Sadist.

Iris' father didn't sound combative, but his words weren't particularly encouraging. As Law met his gaze, he saw the hint of mischief in Iris' dad's eyes. If he didn't know Iris as well as he did, he might have missed it, but the two of them looked very much alike at that moment.

"It's a very respectful sin," he responded solemnly, causing Iris' dad to let out a burst of laughter.

"You'll do." He clapped Law on the shoulder with approval, then released Law's shoulder to hold out his hand. "I'm Diego."

"Lawrence, but everyone calls me Law." Though he'd tried to fight it for a while, he felt more like Law than Lawrence now. "It's nice to meet you. Iris has told me a lot about you."

"She's told me a little about you," Diego said, waiting for Law's reaction, then grinning when he didn't get one. "Which is a lot more than she usually tells me about anyone she dates."

"Only good things, I hope."

"Absolutely. Andrew's the one who says all the bad things."

"Hey, no, I don't," Andrew protested, scowling at his dad, who snickered.

Law grinned. Iris' dad was pretty much exactly how she'd described him.

"I'm going to get back to work, though I don't think there's much left to do," Law said. Diego stayed by the cars they were filling up, opening the back of his van, which had all the seats down, so there was plenty of cargo space to fit extra things.

So many people had offered their vehicles, Iris hadn't needed to rent a moving truck. She also hadn't had to be brave to pack her stuff while Noelle was there. This morning, Law had brought her over to pack. Rae, Domi, and Avery had joined them not long after, and by the time everyone else started showing up, there were boxes ready to be taken down. Now the flow of boxes had slowed considerably, and they really had more people than they needed.

Passing Mitch and Brian on the stairs from the building to the parking lot, each carrying a box, Law nodded his head at them.

*I*RIS

Seeing her empty room was a relief but kind of terrifying. It was crazy how quickly they'd moved everything out. She'd lived here with Noelle for almost four years, and it had only taken about four hours to remove her presence.

Things had gone a lot faster since she'd had so much help.

"I think we're done in here," Rae said, straightening from taping up the last box she'd packed. She looked around and grinned. "Now, we move you into Master Law's."

"Temporarily," Iris said quickly. She didn't want anyone getting the wrong ideas.

"Uh-huh, temporarily." Rae finger-quoted the word.

"It is!" Iris narrowed her eyes. "I'm going to keep looking for a more permanent place. It's way too soon for us to be moving in together."

"Yeah?" Rae lowered her voice, glancing toward the bedroom door. There was a lot of chatter from the main room, where everyone else was. With everything pretty much finished, they were hanging out and waiting to head to Law's, where most of Iris' things would go in his basement. "Wanna move in with me? I'm pretty sure Domi's going to be moving out soon."

"I… oh…" Iris floundered at the unexpected offer. Her initial response was 'no,' although she knew it should be 'yes.' "Um, well, I don't know if I want to do another friend housing share, I mean, you know… no offense."

"None taken," Rae smirked. "Just out of curiosity, what was your *very* first thought before you reached for the whole not wanting to live with a friend again?"

"Ugh, that I don't want to leave Law's yet." Iris rubbed her hands over her face. "This is so going to blow up in my face, isn't it? We haven't even said the L-word yet. This is too soon."

"Kind of late to realize that now." As usual, Olivia blew into the room with a presence that was almost physical. The Dominatrix was dressed casually in shorts and a green tank top with Stronghold's logo across the chest. Her hair was piled on top of her head in a casual, messy bun. Somehow, she still exuded the same authority she did when she was wearing a business suit or her leathers. It was a skill.

"For what it's worth, I think you and Law are on the same page. You two should probably try talking to each other about what that page looks like." Olivia walked over and picked up the box Rae had just packed, hefting it easily. "Come on, let's go get you moved into Law's."

She winked and walked out of Iris' bedroom, leaving Iris and Rae staring after her.

"I hate it when she does that," Iris muttered.

"Does what?" Rae asked, joining Iris as they followed Olivia.

The front room was already emptying, but Law was there, standing by the front door and waiting for Iris.

"Drops the advice I want to take the least, then dashes off before I can ask her *how* I'm supposed to accomplish it." She supposed it wasn't that she didn't know how to talk to Law. She just didn't know how to talk to Law about her feelings.

They were supposed to be going with the flow, not making plans to move in together as a couple.

"Ready to go?" Law asked as she reached him, holding his hand out. Rae gave her a sympathetic smile before ducking out the door and leaving both of them there.

Pausing, Iris turned to look around, giving the main room one last look. Shockingly, it didn't look all that different. Most of her stuff had been in her room, the bathroom, or the cabinets in the kitchen. Noelle's things had taken up most of the main room.

"Yup." Even though she wasn't sure where this thing with Law would lead or if moving in with him even temporarily was a good idea, she knew she didn't belong here any longer. She put the check for the next two months of utilities on the kitchen table. Locking the door behind her one last time, the sense of relief was profound.

She didn't leave the key. Sadly, she wasn't sure she trusted Noelle to return it to the manager. Tomorrow, Iris would take it to the management office, where she'd also sign her end-of-lease paperwork preemptively and also give them her portion of the rent, which would be noted. After that, everything would be up to Noelle.

Iris was done.

Sitting in the backseat of Mitch's car with Law, she took out her phone and stared at it, trying to figure out what to say to Noelle that wouldn't sound antagonistic. Finally, she settled on, *I'm all moved out. Maybe I'll see you around sometime.*

Send.

Her phone quacked almost immediately with a message from Noelle. She could see Mitch glancing in the rearview mirror, and Law looked over, then away, reaching out his hand for her to hold, resting it on the middle seat between them.

Don't think you can come crawling back when everything blows up in your face.

Ugh.

"Everything okay?" Domi asked.

Iris let the phone drop into her lap. Out of the corner of her eye, she could see Law looking over at her again. Reaching to take his hand, her fingers entwined with his. She didn't have to answer Noelle right now. She didn't have to think about being worried Noelle was right. Regardless of what happened with her and Law, she definitely wouldn't be crawling back to Noelle.

Heck, she would happily move in with Rae if things soured with Law.

"It will be."

There was a moment of silence that wasn't exactly awkward but wasn't *not* awkward, either. Then Mitch cleared his throat.

"So, who's looking forward to Renn Fair?" he asked

"Me, me, me!" Domi's hand shot in the air, and she was practically bouncing in her seat, which made Iris laugh.

"Me, too!" She grinned at Law as he squeezed her hand. "I haven't been since I was a little kid. I can't wait." It gave her something to look forward to and think about other than her worries.

———

Law

With Iris' things joining his, Law felt more at home rather than less. He liked seeing bits of her around the house. They'd ended up unpacking a fair amount of her stuff, though some things went in the basement. Rewarding their friends who helped them move with pizza and beer made him feel like he was in college again.

Iris' dad stayed for dinner, which was a lot of fun. He clearly enjoyed giving his kids a hard time, and he adored Kate. While Law wouldn't say Diego was going to adore him anytime soon, he thought he'd made a decent first impression.

"Wow." Iris closed the door behind her family, the last to leave, and leaned against it for a moment. With her hair up in a messy bun, wearing a t-shirt and loose shorts, she looked right at home in his house.

Law didn't think she'd ever looked more beautiful. While it was always enjoyable to see her dressed up in fetwear, he enjoyed seeing her like this just as much. She caught his gaze and smiled at him.

"So… now what?"

Smiling back at her, Law raised his hand and crooked his finger.

Standing in the middle of the room, he waited until she stood in front of him before he cupped her chin and tilted her head back. Lowering his lips to hover just above hers, he heard her swift intake of breath when he stopped short of giving her a kiss.

"Now, we go back to the bedroom and celebrate."

Closing the gap between them, he kissed her deeply. Other than his clavicle, most of his aches and pains had resolved during the week. He pulled her in close, feeling her body press against his. He was moving easier, and it showed.

Iris' hands slid up his chest, gently, and over his shoulders to cling to him.

He turned, angling her in the right direction, so when he broke the kiss, he could spin her around so she was facing the hallway. Law gave her ass a short, sharp smack.

"Get moving, subbie."

Iris' giggles echoed down the hall as she scampered ahead of him, peeking over her shoulder to make sure he was following before giggling again and dashing ahead. Chuckling, Law made his way after her, feeling a bit like a predator on the prowl, his erection thickening with anticipation as he paced after her.

She was waiting for him in the bedroom. Trapped by choice. Eagerly shifting back and forth on her feet, waiting for him.

"Strip, sweetheart," he ordered. "I'm going to get a few toys to play with."

Nothing crazy. Definitely no impact toys. As much as he enjoyed them, he didn't think he was quite recovered enough for that yet. There were a few other things he could play with. Fetching them from the drawer where he kept his favorites, he turned around to see Iris already naked and kneeling in a perfect submissive pose next to the bed.

Well.

Almost perfect.

Her knees were spread, hands resting on the tops of her thighs, palms upward, breasts thrust out... but instead of having her head down, she was watching him. Little brat. Law's lips twitched.

She was incorrigible. Nothing but trouble, as he'd once told Patrick, but she was *his* trouble, and he planned to keep her.

"Naughty girl," he said, shaking his head. "You're supposed to be looking at the floor." He raised his eyebrows at her.

"Sorry, Sir." Iris lowered her gaze but didn't sound particularly sorry.

Amused, Law took a moment to observe her, his thoughts turning over in his head. She peeked up at him before dropping her gaze again.

"Do you think I can't punish you in my current state?" He was curious. Iris had a tendency to push playfully, but he wanted to know if part of the reason she was doing so now was she thought she was safe.

"Um, no, Sir?" There was a hint of question in her voice.

"I can assure you, sweetheart, injured or not, I can make a naughty girl regret her actions."

Iris might be a naughty girl in the fun sense of the word, but she was also a subbie who liked a bite of pain with her sex. She'd not only been missing out on sex this week, she'd also been missing out on the pain and punishment she craved.

The flare of need in her eyes confirmed his guess that she'd needed a little something more than he'd given her. Well, that was easily remedied.

"Offer me your breasts, sweetheart."

It was a good thing he'd already picked out the electric nipple clamps instead of the regular ones.

This was going to be fun.

CHAPTER THIRTY-FIVE

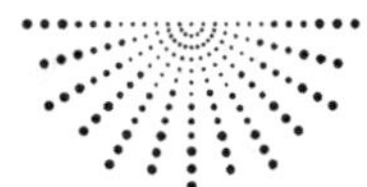

IRIS

It was a damn good thing she trusted Law as much as she did. Her body quivered when she got a good look at the clamps he intended to put on her. The actual clamps weren't that intimidating, but the wires and the little box they were connected to did.

Holy shit!

"Um, are those electric?" she asked, cupping her breasts the way she was supposed to and glancing nervously up at Law.

His smile was not at all reassuring.

"Why yes… yes, they are."

Warm fingers rubbed her breasts, playing with her nipples and making the tiny buds even harder. Iris' insides clenched as Law stood above her, fully clothed, toying with her body, preparing her for pain and pleasure. She wanted the pain. She did. In fact, she'd been bratting a little, hoping to get it.

But she wasn't sure she wanted electric nipple clamps. She hadn't even known electric nipple clamps were a thing.

That's why you don't poke the Dom, dumbass. It gets your nipples electrocuted.

Granted, she was hardly the only sub to poke a Dom, but she'd never heard about any of them having their nipples electrocuted. This was what she got for poking Master Law, who she knew was into electrical play.

You didn't think he'd already shown you everything, did you?

At the very least, she'd kinda thought he'd already shown her most of what he could or would do.

Her treacherous nipples were getting harder as he played with them, uncaring of their fate. The thought was a little exciting, even if it was terrifying. If it was anyone else but Law, she was pretty sure she'd be safewording right now.

If you were really smart, Law wouldn't be an exception.

Except that dangerous and painful was also arousing and exciting because that was how her brain worked.

She sucked in a breath as he applied the first clamp. The tight pinch was no worse than any other clamp, sending a jolt of pleasure and pain through her body. She moaned as he applied the second one, his eyes scanning her face as he watched her reaction. On her knees with her hands still holding her breasts, offering them to him to torture, she was right on level with his cock and could see the hard bulge at the front of his pants.

"Now what?" she asked as he straightened, holding the little box in his hand.

Law's eyebrows lifted, and he pushed something on the controller. A little shock hit both breasts, and Iris squealed, jerking. It was like a static shock, straight to her nipples, which hurt like crazy... but also fueled the throbbing need between her legs.

There was only the one hard shock, then the intensity drew back, turning into a steady pulse that made her moan again. Her fingers had tightened during the initial shock, squeezing her breasts, and now they did again as the pulses throbbed through her.

"I believe what you wanted to say was, 'Now what, Sir?'"

Iris whimpered. "Now what, Sir?" she whispered.

Do not poke the Dom. Lesson learned this time. Promise.

His smile widened.

"Now, stand up and bend over the bed."

Gingerly, Iris got to her feet, moving slowly, carefully, so as not to disturb the wire connecting her to the remote he was holding. The pulsing electricity continued to flow, like a steady throbbing bass beat she could only feel through the little buds. It felt great, but she couldn't forget how much that first zap had hurt.

The clamps felt as if they were even tighter when she bent over, and they hung from her breasts. She propped up on her elbows so the clamps didn't touch the bed. The position put her ass high in the air, her legs parted wide enough to give Law easy access to her pussy. What he was going to do next, she didn't know. He'd been holding something else in his hand, but she hadn't gotten a good look.

A short, sharp blow against her sensitive pussy lips made her gasp and rock forward. The movement pushed against the clamps, which made her nipples throb even more in a pleasure-pain response that curled her toes. In her current position, she went up onto her tiptoes.

"The thing about punishment is I don't need a whip or a paddle." His fingers landed against her pussy again with a sharp sting.

Iris groaned, rocking back and forth as the pain and pleasure curled through her, and the clamps jiggled on her breasts.

"I can use my hand."

Said hand slapped her pussy again, and Iris cried out, going up on her toes. It hurt... it hurt so good. The stinging fire tingled and buzzed through her sensitive flesh, leaving her aching all over, a painful counterpoint to the pleasurable pulses stimulating her nipples.

"And when I'm spanking this pretty little pussy, I don't need to do it very hard for it to hurt."

Swats rained down, fast and furious. Iris cried out, arching her back and doing her best to stay in place while her arms trembled from holding her up. She couldn't imagine how much it would hurt if her breasts were squashed against the bed, so she did her best to keep herself upright as her lower body throbbed and burned.

A few more particularly hard swats made Iris cry out, then there was a pause. She shuddered in position, her body buffeted by the sensations. Everything was still throbbing, then she felt the slick press of something against her anus. Iris moaned as Law's finger pushed inward, stretching her open.

Her pussy wanted his attention, but this felt damn good. Pumping his finger, he twisted it inside her, and Iris whimpered, pushing back against him. She felt delightfully full, and her nipples were still buzzing happily in their electrified confines.

What she didn't expect was when he pulled his finger out, it wasn't replaced by a plug. No, the pressure on her opening was completely different—not slim, not tapered, and not plastic. Iris gasped, rocking forward, away from the thick cock pressing against her anus, more out of surprise than anything else.

Hands gripped her hips, holding her in place as the thick shaft pressed inward, stretching her open.

"Oh God..." She clenched around him, shuddering, but her muscles could do very little since he'd lubed both his cock and her insides. The increased friction made her passageway burn, but that was hardly a deterrent for him.

"Be a good girl and take my cock, Iris." As he said the words, he thrust in deeper, and she cried out, taking his cock up her ass like a good girl, just like he'd told her to.

The pain and pleasure, heat and need, clashed inside her, leaving her shuddering as Law filled her with his cock. The exquisite agony, the deep intimacy of taking him in her ass on the day she'd moved into his house, felt so very right. An acknowledgment of how they belonged together, how their relationship had advanced to another level, whether or not they admitted it out loud.

Law

The tight grip of Iris' ass massaged the length of Law's cock as he buried it inside her. Velvet heat wrapped around him, squeezing his dick and heightening his pleasure. Reaching down, he tapped the controller for the clamps, enjoying her cry and the way her ass convulsed around him at the slight increase in voltage.

Holding onto her hips, he slowly thrust, pulling halfway out, then pushing back in, helping her remain mostly upright. He didn't want her upper body flat on the bed—yet.

Dropping her head between her arms, Iris moaned as her hips lifted, moving to meet his thrusts.

Looking down, he could see her tiny hole stretching around his cock as the slick length of his dick slid into her over and over. The combination of visual and physical pleasure was intoxicating.

"Whose good girl are you?" The words slipped out of his mouth before he knew he was going to ask. He hadn't felt possessive in years or had the urge to claim a submissive, much less conquer one. With Iris, he felt it all.

He wanted it all.

Maybe he couldn't bring himself to say 'love' out loud yet, but part of him wanted her acknowledged as his in some way.

Claiming her ass was only part of it.

"Yours, Sir. I'm your good girl."

Fuck.

The need driving Law amped up, and he moved harder, faster, riding her and ignoring the ache growing around his injury.

Before he lost himself, he reached down to turn off the electricity to the clamps and heard her small sound of disappointment. Sliding his hands up her sides, he leaned forward, cupped her breasts, and pulled the clamps free. Her ass clenched around him as her nipples were released from their confines, and the blood flowed back into them.

Cupping her breasts, Law massaged, rubbing them, using them as leverage to pound harder into her ass.

"Oh, fuck... Master Law... fuck... please..."

Iris' pleas drove his passion higher. He squeezed her breasts harder as he rode her and pulled harder on her breasts, pushing her upper body up, so he could kiss the back of her shoulder, biting and nipping her soft flesh.

Kneading her breasts, he pinched her already tortured nipples between his fingers before sliding his left hand down her stomach to her pussy. Iris cried out, writhing against him. Her hands wrapped around his neck, helping her hold her position as he fucked her ass and fingered her clit. The slick heat of her arousal coated his hand as her body moved against it, grinding against his palm and working her way up to orgasm.

IRIS

Oh fuck, oh fuck, oh fuck...

This was more than sex... this was primal. Law's low growl in her ear as he ravaged her, his hands all over her body, his breath hot against her throat, teeth nipping at her shoulder... Iris was lost to the hot passion consuming both of them.

"Please..." Her voice came out on a sob as he rubbed harder against her throbbing clit. "Oh God, Law..."

Hot bliss exploded inside her in a fiery burst of rapture, and Iris cried out. She rode his hand as his cock thrust into her ass, filling her so deliciously while his fingers pushed into her pussy, sending her soaring as the filthy sensations rocked her core.

As the initial intensity of her orgasm wore off, Law's arms moved away, and Iris fell forward, so she was bent over the bed again. She didn't land on her elbows, though she tried, and her breasts flattened against the bed, her sensitized nipples rasping against the fabric. The sudden glut of new sensations and Law's cock driving harder, deeper into her ass at this angle set off another, more intense orgasm. Iris screamed into the comforter as the overstimulation sent her soaring.

Her pleasure went on and on and on as Law's cock dragged back and forth in her ass, every thrust sending her to new heights of dizzying pleasure and ecstatic pain. By the time he buried himself inside her, his own pleasure spurting and filling her, she was nearly insensible from the sexual overload.

Panting, Law fell on top of her, his body curved over hers, his cock firmly embedded in her ass. The sensual haze Iris saw the world through made their positions feel like the most cuddly, warm, wonderful place to be.

She closed her eyes, smiling, as their breathing and heart rates slowed. It was a perfect end to what could have been a really stressful day.

CHAPTER THIRTY-SIX

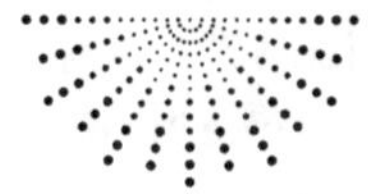

IRIS

The Renaissance Fair was everything Iris remembered. Even though she hadn't been in years, it didn't seem to have changed. It had permanent structures, which probably helped, but she was pretty sure all the shops in those structures were still the same, too. It was like stepping back in time, though not all the way back to the Renaissance. Just back to her childhood.

The only thing that really seemed to have changed were the acts.

Her head snapped around.

"Did that guy just say he needs a gag in his mouth?" Surely, she couldn't have heard that correctly, but the audience laughing uproariously at the four-man music troupe on stage had definitely heard something funny.

Law glanced over.

"Possibly. Those are the Hooligans. They can get pretty raunchy. Come on, we have to get over to the joust, or we won't be able to get seats." Law tugged on her hand, and bemused, Iris followed.

They kept getting funny looks as they walked around, probably because Iris' outfit resembled a tavern wench, the corset she'd borrowed from Angel pushing her boobs up like a shelf. Law was wearing monk's robes. Yeah, a celibate monk, he was not, but it worked well with his bald head. She found it hilarious. Thankfully, he didn't have to wear the sling any longer, so it didn't detract from the look, making him appear very authentic... like a very naughty monk. It was like being at the club, except there were a lot of kids running around.

As they passed by one of the taverns, Law slowed.

"Did you want to grab a drink?"

It was the third or fourth time he'd asked, and Iris answered the same way she had the other times.

"No, I'm good." She really was, but Law brought them to a halt, his brow furrowed.

"You don't have to not drink because of me." He faced her head-on, so she could see his expression clearly. "I hit a point a long time ago where being around people who are drinking is fine." He gestured around at the festival goers, and Iris had to laugh because... yeah.

Dragging everyone with them, the first thing Asad and Connor had done was hit the first bar they'd come to and order oyster shooters. Iris had demurred there as well since she didn't like raw oysters.

Part of the reason she wasn't drinking was because of Law, but she also didn't feel the need to or even want to. There were lots of things to do and see, and while she enjoyed having a drink when the occasion warranted it, she was just fine without.

"I hit a point in my life where I don't need to drink to enjoy myself," she replied, squeezing his hand. "I really am good. I'm having fun and don't feel the need for a drink. It's also hot as balls, and I'm a little worried about dehydration. Which... we should really check on the others when we meet back up with them."

They'd split up to do different things—as big as the grounds were, it was surprisingly hard to keep everyone together—and would regroup at the joust.

"I don't want you to feel like you're missing out on anything." Law's jaw worked, clenching and unclenching, trying to figure out what to say.

A rush of warmth filled Iris. He was such a good guy. Sure, he sometimes had a stick up his ass, but that's why she was there to loosen him up. This was one of those times.

"If I suddenly start feeling I'm missing out on anything, I'll be sure to let you know," she teased. The warning look he gave her made her laugh even harder. God, she loved him. They'd been living together for a few weeks, and that hadn't gone away. She wasn't looking for a new place to live at this point, though she probably should be. He was more than healed enough to be on his own, but he hadn't brought it up, so neither had she.

Suddenly, under his dark stare, she didn't feel like she could hold back the words anymore. "I love you, Law."

His reaction—eyes widening so far, they practically bulged, his jaw dropping to hang open—was more than a little satisfying.

"I know you probably think it's too soon, but that's how I feel. So, trust me, I'm not missing out on anything. I'm having a blast." Iris smiled serenely, incredibly amused that Law was still slack-jawed. "I don't expect you to say it back right now, by the way. I can wait till you're ready."

Did she want him to say the L-word? Of course, but if she'd learned anything about Law, it was he was a very deliberate person. While she knew he cared about her deeply, she wasn't sure he was in a position to be comfortable saying it back to her, and she'd known that would be the case. Whereas she'd always been more of a "ready, fire, aim" person. It had been on the tip of her tongue for days, and she was tired of holding back. Whether or not he said it back was… well, not immaterial, but it didn't change how she felt or what she'd wanted to say.

She felt lighter as if a weight had been lifted off her.

"Miss Iris, Miss Iris! Look! Mitch bought me a sword!" Ana, Domi's daughter, came running up, brandishing the wooden weapon. Turning to her, Iris made an awed face. Truthfully, she was a little awed, mostly by how much the little girl's outfit had changed since they'd parted ways an hour ago.

Angel had lent Iris a bunch of garb to give her 'options,' with instructions that her friends could use some as well if she wanted. There had been enough options in different sizes that Iris, Avery, Domi, and Rae were all decked out. Mitch had put on a knight's costume he'd worn for Halloween, so while he didn't look as authentic as Law, Asad, Connor, and Q, he fit right in with the crowds —only about half the people around them were dressed up.

Surrounded by people in garb, Nick had decided he needed an outfit, which had spurred Ana to ask if she could have an outfit, which had caused the group to split up for a bit. That had been fine since Asad, Connor, and Q had wanted to go back for more oyster shooters, and Iris had wanted to see the jugglers. After, she and Law had wandered until it was time to meet everyone at the joust.

Ana had made out like a bandit—not just a new sword but also a new purple dress, a little black vest with white lace that laced up the front, and a pink-and-purple flower crown. The only thing that hadn't changed was her sneakers, but since they were purple, they didn't look completely incongruous with the rest of her outfit.

"My goodness, look at you! You're a little lady knight."

"A lady knight?" Ana asked, sounding fascinated, lowering the sword a bit as she stared up at Iris.

"Yes, like… like…" Hm. There weren't any references Ana would recognize at her age that immediately came to mind. "Well, when you're old enough, I'm going to introduce you to Alanna of Trebond, my favorite lady knight."

"Cool!" Ana turned around to where Mitch and Domi were coming up, hand in hand. Mitch was grinning so wide, it nearly split his face, whereas Domi was shaking her head in resigned amusement. Iris had a feeling Mitch had done the majority of the purchasing.

"Where's Rae?" she asked as their friends joined them. She had started off with them.

"In line for a crab pretzel, then she'll join us." Domi waved her hand behind her. "Let's go see the joust."

"I'm going to be a lady knight when I grow up!" Ana announced, and Mitch reached out to ruffle her hair.

"Damn right you are."

LAW

Coward. You're a big, stinking coward.

Holding Iris' hand and moving through the crowds, Law couldn't stop the chiding thoughts filling his head.

To be fair, he'd been blindsided and fumbling to find the words when Ana came running up, but he wasn't even trying to draw Iris to the side to tell her he loved her, too. Would she think he was only saying it because she had? He hadn't known whether to say it back when she was telling him he didn't have to, then Ana interrupted them, and it was too late. Now, he felt like he'd lost the opportunity.

As they neared the joust, they could see their group of friends gathered at the bottom of the little hillside next to the jousting arena, right next to the fountain and lovers' bridge. Asad was taking a picture of Nick and Avery on the bridge. Nick appeared to have bought a shirt and hat. Iris cracked up when the two of them came off the bridge, and Nick's lower half remained unchanged in his cargo shorts and sandals. Law grinned. He always enjoyed the half and half look that so many new visitors, like Nick, ended up wearing.

"Oooh, we should get a picture, too," Mitch said, grabbing Domi's hand and pulling her toward the bridge. Ana had already run ahead to show Connor her sword. Much to the big guy's confusion, she'd latched onto him immediately when she met him. Maybe it was the Viking helmet, or maybe Ana had an instinct for knowing who the biggest softie in a group was.

"Do you want a picture?" he asked Iris, his mind already working furiously. Maybe being on Lover's Bridge for a picture would be a good time to tell her he loved her. She'd stolen his thunder, but he could still make it special when he said it. Memorable.

"Sure." The saucy look she sent his way was more than worthy of her wench attire, and he had to chuckle. Sliding his arm around her waist, they moved toward the bridge. Avery and Nick were making their way off one end while Mitch and Domi filed onto the other end.

The tiny fountain pond in front of the bridge had plenty of flowers and greenery and looked particularly pretty against the small white bridge. Domi and Mitch moved to the center, where they posed for the picture, arms around each other, facing their friends, each with one hand on the rail in front of them.

Then, instead of turning to leave, Mitch turned toward Domi and went down on one knee.

Domi gasped, her hands flying to her mouth.

"I can't see!" Ana wailed. Connor lifted her onto his shoulders, where she grabbed onto the horns of his Viking helmet, but Law was sure it didn't help since the bridge railing was high enough, they could only see the top of Mitch's head over it. Next to him, Iris burst out laughing.

"We can't see you, Mitch. You're too far down!" Rae yelled at him. "Get in front of the bridge to do it!"

Glancing at Rae, he could see that she was grinning. Unlike Domi, she obviously wasn't particularly surprised.

"You're all ruining the spontaneity and romance of the moment!" Despite that, Mitch popped up to his feet and pulled a now laughing Domi off the bridge and around to the front of the pond, where he dropped to one knee again.

The number of phones that came out in the meantime was epic, recording or taking pictures. They'd drawn a bit of a crowd and not just strangers. There were multiple people from Stronghold and Marquis at the fair—not surprising since the kink community loved Renn Fair—and a lot of them were among those watching Mitch's proposal.

On his knee again, ring box in hand, Mitch cleared his throat.

"Domi, when I met you, I had no intention of being in a serious relationship, and neither did you. Obviously, I've changed my mind."

Groaning, Domi covered her face with her hands, her shoulders shaking with laughter. Mitch was grinning like a fool. There was some confusion on the faces of people around them, but everyone who knew the two of them was shaking their heads, laughing, or both.

"I didn't know when I was going to ask you, so I've been carrying this ring around for a few weeks, waiting for the perfect moment. I thought this was it. I might have gotten it a little off, but you took a chance on me when I made a fool out of myself the last time. I'm hoping you'll do it again. Will you marry me?"

"Say yes!" Ana yelled before her mom could answer, causing raucous laughter from the witnesses. With her sword held high, on top of a Viking's shoulders, she made a rather threatening visage for being only six years old.

Lowering her hands from her face, Domi wagged her finger at her daughter before turning back to Mitch.

"You're a twit, but you're my twit," she said.

"That's *Sir* Twit to you," he replied, causing another round of laughter, including those who probably thought he was referencing his knight costume and didn't realize the double entendre. "So... that wasn't an answer."

"Yes, I will marry you," she said, shaking her head. "As if there was ever really a question."

Grinning, Mitch popped open the box and slid the ring onto Domi's finger.

The crowd surged forward, filled with people wanting to congratulate them, and Iris was almost one of them, but Law held her back. Turning to look at him, questions filling her eyes, she tilted her head, trying to figure out what was going on. His mouth was dry, but...

Well, proposals were romantic moments, right?

And he needed to say it back.

He pulled Iris toward him, his hands on her hips. A little smile curved her lips as she went willingly, curiously.

Law cleared his throat.

"In the light of grand declarations and making fools of ourselves... I want you to know that I love you, too."

Happiness flashed across her face, her smile brighter than the sun.

"I know," she smugly. "I just didn't know if you knew."

Growling under his breath, Law pulled her in for a kiss. They didn't need a bridge or even a grand declaration. They just needed each other.

She was everything he wanted for his future, and he would never let her go.

Law and disorder. A perfect match.

Dun-dun.

EPILOGUE

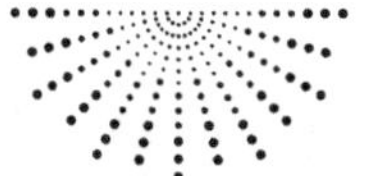

<u>Q</u>

The second time walking into Marquis for a class was more daunting than the first. Maybe because the first time he'd gone to a class, it had been for Dominants, not submissives. Somehow, being a submissive was scarier, even though he had nothing but respect for them after going through the Dominance class. Admitting that part of him resonated instead of rejected being submissive didn't fit the image he'd always had of himself.

More than the other Doms had, he'd really liked the parts of the Dominance class when they tried things they'd want to do to a submissive.

He didn't always feel satisfied being the one in charge. Sometimes, he wanted to give up control. Sometimes, the idea of having a woman bossing him around, telling him what to do, was hot as hell.

Even if his brain told him it was wrong and he shouldn't want it.

He wondered if it was a holdover from living with his friend, Angel, for so long before she'd started going to Stronghold and met Adam, her now-husband. She could be incredibly bossy when she wanted but was submissive in the bedroom—all the time, not just some of the time like Q felt he might be. Q had gotten used to her bossing around him and their other two roommates, Sam and Mark.

Thinking about Sam made him shake his head. He knew that was another reason he was nervous tonight. Not because of his old roommate, Sam, but because of Samantha Dupre, who preferred to go by Sam. In his head, she was always Samantha... or Samwise—the nickname he'd given her in high school when they were butting heads.

Calling her that had never been a good idea, but tonight, in particular, it would be a mistake.

This whole thing was probably a mistake.

He was still questioning the wisdom of putting himself and his tenderest bits at the mercy of someone who didn't seem to particularly like him very much. Not that he understood why *she* was holding a grudge. Of the two of them, he had the better reason, that was for sure.

He wouldn't ask for special treatment because of high school bullshit. If Samantha didn't want to work with him during the class, that was her thing. Q would not be the one to back down.

Bounding to the top of the stairs and into the main lobby of Marquis, he looked around. Master Law and Mistress Julie were standing in front of the desk outside the door to the main stage area. It looked like they were arguing, though they were keeping their voices low. A vase filled with red roses was sitting on the desk beside them, and Master Law kept gesturing to it.

Curious, Q moved toward them, and they glanced up when they saw him.

"Hey Q, head inside. All the other submissives are here... no, you're not late. They were just very early." Julie gave him a reassuring smile before turning back to Law, who still had a scowl on his face. "Give it up, Law. They're just flowers. It's fine."

"This is the second time—"

Whatever it was the second time of, Q didn't hear. Taking his cue from Mistress Julie, he headed into the main room of Marquis. It looked a lot like it had for the first Dominance class, with the round stage in the center of the room cleared off except for chairs. There was one still open, and everyone turned as he entered.

Relief flooded him when he saw he wasn't the only male submissive. He thought… oh. Master Law said he was the only male submissive who preferred a female dominant. Got it. Talk about being forced to examine his own internal biases. He'd try not to make that assumption again.

"Hey, everyone," he said, smiling and pretending a casualness he didn't feel. *Fake it till you make it.* "I'm Q. Nice to meet you."

They all stood, almost as a group, as he got closer.

"Hey, we've met before. Steve, I'm Chris' brother." As soon as he said the words, Q recognized the guy. They'd met in passing at a group event. Chris was the husband of Jessica, who was one of Angel's friends. Sometimes, it was like six degrees of kinky separation. Steve was still holding out his hand. Tall and dark-haired, although lankier than his brother, there was a strong resemblance between them.

"Right, hi, sorry." Q shook his hand.

"No worries." Steve grinned as they let go of the handshake. "It's been a while."

"Hi, I'm Emerson, they/them pronouns," said the person next to Q, holding out their hand. "I'm non-binary."

"Right, sorry, I'm he/him," Steve said, shooting Emerson an apologetic glance. They grinned back at him. With short-cropped reddish hair and a slim build, they were a few inches shorter than Steve and seemed perfectly at home as everyone fumbled around them. Maybe even as though they were enjoying it a little. Another brat in the making. Q smiled back.

One thing he'd learned from dominance class, he enjoyed the brats.

"Q, he/him." Q shook their hand.

"Cassidy. Um, she/her." The pretty blonde next to Emerson whispered before offering her hand. She seemed nervous, and Q was ninety-nine percent sure she was the one Iris had rescued from an abusive Dom a few months ago. Interesting that she was in the new submissives class when he'd thought she was experienced.

The woman beside her was much more chipper, smiling brightly at him. She was also blonde.

"And I'm Noelle, she/her pronouns. Nice to meet you." They shook hands. "So, I guess that's all of us."

Everyone sat down.

"So, you're submissive?" Steve asked, leaning forward to look at Q a little curiously. "I thought I heard you took the Dominance class."

"I did. I think I'm a switch." Noelle and Emerson looked a little confused at the term. "That means, sometimes, I tend to be more dominant, and other times, I tend to be more submissive. I can go back and forth between."

"Oh." Emerson's expression cleared, and they laughed. "Well, I know what that's like." Which made everyone else laugh.

Q started to relax. It seemed this was going to be a fun group. No one seemed judgmental, which was reassuring. Not that he'd run into anyone judgmental yet, but he kept waiting for it to happen. There was a part of his brain that insisted it couldn't possibly be this easy.

"I'm excited. My old best friend was into BDSM, but I never really understood it." Noelle's expression turned a little sad. "I'm hoping I'll be able to reconnect with her once I understand it better."

Huh. Wasn't Iris' old best friend named Noelle?

It had to be a coincidence. Iris had moved in with Law months ago after a big blowup with her old roommate and best friend, and *that* Noelle had basically kicked her out. Couldn't be the same one.

Could it?

The door behind them opened again, distracting Q from his thoughts. Master Law and Mistress Julie came in, followed by five other dominants, including Samantha Dupre. Their gazes meeting for a moment, she arched her eyebrow and lifted her chin, then she looked at the Dom next to her and smiled at something he'd said.

Q's chest tightened.

So, she hadn't backed down.

It was just like old times.

Samantha Dupre had been his greatest rival in high school.
She'd also been the one who got away.

IT'S A POWER STRUGGLE THAT GOES BACK YEARS - WHO WILL COME OUT ON top when Sam and Q finally face off? Find out in Book 4 of the Masters of Marquis series, Switch Play!

ACKNOWLEDGMENTS

As always, a huge thank you to my beta readers. Candida, Marie, Marta, Annie, Karen, and Katherine - these books would not be the same without you. I am so blessed to have such amazing supporters.

Thank you to Sandy, from Personal Touch Editing, whose work always makes my own so much better.

A huge thank you to my husband, whose support is so integral to my own success.

For this one, I also want to thank all the readers who requested that Andrew's little sister Iris get her own story. I think she absolutely deserved it.

An additional shoutout to Reggie Deanching, who - when I asked if he had any male Asian cover models - immediately showed me Jerry and told me they had a shoot coming up. He asked if there were any poses in particular I wanted and they came through in an amazing manner. I adore this cover. Which, of course, also leads me to my next shoutout - Eris Adderly, whose amazing cover skills make this series look so fantastic.

And, finally, thank you to you, all my readers. I never had any idea that Venus Rising would lead to Stronghold or that there would be another series following it. But as long as you keep reading, I'll keep writing!

Stay Sassy,

Angel

ABOUT THE AUTHOR

Golden Angel is a USA Today best-selling author and self-described bibliophile with a "kinky" bent who loves to write stories for the characters in her head. If she didn't get them out, she's pretty sure she'd go just a little crazy.

She is happily married, old enough to know better but still too young to care, and a big fan of happily-ever-afters, strong heroes and heroines, and sizzling chemistry.

When she's not writing, she can often be found on the couch reading, in front of her sewing machine making a new cosplay, hanging out with her friends, or wandering the Maryland Renaissance Fair.

www.goldenangelromance.com

OTHER BOOKS BY GOLDEN ANGEL

CONTEMPORARY BDSM ROMANCE

Venus Rising Series (MFM Romance)

The Venus School

Venus Aspiring

Venus Desiring

Venus Transcendent

Venus Wedding

Venus Rising Box Set

Stronghold Doms Series

The Sassy Submissive

Taming the Tease

Mastering Lexie

Pieces of Stronghold

Breaking the Chain

Bound to the Past

Stripping the Sub

Tempting the Domme

Hardcore Vanilla

Steamy Stocking Stuffers

Entering Stronghold Box Set

Nights at Stronghold Box Set

Stronghold: Closing Time Box Set

Masters of Marquis Series

Bondage Buddies

Master Chef

Law & Disorder

Dungeons & Doms Series

Dungeon Master

Dungeon Daddy

Dungeon Showdown

Poker Loser Trilogy

Forced Bet

Back in the Game

Winning Hand

Poker Loser Trilogy Bundle (3 books in 1!)

Standalones - Daddy Doms

Chef Daddy

Little Villain

HISTORICAL SPANKING ROMANCE

Domestic Discipline Quartet

Birching His Bride

Dealing With Discipline

Punishing His Ward

Claiming His Wife

The Domestic Discipline Quartet Box Set

Bridal Discipline Series

Philip's Rules

Gabrielle's Discipline

Lydia's Penance

Benedict's Commands

Arabella's Taming

Pride and Punishment Box Set

Commands and Consequences Box Set

Deception and Discipline

A Season for Treason

A Season for Scandal

A Season for Smugglers

A Season for Spies

Bridgewater Brides

Their Harlot Bride

Standalone

Marriage Training

The Duke's Pursuit

Rogue Booty

SCI-FI ROMANCE

Tsenturion Masters Series with Lee Savino

Alien Captive

Alien Tribute

Alien Abduction

Standalone

Mated on Hades